# BLUEWATER REVOLUTION

---

## THE 12TH NOVEL IN THE SERIES - MYSTERY AND ADVENTURE IN FLORIDA, CUBA, AND THE CARIBBEAN

## C.L.R. DOUGHERTY

Atlantic Ocean

Florida

The Bahamas

Gulf of
Mexico

Shark River →

Miami

Marathon →

Andros
Island

Havana

Cuba

Caribbean Sea

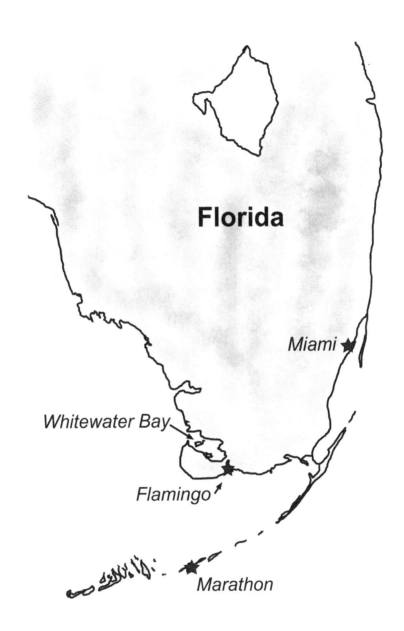

Florida

Miami

Whitewater Bay

Flamingo

Marathon

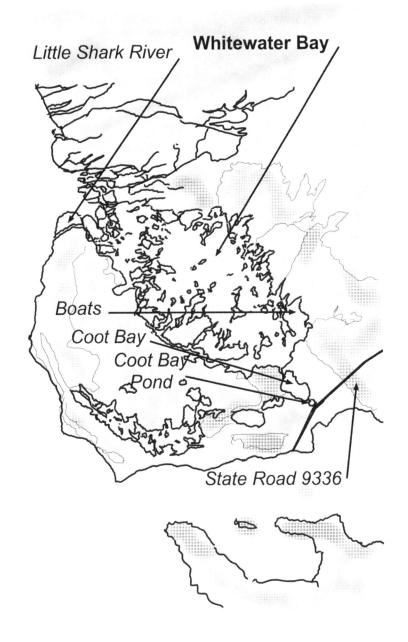

Little Shark River

**Whitewater Bay**

Boats

Coot Bay

Coot Bay
Pond

State Road 9336

# 1
---

"Dani, what are we doing here?" Liz Chirac asked, starting to rise to her knees.

"Shh!" Dani Berger clapped a muddy hand over Liz's mouth. She glared at her friend until Liz nodded and lay back down in the mud. Liz watched as Dani parted the undergrowth that blocked their view of the beach. Dani moved the leaves in tiny, imperceptible increments.

She turned her head until she faced Liz. Raising her eyebrows, she gestured toward the beach with her head. Liz nodded, indicating that she could see. Dani reached back with her free hand, patting the mud until she found a fist-sized rock. She picked it up and placed it where it would keep the scrub from springing back to cut off their view.

Noticing the look on Liz's face, Dani raised a finger to her lips and shook her head, pointing at the beach with her other hand. Liz frowned and looked back out at the moonlit sand. In a few minutes, she sensed movement in the shadows to their left. A man was walking down the steps from the boardwalk under which the two of them were concealed. Liz stole a glance at Dani. Her friend followed the man's movements with a cold stare.

He stopped about halfway to the water's edge, waiting, staring out at the small waves that rolled in. Even at night, there were people on the beach. Couples lay entwined on blankets, dark splotches on the silver sand that stretched from the boardwalk down to the waves that broke with a soft hissing sound every few seconds.

After a minute or two, a shadowy form approached the man and paused, greeting him. A woman, Liz realized, when the shadow stood on tiptoes and embraced the man, kissing him on each cheek. A friend, she guessed, as opposed to a lover. Liz was relieved for Dani's sake.

The man and woman stood chatting in quiet tones for perhaps thirty seconds. Then they turned and strolled to the north along the hard sand exposed by the receding tide. They continued to converse softly.

"Bastard," Dani hissed.

"What happened?" Liz asked. "From the bar, it looked like you two were getting along nicely until he took that phone call."

"I thought I was going to get lucky, finally," Dani said, nodding. "Did you get a good look at him?"

"Yummy, wasn't he?" Liz asked.

"He sure was. He'd just asked me to join him for dinner, too. Then his phone rang."

"He took the call at the table," Liz said. "Did you eavesdrop?"

Dani cut her eyes at her friend, then realized Liz couldn't see her sarcastic look in the gloom under the boardwalk. "Yes, of course. The arrogant prick was speaking Spanish, so he thought I couldn't understand what was going on."

"Well?" Liz prompted.

"I could only hear his side, but apparently *she* demanded that he meet her on the beach, right away. He tried to explain that he was busy. He told her that he had dinner plans with me, but it didn't matter to her. She was screeching at him. I couldn't make out what she said, but I could tell she wasn't happy. He discon-

nected and apologized to me. Said something about a crisis, and
that we'd have to do it another time. He said he'd call me later.
Bastard."

"So he got your phone number?"

"Yes," Dani said. "And I have his."

"Any idea who the woman is?"

Dani shook her head. "He said he was single."

"What made you decide to follow him?" Liz asked.

"Just my gut reaction. His side of the conversation seemed
really odd."

"There's something you didn't tell me, then," Liz said.

"Yes. He made some reference to dinner with the *béké's*
daughter."

"*Béké*? The Creole word, like in Martinique?"

"Yes."

"Had you told him about J.-P. being from there?"

"No. I hadn't told him anything that would have made him
think I was a *békée*, either."

"So he knew who you were, then?"

"So it seems," Dani said. "I've never heard that term used to
describe someone of French descent except in the French
Antilles."

"You think he was from Martinique?"

"I don't know. He *said* he was Cuban-American. David Ortiz.
He told me his parents came here on a raft when his mother was
pregnant with him."

"Interesting," Liz said.

"That's why I followed him. We may as well go back to
*Vengeance* and clean up. I'm not in the mood for picking up guys
anymore."

Liz looked at her mud-covered friend and suppressed a laugh,
shaking her head.

∾

GUILLERMO MALDONADO SAID, "I heard from Havana; Raul Castro's decided to personally call the shots on this one. He wants to set up a bogus invasion, an anti-Castro revolution. He says it's critical that it must appear to be an American-initiated operation. He wants it to look like the CIA put the exiles up to it." Maldonado was on a secure satellite phone link, talking with José Martínez, his lead operative in South Florida.

José Martínez chuckled. "Like Avila? Back in the early '90s?"

"You have a good memory," Maldonado said.

"Yeah. Raul's assuming the Americans don't, I guess."

"Don't what?" Maldonado said.

"Don't remember Avila," Martínez said.

Francisco Avila Azcuy had been Chief of Operations for Alpha-66, a militant group of Cuban exiles. In 1992, Avila confessed that for many years he had been working for DGI, Cuba's *Dirección General de Inteligencia*, in south Florida. He claimed DGI funded several attacks on Cuba by Alpha-66. When Avila gave himself up to the FBI, he said that Fidel Castro had ordered the operations to justify some of his anti-American policies to the Cuban people and the rest of the world.

"Your latest report got Raul to thinking, José. When you mentioned that big birthday celebration for Mario Espinosa, Raul came up with this idea. You have to admit, having J.-P. Berger and his whole team right there in Miami is too good an opportunity to pass up."

"I thought it might interest him," Martínez said. "I know he's always kept up with Espinosa. The guy's like the elder statesman of the exiles. So what's the plan, now? What kind of opportunity does he see?"

"You used to know Phillip Davis, right? Back when you were both working in Central America in the bad old days?"

"Yeah. He's been retired for a few years now, supposedly. Lives in Martinique, and his wife's a senior French customs official there."

"That sounds convenient for a spy," Maldonado said. "You sure he's retired?"

"Who knows, with these guys?" Martínez said. "Nobody ever knew for sure who he worked for, anyway. He was a career Army officer, but he was always hanging around embassies in the Caribbean basin. Whenever there was any kind of shooting war going on, he was on the fringes. Espinosa and Berger were only a step removed, shipping in weapons and everything else."

"Davis was CIA."

"We never confirmed that," Martínez said.

"Close enough for our purposes, anyway, José."

"And what does that mean?"

"It means Raul wants you to approach Davis, posing as the front man for a consortium of the exile organizations."

"I've already taken steps to infiltrate Berger's party," Martínez said. "Should we wait and see what he finds?"

"You did what? Why, and on what authority?"

"You heard me. When I picked up that Berger was renting that place on Star Island, I decided we needed to know what he was doing."

"But what agent are you using?" Maldonado asked.

"Relax, Willy." Guillermo Maldonado had adopted the nick-name, Willy, years ago. When he had been a field agent in Florida, he thought Guillermo sounded too foreign. "He's flying blind. He has no idea who's behind his mission. It's low risk."

"Who is he?" Maldonado asked, again.

"A kid named David Ortiz," Martínez said. "His parents came on a raft in the late '80s, early '90s. He's active in Alpha-66, and he's working for Manny Cruz."

"In the real estate business? Or the other?"

"The real estate business," Martínez said. "He's a sales agent, just getting going. Mostly an errand boy, but he's a real ladies' man."

"Have you met him?"

"Of course not. He's got no clue what's going on. He thinks Manny's sent him in there to pave the way for Lupita to kidnap Berger's daughter."

"Lupita Vidal?" Maldonado asked. "But why does he think she's going to kidnap Berger's daughter?"

"To force Berger to sell weapons to Alpha-66."

"Jesus, José. Did you make that shit up? Or did you know?"

"Made it up. Actually, Manny and Lupita thought of it as a way to keep the kid in the dark. Ortiz is scared shitless of Lupita."

"Yeah, I can imagine," Maldonado said. "I don't blame him. You trust this kid?"

"Enough to do this. He's already picked Berger's daughter up in a bar at South Beach this evening."

"Who's running him? Cruz?"

"Lupita," Martínez said. "She likes jerking him around."

"Okay, I guess. Don't let her get carried away, though."

"She'll be okay, Willy. Now that we've got a clear mission, Manny can give her a little more direction."

"All right. Raul wants you to make the approach to Davis," Maldonado said. "You think he'll trust you?"

"We've got some history. He always thought I was a pure mercenary. We weren't quite on the same side, but we weren't trying to kill each other, either," Martínez said.

"Good. We're sticking to that old mercenary cover. Your story's going to be that the exile community in Miami isn't happy with the rapprochement between Raul Castro and the U.S. government. We want it to look like the exiles have hired you to lead an invasion."

"That's a good story," Martínez said. "They definitely are not happy, but what's in this for Raul? I mean the situation has changed a lot since Avila. There was reason to embarrass the U.S. back then, but they're not bothering us now. What's he want out of this?"

"Raul Castro is worried that the Cuban people are going to be seduced by capitalism, just like all the other socialist countries have been," Maldonado said.

"Why doesn't Raul just tell the U.S. to fuck off, then?"

"World opinion's on the side of the U.S., since they dropped the embargo. Raul is cornered, José. Cuba's more or less forced to make nice with the U.S. If Raul tells them to fuck off, he looks like the bad guy. Fidel already mouthed off enough to mess things up before he died. He made Raul decline U.S. disaster aid after the last hurricane. The people didn't like that, so Raul's looking for some overt signs of bad faith from the U.S. to explain his brother's attitude."

"I think I understand," Martínez said. "If the rest of the world thinks the U.S. is pushing the exiles to overthrow the Castro government, they'll side with Cuba. *Then* Raul can tell the U.S to go to hell."

"Yes," Maldonado said. "And it's not just the rest of the world that will take Cuba's side. The most important thing is that the Cuban people will be upset with the U.S. for trying to interfere. They'll turn against the Americans. Now you see why it must appear that the U.S. government is behind this initiative?"

"Yeah," Martínez said. "Raul is a genius."

"Maybe. Just set it up so nobody will ever figure it out. That's the point. If we're successful, the U.S. government can deny that they were involved in this effort to overthrow our government, but there will be plenty of people who believe otherwise."

"But what if Davis tells people I came to him, instead of vice-versa?" Martínez asked.

"No matter. Who's going to take the word of a CIA agent? Of course he'd say the exiles started the whole thing."

"And the Cuban people will believe the U.S. wants to make us a colony," Martínez said. "We've poisoned their minds for so long that no matter how much they want automobiles and cellphones, they won't trust the U.S."

"That's the idea," Maldonado said. "When can you get to
Davis?"

"I'll let you know. Soon, though. Very soon. But I need your
help with something."

"What do you need?"

"Nothing big, but if I'm going active, I need to put some
distance between me and Cruz. Can you take over running him?
Make like it's a big promotion for him; he eats that kind of shit
up. I need to break off contact with him, at least until this
is over."

"Yeah, sure, José. No problem. Just work through me for what
you need from him."

"I TOLD YOU, I don't know when we're going to snatch her," Lupita
Vidal said, walking along the beach beside David Ortiz.

"Okay. I didn't have a good feeling about this evening,
anyway," Ortiz said. "I was relieved when you called me and interrupted us."

"Why's that?"

"She was squirrely," Ortiz said, with a shrug.

"What do you mean by that?"

"She gave off a strange vibe, like she was always looking over
her shoulder. Jumpy, maybe, like she was ready for a fight to start.
I dunno how to say it better."

"Yeah. We don't keep you around because you're articulate,
that's for sure. Good thing you're so handsome."

"You got a lot of room to talk. I know why Manny keeps you
around. It sure as shit ain't for your brains."

"He put me in charge of this part of the operation, David. If
you've got a problem with that, I can handle it. Just keep up your
shit and I'll kick your ass."

"Is that a threat?"

"You're smarter than I thought. Now shut up and listen." She walked in silence for several seconds.

"We're not going to snatch her," she said. "Not right away, anyhow." She glanced his way to make sure he was listening. "But your new job is to suck up to her. We've got other plans to get what we need from her father and his friends, but you need to stay close to her."

"What for?"

"You're going to be our inside man. Court that girl for all you're worth. We need somebody that can come and go from that compound on Star Island where they're all hanging out."

"She's on that damn boat with the other girl, the French one," Ortiz said. "Not in the compound."

"Belgian," Vidal said.

"What?"

"Liz Chirac is Belgian, not French. Dani Berger is half-French. And the boat is tied to the dock at the compound. I don't care if you're hanging out on the boat with her or somewhere else, as long as you're part of her crowd. You need to become a regular with them."

"She's got an American accent."

"Yeah?" Lupita Vidal asked, raising her eyebrows and shaking her head. "So?"

"You said she was half-French."

"She is," Vidal said. "You know that. Her father's from Martinique, like you said on the phone when you screwed up."

"What are you talking about, 'screwed up?'"

"Talking to me on the phone while you were at the table with her, dumbass."

"What was I supposed to do?"

"You could have excused yourself to take my call."

"Shit, Lupita. She doesn't know what I said. I spoke Spanish, remember?"

"Yeah, I noticed. You also called her the *béké's* daughter."

"So?"

"It didn't occur to you that she might have picked up on that? Realized you were talking about her?"

"I was speaking *Spanish*; she's a fuckin' *Anglo*, Lupita."

"You know who her godfather is?"

"Her godfather? What's he got to do with anything?"

"Mario Espinosa's her godfather, you moron. You do know who he is, right?"

"Now you're insulting me. Of course I know who he is."

"He's her father's business partner and best friend. She spent a lot of time with Espinosa and his family when she was little."

"So? I knew that from the briefing Manny gave us."

"At least you were listening. Too bad you don't have the brains to use what you heard."

"You're starting to piss me off, Lupita. What's your point?" He stopped walking and turned to face her.

Without missing a step, she whirled and delivered a snap-kick to his groin. He grabbed himself and sank to his knees on the hard sand of the beach. He swayed back and forth, gasping.

"Two things, David," she said, putting a hand under his chin and turning his face up toward hers. "First, I'm running this operation. I demand respect. I don't have time for your male-ego bullshit. You got that? Or do I need to give you another lesson?"

"I got it," he mumbled.

"Good. If you keep pushing back, I'll get angry. You won't like that. Now, we were talking about Dani Berger, remember?"

"Yeah."

"And the fact that she spent parts of her childhood in Espinosa's household."

"Yeah. I got that. But I still — "

"She speaks Spanish, *pinguero*. And she's way smarter than you."

"So?"

"So, she now knows that you know who her father is."

"How?" Ortiz asked, frowning as he struggled to make the connection. "Because — "

"Because you called her the *béké's* daughter. That means you know about her father, that he's from the French islands."

"Oh," he said. "Maybe I can — "

"Maybe you can shut up and let me tell you how you're going to cover your ass."

"Okay, okay," he said, rising to his feet with care. "Can we walk again? I need to walk and breathe deep. You hurt me bad."

She nodded. "I meant to. At least now I know. I can tell the others, settle our bet."

"Know what? What bet?"

"Some people don't think you've still got your *cojones*. Rumor was some irate husband cut you. But I know better now. You're just a *págaro*."

"I don't have to take this from you."

"Yeah, actually you do have to. Now, here's how you're going to explain yourself to Dani Berger. You ready to listen?"

"Yeah."

"All right. You tell her that the call was from your sister, Lupita. Your mother's from Martinique originally. She's been visiting a friend of hers down there that everybody calls the *béké's* daughter. Your mother's had a stroke, and your sister had to see you to get money for an emergency trip to Martinique to take care of her. Got it?"

"Yeah, but I — "

"Shut up. You're to call Dani and apologize for this evening; explain the whole thing to her like I just told you. Take her out to a fancy meal somewhere and work your magic on her. Think you can do that?"

"Yeah."

"Good," she said. "Repeat that cover story for me. Make like I'm her, and make me believe it's true, or else."

He rattled off the explanation with conviction. "Okay?" he asked, eyeing her with caution.

She smiled and flipped her long, curly black hair over her shoulder. "Good."

"Suppose she doesn't buy it?" he asked.

"Your mission is to make her buy it; you have to make her fall in love with you. Can you do that?"

"Yeah, sure. But then what?"

"One step at a time, David. I don't want to overload your cute little brain."

## 2

"How'd you first meet Sharktooth?" Paul Russo asked Phillip Davis.

"We were in the jungle, and — "

"Where?" Paul interrupted.

"Can't tell you that," Phillip said. "Not when, either. It's classified, kind of."

Paul nodded, looking perplexed. "Kind of?"

"Yeah," Phillip said. "Anyway, this guy had just dropped from a tree and landed on my back — knocked the shit out of me. I was struggling to get enough air in my lungs to fight back when somebody pulled him off me. When I turned over, I found myself staring up into the biggest, blackest face I'd ever seen." He paused, smiling.

"And?" Paul prompted.

"He grinned at me and said 'Who d' hell are you, white boy?'"

"What did you tell him?"

"I can't remember exactly. I was too stunned. Whatever I said, I guess it was all right with him, because he pulled the knife away."

"The knife?"

"Yeah, I hadn't noticed it until then."

"Pulled it away from where?" Paul asked.

"My throat. He wasn't taking any chances on me, you know?" Phillip stared off at the boats in the anchorage to the north. They sat on the veranda of a rented mansion on Star Island in Biscayne Bay.

After a while, he said, "Anyway, I asked him, 'How come you saved my ass if you didn't know who I was?'"

"How'd he answer that?"

"He said, 'I knew who the other mon was. Bad mon. Figured you might be okay if he was gon' kill you.'"

"And I guess he decided you *were* okay, then?" Paul asked.

"I guess. I'm here."

"What about the other guy?" Paul asked.

"Broken neck," Phillip said. "Sharktooth palmed his head like a basketball when he pulled the guy off me."

"Jesus," Paul said. "That's hard to imagine. Did you see that happen? You said you were stunned."

"I was. He told me about it, but I didn't believe him until I saw him take out another one a little while later. He just grabs and twists. His hands are the size of baseball gloves."

Paul shook his head. "He seems so gentle."

"He is. Wouldn't hurt a fly, as the saying goes. Unless ... " Phillip was looking past Paul, distracted.

Connie Barrera stepped out onto the veranda behind Paul. "There you are," she said, putting a hand on Paul's shoulder. "We've only been married for a year, and you're already sneaking off to have a beer with the boys. What's up?"

"Oh, not much. Just swapping war stories."

"You never tell me war stories," she said.

"I don't really have any. I was egging Phillip on, that's all. He was telling me about how he and Sharktooth met."

"Was Dani involved?" Connie asked.

"Ah, Dani was too young; she was still playing with dolls,"

Phillip said, a teasing grin on his face. He was watching Dani walk up behind Connie.

"She played with dolls?" Connie asked. "*Our* Dani?"

"Voodoo," Dani said. "I was trying to put a curse on Phillip, because he didn't let me go with them."

Connie turned, startled, taking in Dani's mud-encrusted cocktail dress. "What happened to you?"

"This jerk I met in a club had just asked me out to dinner, and then he got a phone call and ran out on me."

"Was that before or after your turn in the mud-wrestling pit?"

"Don't start something you aren't prepared to finish." Dani glared at Connie.

"I didn't mean to aggravate you," Connie said.

"I know. Sorry, I'm just generally pissed off right now. Did you and Paul just get here?"

"We've been back in the States for a few days. We cleared in at Key West and chilled out in the Keys for a while. We sailed up from Rodriguez Key this morning and got in a little while ago. How about you and Liz?"

"We came from the Bahamas a couple of days ago. Papa and Anne spent some time with us, poking around in the Exumas."

"We saw them a little while ago," Paul said. "Where's Liz?"

"On *Vengeance*, rinsing off the mud. When I saw *Diamantista II* rafted up to us, I decided to come find you and say hello."

"It's nice to see you again," Connie said. "I think the last time everybody was together was when Paul and I got married."

"Yes, that's right," Dani said. "I'm glad Papa thought of doing this."

"How is he going to get Mario here without tipping his hand?" Phillip asked.

Dani shrugged. "I don't think he's worked that out, yet. He'll think of something, though. Where's Sandrine?"

"Not here yet. She's still working, but she'll be here. Sharktooth's not here yet, either. It's still a few days until Mario's birthday."

"Right," Dani said. "Is he bringing Maureen?"

"Yes. No way she'd let him come to Miami without her."

Dani chuckled. "Guess I should go get cleaned up."

"You should check out the shower in the master suite," Connie said. "It's like being in the rain forest. How did J.-P. find a place like this to rent for the party?"

Dani grinned. "Who knows? For all I know, he might have bought it. You know Papa."

Connie nodded. "Every kind of toiletry you can imagine is in the linen closet in there; it's like a designer cosmetics store."

"I'll pass. All my stuff's on *Vengeance*. See you later."

"DID LIZ SAY what she and Dani were up to earlier this evening?" Paul asked. He and Connie were back aboard *Diamantista II*, turning down their bed.

"They were making the rounds of some of the clubs at South Beach," Connie said.

"How did they get all muddy?" Paul asked. "There's gotta be a story there."

"You heard Dani's response when I asked her?" Connie asked.

He chuckled. "Mud wrestling? You were poking at the hornets' nest, weren't you?"

"I really didn't mean to provoke her; she usually has a better sense of humor. Liz said she's going through a crisis about not being able to find a boyfriend. I guess I hit a nerve."

"I guess," Paul said, grinning. "Did Liz tell you what happened? I saw you two talking while Phillip finished telling me his Sharktooth story."

"Yes. This good-looking hunk hit on Dani, and Liz excused

herself. She left them at the table and sat at the bar where she could keep an eye on them."

"Like Dani might need protection," Paul said, shaking his head. "Not that girl. Were they really in a club with a mud wrestling pit? I thought that was passé."

"No. That was just my smart-aleck remark. Dani and the guy were going through the pick-up ritual when he got a phone call and bailed out on her. He'd just asked her to go to dinner, and then he ran off."

"Okay. So what about the mud wrestling?"

"There was no mud wrestling, Paul. Forget that and listen to me, damn it. Dani overheard enough of the call to know that he'd agreed to meet this woman named Lupita on the beach east of the club in ten minutes. She grabbed Liz and they hid under the boardwalk to see what he was up to."

"That's a little odd, even for Dani," Paul said. "And I thought you were the suspicious type."

"Watch it, mister. This jerk spoke Spanish on the call, apparently thinking Dani was too white-bread to understand. She didn't catch everything, but she heard him say something about dinner with the *béké's* daughter, and Dani thought that he was describing her."

"Okay," Paul said, "but why follow him?"

"Because she hadn't told him enough about herself for him to know anything about her father."

"I see. So she thought this guy knew who she was before he moved in on her. That is a little suspicious."

"Yes," Connie said. "I guess it was. Following him might have been over the top, but this is Dani we're talking about."

"Right. So did they learn anything about the guy?"

"A woman met him right after he stepped onto the beach. Liz said from the way she greeted him, they looked to be friends rather than lovers. They walked off up the beach, talking, but they were out of earshot, so Dani was even more frustrated."

"What's she going to do about it?" Paul asked.

Connie shrugged. "Who knows? She's got his name and phone number. They swapped numbers early on, I guess. Liz told her to wait and see what happens. She figures he might call Dani, but she's not sure how Dani will react. Or how she *should* react."

"What's your take?" Paul asked.

"Mine?" Connie smiled. "I'm glad I'm married. I never did like that dating stuff. But I agree with Dani. From what I heard, this man's behavior's a bit off. I hope she steers clear of him."

"Will you tell her that?"

"Only if she asks for my opinion. It's not really any of my business," Connie said.

"Mm," Paul said. "I could make a call and check this guy out. Maybe you should make the offer; get his name and number."

"I don't think so, Paul. Not unless she asks. She knows your connections to the MPD, and she's not shy about asking if she wants help. Wait and see. She's sort of tense over this whole dating thing, from what Liz said. Let's leave her alone unless she brings it up, okay?"

"Yes ma'am. And for the record, I'm glad you're married, too."

"WHAT DO you think I should do about him, Liz?" Dani took a sip of wine. She and Liz were sitting at the table in *Vengeance's* main cabin having a nightcap.

"I thought we decided earlier that you should wait and see if he calls. Have you changed your mind?"

"Maybe. Whether he calls or not, I want to know why he knew about Papa."

"Is there any chance you misunderstood? He was speaking pretty softly, from what I could tell."

"I didn't catch everything," Dani said, frowning. "He definitely said something about eating with the *béké's* daughter, though."

And he called that woman Lupita. The way he said her name, it didn't sound like they were strangers."

"No," Liz agreed. "It didn't look that way on the beach, either. But I don't think they're lovers."

"Why do you say that?" Dani raised her eyebrows.

"Two things. First, if they were lovers, she would have probably been angry with him for picking you up in the bar, don't you think?"

"I see. Yes, that makes sense. She didn't seem angry, did she?"

"No, she didn't, and the kiss on each cheek isn't the way I would have expected her to greet her lover. Especially not if he was trying to pick up a girl in a bar."

"Right," Dani said. "So, what do you think? Should I call him?"

"I think you should see if he calls you. Put aside your curiosity; think like a girl who was abandoned."

"So I should be pissed off? Is that what you're saying?"

"Not necessarily pissed off, but I don't think it would be normal for you to initiate contact with him so quickly. Forgetting the '*béké's* daughter' comment for a moment, I think a normal reaction would be to wait and see. It's not like you had any kind of relationship with him."

"But I still want to know who he is, whether he calls or not. In fact, I'd like to know before he calls. It might be important."

"Why?" Liz asked.

"Because if he knew who I was before he hit on me, he was most likely looking for me."

"How would he have known where to find you?"

"Good question. Maybe he followed us. Or had someone follow us."

"That's a scary thought," Liz said. "Why would he do that?"

"Another good question," Dani said, draining her wine. "You're learning."

Liz chuckled. "I'm supposed to be teaching you, I thought."

"About dating, yes. But I don't need any help being ... um ... "

"Paranoid?" Liz prompted.

"It's not a sign of paranoia to be worried when someone's really after you," Dani said.

Liz grinned and shook her head. "Okay, but I still think you should wait and see if he calls before you call him. Maybe Mario can find out something about him for you in the meantime."

"I can't ask Mario, Liz. That would spoil the surprise. He doesn't know we're here."

"Oh, right," Liz said. "Well — "

"Wait," Dani interrupted. "I can ask Paul. Thanks for the idea. I kind of forgot where we were."

"Uh-huh," Liz said. "I'm exhausted. Are you ready to go to sleep yet?"

"Sure. Thanks for listening, coach."

"My pleasure," Liz said, finishing her wine.

# 3

---

Phillip Davis sat in the gazebo, sipping his first cup of coffee and watching the seagulls swooping over a school of bait-fish near the shore. He dropped his gaze to admire *Vengeance* and *Diamantista II*, tied side by side at the dock. His thoughts were interrupted by the approach of a man in work clothes, his face shaded by a rough straw hat. Phillip had noticed him working in one of the flower beds near the gate when he brought his coffee out a few minutes earlier.

The man stopped a few paces from Phillip and removed his hat, mopping his forehead with a red bandana before he said, "Good morning, *Señor* Davis. Can you spare a moment?"

Surprised that the man addressed him by name, Phillip put his mug down on the table and turned to look at him. He couldn't place the man, but he knew the face from somewhere. "Good morning," Phillip said, as he searched his memory.

The man grinned, holding the hat by his side with his left hand. He gave Phillip a moment before he spoke. "You may not remember, but we — "

"Martínez, right?" Phillip interrupted him. "Give me just a ... José Martínez, isn't it?"

The man nodded, a pleased look on his dark face. "Yes, Colonel Davis. You have a good memory. It has been some years since you last saw me. You are looking as fit as always. You are retired, I hear."

"Yes." Phillip extended his hand, and the man took it. "I'm not Colonel Davis any longer. Phillip will do, if I can call you José. You haven't changed much, either."

"You are kind, *señor*," the man said, releasing Phillip's hand from his callused grip. "Of course, call me José, but I will call you *Señor* Davis. I must stay in character in case we are overheard. Please, will you walk with me while we talk? Pretend to be interested in the flowers; we may be watched."

Phillip nodded and stood up, picking up his coffee. Martínez turned and they strolled toward the flower bed where he had been working, walking side-by-side as Martínez gestured at the plants around the perimeter of the property.

"I take it that you are *not* retired, José?"

"Never, *señor*. If I stay in one place too long, my past will catch up to me, I fear."

"But you're not really a gardener, either, are you?"

Martínez put the hat back on and turned, pointing at the flower bed where Phillip had first seen him. "Only when it suits me. Perhaps in another life, I could be. But in this life, I have too much to do to spend my time on such things."

"I won't take up your time unnecessarily, then. I'm sure you came to me for a reason."

"Thank you, *señor*. Your manner has not changed any more than your appearance. I will cut to the chase, as they say. We may both be old soldiers, but me, I am still fighting the same war, you know?"

"Against the Castro regime?" Phillip asked.

Martínez shrugged.

"Then I don't understand your caution this morning. Surely, you must feel safe enough here in Miami."

Martínez dropped to one knee and poked at the loose, black soil in the flower bed with his right hand. "They are everywhere, the DGI. Even here in Miami. Especially here, because we are here, and they watch us. My people watch over us just now, but the younger ones, they are sometimes working both sides. So, we old soldiers, we are cautious. There are bold soldiers, and there are old soldiers, but not so many old, bold soldiers, yes?" Martínez smiled at Phillip.

"Yes. So you still hope to overthrow the Castro regime?"

"It is more important now than ever, *señor*. Fidel is dead, and Raul, he is old. When he dies, the country will be in some real trouble. With no one to provide a path into the future, the crooked ones will take over. Poor Cuba. You understand me?"

"I think so. Why have you come to me?"

"We need weapons my friend. Even though you are retired, I think you may know people who can help us, yes?"

"I don't know, José. I'll have to make some calls. Perhaps someone will remember me."

"That is all I ask, *Señor* Davis. Thank you for listening. Now I leave you to your coffee."

"Wait," Phillip said. "How will I reach you?"

"You cannot, but I'll be back in touch."

"It may take me a little time," Phillip said, frowning. "I'll have to signal you somehow."

Martínez smiled. "We will know, *señor*. We will hear. Do not worry; I will be in touch when you have something for me. Now, I must go. The roses, they need my attention. Good day."

Phillip went back to his coffee and thought about what Martínez had said. His first reaction was to tell Martínez that he couldn't help. He'd retired from the military years ago. Like many before him, he had used his military experience to pursue a second career with J.-P. Berger.

In the last few years, clandestine military activity in the Caribbean basin had waned. Phillip could have worked in other, less settled parts of the world, but he was reluctant. He didn't need the money, so he had withdrawn from the business. Presented with this opportunity, he realized he missed the action. The chance to work with Martínez and J.-P. excited him.

"WE SLEPT LATE," Liz said, filling a kettle at the galley sink and putting it on the stove to boil.

Dani yawned, nodding as she watched Liz spooning finely ground coffee into a funnel-shaped filter. "It's a luxury not to have to worry about the anchor dragging every time the wind shifts during the night."

"I can't remember the last time I slept until nine o'clock," Liz said, nodding. "I don't like being tied to a dock, though. The motion of the boat is awkward when she jerks against the dock lines."

"It is," Dani agreed. "And I feel like we have to be extra quiet because Connie and Paul are right next to us."

"It's good to see them," Liz said. "Especially with no — "

The ringing of Dani's phone interrupted her. Dani turned and scooped it up from the chart table, glancing at the caller i.d. "Unknown caller," she said, sliding her finger across the screen to accept the call. "Hello?"

"Dani?" a man's voice asked. Dani had the phone set to default to speaker mode, a habit born of living life outside in the trade winds, which often made it difficult to hear a caller.

"Yes. Who's calling, please?"

"It's David Ortiz, from last night. I hope I didn't wake you."

"No, I was up," Dani said, a chill coming into her voice.

"Look, I wanted to apologize for running out on you last night. My sister called; it was a family emergency."

"Oh?" Dani said, still in a cold tone. "I hope everything's all right, then."

"I don't know yet; she's still on her way to Martinique, and I haven't heard from her. Our mother's down there, visiting a friend. Mom had a stroke, they think, and the friend called Lupita."

"Lupita's your sister?"

"Right, and she needed some money for the flights. Sorry I didn't take time to explain last night, but she was upset. The *béké's* daughter doesn't speak anything but French, so she and Lupita couldn't really communicate well."

"The *béké's* daughter?" Dani asked. "Who's that?"

"Sorry. That's what Mom always called her friend. *Béké* is Creole for, like, a white person, a French person, mostly."

"Uh-huh," Dani said. "Well, I hope everything's okay with your mom, anyway."

"Thanks," Ortiz said. "That's kind of you. I'd like a chance to make up for last night, if you're still interested."

"I don't know, David. I'm not going to have a lot of free evenings while we're in Miami." Dani smiled as Liz nodded and gave her a thumbs up.

"How about lunch then?" Ortiz asked.

"Lunch?" Surprised, Dani looked at Liz, raising her eyebrows. "Today?"

"If you can make it," Ortiz said.

Liz shrugged, looked pensive for a moment, and then nodded, shrugging again.

"Okay, but it'll have to be a quick one. I'm here to see a lot of friends I haven't seen in a long time."

"Great!" Ortiz said. "Where are you staying?"

"On my boat," Dani said. "We're at a private dock on Star Island."

"Wow! You're living large. Do you know the yacht club?"

"The Miami Yacht Club?" Dani asked.

"Yes. It's pretty close to where you are, and the food's excellent."

"Right," Dani said. "I know it well."

"Okay, then. I'll book a table there for noon. How's that?"

"Okay," Dani said.

"I'll pick you up around 11:45, then."

Liz shook her head and mouthed, "Meet him there."

Dani nodded. "Actually, David, it would be better if I met you there. I have some errands to run this morning."

"Okay, great," Ortiz said. "I'll look forward to it. Thanks, and 'bye for now."

Dani disconnected the call and put the phone down, taking the coffee that Liz offered her. "How'd I do, coach?"

"Great. I thought it would be better if you had your own transportation, though, just in case," Liz said.

"I think so, too. I'll take the dinghy; it's a short trip, even at no-wake speed."

"What did you think of his story?" Liz asked.

Dani shrugged and took a sip of coffee. "I don't know."

"Was it a plausible explanation of what you overheard last night?" Liz asked.

"Maybe. It almost seems contrived, though."

"Why?"

"The way he dropped in the '*béké's* daughter' reference, like he knew it would have made me suspicious."

"Poor guy," Liz said, grinning. She raised her coffee mug to her nose and inhaled, closing her eyes. She sighed and then took a sip. "You're the most suspicious person I know. He doesn't stand a chance."

"Does that mean you agree with me?"

Liz peered into her coffee mug for a moment, thinking. She looked up at Dani and nodded. "Maybe so. But he could have been telling the truth."

"Why didn't he just call her 'mom's friend,' or something? Why explain what *béké* means?"

"Your first question is a good one, but he's probably a little upset about his mother, and maybe that really is what they call her friend, and it just came out naturally."

Dani shook her head. "But why explain it, then?"

"Because you asked, Dani."

"I still don't like it, Liz. It was too convenient, and then there's the coincidence of my being a *béké's* daughter."

"That's why I thought you should have your own transportation. Don't get in a car with him, at least not until you know more about him."

"That's how I feel, too," Dani said. "I think I'll go see if Paul's awake. Maybe he can check this guy out with the MPD."

"DID he say which exile groups are working with him?" J.-P. Berger asked.

Phillip shook his head. "No. But then he wouldn't, normally. Martínez was always good at being discreet."

"But he did say that they wanted to overthrow the Castro government?" J.-P. asked.

Phillip hesitated. "No, now that I think about it, he didn't. Not outright. I asked twice, and he never quite answered. He didn't say anything to indicate that I was wrong about him being anti-Castro, but he was careful. He also mentioned that we might be overheard, so he gave himself an out, I guess. Both with me and with anybody who might have been listening."

J.-P. nodded. "He has the reputation of being a smooth operator. When do you think you'll hear back from your contact at the agency?"

Phillip shrugged. "It's not an emergency, so I didn't put any pressure on them. I just told them I needed advice on how to proceed with Martínez."

"What do you think they'll do?"

"It's hard to say, J.-P. I'm sure they'll check him out, but beyond that, your guess is as good as mine."

"Will they have you get back in touch with him?"

"Probably, unless they decide to ignore him."

"Would they not tell you that?"

"I don't know, J.-P. This is new territory for me. I haven't called them since I retired."

"How did Martínez want you to contact him once you had an answer?"

"He didn't. He told me they'd know once I made my call and that he'd get in touch then."

J.-P. frowned. "That is strange, to me. What do you make of it?"

"Whoever Martínez is working with must have someone on the inside," Phillip said. "Either that, or they're monitoring my communications."

"Is either of those things likely?" J.-P. asked.

Phillip shook his head. "Neither is likely, to my way of thinking. But we both know that either is possible."

"You are better versed in this part of the business than I, Phillip. Which do you think is more probable?"

Phillip studied his friend for a moment as he considered his answer. "It's more probable that they have a mole somewhere in our government, I think. Not that my communications are so secure, but my movements and patterns of use are too erratic, these days. Monitoring my communications would be more difficult than planting a mole, I think."

"I don't quite take your meaning," J.-P. said. "It seems to me that penetrating the agency would be more difficult."

"In some ways, yes," Phillip said. "But the scope of an effort to monitor all my possible means of communication would be so broad that it's probably beyond any of the organizations Martínez might be allied with. I don't mean it's impossible, but it would take the kind of infrastructure that the NSA might have. It's not something a coalition of exile groups could do, in my opinion."

J.-P. nodded. "Then why would they involve you?"

"Now I'm the one who doesn't understand," Phillip said. "Can you ask that a different way?"

"Perhaps I was ahead of myself. If they have an inside source, why would they need you? Why not go to their inside person?"

"Ah! I see your point. First, their inside source could well be someone at a low level; someone who can monitor and report, but who has no authority within the organization."

J.-P. nodded. "I understand that now, thank you. But you said, 'first.' That implies that there may be a second possibility."

"There are many possibilities, J.-P." Phillip smiled. "The one I was thinking of is that for some reason, they want *my* involvement."

J.-P. frowned and shook his head. "But why?"

"They could have a mole in any of several places, but I have a certain track record. If I'm involved, it could imply endorsement by certain parts of the U.S. government. That could be important to them for a lot of different reasons."

J.-P. nodded. "Thank you for explaining. I was overlooking the international political aspects."

"Or it could be as simple as the fact that Martínez remembers me," Phillip said. "It could also be because he knows about my connection to you, and he wants something that only you could supply."

"And what would that be?" J.-P. asked.

Phillip smiled. "I wouldn't know. I'm retired, remember?"

"You will always be a partner in our business; you know that. Any time you wish to take an active role again, you may."

"Thank you. Yes, I do know that. But it's best for all of us if I don't know the latest about what's in the portfolio. Unless I do resume an active role, at least."

J.-P. nodded. "Did Martínez say whether they had money to pay for these weapons?"

"It didn't come up," Phillip said. "That could be another

reason he approached me. He knows I used to arrange financing. Or maybe not. There's plenty of money in the exile community."

"How many men does he want to equip?"

"He didn't say. Why?"

"Just curious," J.-P. said, with a smile. "Business is business. Training? Did he mention that?"

"Not yet, J.-P. You almost sound hungry for business," Phillip said, a teasing smile on his face.

J.-P. chuckled. "Always. So, while you are thinking like a super-spy, let's talk about how I'm going to get Mario and his wife out here without telling him what's going on."

# 4

"How well do you know José Martínez?" The man in the dark glasses asked. He and Phillip sat at an outside table in front of a tiny Cuban restaurant on Lincoln Road Mall in South Beach.

"Not all that well," Phillip said. "I encountered him on several of my assignments in Central America. We've met often enough in strange places over the years. Either of us would have guessed the other wasn't there as a tourist; you know what I mean."

The man nodded and took a bite of pastry. "Don't be offended, but I have to ask you some questions." He pulled his dark glasses down his nose and peered over the top at Phillip, waiting for a reaction. When Phillip nodded, he settled the glasses back in place and continued. "Did you and Martínez ever pass information back and forth?"

"No."

The man nodded. "Good. Did you ever tell him who you were working for? I mean, besides being a military attaché?"

"No," Phillip said, smiling.

"Did he ever tell you who he was working for?"

"He was a mercenary. It was always clear who he was working for from what he was doing each time I encountered him."

The man nodded. "Do you have any reason to think he might have been working for a foreign intelligence organization besides being a mercenary?"

"No, but I can't say that he wasn't, either."

"You were in this game for a long time — a lot longer than I have been, obviously. You're well respected by my superiors. They told me to ask you something that I find odd, but they said you'd understand the importance." He slid the glasses down his nose again and looked at Phillip.

Phillip nodded, smiling, and said, "They want my opinion on this."

His glasses back in place, the man said, "Yes. I'm to ask about your gut reaction."

Phillip lifted his tiny cup of *colado* to his lips and took a sip, his eyes taking in the people passing on the pedestrian mall. Swallowing the sticky-sweet, bitter Cuban espresso, he turned to face his companion. "I think you should check him out thoroughly before making a decision. His story's plausible, but the timing makes this suspicious, to me."

"Can you expand on that?"

"Yes. Why wait until we're normalizing our relations with Cuba? What he says about the potential instability that would result from the death of Raul Castro rings true. I can see a big risk for the U.S. in that scenario. Living with Castro next door is one thing, but we could get a much worse neighbor. Fidel's focus was on what was good for him and his country. Raul is a little more open, but imagine Cuba in the hands of people who want to do serious damage to the U.S. Somebody aggressive and suicidal, like ISIL, for example. That's an argument for supporting Martínez and his people, maybe." Phillip paused and finished his coffee.

He drank some ice water and started talking again. "But if we back his effort, the risks are significant as well. We can't do it in a way that will hide our involvement. The world will know the invasion was staged from our soil, so our complicity will be assumed by the rest of the world. No amount of insulation or denial will change that."

"You're saying you don't trust Martínez, then?"

"I'm saying the stakes are too high to make a bet based on my gut reaction. I don't have any reason to trust him or not to trust him. I've known him casually for a long time, but that's it. He's not family, or even a friend. You know?"

"If your mother says she loves you, check it out? Is that it?"

"Yes, exactly."

"Okay, good. Now, another question. Given what you just told me about your relationship, or lack of relationship, why do you think Martínez came to you?"

"Good question. I don't know the answer, but it could be critical," Phillip said.

"Okay. I'll pass all that up the line, and we'll get back to you. In the meantime, we'd like for you to do two things when you see Martínez again."

Phillip waited for a moment, and asked, "What two things?"

"Ask him to be specific about which exile organization or organizations he's working for."

"That's one," Phillip said. "What else?"

"Ask him why he came to you."

"Okay," Phillip said. "Anything else that you need?"

"How are you to contact Martínez?"

"Don't call us; we'll call you."

"When is he supposed to call?"

"I don't know. He said he'd know when I had something."

"So he's following you, or he's got you wired, somehow."

Phillip nodded. "Either that, or you."

"What?"

"He could be watching you, or have you — or somebody else who knows your actions — wired."

"Impossible," the man in the dark glasses said.

Phillip smiled.

"Why are you smiling?"

"Gut reaction," Phillip said.

"What's your gut reaction? To what?"

"Ask your superiors."

"I don't get it. Ask them what?"

"About what's impossible. I'm leaving now. You should stay here and watch the people for a few minutes."

"Why?"

"See if you spot anyone watching me or tailing me."

"If I do?"

"Call me and tell me. And if you don't spot anyone, watch your ass, because if they aren't tailing me, they're probably tailing you. Take care, and tell your superiors they owe me one." Phillip stood and blended into the crowd of pedestrians meandering along the mall.

"YOU DON'T NEED to do this, you know," Dani said to Liz.

"I know I don't need to, but I'd like to, if you don't mind. What else am I going to do? Sit around here? Everybody else is out and about." Liz suppressed a chuckle as she watched Dani trying to put on mascara.

"I don't mind. I just don't want you to feel like you have to be my nursemaid. Paul said David Ortiz doesn't have a criminal record. I'll be okay having lunch at the club with him."

"I thought it might be fun to sit out by the pool and sunbathe. And I can watch the children's sailing class. Maybe I'll pitch in on the committee boat if they organize a race for them. If not, I'll just get one of those grilled mahi sandwiches and read *Sails Job*."

"*Sails Job?*"

"The latest book about Connie and Paul. Bud just released it a few weeks ago."

"Suit yourself. You ready?"

"Yes. Don't forget your lip gloss."

"Trying to look like a girl on the make can be a pain. I hope David appreciates it," Dani said, turning to the mirror and puckering her lips.

"I'm sure he will. You look stunning."

"Thanks. I feel stark naked."

"Stark naked? That sundress comes down to your knees."

"But there's no back to it. I can't even wear a bra. And I'd rather be wearing shorts. Dresses are so ... "

"So what?"

"I don't know. My legs feel exposed when I sit down."

"That's the idea, Dani. You have great legs; use them for something besides walking and kicking people."

"And there's nowhere to put my multi-tool, or my rigging knife."

"How about in your purse?"

"No room, with my wallet and phone and all this girl stuff."

"If you get in a bind and need tools, call me. I have mine."

Dani put the lip gloss in her purse and turned to look at Liz. "You're wearing shorts and a polo shirt? I thought you were going to sunbathe."

"I'll change at the club, if I feel like it. My suit's in my shoulder bag, with my multi-tool and rigging knife."

"Oh, sure. Rub it in. Why can't I carry a shoulder bag?"

"I told you. That canvas monstrosity of yours wouldn't go with your outfit. You'd look like a call girl with a bag full of sex toys."

"How would you know?"

"Movies. Blot your lipstick and let's go."

"Are you driving the dinghy, or am I?"

"I will. You'd break a fingernail."

"And that's another thing. I hate these glued-on nails. Why do women do stuff like this to themselves?"

"Men, Dani. Come on; it's time to get moving."

MANNY CRUZ WAS EATING lunch at his desk when Maldonado called. "What's happening, Willy?" Cruz asked when he took the call. He put his sandwich down on the wrapping paper and swung his feet off his desk to the floor, sitting upright, as if his boss could see him. For all he knew, Maldonado had a webcam right here in his office. The man didn't trust anybody, and reporting directly to him made Cruz nervous.

"Is Ortiz in place yet?" Maldonado asked.

"He should be having lunch with the girl about now," Cruz said. "He made a date with her for noon at the yacht club, I think. Why? Is something going on?"

"Not yet, but the sooner he becomes part of her routine, the better. Martínez spoke with Davis early this morning. It's starting to move."

"So soon? Where did Martínez — "

"You don't need to know that," Maldonado said, interrupting Cruz.

"Right. I just want to be sure I'm positioned to help."

"Do as I tell you and it will all work out," Maldonado said. "Davis has already called his former employers. He had a meeting with one of their field agents not long ago. Unfortunately, we didn't manage to get a recording, but that's okay. It's too early for them to have said anything important. But we'll need your help this afternoon."

"No problem. Whatever you need," Cruz said.

"A car and driver, non-descript, but classy enough to look like it should be picking up a passenger on Star Island."

"You care about the plates?" Cruz asked.

"Of course. It's picking up Davis and taking him to a meeting with Martínez. Davis will no doubt run the plates as soon as he gets back to the villa on Star Island. They should be a dead end."

"Stolen okay?" Cruz asked.

"The car? Or the plates?" Maldonado asked.

"The plates. Car's too big a risk; I can send one of the company cars, but it'll come back to me unless we change the plates."

"Stolen plates would be okay. Borrowed would be better, especially if you could return them before the owner notices. That'll send them on a false trail."

"But wouldn't it make sense to have the plates lead back to someone in the exile community?" Cruz asked.

"No. That would look sloppy. We want Davis and his people to think Martínez is with a serious organization. Plates that lead back to anyone who might know Martínez would look amateurish."

"Got it. We can handle that. Where are we going to take Davis?"

"That's your next step," Maldonado said. "You have a vacant rental property? Or one of your listings that's unoccupied for a few days?"

"Sure, I can do that, but won't Davis trace the house?" Cruz asked

"Blindfold him when he gets in the car."

"Think he'll allow that?"

"Yes. He's done this kind of thing before." Maldonado kept his impatience out of his voice. Now he had a better appreciation for why Martínez wanted him for a buffer. Cruz was a rank amateur. "He'll probably expect it," Maldonado said. "You can let him take it off once he's inside the house for the meeting; we want him comfortable. Just make sure there's nothing sitting around that will tell him where he is. No mail, no brochures, that kind of thing."

"Right. Got it. When's the pickup?" Cruz asked.

"I'll call you. How much lead time do you need?"

"I'll send somebody to grab a license plate right now. Figure I'll have a car ready in thirty minutes. I've got a house ready now; we just staged it for showing yesterday. I was going to send Ortiz to put the brochures in it this afternoon after he's back from his lunch with the girl."

"Good," Maldonado said. "Make sure Ortiz understands. He needs to seduce that girl; we want her under his spell. Besides what he can pick up from her and her friends, we may need her for leverage before this is over."

"Got it. Ortiz is dumber than a stone, but the women can't leave him alone. Even Lupita thinks he's hot."

"Why do you say 'even Lupita?'" Maldonado asked. "I always thought she was strange."

"Me too, but I keep my mouth shut. I've seen what she does to people that rub her the wrong way."

"Yeah. No matter. She's good at what she does. She still doing that cage fighting shit?"

"Yeah," Cruz said. "She's good enough to turn pro, what I hear."

"Don't lose her, Manny. Whatever it costs, keep her around. We need her."

"No problem, Willy. I gotta get moving on the plates."

"Good. You can tell me where the house is when I call you back, so I can get Martínez there."

Maldonado disconnected the call without saying goodbye. Cruz called his secretary and told her to find one of the drivers and send him in. He picked up his sandwich and swiveled his chair, putting his feet back on his desk.

# 5

---

"If you don't see me, just give me a call when you're done," Liz said, as Dani stepped onto the floating dinghy dock at the Miami Yacht Club. She chuckled as she watched Dani's barefoot walk up the gangplank, her high-heeled sandals dangling from her right hand. As Dani reached solid ground, she leaned against a dinghy rack and put the shoes on, wobbling away across the grass toward the clubhouse.

As they had planned, Liz pushed off from the dock and motored out into the anchorage. They were early for Dani's date with David Ortiz, but Dani didn't want to chance having him see Liz hovering in the background. She'd asked Liz to drop her and then kill a little time before coming back to the club, in case Ortiz had arrived early.

Liz smiled and shook her head at the memory of her friend's jitters. Dani could plan and execute a single-handed attack on a drug smuggler's boat with a heavily armed crew without showing the least anxiety. Going to lunch with a handsome man was a different thing entirely.

Liz skirted the densely packed anchorage that extended from the club out to the first of the Venetian Islands. When she could no longer make out the club through the anchored boats, she checked her watch. It was ten after twelve; by the time she got back to the club, Ortiz and Dani would either be seated, or Dani would be devastated at having been stood up.

As she wedged the dinghy in between two others at the now-crowded dock, Liz spotted Dani and Ortiz seated at a table on the patio. She picked up the padlock from the pouch in the dinghy's bow and grasped the end of the 20-foot-long stainless steel security chain they used to lock their dinghy. She scrambled across another dinghy that was tied up short, blocking her path to the dock. After she stepped onto the dock, she crouched and looped the chain around the low railing, locking her dinghy to the dock. As Liz straightened up from her crouch, a flash of light from the parking lot caught her attention.

She dropped back into a squatting position, pretending to check the lock as she studied the cars. She spotted a woman sitting in one, holding a camera with a big telephoto lens. As Liz watched, the woman snapped photos of Dani and Ortiz, the only people on the patio. The woman lowered the camera and sunlight reflected from the lens, replicating the flash that had caught Liz's attention.

Liz stood up and mounted the gangway that led to the shore. Instead of taking the direct path to the patio and pool area that Dani had chosen, Liz turned left at the top of the gangway. She walked around the racks of stored dinghies, coming out into the parking area. With a clear view of the back end of the woman's car, Liz looked at her smartphone as if checking something. She snapped a photo of the license plate and put the phone back in her pocket.

On her way to the women's locker room, Liz strolled past the driver's side of the car. With a sideways glance, she saw that the woman was young, with a mass of curly black hair. Looking at the screen on her camera, the woman didn't notice Liz.

Once inside, Liz decided to skip changing into her bikini.

Since Dani was sitting outside, Liz would sit at the inside bar where she'd be out of Ortiz's view. She wasn't sure if he'd remember her from their brief encounter last night when he'd approached their table at the nightclub, but she didn't want to chance it. She ordered a grilled mahi-mahi sandwich and a heart of palm salad from the bartender.

"Great!" the bartender said. "Good choice. The mahi-mahi was caught just a few hours ago by one of the members. And what can I get you to drink?"

"Iced tea, please," Liz said.

"I'll get your order back to the kitchen and bring your tea right out, ma'am."

"Thanks," Liz said.

As the bartender left, Liz put her phone on the bar and sent a text to Paul Russo, asking if he could get someone to run the license plate number for her.

"Are you meeting someone?" the bartender asked, setting a tall glass of iced tea on the bar in front of Liz.

"No. Why?" Liz asked.

"Oh, I was just going to suggest that you grab a table if you were. It'll fill up in a few minutes with the lunch crowd."

"I see. Well, thanks, but I'm by myself today."

"I don't remember seeing you here. Are you a new member?"

"No, I'm an out-of-state member. My partner and I run charters down in the islands, but we get up here often enough to make the membership worthwhile. Did you need my club card?"

"Oh, no. That's fine. Just making conversation. I like talking to visiting sailors; I'm going to take off cruising myself, one of these days."

"What kind of boat do you have?" Liz asked.

"I'm shopping. I was all set to go down island with my fiancé. We left from Annapolis last year and got this far before we broke up. The boat was his, so here I am."

"Not a bad place to be shopping for a cruising boat," Liz said.

"Not bad at all," the bartender agreed. "A lot of people get this far and lose their nerve at the prospect of finally going offshore. Then they put their boats on the market. Only problem is, most of the boats are way too big for me to single hand."

"Newbies do tend to buy boats that are too big," Liz agreed. "So you know most of the members by sight, now?"

"Well, most of the regulars. That guy out there on the patio with the pretty girl is in here all the time."

"Handsome guy, isn't he?" Liz said.

"Yeah, and he knows it, too. Thinks he's a real ladies' man, that one does."

"One of those, huh?" Liz said.

"Oh, he's not so bad," the young woman said. "I mean, he's polite and everything. Actually, he's a real nice guy, but he's got a different girl every time I see him. I went out to dinner with him a couple of times. He still hits on me every so often, but he's not my type."

"Why's that?"

"Not a serious sailor. He uses a company membership to entertain here."

"What kind of company does he own?" Liz asked, fishing.

"Real estate. But he doesn't own it. The owner's a guy named Manny Cruz. That guy just works there. He's like, some kind of sales agent, or something."

"I see," Liz said.

"Excuse me; that chime means your order's up." The woman stepped back into the kitchen and returned with Liz's lunch. "Well, nice talking with you. Guess I'd better get busy and set up for the crowd. Flag me down if you need anything."

"Will do," Liz said. "Thanks."

As she reached for her sandwich, her phone buzzed, vibrating on the bar top. She looked down and saw that Paul had sent her a text. She tapped the screen and read, "Car registered to Lupita Vidal. Cops know her; be careful. More when we see you."

She tapped out a quick response. "Thx. Don't mention to anyone, esp. Dani. Will explain later."

"Forgive the excessive caution of my associates, *Señor* Davis," Martínez said, handing Phillip a small cup of strong, sugar-laden coffee. "They trust no one these days, not even their fellow Americans. They treated you well, I hope — except for the blindfold?"

Phillip smiled and took a sip of the coffee. "Yes. Well enough. That's okay; I understand. My associates feel the same way about you, I'm afraid."

Martínez chuckled and shook his head. "The one you met with on Lincoln Road this morning, he is too young to have much experience. I am surprised his superiors trusted him with such a sensitive mission."

"They're all young, now, José. People our age have been put out to pasture."

Martínez nodded. "Yes. Or buried. So what did this child have to say? Your meeting was quite brief."

"He's just a messenger boy," Phillip said.

"We have guessed this; it's not our first encounter with him. He had some questions, no doubt."

Phillip nodded and took another sip of the coffee. "Yes. They wanted to know if I trusted you."

Martínez laughed. "Fools. And I'm sure you told them you did not."

"Almost. I told them I had no reason to trust or distrust you, that our acquaintance was casual."

"Then, of course, he wanted to know what is your instinct about me, yes?"

Phillip chuckled. "Were you listening in?"

Martínez shook his head, smiling. "No, *señor*. But this is not my first time. What else do they want to know?"

"The names of the organizations in the consortium you work with."

Martínez looked away, a somber look on his weathered, brown face. After a moment, he turned back to Phillip. "No."

"No?" Phillip asked. "It's a reasonable question."

"Perhaps to someone not involved in this business, it is reasonable. I could, of course, name the 'usual suspects,' but that would prove nothing. Next they will want names of people."

"You're worried that they'll arrest the people, or investigate them? Spoil the plot, somehow?"

"No, *señor*. They have a track record of ignoring such activity, even though the rest of the world thinks they're allowing terrorists to operate with impunity. I don't think they would bother us that way."

"What's the problem, then?" Phillip asked.

"The problem is that the DGI has infiltrated all of these organizations, my friend. So has the FBI. Miami is overrun with double and triple agents."

"You're saying you don't trust your own people, José?"

"You and I are both alive after all these years because we are cautious men. They asked that question as a test, I think, not because they expected me to answer."

"A test?" Phillip asked, frowning.

"To see if I am a fool. This is what I think. To answer their question would be foolish. They know this. They are testing me. And to answer your question, I trust very few people. I don't trust any organization — only a few individuals. You understand?"

"Yes."

"I knew that you would. You are the same, I think."

Phillip held Martínez's gaze for several seconds. "I understand your position, but how can we move forward?"

"I will send them a signal. They will recognize it, and they won't question my bona fides. Afterward, you will be dealing with someone at a higher level in their organization. I'm sure they won't trust that child with this, once they know I am serious. Did they have any other questions?"

Phillip shook his head. "No, but I have one."

Martínez grinned. "Perhaps I can answer it. Ask, *señor*."

"Do you have funding for this?"

"You mean, am I expecting your government to pay for it?"

"Correct. That's my question."

"The money is not a problem. What I need is for your government to stay out of our way. They have too many people watching us for me to do this without their blessing. As you no doubt guessed, we have staging areas in South Florida. They know where these are already. They must not interfere. That is one thing. The other is that they must allow our shipments to pass unquestioned. Our matériel will come from outside the U.S., to afford them deniability, as they call it. But it must reach our staging areas without U.S. Customs finding it."

"You have a supplier already, then?"

"In the fullness of time, my friend, we will discuss this. If you have nothing else, please put the blindfold on, and I will summon the car to take you back to the villa. And give *Señor* Espinosa my regards on his birthday, please."

"I ENJOY your company very much, Dani," Ortiz said, his demeanor matching the sincerity of his tone of voice. "I hope we can do this again, soon."

"Oh, so do I," Dani said, annoyed as she felt the flush spreading up from her chest. She envisioned the red blotches that she could sense creeping up her neck. Her cheeks felt hot, and she fought down the urge to hop into his lap. Disgusted with her hormonal reaction, she reached for her water glass and knocked it over. "Shit!" she yelped, feeling her flushed skin burn with embarrassment.

"It's nothing," Ortiz said, leaping to his feet and stemming the spreading puddle with a napkin. "It was almost empty."

"I'm such a klutz," Dani said.

"Nonsense. Could have happened to anybody. In this humidity, the moisture forms on a cold glass and makes it slippery as all get out. It's my fault for choosing an outdoor table. It wouldn't have happened inside in the air conditioning. You okay?"

"Yes. Thanks for being so nice."

"Like I said, it's just one of those things. It happens a lot in this climate."

Dani felt a smile on her face. "I didn't mean just about my clumsiness. I had a wonderful time. I don't know when I've enjoyed anyone's company so much."

Ortiz, still standing, beamed his sexiest smile. "Me, too. I'd better go, though. Can't keep my client waiting. Can I call you this evening?"

"Yes, please. I hope you will."

He nodded. "Count on it," he said and stepped around the table. He leaned over, bending close to her, holding her gaze. "May I?", he asked, in a soft, husky tone.

Dani suppressed a grin and nodded, turning her face up to him and closing her eyes. She was disappointed to feel his chaste peck on her cheek.

"Talk to you this evening, then," he said, turning to walk through the breezeway and out the front door.

Dani was still in a warm daze a minute later when she heard Liz say, "Well, tell me about it!" as she took Ortiz's chair.

Shock on her face, Dani asked, "Where were you? I didn't see you by the pool."

"Inside at the bar. When I saw you two out here, I thought I'd be less conspicuous there. Nice flowers, by the way," Liz said eyeing the six long-stemmed roses in a box that was open on the table.

"Oh, Liz. It was going so well, and then ... " Dani shook her head, her dazzled look fading to one of dismay.

"And then what?"

"I was so rattled that I knocked over my water."

Liz laughed. "That's all? Nothing else went wrong?"

"I'm such a social dork," Dani said.

"From what I could see through the window, he was mesmerized by you. How did you part company?"

"He said, 'I enjoy your company very much, Dani, and I hope we can do this again, soon.'"

"That's nice. How did you respond?"

"By spilling my water."

"No, silly. I saw all of that. What did you say afterward? Did you tell him you had a nice time?"

"I thanked him for being so nice, and told him I couldn't remember ever enjoying anyone's company so much."

"Good job. Is he going to call you?"

Dani nodded. "I think so. He asked if he could call me this evening." She frowned.

"What's wrong?" Liz asked.

"Do you think he will? Call, I mean?"

"I'd bet my share in *Vengeance* on it," Liz said.

"Really?"

"Really. You did a good job. Now that he's hooked you need to think about whether you want to land him or not."

Dani was silent for a moment, a distant look on her face as she thought about what Liz said. Breaking the silence, she said, "Let's go back to the boat. I want to put some real clothes on, and wash this sticky mess off my face."

## 6

Ortiz, a cardboard cup of overpriced coffee in hand, pressed the key fob to unlock his car. He opened the driver's door and sat down, putting the coffee in the cup holder in the center console.

As he closed the door, he heard a woman's voice from the back seat. "Don't turn around or acknowledge me yet. Pull out of the garage and head south for the MacArthur causeway, back to Miami." He flicked his eyes to the rear-view mirror, but saw no one.

Ortiz pressed the start button, put the car in reverse, and backed out of the parking place. He drove to the nearest exit and inserted his claim check in the machine, followed by a five-dollar bill. He retrieved his change and pulled out of the garage, following the woman's instructions.

"Anyone following?" the voice asked after a couple of stoplights.

"No," Ortiz said.

"Good. Tell me how things are going with Cruz."

"Well enough. He's assigned me to a project with Lupita Vidal."

"Excellent. In Little Haiti?"

"No, it's not."

"What, then?"

"I think it's Alpha-66 business, but that's kind of a guess, so far."

"Well, at least he trusts you. Tell me more about the project."

"I'm supposed to set a honey trap for a woman whose father's apparently an arms dealer. He's rented a big place on Star Island for some kind of family gathering."

"Name?"

"J.-P. Berger. The daughter is Danielle. Dani, they call her."

"Where are these people from? The States?"

"No. The father's from France, although he's originally from Martinique. Dani and another woman own a charter yacht that they run in the islands. She's got an American mother, but she's divorced."

"She who? Dani's divorced, or the mother? Or the other woman? Whose mother?"

"Jeez. Dani's mother's divorced from her father. The other woman's named Liz Chirac, and she's Belgian. Okay?"

"Yes. Thanks. So why a honey trap?"

"I'm guessing now, but I think Cruz is trying to score weapons for Alpha-66."

"You think they're planning something?"

"I don't know yet. It could be opportunistic, because Berger's here."

"Try to find out what they're up to."

"All right, but it's off the track of our mission. I'm not happy about being pulled away from the Haitian thing."

"I understand, but the boss says you should go with it. It'll build trust with Cruz, and Lupita Vidal is the link between Cruz and Santos. Try to get close to her, if you can."

Ortiz laughed. "That's like trying to tame a wildcat; she's nuts."

"Try. That's an order."

"Yes, ma'am. Where are we going?"

"Head on into downtown. Park in one of the garages close to city hall and take a walk for a few minutes. I'll be in touch."

"WHERE'S DANI?" Connie asked, as Liz settled into the cockpit cushions aboard *Diamantista II*.

"She's gone to a day spa with her stepmother," Liz said.

"I can see Anne pampering herself, but that doesn't sound like Dani," Paul said.

"I called Anne during Dani's lunch date and asked her to insist that Dani go with her," Liz said. "It turned out not to be such a hard sell. Dani jumped at the chance to get her hair done."

"Dani?" Connie asked, wide-eyed. "I thought you cut each other's hair."

"She's had a sudden onset of vanity," Liz said.

"The date went well, then?" Connie asked.

"She's in love, or thinks so, anyway," Liz said. "I've never seen her in such a dopey state. It's like he put something in her drink."

"Really?" Paul asked. "You think he drugged her?"

"No, but he might as well have done."

"Good for her," Connie said. "She's been needing this for a while, ever since that Ralph guy dumped her."

"Well, I don't know about that. I think a lot of the Ralph thing was in Dani's mind, but don't tell her."

"You think this guy's serious?"

"That's why I asked Anne to take her to the spa. I wanted time alone to talk with you. I don't know what he's up to, but I'm worried." Liz told them about Ortiz's explanation for abandoning Dani the night they met.

"His sister's named Lupita?" Paul asked. "That's a coincidence. That plate you asked me to run earlier?"

"Yes," Liz said, "but the last name's different. I suppose she could be married, but that still doesn't explain why she was sitting in the car at the yacht club, taking pictures of Dani and Ortiz. Or why she's here when she's supposed to be in Martinique."

"She was what?" Paul asked, raising his eyebrows.

"That's why I asked you to run the plate."

"Somebody might have borrowed her car," Connie said. "Did you get a good look at the woman? Was she the same one who was on the beach last night?"

"I got a good look at the woman in the car. She could be the same one; the hair's the same. But it was pretty dark last night on the beach. I can't be sure."

Paul fussed with his smartphone for a few seconds and handed it to Liz. She studied the mug shot and nodded. "Maybe. Same hair, but I saw her in profile."

"Swipe right to left," Paul said.

"This is the woman in the car," Liz said, looking at a profile shot. "No question. Is she Lupita Vidal?"

"Yes," Paul said. "And that's her maiden name. She's a serious bad-ass."

"You think she could be this guy's sister?" Connie asked.

"Not if he's who he says he is," Paul said. "This woman's an only child. Her parents came from Cuba, all right, but they settled in Savannah, and they're dead. She's got quite a record."

"She has a police record?" Liz asked. "For what?"

"She's been arrested several times for assault, assault and battery, disturbing the peace, that kind of thing. Never been charged. Witnesses didn't want to follow through."

"Isn't that odd?" Liz asked.

"Not too odd," Paul said. "The people she picked on are as scared of the police as they are of her. She's muscle for a slum lord named Tony Santos who rents to poor immigrants. She collects overdue rent, and kicks people out when it suits him. That kind of thing."

"A woman? Doing that kind of work?" Liz asked.

"She's a tiger, apparently," Paul said. "She's a semi-pro cage fighter."

"A what?" Liz asked.

"Mixed martial arts," Paul said. "It's a blood sport. Bare knuckles, anything goes. No rules. They shut two opponents in a cage and let them go at it until one gives up or gets knocked unconscious."

"That sounds like it should be illegal," Connie said.

"It is, in some places. Lupita Vidal is undefeated, so far."

"Why would someone like that be tailing Dani and Ortiz?" Liz asked.

"I don't know," Paul said, "but you'd better warn Dani."

"That's what my reaction was earlier," Liz said. "Then I saw how excited she was. She'll be devastated."

"You have to tell her, Liz," Connie said. "She can ask David Ortiz about it. Maybe there's some explanation. Maybe this Lupita's got him confused with someone else, or ... " She shook her head.

"You're clutching at straws, Connie," Paul said. "He told Dani that Lupita's his sister, remember?"

"But Liz isn't sure she's the same woman."

"Liz can't positively identify her as the woman on the beach, but she had to be. One guy, two women of similar appearance within a 24-hour period? Both named Lupita? No question. You need to tell her, Liz. This woman's dangerous."

"How do you feel about that, Liz," Connie asked.

"Awful." The look on Liz's face was more eloquent than her answer. "Thanks for your support. I have a feeling I'm going to need you two to help pick up the pieces."

"I think some of Paul's rum punch is in order," Connie said. "When are she and Anne due back?"

Liz glanced at the screen of her phone. "About an hour. Make mine a double, please."

THE MERCEDES SEDAN with the dark windows pulled to a stop under the portico of the Star Island mansion. Phillip sat in the back, blindfolded. The man in the front passenger seat said, "Okay, *señor*. You may remove the blindfold."

Phillip pushed the black cloth band up over his forehead and put it in the man's waiting hand. "Thank you."

"My pleasure," Phillip said. "Have a nice evening."

"Thank you, *señor*, and you as well."

He glanced at his watch as he opened the front door of the house. He turned to watch the car leave, checking the license plate. As he expected, it was the same car that had picked him up. He'd committed the number to memory, planning to ask Paul Russo to check with his former colleagues at the Miami PD.

Entering the sunken living room, Phillip was surprised to find J.-P. sitting on a big leather couch, reading a local newspaper. When he saw Phillip, he folded the paper neatly and put it on the coffee table.

"Well?" J.-P. asked.

"Hey, I thought you'd be out sightseeing with Anne. I didn't expect to see you until later."

"Liz called and asked Anne to keep Dani amused this afternoon. When Dani and Liz returned, Anne took her to a day spa. I was surprised that Dani went; it is not like her. Liz wanted to talk with Paul about investigating this gentleman friend of Dani's."

"Sounds mysterious," Phillip said.

J.-P. shrugged. "Dani is Dani. She will tell us when she wants us to know. Was that Martínez in the car that came for you?"

"No. Two men. They were sent to take me to him." Phillip said. "Same two brought me back. They blindfolded me, so I don't know where they took me. Not far, though. Ten minutes, each way, some of it on the Interstate. Probably into Little Havana, but that's a pure guess. Martínez was waiting, apparently alone, in a modest house. All the shades were drawn, so I have no clue where it was. I'll get Paul to run the plate, but it's probably stolen."

"What did he want?"

"He was following up on my contact with the agency earlier this morning. Apparently, they watched. Maybe they eavesdropped; I couldn't say. He implied that they knew the kid who met me from previous encounters."

"So who is he working with?" J.-P. asked.

"He wouldn't say. He implied that it was 'the usual suspects,' as he put it, but he declined to name anyone. He says the exile organizations are all full of double and triple agents. He doesn't trust them, or the kid from the agency, either. He's worried that word of what he's doing will get back to the wrong people."

"That is interesting," J.-P. said, "but how will you proceed?"

"He said he would send a signal that they couldn't miss. It will prove he's serious and positioned to move forward."

"What is this signal to be?" J.-P. asked.

Phillip shrugged. "I don't know. I guess the agency will know it when they see it."

"Very strange. Did you discuss the money?"

Phillip smiled. "Yes. He said the money's not a problem. He has funding."

"And did you ask about a supplier?"

"Yes. He chuckled and said that 'in the fullness of time,' he would tell us."

"So, we wait, then," J.-P. said. "Would you like a drink?"

"Sure, but I'd best call in this contact first. What time are Anne and Dani coming back?"

"I do not know. Anne called a few minutes ago; she and Dani are going shopping. Dani needs some clothes, so they are delayed. Anne said she will explain when she gets back."

"Dani needs clothes?" Phillip shook his head. "Now *that* is strange. Let me make my call while you mix us drinks."

"Rum?" J.-P. asked. "I have Saint James Reserve."

"Good. Make mine on the rocks, please."

PAUL HAD JUST OFFERED Liz and Connie refills on their drinks when Liz's phone rang. She nodded her thanks and extended her glass toward him while she slipped her phone out of the pocket of her shorts.

"Dani," she announced, as she accepted the call. "Hi. How's the haircut?"

She listened for a few seconds. "Good. So are you and Anne on your way home?"

She listened again. "No, you're not on the speaker. I'm having a drink with Connie and Paul. I can talk. They're both below, fixing a snack tray."

Connie, taking the hint, got to her feet and went below to join Paul, leaving Liz to converse in privacy.

"He called while I was getting my hair cut, Liz," Dani said, her voice squeaking with excitement.

"I see," Liz said. "And?"

"And I'm going to dinner with him! He had a client meeting scheduled, so he didn't ask me earlier, but it got changed, so he called. I'm pumped up!"

"I can tell. You're coming back here first, right?" Liz asked, looking at her watch.

"No. there's no time. I just called to — "

"Dani, you can't go to dinner with him dressed the way you are."

"I'm not. Anne and I are shopping for a dress and shoes for me to wear right now. After he called, I showered at the spa and got my makeup *and* my hair done. I'm a new woman. You won't recognize me. I've got a *date*, Liz!"

"Um, that's great, Dani. I'm happy for you. Where is he taking you?"

"He didn't say; he hadn't booked a table yet when he called, so it'll be a surprise."

"Okay. Thanks for letting me know. Call me if you need me for anything."

"I will. I mean, I probably won't, but thanks for everything. All your help's paying off, finally."

"Any idea what time you'll get home?"

"Now you sound like my mother. No, I have no idea. He might ask me to ... should I ... what if he wants me to go to his place, and ... you know?"

"Take it slowly, Dani. It's your first date with — "

"Second date!"

"Yes, technically it's your second date, but what I was going to say is that you shouldn't rush into anything physical with him until you're sure how you feel about him. If you're feeling the need to ask me, it's a sign you've got some questions in your own mind."

"But I don't want him to think I'm, you know, some kind of prude or something. He might not call again if I don't ... "

"Trust your judgment, Dani. Think this through. You could blow it by being too easy. That can be just as bad as the other. Wait and see what happens before you decide, okay? You'll do the right thing for you. That's what matters."

"Okay, but don't wait up for me. I'll probably be late, and I'll just sleep in the guest cabin so I won't wake you."

"Okay, Dani. Thanks for calling, and have a nice evening."

Liz put the phone down and called, "Thanks. I'm off the phone now."

Connie climbed back into the cockpit and turned to take a tray from Paul before he joined them. She put the tray on the cockpit table and sat down across from Liz. Paul passed the fresh glasses of rum punch and sat down beside Connie.

"Can you talk?" Connie asked. "We don't want to pry."

Liz, a wry smile on her face, took a sip of her drink. She swallowed and said, "He called her and asked her out. She's going to dinner with him."

"Ortiz?" Paul asked.

"Yes. She's so excited ... "

"Did you tell her about Lupita?" Connie asked.

"No. I didn't get a chance to do much except listen. She's really wound up. I've never seen her like this." Liz grimaced and shook her head.

"Where are they going?" Paul asked. "I could ... "

"No, Paul," Connie said. "She's a grown woman."

"And she doesn't know where he's taking her, anyway," Liz said. "Look, she may be dazed and excited, but she's still Dani. She can take care of herself."

Paul looked dubious. "You're at least going to wait up for her, aren't you? I mean, this Lupita Vidal thing ... it doesn't sound right."

"I may," Liz said, "but I'm not going to let her know. She's already said she'll take the guest cabin so she won't disturb me when she gets back."

"Let us know if you get worried," Connie said. "We can at least all worry together."

"Thanks. Now I'm *really* not looking forward to telling her about Lupita." Liz took a long drink of rum punch. "Or maybe he'll make her angry and Lupita won't matter. This is Dani we're talking about, after all. It wouldn't take much of a misstep on his part. For once, maybe her thin skin and hair-trigger temper will be assets."

## 7

Ortiz heard himself groaning through his clenched teeth, his hands tangled in her hair. He was fighting for control, right on the edge of losing it. He'd been so close several times, and each time, she'd let him down, the bitch. He was sure he was going to make it this time, though. He'd been careful to hide his arousal from her this time. Just when he was almost there, she stopped cold and pulled his hands from her hair, digging her nails into his wrists. She slithered up and put her head on the pillow next to him, laughing.

"No," he moaned. "Don't stop, please?"

"You want more?" she murmured in his ear. "You like what I was doing?"

"Why are you doing this to me?" he asked.

"Because I can. And I like it, this tormenting you. It's fun to make you beg."

"I didn't think we were going to — ," Ortiz said.

"No, I know you didn't. But I did. I was just waiting for the right time."

"But I — "

"After you failed to get in Berger's pants, I wanted to know if you had what it took, *pinguera*. You stupid little gigolo, don't you understand what you are hired to do?"

"My orders were to make her fall in love with me. There are different ways of doing that. I have to charm her, first. She's not some cheap *puta*; I know what I'm doing."

Moving with blinding speed, she brought her left knee up into his hip with such force that his head cracked against the headboard. "You don't call me *puta,* you little fairy. Or I'll knee you somewhere else." She laughed as he rubbed his head. "I'll fix you so you don't even want a woman. You got that?"

When he didn't answer, she dug the tip of her left index finger into the small hollow below his left ear until he screamed for relief, writhing in pain but trapped in her grasp.

"Answer me, *comepinga.*"

"Yes. No. I mean, I never meant that you were a slut. I — "

"Enough. You are moving too slowly with Berger."

"You want me to take her against her will?"

"I don't care whether you *take* her or not. You need to get closer to her and her friends. You are to become part of her group, so none of them will think it is strange if you are at that place on Star Island, with her or without her. Time is passing. We need you on the inside. Tell her you want to meet her family; tell her anything. Make love to her, if that's what she wants. Get down on the floor and lick her feet. I don't care. You do whatever it takes; you understand?"

"Yes, but what if she wants to meet *my* family? She's already asking about them. Then what?"

"You play on her sympathy, *estúpido.* Your father is dead, and your only sister is in Martinique with your poor, ill mother. Make her feel sorry for you. Bring out her maternal instincts; be a poor, lonely little boy, so she will take you home."

"Okay, okay. I got it, Lupita. Now, can we finish what — "

She kneed him again. "I only like real men, *págaro.*" With that, she sat up and picked her clothes off the floor, dressing as he lay there, clutching himself and moaning.

"Were you surprised to hear from me?"

Phillip sat down; he studied the man across the table for a few seconds. A retired Brigadier General, Rick Olsen was at least 15 years older than Phillip, but he didn't look it. "A bit surprised, yes."

Olsen grinned. "Have you had breakfast?"

"Yes. I'm still an early riser."

"Good. Let's walk and talk." Olsen left a $20 bill on the table next to the check for his breakfast and stood up.

Phillip rose and followed his old boss out of the diner. They were on Collins Avenue in South Beach. Olsen turned a corner and walked a block further inland, turning again on Collins Court, which paralleled Collins Avenue. In contrast to Collins Avenue, it was deserted.

"This should do," Olsen said. He continued in his flat, Texas drawl. "You've stirred up some kind of trouble, boy."

"Sir?" Phillip asked.

"No need to call me 'sir.' We've both put that behind us. At least, I thought I had, until the Director called. You're not still active are you? I mean in that business you were in with J.-P. I know you quit the other, years ago, when I did."

"That's right," Phillip said. "What did the Director want?"

"He's put us both back on active status until this Martínez business is settled. I'm reporting to him and you're reporting to me. But only the three of us know that."

"I see. He must have guessed that Martínez had someone inside, then."

"No guesswork involved. That young fellow that met you the other morning after you called the emergency number?"

"Right. What about him?"

"He's dead. Cops were called by one of his neighbors; they complained about a disturbance in his apartment. They found him with a bullet in the back of his head and a briefcase full of documents that could cause no end of problems."

"Problems for whom?" Phillip asked.

"The FBI, or maybe DHS, or the CIA. Whoever the hell he was nominally working for."

"What kind of problems?"

"Well, that would depend on who got their hands on the documents. Looks like the kid was working both sides; there's some strong evidence that he was a DGI agent."

"A double agent, maybe," Phillip said.

"At the very least," Olsen said. "Or triple, or ... who can tell?"

"That's why we're back in the game?" Phillip asked.

"Yes, exactly. There's a grade-A witch hunt brewing, and the Director doesn't want to lose the Martínez contact. Speaking of which, have you heard from him?"

"Not since I called in yesterday."

"You called in yesterday?"

"After I met with Martínez."

"There's no record of that."

"Surprise, surprise," Phillip said. "They sent me to ask Martínez who he was working with before they made any decisions."

"And?"

"And Martínez is no fool. He knew I'd met with the young guy, and he said they'd encountered him before. He wouldn't give me any names — neither people, nor organizations."

"So how did you leave it with him, then?"

"He said he was going to send a *signal* to the young man's superiors that would prove his bona fides. He also said that I would probably be working with someone much higher in the organization."

"Prescient, wasn't he?"

"Yes. I don't know about you and the Director, but I think he's serious about this."

"I agree. But it would still be nice to know what's driving him."

"You got the first intel that I forwarded?" Phillip asked.

"About wanting to forestall the chaos that would be precipitated by the death of Raul Castro?"

"Yes, that's it."

"That's plausible enough," Olsen said. "But you see the problem, I'm sure."

"I see several opportunities for this to blow up in our faces," Phillip said.

"What do you think we should do?"

"We who?"

Olsen chuckled. "You and me."

"Pass along what Martínez wants to the Director," Phillip said.

"And?"

"And follow legally binding orders."

Olsen smiled. "Yes. And what should those orders be?"

"You're asking for an opinion that I'd have to form without policy information that's above my pay grade."

"Mine, too," Olsen said. "How do you contact Martínez?"

"Don't call us, we'll call you," Phillip said.

"You can reach me using this; the number's programmed." Olsen handed Phillip what looked like an ordinary iPhone. "But don't use it to call anywhere else. That could be fatal. I'm told it could blow your head off if you dial a number besides mine."

"Got it," Phillip said.

"The technology's changed a lot since the last time we did this," Olsen said.

"It certainly has," Phillip said.

"You're here with some of your friends to celebrate Mario Espinosa's 75th birthday, I hear."

"Yes, that's right."

"Time flies. I hear that you're married, too. Your wife here?"

"Not yet. She's catching a ride with Sharktooth and his wife. They'll be here before the big day."

"Sharktooth." Olsen grinned and shook his head. "I wish I could see everybody."

"You'd be welcome, Rick."

"I know. But given our situation, it wouldn't be a good idea. Don't even mention me."

"All right. It's nice to be working with you again, anyway."

"It's always a pleasure, Phillip. Glad you're well."

"And you, sir. I'll be in touch as soon as I hear from Martínez."

Olsen nodded. "I'll turn off here. You keep going."

"I DIDN'T WAKE YOU, did I? When I came aboard last night?" Dani filled a mug with coffee and sat down across the saloon table from Liz.

Liz shook her head. "I didn't hear a sound. You were very quiet. Was it late?"

"Not too late. I'd say it was maybe one, one-thirty."

"Did you have a nice evening?" Liz asked.

"Oh, I really did, Liz. He's such a gentleman."

Liz took in the dreamy tone of voice and the faraway look on her friend's face. She tried to find the courage to tell Dani about Ortiz's deception, but before she spoke, Dani went on.

"We had a fabulous dinner at this Thai place in South Beach, and we hit a couple of clubs afterward, just to see what was going on. Everybody knows David; he's really popular. At first, I thought it must be because he tipped well, but it wasn't just the help. The other patrons all spoke to him, too."

"How did he react to them?" Liz asked.

"He was pleasant to everybody, asking about their business, or their family. You know. He had a little something to make each one of them feel special. And they were all so welcoming when he introduced me. I can't ever remember a more pleasant evening."

"But you didn't go back to his place?" Liz asked.

"No." Dani frowned. "I told him I'd really like to see where he lived. You don't think that was too forward of me, do you? I mean it seemed okay at the time. He and some of the others were talking about neighborhoods, and it just kind of slipped out. I probably blushed, but I think it was dark enough so nobody noticed."

"I'm sure it was fine in that context," Liz said. "How did he react?"

"Oh, he said something like, 'Sure. You'll like it, I hope,' and moved the conversation along to something else about new condos in South Miami, I think. He's in the real estate business."

"I see. How about later? When the two of you were alone?"

"What about it?" Dani asked.

"Did he mention taking you to his place?"

"Well, sort of. He was talking about how well I fit in with his friends, and how much he enjoyed the evening. But then he said he wanted to go slowly with me; he's just getting over a breakup, and he doesn't want to get too deep into a relationship until we know one another better. I thought that was good, the way he said it. I told him I understood, and I appreciated his openness. Was that okay?"

"Perfect," Liz said.

"One time he excused himself for a few minutes and one of the other women at the table told me that she was glad to see him spending time with somebody like me, for a change. 'You're good for him,' she said. 'You bring out the best in him, not like the other women he's dated.'"

"That was a nice thing for her to say," Liz said. "Do you know how she came to know him?"

Dani shook her head. "She didn't say. But I don't think she was somebody he'd ... you know, dated, or anything."

"Probably not," Liz said, "but you can never tell about people and their exes."

"Oh, I really didn't get that kind of feeling from watching the two of them. She was there with her husband, too."

"Did anybody ask about his mother?"

"Huh?" Dani asked, frowning. "His mother?"

"Her stroke? I thought if these were friends, at least some of them might have asked about her health."

"No, it didn't come up. But I don't know that any of them were *that* kind of friends," Dani shook her head.

"Then how about his sister?" Liz asked.

Dani looked puzzled. "She's in Martinique, remember? We didn't see her."

"Did anybody mention her?"

"No. Why?"

"I thought maybe she hung around with him and his friends; she looked to be about his age, from what we saw the other night."

"No. No mention of her."

"Dani," Liz said, "I have to tell you something, and there's no way I can sugar coat it."

"You think I blew it?"

"No. It's nothing you did. It's — "

"You don't like him! Because he's Cuban?"

"No. It's nothing to do with liking him. It's about this Lupita."

"His sister?" Dani asked, perplexed. "What's she got to do with me and David?"

"I don't know the answer to that, but there are some things you need to know. You're like my sister, and this isn't easy. Please, just hear me out, okay?"

Dani frowned, her deep blue eyes locked on Liz's. Several seconds passed, before she nodded and said, "Okay."

"Lupita was in a car in the parking lot at the yacht club yesterday while you and David were having lunch."

"No!" Dani blurted. "She couldn't have been. She — "

Liz took a deep breath and held up her hand, palm toward Dani. When Dani paused, she said, "Please, Dani, let me finish."

Dani's face was flushed, but she nodded. "Go ahead."

"When I came back to the dinghy dock after I killed a few minutes to let you get settled, I noticed a woman in a parked car taking pictures of you and David with a telephoto lens." She paused, holding Dani's eye until she nodded for Liz to continue.

"I got the plate number and walked right by the side of the car on my way into the locker room. I got a good look at the woman, but I couldn't tell if she was the one he met on the beach."

Dani sighed, the tension fading from her features. She nodded. "Okay. Go ahead."

"You and David were the only people on the patio, so she had to be taking pictures of you. That worried me, so I sent Paul a text and asked him to run the license plate."

"And?" Dani asked, "Whose car was it?"

"Lupita Vidal is her name. She's got a lengthy record; she's not a nice woman."

"Did you check to see if this Vidal woman was married or single?"

"Single. Vidal is her maiden name, and she's an only child. Cuban parents, from up in Georgia."

"So, even if she's the one driving the car, she's not David's sister, then. And whoever it was could have borrowed the car. Still, why would she be taking pictures of us?"

"That's the question, but there's more. Paul had mug shots. The woman was Lupita Vidal; there's no doubt in my mind."

"But you said you didn't think she was the one David met on the beach."

"I said I couldn't be sure, but think this through. Forget about you and David for a minute, okay?"

Dani nodded. "Okay."

"Remember the woman on the beach? Think about her hair."

Dani, eyes closed, said, "Curly, dark, down past her shoulders. Like Connie's hair, but curly instead of wavy."

Liz slid her cellphone across the table, the profile shot of Lupita Vidal on the screen. Dani studied it for a moment.

Looking up at Liz, she said, "It could be, but lots of women have hair like that, and David's sister is in Martinique."

"That would be a huge coincidence, don't you think?" Liz asked. "Two women with similar hair, both named Lupita, both hanging around David in the same 24-hour period."

Dani, her face red, her voice cracking, said, "What should I do, Liz? I'm ... "

"Take a deep breath, Dani. First, Lupita Vidal is an enforcer for a slum lord. Paul says she's viewed as dangerous by the MPD. She's also a semi-professional cage fighter, which is something I never heard of until Paul told me about it. Do you know about cage fighting?"

"Yes. Big deal. I'm not scared of her."

"No, I didn't think you would be, but forewarned is forearmed, as the saying goes. Can you think of a way to ask David what's going on?"

"Yes. We're having lunch at the yacht club in a couple of hours. I'll just ask him outright. That's all. There's probably a good explanation."

"Maybe so," Liz said. "I hope so." She saw tears running down her friend's cheek and felt her own eyes overflow. She leaned across the table and gave Dani a hug, patting her on the shoulder. "It'll come right, somehow. It always does, and you've got all your friends and family close by to help you through, whatever happens."

"Thanks, Liz," Dani sobbed. She took several deep breaths and then sat up straight. "If he's leading me on for some reason, he's dead," she said, in a calm voice that gave Liz a chill.

---

## 8

"One of the problems with a guy like Martínez is that he's beyond control," Maldonado said. "But then again, that's part of what makes him successful."

"I'm still struggling with this one, Willy," Cruz said. "He killed a CIA agent?"

"Or whatever kind of agent he was. Who knows? They don't carry badges; it's hard to tell who's who."

"But I thought that guy was one of ours. Why did Martínez kill him?"

"Manny, he didn't just kill him. He planted a bunch of shit on him to make sure they could tell he was working for DGI."

"But why?"

"He said he was establishing his credentials with them."

"Jesus. So now we don't have an inside source any more. What a way to establish his credentials. He's nuts."

"Maybe. He's never failed before. He may know what he's doing."

"But to kill our only source of inside information ... " Cruz shook his head.

"Relax, Manny. I never said he was our only source."

"Yeah, but ... okay. Martínez is out of control. So now what?"

"Now we watch carefully; we'll see who steps in as Phillip Davis's contact and go from there. Martínez certainly showed them he's serious. And committed, too."

"What do you want me to do?"

"Ramp up Lupita and David Ortiz; we may need a plan 'B' in case Martínez blows it."

"You're thinking a snatch, again?"

"Maybe. But not necessarily. Is Lupita keeping track of Ortiz and the Berger woman's romance? Pictures and everything?"

"Yeah. She planted a bug and a video camera in his place last night, in case he takes Berger there. What are you thinking, if not a snatch?"

"Disinformation. We've got all we need to show that Ortiz is active in Alpha-66, right?"

"Right."

"And with Lupita's help, we're able to connect him to J.-P. Berger's daughter, right here in Miami," Maldonado said.

"Yeah, okay. We can set it up to look like Alpha-66 planned the invasion and hooked up with Berger for weapons, but I thought we wanted to lock in the CIA. Or some other U.S. agency."

"That's right. It's in the works. We have the pistol that was used to kill Davis's contact."

"You're going to plant it on somebody?"

"It's an option."

"But who?"

"Don't get ahead of yourself. Your mission is to get Ortiz established as part of Berger's entourage. How's that going?"

"Well enough. He's meeting her for lunch today. She practically asked him to take her to his place last night."

"And did he?"

"No. He had a scheduling problem. He had a late date with Lupita to wire his place, remember?"

"Shit, Manny! Does he know his place is under surveillance? That's not — "

"Easy, Willy. No, of course not. Lupita made him think she was hot for him; she told him she'd be waiting for him at his place when he was done with Berger. He's got no idea what she was really up to."

"So what did he tell Dani Berger when she put the moves on him?"

"He played hard to get. Gave her some line about a bad breakup recently; said he didn't want to risk hurting her. He's playing the gentleman card, bigtime. Lupita says it's working. She's been watching. Berger's falling hard."

"Okay, good," Maldonado said. "Tell Lupita to get with him this afternoon after his lunch date. They need to figure out how and where to snatch the girl."

"I thought that was plan 'B.'"

"Yeah, it is," Maldonado said, "but we need to be ready. The way Martínez operates, this whole thing could spin out of control on a moment's notice."

"Okay. Got it. I'd better get Lupita in here and work through this with her while Ortiz is at lunch with Berger."

"Do it," Maldonado said. There was a click as he disconnected the call. Cruz put the encrypted phone away and picked up his desk phone. He hit a speed dial key, and in a moment, he was connected to Lupita's cellphone.

DANI SAW David Ortiz sitting at the table where they had lunch yesterday. She locked her dinghy to the dock and took the same circuitous route into the club that Liz had used, checking the parking lot on her way. Seeing no sign of Lupita Vidal's car, she entered the club through the front door and walked out to the patio.

"Hi, David," she said, coming up behind him and laying a hand on his shoulder.

Startled, Ortiz shoved his chair back and scrambled to his feet, turning to greet her. Smiling, he said, "Hi! You surprised me. Where'd you come from?" He leaned in to kiss her, but she turned her head enough so that his lips grazed her cheek. A puzzled look on his face, he pulled out a chair and held it for her. "It's great to see you," he said. "You're more beautiful every time we meet."

She sat, waiting until he was back in his own chair before she asked, "Where's Lupita?" She stared at him, keeping her expression as neutral as her tone of voice.

His eyes darted around the patio before he locked on her gaze. "Lupita?"

"Your sister? Lupita Vidal, from Georgia? Is she watching us today? I didn't see her in the parking lot."

"In the parking lot?"

"She was there yesterday, David. In her car, with a camera and a telephoto lens, taking pictures of us."

"She was? I ... I ... um, I thought she was in Martinique with Mom."

"Don't lie to me, please. I'm hurt, and on the verge of being angry. I know she's supposed to be a bad-ass, but you have no idea what happens to people who make me angry. Don't do it." She felt the muscles in her jaw twitching as she clenched her teeth.

"I can explain. It's ... uh .. it's nothing to do with you, Dani. I'm really sorry you got caught up in this. My sister — "

Dani lurched to her feet and leaned across the table, getting right in his face. She hissed, "Stop, David. I'm warning you. She's not your sister. What's she to you? Wife? Girlfriend? One last chance to come clean with me; that's all you get."

He nodded, his face twitching. He swallowed hard, waiting to see if she sat down. He glanced around. Just as it had been yesterday, the patio was deserted. Most people ate inside during the heat of midday. When she settled into her chair, he said, "Okay. I'll tell you everything. It's just that it's so embarrassing, Dani, this business with Lupita. First though, I have to tell you, I've fallen for you in a way that's ... I don't even know how to describe it. There've been other women in my life, but not like this. It's like you're the first woman I've ever been in love with, you know?" He paused, watching her, and took a sip of water.

"Lupita," Dani said, in a flat tone, her dark blue eyes flashing a warning.

"I ... I dated her, briefly. I m-met her at a seminar one of the banks held for property managers. She works for a guy who has a lot of rental property." He took another sip of water, waiting, watching for her reaction.

She blinked, but her expression didn't change. She kept staring at him, her fury obvious.

"Anyway, we went out for a while, but she's just, I don't know, not my type. She's a tough chick; I found out her job is to evict people. Sometimes, she beats them up if they're late with their rent. I tried to break up with her, but she won't leave me alone. She's stalking me."

"Why did you jump up when she called that first night we met? You ran out to meet her like some whipped puppy and left me sitting there."

"She demanded money; she said she'd hurt you if I didn't meet her and give her a thousand dollars."

"That sounds like bullshit, David. You didn't even know me then. We'd just met."

"Well, it's more complicated than that, you're right. She did say she'd hurt you, though, if I didn't do what she wanted. Sh ... she threatened my mother."

"You told me your mother was in Martinique, with her friend, the *béké's* daughter. Was that a lie, too?"

"Nn ... well, kind of."

Not reacting to his contrite tone or his dejected look, Dani pushed him. "Kind of a lie? I'm losing patience, David."

"She's blackmailing me," he said. "About my mother."

"If I have to ask one more time, we're done, David." Dani's manner was cold, but her face was flushed.

"My mother's in Martinique. *She's* the *béké's* daughter. She's visiting her family. She was born there, not Cuba. She's an illegal, Dani. She and my father came here when she was pregnant, just like I said. They came from Cuba; he was Cuban. Her parents weren't. They were from Martinique. They had a business in Cuba, but they went back to Martinique to escape Castro, because that's where her mother's family was from. So technically, since she wasn't Cuban, she couldn't get asylum." He paused and took another sip of water.

"That doesn't sound right," Dani said.

"I don't know. They weren't wealthy, or well educated, my parents. Maybe they didn't do things right. Maybe they didn't understand about immigration and all. Anyway, my father's dead, and she doesn't have papers."

"How does she travel to Martinique, then?"

"A French passport that belongs to her sister. Going there's not hard. Getting back here, she flies to Nassau and then sneaks back into the U.S. There are plenty of people with fast boats in the Bahamas that can sneak people and stuff into Florida, but you probably know that."

"Yes," Dani said. "So how was Lupita blackmailing you?"

"She knows all about illegals. The guy she works for rents to illegals, mostly from Haiti and the D.R. She threatens them all the time, says she'll call ICE and turn them in."

"ICE?"

"Immigration and Customs Enforcement. She's got some contacts there. She said she'd turn my mother in if I didn't pay her."

"And you put up with that?"

"My mother's whole life is here, now. I couldn't risk her getting deported, Dani. Since my father died, I'm all she's got. Don't you see? What could I do?"

"There have to be other options," Dani said, staring out at the boats in the anchorage. After several seconds, she asked, "Why would Lupita Vidal be taking pictures of us?"

Sensing a thaw in her demeanor with the change of subject, Ortiz sighed and shook his head. "I don't know. Probably it's me she was interested in, but who can say? I wasn't kidding about the stalking. Blackmail aside, she won't leave me alone."

"Have you dated other women since you broke up with her?" Dani could see that the question made him nervous. "I mean, before you met me?"

"A few," he said. He hesitated for a moment and continued. "She, um ... interfered. She'd do stuff like call me when I was out with somebody else, or come up to our table and act like she was my ex-wife, one time. She's dangerous."

"She sounds like a real pain," Dani said.

"No," Ortiz protested. "I mean, yes, she's a pain. But when I said she was dangerous, I meant physically dangerous. I told you she beats people up, but she's a professional fighter. For all I know she could be a killer. I don't want her anywhere close to you; she scares me. Maybe we should stop seeing — "

"No, David. Don't let some psycho mess us up. I wasn't kidding when I said I was hurt. I haven't been serious about many other men — one, to be exact. I'm enjoying the time we spend together."

"Oh, me, too, Dani. But I don't want you hurt. Not emotionally, and not physically, either."

"Let's see what happens, David. We don't have to make any decisions right now. We need to give this a little time, anyway, like you said last night." She reached across the table and took his hand. "Was it true? What you told me about needing to go slowly because of ... "

"Yes. I was engaged to this girl. At the time, I thought I was in love, but that was before l met you and learned what it really feels like to ... anyway, she dumped me for a rich guy. I'm still not over it, but with you in my life, I don't think it'll take long." He shook his head and looked away from Dani.

She sat, saying nothing, and held his hand until he turned back toward her.

"Are we okay?" he asked, in a beseeching tone.

Dani held his gaze for a moment before she nodded and said, "I think so. I'm still upset, but I'll get over it. I wish you'd been honest with me to start with, but I understand why you weren't. I need some time to work through this, okay?"

"I understand, Dani. Thank you, so much. I'll give you all the time you need. I promised lunch? Should we order now?"

"I'm afraid I don't have much appetite right now, David. I need to go, okay?"

He nodded, looking sad. "Can I call you this evening, or is that too — "

"That will be fine," she said, forcing a smile. "Please do."

She gave his hand a final squeeze and stood up, motioning for him to keep his seat. She walked back to the dinghy dock, lost in thought.

ORTIZ FOUND Lupita in his living room when he got back from his aborted lunch. She was sprawled on the couch, her shoes off, reading a mixed martial arts magazine. He wasn't surprised; he knew she'd want the details of his latest date with Berger.

"Hey, lover boy," she sneered. "How was lunch with your sweetie?"

Ortiz had been struggling with what to say to Lupita ever since he parted with Dani. He was sure that he'd spun Dani a convincing tale to explain his relationship with Lupita, but he couldn't figure out why Lupita had been in the parking lot at the club, taking pictures. For that matter, he wondered how Dani had spotted her, and how she knew so much about her. Women were mysterious creatures.

Lupita would get a kick out of his characterization of her as a stalker and a blackmailer. He was pleased that he'd come up with such a plausible story in his moment of crisis with Dani. He'd considered whether sharing it with Lupita might impress her.

There was some serious upside to impressing Lupita. All her violent tendencies aside, she was one hot babe. Despite several interludes like the one they'd had last night, though, he'd never managed to score with her. And that bothered him; it was a matter of pride.

As he'd drawn close to his condo, he'd concluded that telling Lupita about his latest conversation with Dani could be risky. He decided to hold back. He didn't want Lupita upset with him; what she didn't know couldn't hurt him. It would be best just to play along; let her tease him about his lunch date.

"Fine," he said. "It was good. She's pretty well hooked, now."

"It's about time, *pinguera*. You need to reel her ass in. Manny's not happy you're moving so slow."

"What's the big rush, anyhow, Lupita? I thought Martínez was — "

"Martínez? Who is Martínez, *pendejo*?" Mindful of the recording devices she'd installed last night without Ortiz's knowledge, she leapt to her feet, cat-like, and embraced him, thrusting her tongue down his throat and grabbing his crotch. That never failed to distract him. She dared not let him announce that she'd shared the details of the operation with him. Cruz would have her ass for that if he found out. He didn't want anybody to know about Martínez; he'd told her about the mercenary in a fit of passion one night.

As she expected, Ortiz responded in kind, his hands all over her. She let him grope her for a minute, pretending she enjoyed it. When she thought he was about to lose himself, she pushed him away and said, "Whoo! You better save it for Berger, big boy. But I gotta say, she's one lucky lady. You gonna score tonight?" She suppressed a laugh as she watched him fighting for control.

"I'm working on it," he said. "I should get inside the compound this evening, anyway, meet some of the others."

"Good. You get real close to as many as you can. It's sounding like I may need to snatch her for some leverage when they start negotiating with her father. If that happens, your job's to hang out with her parents acting heartbroken so you can tell us how her old man's reacting, okay?"

"How long have I got before this happens?"

"That's why I'm kicking your ass to move faster. We don't know. It could be any time."

"Any time, like days? Weeks? What?"

"Days. Maybe real sudden. Not hours, but no more than a few days, I think. Maybe even tomorrow or the next day."

"Thanks. That helps. You gonna need me to help set her up for the snatch?"

"You shouldn't be anywhere near her when it goes down. The best thing would be if you were sitting there with her parents when they got the word, like you were waiting for her to come back from some kind of girl thing."

"Girl thing?"

"Yeah, you know. Like a manicure or a pedicure. Maybe a massage."

"She just did something like that with her stepmother yesterday. If you give me enough lead time, I could set it up with like a gift certificate, or something, for both of them. Then I could maybe take her old man some real expensive cigars and shoot the shit with him while we sit out by the pool waiting for them to come back."

"That's a good idea, David. How long would it take to set it up?"

"A few hours. I have a client in that business, and she owes me one."

Lupita laughed. "I'll just bet she does. Okay, I'll keep that in mind, depending on the timing. Now, I gotta go." She sat down on the couch, and picked up her shoes.

She was careful to let him see plenty of thigh as she pulled the shoes on. She caught him staring at her filmy panties and laughed at him. "Maybe tonight you'll get lucky with that skinny little blonde, *pinguera*. You're not ready for me yet." She tugged the skirt down and stood up, patting him on the cheek as she strutted to the door and let herself out.

# 9

---

Ortiz, relishing the prospect of an evening to himself, mixed a drink and kicked off his shoes. Before he had time to sit down, his cellphone rang. He glanced at the number. Recognizing it, he didn't answer. With a sigh of resignation, he put the drink in the refrigerator and slipped on his shoes. He snatched his car keys from the hook by his front door and decided on the three flights of stairs rather than the elevator.

Less than two minutes after the call, he approached his car in the basement garage. As soon as he sat down and closed the door, he heard a woman's voice from the footwell in the back seat.

"Take me for a ride, Ortiz; anywhere will do. Just keep driving."

"You didn't leave a message," he said. "You think my phone's being monitored?"

"No. it's encrypted, remember? I was afraid you'd retrieve the voicemail in speaker mode. Your place is wired."

"Shit! Video? Or just audio?"

"Both."

"Who?" he asked.

"Probably Vidal. She was there for a while before you got in last night."

"She's a pain in the ass," he said.

"You're doing it wrong, then, David. You need to relax, don't fight it. Maybe use some — "

"Fuck you."

"Is that any way for you to talk to your boss?"

"Now you sound like her."

"Just trying to be helpful. Is she really messing with you?"

"So far, just hard-core teasing. She's on some kind of power trip. What's up, Mary?"

"Routine follow-up. Mostly, I wanted you to know your place was compromised. But since we're talking, what's new with Vidal? She spent some time with you this afternoon."

"Not much new. She dropped by to debrief me on my lunch with Berger. Besides that, just her normal crap."

"She trying to make you do things you're not comfortable with?"

"Seriously? What are you? Some kind of voyeur?"

"No. All kidding aside, do you need some help with her?"

"Not so far. She's a class-A bitch, though. Are you going to have my place swept?"

"No. we don't want them to know that we know. We've tapped their feeds, though, just so you know. Whatever they get, we get."

"That's comforting."

"Don't be sarcastic, David. We got what you gave her on Berger. Is there anything else you think we might have missed?"

"Maybe. Did you catch the reference to Martínez?"

"Yeah. But then she jumped you, and I was too embarrassed to keep listening."

"Look, I have to put up with shit like that from her, but not from you."

"Sorry, David. You're right. What about Martínez? Who is he?"

"I'm not sure. I think he's behind this whole Alpha-66 weapons deal. He's apparently able to give Cruz orders."

"Have you met him? Could you i.d. him from photos?"

"No. I've only got what I've given you, but Lupita was dropping his name a while back like he was hot shit."

"Did she say anything that connects him with the Haitians?"

"No. Only the Cuban exile stuff. But she clearly didn't want me talking about him tonight. At the time, it didn't make sense, but now that I know we were being watched, I think she jumped me to shut me up."

"Okay, that's good info. I'll see if we can dig up anything. You got anything else?"

"What about this Alpha-66 business?" he asked.

"What about it?"

"You want me to chase it?"

"No. Stick to the Haitian angle. I mean, sure, if you can find out more about him, let me know. I'll ask up the line, but Alpha-66 is kind of ho-hum, these days. Use it to worm your way into Cruz's confidence, but that's all it's good for. They're just a bunch of old men. They're always trying to stir up something, but nobody takes them seriously any more — not even the Cuban government. I'll let you know if I hear different."

"What a marvelous dinner," Anne Berger said, as Paul and Liz brought platters of food to the table in the outdoor dining room of the mansion. "It's too bad Dani had other plans."

"Is she out with her new friend?" Phillip asked. "What's his name, again?"

"David Ortiz," Liz said.

"Have you met him, Liz?" J.-P. Berger asked.

"Only briefly. He's pleasant enough, and very handsome," Liz said.

"She seems smitten, from the little I've heard from her," Connie said.

Seeing that everyone's plates were filled, Liz and Paul sat down with the others.

J.-P. raised his wine glass. "To old friends and new," he offered. They all touched glasses and sipped the wine. "We should do this more often," J.-P. said. "We should have insisted that Dani bring this new man to meet us all."

"She's certainly charmed with him," Anne said. "That's all she talked about when we were at the spa; that, and how much she appreciated your advice, Liz."

"Not that she needs it, or heeds it," Liz said, with a smile. "This is Dani we're talking about."

"I wonder why she didn't invite him to dinner here?" Connie asked. "It's not like this is a first date, and we would have behaved ourselves. Were they going somewhere special? Or are you sworn to secrecy, Liz?"

"No, neither," Liz said. "I don't think she's out with him tonight."

"Uh-oh," Anne said. "Is there a problem? Can you say?"

"She didn't discuss it with me," Liz said, "so I shouldn't speculate. But she did say she needed some time to herself; she was planning to go for a long walk on the beach this evening. 'To think things over,' she said." Liz took a sip of her wine and cut into the seared ahi steak on her plate.

As the silence began to weigh on them, Phillip put his fork down and drank a swallow of water. "J.-P., have you come up with a way to get Mario out here for his surprise party?"

"Yes and no. In all the years we've known one another, I've never managed to trick him; he is too crafty for a simple, straightforward person like me."

That brought a round of laughter from his tablemates, and he waited, letting them enjoy a moment of levity at his expense. "There is only one person I know who can fool Mario, so I asked for professional help." J.-P. let the suspense build for a moment, and then said, "Gina is going to tell him that she's booked a table for two for his birthday dinner at a new place in South Beach that she learned about from a friend. She will tell him they must stop on the way so that she can retrieve his gift from another friend who is hiding it for her. That stop will be here."

"Will he fall for that?" Phillip asked.

"Mario is a smart man; he has had over 50 years to learn not to ask questions about what Gina tells him," J.-P. said. "Speaking of getting people here, Phillip, have you heard any more from Sandrine about when she and Sharktooth and Maureen will arrive?"

"Yes. We spoke a little while ago. A friend of Sharktooth's will fly the three of them in from Dominica on the afternoon of Mario's birthday. Sandrine's planning to catch a LIAT flight from Martinique to Dominica that morning."

"Excellent. Then we will all be together for the big moment."

LUPITA VIDAL WAS DRESSED for nightclubbing when she emerged from the elevator lobby into the underground garage in her condo building. As she covered the 25 meters between the lobby doors and her car, she pressed the unlock button on her electronic key fob.

The interior lights on her car came on and she heard the soft chirp of the access system announcing that the car was unlocked. As she reached for the driver's side door handle, she sensed movement behind her. Whirling, she adopted a defensive stance, dropping her purse and stiffening her hands.

A slight figure about her own height stood no more than a foot from her. The dark clothing and the balaclava told her everything she needed to know. She tried to shift her right foot back to give herself room to strike, but her car blocked her movement. She lunged toward her attacker, thrusting against the car with her hips, putting her weight behind her right hand, which was bent back at the wrist for a heel-of-palm strike to her opponent's nose.

She realized she was a fraction of a second too slow when she lost the feeling in her right arm. Unsure what had happened, she rolled slightly to her left, preparing to drive the stiffened fingers of her left hand into the other person's solar plexus. Her right arm hung at her side, useless.

This time, she saw the blow coming, but the arc was too short for her to react. She caught a glimpse of braided black leather milliseconds before the blackjack struck her left shoulder. She felt no pain, but now her left arm was numb, too, dangling by her side.

Undeterred, she rolled to the right, raising her left foot, preparing for a short kick to the other person's kneecap. Unable to use her arms, Lupita couldn't block the blow to the big muscle in her upper left thigh. She leaned against her car, balanced on her right leg, helpless.

"What's this about?" she asked.

"David Ortiz," the masked attacker said, grabbing the left shoulder-strap of Lupita's cocktail dress and casually pulling her off balance, chuckling as Lupita crashed to the pavement.

"You bitch!" Lupita screeched, furious at having been taken down by another woman, one who appeared to weigh well under her own 139 pounds. "Who are you?"

"*No es importante, grilla,*" the woman said, smashing the black-jack into Lupita's right thigh. "*Comemierda, puta palestina!*"

With all four limbs numb, Lupita screamed in anger and frustration when the woman raised the blackjack again.

"*Cállate, tortillera!*" the woman barked, shifting her position and landing a brutal blow on Lupita's nose. She laughed as Lupita choked on her own blood, the scream cut off by her gagging.

"*Ahora, trabajo,*" the slight woman said, as she began to methodically hammer every muscle in Lupita's body.

LUPITA WENT into shock not long after that, but the beating continued until every square inch of Lupita's body was bruised. The woman was thorough and experienced; she knew from her own mishaps that Lupita would be weeks recovering from the first few blows. Her intention was that her victim would spend months in physical therapy before she could think about walking unassisted, let alone practicing martial arts.

For all her thoroughness, the woman worked quickly. In less than three minutes, she pocketed the blackjack and walked to the vehicle exit. She'd spotted the security cameras earlier, when she'd slipped into the garage by scurrying behind another resident's car. Once past the cameras, she rolled the balaclava up over her face so that it looked like a stocking cap.

Careful to keep her blonde curls tucked underneath, she stepped out onto the sidewalk and walked away into the darkness, whistling a sailor's hornpipe. Her hands in the pockets of her dirty black jeans, she could have been mistaken for one of the many lost souls who wander the streets of South Beach after dark.

CRUZ SAT in the dimly lighted club, listening to the jazz combo and nursing his drink. He looked at his watch, growing more worried by the minute. Lupita should have arrived half an hour ago. Unlike most women of his acquaintance, Lupita was rarely late, at least for appointments with him. He was due to call Maldonado in a couple of hours with the latest update on Ortiz and Berger.

He'd been too busy to talk to Lupita this afternoon when she'd called, so he'd agreed to take her out for dinner to hear her report. Not that he minded; she was easy on the eyes, and they'd enjoyed a casual, no-strings relationship for several years. From her flirtatious tone earlier, he'd been looking forward to the next installment in their ongoing exploration of the world of bondage.

Forty minutes, he noted when he looked at his watch again. Something was definitely wrong. He checked to see if his phone was turned on and saw he'd missed a call from Tony Santos. He hadn't felt the phone vibrate; he'd set it to silent mode, not wanting to attract attention in the quiet, upscale jazz club.

Santos managed Cruz's low-rent properties, as well as Cruz's other, less savory interests in Little Haiti. As far as anyone knew, Santos was an independent, somewhat shady entrepreneur. Cruz was an invisible, silent investor. Besides handling rough work for Santos, Lupita was their go-between. Santos and Cruz rarely spoke to one another, hiding their relationship, depending on her to carry messages back and forth. Her absence and the call from Santos could well mean trouble.

Looking around the club to see if anyone was within earshot, Cruz decided to risk a call from his table. Santos answered immediately.

"Manny?" Santos answered.

"What? Why'd you call?"

"She's in trouble."

"Where is she?"

"Mount Sinai. The emergency room called me. My card was in her purse."

"What happened? Accident? She okay, or what?"

"No accident. Somebody beat the shit out of her. She's okay. Semi-conscious, but they say that's mostly from the pain medication."

"Who did it? Where?"

"In the basement garage at her place, when she was gettin' in the car. She don't know who. Woman, about her height, wiry and fast. Only said a few words, Cuban Spanish, like a native."

"Any idea why?"

"She asked what it was about before the woman tore into her. All she said was, 'David Ortiz.' Other than that, just a bunch of Cuban curses."

"Jesus. What kind of woman could get the drop on Lupita?"

"My papa always said, 'It don't matter how tough you are; there's always somebody tougher.'"

"Yeah, I hear you. Anything else?"

"Yeah. She said the woman used a blackjack; knew exactly where to hit. She hit her four times and immobilized her. After that, she worked her over from the neck right down to the soles of her feet. Rolled her over; got the front and the back. Never hit her on the head, except to break her nose so she couldn't scream. She meant to punish her."

"Sounds like a pro of some kind. I never heard of anybody using a blackjack lately."

"Me neither. ER doc says she's got months of physical therapy ahead of her. Serious muscle damage. Like she said, whoever it was knew what the fuck she was doin'."

"Who could be behind it? She been crossways with anybody in the rentals that could have done this?"

"Not that I know of. You don't buy the story about Ortiz?"

"Ortiz would piss his pants just hearing about this, Tony."

"He been into anything might cause somebody to want to get your attention, maybe?"

"I don't think so. We got him tied up in something right now — nothing that might cause this kind of thing."

"What do you want me to do?" Santos asked.

"Take care of her. Tell her I'll catch up with her soon. I got my hands full right now with her out of commission."

"Okay, then. See ya," Santos said.

"Yeah," Cruz said, disconnecting the call. He put the phone back in his pocket and waved for the check.

## 10

———————

D avid Ortiz was surprised by the tapping on his door so late at night. Normally, no one except Lupita would be visiting him, and he knew she'd gone out with Manny Cruz. She claimed it was to report on their progress with Dani Berger, but he knew what she and Cruz were doing in their spare time.

As he approached the door, he wondered who it could be. He kept his conquests away from his apartment. He was prepared to make an exception with Berger, but he would relocate after he was done with that piece of work. And she didn't have his address yet. He put an eye to the peephole, stunned when he saw Manny Cruz. Cruz appeared to be alone; there was no sign of Lupita.

Ortiz turned the deadbolt and opened the door. "Hello, Manny. I thought — "

"Let me in, first," Cruz said, stepping forward, crowding him.

"Sure. Come in," Ortiz said, stepping back and swinging the door wide.

Cruz entered and jerked the door from Ortiz's hand, pushing it closed behind him. "You and Lupita into something I don't know about?" he asked, continuing to crowd into Ortiz's personal space, backing him against the wall in the small entryway.

Ortiz blanched, frowning and shaking his head. "No! I — "

"You been fuckin' somebody on the side?" Cruz growled. "Somebody we don't know about?"

"No, Manny. I haven't been doing anything like that since Lupita put me on this Dani Berger thing."

Cruz stared at him for several long seconds, studying him, watching him tremble.

"B-believe me, Manny! Honest, I haven't been doing anything except what she told me since — "

"You been fuckin' Lupita?" Cruz barked.

Ortiz swallowed hard, and the trembling increased. He shook his head and tried to utter a denial, but he only succeeded in making unintelligible sounds.

Cruz grinned, watching for a moment before he said, "Relax, David." His tone of voice was almost pleasant, no longer threatening. "I don't care if you and Lupita are screwing one another. I know what she is; she's hot. I wouldn't blame you, if she gave you the chance. I just need to know. One of you has pissed off somebody. Somebody with some serious juice, kid."

"N-no, Manny. I swear. She teases the shit out of me, but that's as far as it gets. What's wrong?"

"What makes you think something's wrong?" Cruz asked, his tone still affable.

Ortiz had calmed down somewhat. "I thought she was supposed to have dinner with you, update you on the Berger thing."

"She tell you that?"

"Yeah. Yeah, she did. She said you couldn't talk with her this afternoon when she called. I was tryin' to get Berger to invite me into the compound tonight, and Lupita was gonna call me later, after you guys had dinner. She figured you'd take her to your place afterward."

"She figured that, did she? And she told you?" Cruz shook his head. "She tell you about what she did with me?"

Ortiz went pale again. "No. Just kind of hints that you two were ... um ... "

"Crazy bitch," Cruz said. "If she told you that, did she ever tell you if she was gettin' it on with anybody else?"

"No," Ortiz said, the color returning to his face. "As far as I know, she didn't have anybody else. At least not right now."

"How about recently? Like in the last few months?"

"I don't know, Manny. Nobody she told me about."

"Did she usually tell you who she was dating?"

"Not who, except for you. But she'd let me know when she was doin' somebody. It's part of the way she likes to tease me. I don't think she was seeing anybody recently. Where is she?"

"The emergency room. Somebody jumped her when she was on her way to meet me earlier."

Ortiz gulped. "She okay?"

"Yeah, more or less. They fucked her up pretty bad, though. She's out of action for several months, probably."

"A street gang, or what?"

"No street gang. A Cuban woman with a blackjack beat the shit out of her."

"Jesus!" Ortiz said. "One woman? That's fuckin' unbelievable, man. I've seen Lupita — "

"Yeah, yeah. I know. Me too. Listen, Ortiz. When they first got crossways, Lupita asked the woman what she wanted, what it was about. And the woman said your name."

"My name? That's it? Nothing else?"

"Nothing else. Then she hit Lupita a few times to paralyze her and went to work on her."

"How could one woman ... was she what, some kind of Amazon, or something?"

"Not from what Lupita said. About her own height, and skinny. Bitch knew what she was doing. This wasn't any random thing. She had to be a pro, to give Lupita that kind of beating without killing her. It was deliberate and methodical. She was sending a message."

"What message, Manny? I don't get it."

"Me, either, kid. I was hoping maybe you had some idea what the fuck was going on."

"Me? Uh-uh. You said she was Cuban?"

"Except for your name, all she did was curse Lupita in Cuban Spanish. Spoke it like a native. Words only a Cuban would have used, mostly."

Ortiz shook his head. "No idea, Manny. Maybe Lupita was up to something she didn't tell me about."

"Whatever it is, whoever's behind it, they got your name, kid. If I were you, I'd watch my ass."

"Yeah, I will."

"Okay, Ortiz. If anything comes to mind, let me know. Meanwhile, how come you're not screwing Dani Berger tonight?"

"She had some kind of family thing going on tonight at the compound. I talked to her late this afternoon to see about making some plans for tonight, but she couldn't do it. I tried to get her to invite me to whatever it was, but she said it wouldn't fly — too small a group, but she wanted me to meet everybody. She said there'd be another chance; they're all going to be around for several days."

"Okay. I need you in there. Your job's to become part of that family gathering, as quick as you can. Understand?"

"Yes, Manny. I got it; I'm pushing as hard as I can. I don't want to piss her off."

"No, don't do that. But anything you can do to speed it up, anything you need, just let me know, okay."

"Okay."

"With Lupita laid up, you're going to be working directly with me. I like to be kept in the loop — even dumb stuff. You never know what might be important. Don't feel like you need to hold anything back because it seems trivial, okay?"

"I understand, Manny."

"Good. Now get some rest and get to work on Berger tomorrow."

"Uh, Manny?"

"Yeah, kid. What is it?"

"Lupita did say something about somebody named Martínez."

"Martínez?"

"Yeah. She'd never mentioned him before."

Cruz stared at him for a moment. "You said, 'him.' This Martínez is a guy, then?"

Ortiz frowned. "Yeah, I guess. I can't remember exactly what she said, now. But I must have gotten the impression Martínez was a guy, huh?"

"I guess. Why'd she mention him?"

Ortiz shrugged. "Had to be something about this Berger business. I thought maybe it might be important, you know?"

"Maybe, kid. If you remember anything else about this Martínez, let me know, okay?"

"Sure, Manny. The way she said it, it somehow made me think you knew him."

Cruz shook his head. "Common name, but it's not ringing any bells right now. I gotta go. Have a good evening."

Ortiz nodded, and Cruz opened the door and left, closing it behind himself. Ortiz went into the kitchen and put three ice cubes into a highball glass. He reached far into the back of a cabinet and took out a bottle of the best rum he had. He filled the glass and took it into the living room. He needed to think his way through this.

WHEN DANI RETURNED to the Star Island mansion, she saw that everyone was still in the outdoor dining room. In no mood to socialize with them, she crept around the perimeter of the grounds and slipped aboard *Vengeance.* She stowed the small duffle bag that she'd been carrying, and stretched out on her bunk to consider how she wanted to deal with David.

Although she was still bowled over by his attention, she recognized that she'd lost considerable respect for him. She couldn't comprehend his attitude toward this Lupita Vidal. As handsome as he was, and as sweet as he had been to her, she had to admit that he might be a coward. To knuckle under to someone like the Vidal woman was incomprehensible to her.

But she liked him; he was kind and gentle. Of course, those traits helped explain why he let the woman push him around. She couldn't help comparing him to the other men in her circle, but she knew that wasn't fair to him. He was attractive to her because he was a regular guy. Her father, Phillip, Shark-tooth — they shaped her notion of how a man should behave. But would she want a man like that as a lover? She didn't know.

She reflected on her half-brother and her former fiancé; both were despicable weaklings. Not just physically — she could excuse that. It was their lack of grit and determination that she found unattractive. Ralph Suarez, the one man she'd ever thought she could love, had his failings, as well.

She knew now that she'd misread Ralph's interest. A gentleman to the core, Suarez had treated her as an equal, a responsible, competent person. She'd been swept off her feet by his consideration and respect, only to discover that he was unavailable. She had been stunned when she learned he was gay. Hurt and angry didn't even come close to her feelings when she'd discovered that.

Now, with some time to dull her pain, she knew that Ralph wasn't to blame. He'd done nothing to encourage her amorous feelings; he'd been looking for a business partner, not a soulmate, and had been as upset as she was when her misunderstanding surfaced. They'd parted on good terms. Dani was still embarrassed by the memory of her naïveté, though.

She could imagine how Suarez would have dealt with someone like Lupita. It wouldn't have involved paying her blackmail, nor would he have responded to her summons the way David had. He might have gone to meet her once or twice, but only to set her up.

It wasn't that she was worried about Lupita's interfering in her future relationship with David. She was certain that wouldn't happen — not after tonight. But would a man who had let himself get into that kind of situation be able to avoid falling into a similar trap another time? She had a strong view on that, and it didn't augur well for a future with David.

Still, he was handsome and polite. She was only here for another few days — maybe a week or two at the outside. What was the harm in a little dalliance? She wished Liz were back; she needed to talk this over with her. And she needed to decide what she wanted to do before she met him in the morning.

She'd made the excuse of a mandatory family dinner when he asked her out tonight. He'd been obvious in his willingness to accompany her, suggesting that he'd really like to meet her family and friends, but she'd managed to stall him. She knew she couldn't keep putting him off. She either needed to dump him or bring him into the fold.

She heard footsteps on the dock outside and stood up to peep through the port light. Paul and Connie were coming back to *Diamantista II*. Liz wouldn't be far behind.

"Dani!" Liz yelped when she came down the companionway and turned on the light.

"Sorry. I didn't mean to startle you."

"Why are you sitting here in the dark?"

"I didn't want to deal with everybody, so I sort of sneaked in."

"I've been watching for you to come back. I was a little

worried, to tell the truth. Are you okay? How long have you been here?"

Dani shrugged. "Yes, I guess. I got back ... I don't know. Maybe half an hour?"

"Did you get something to eat?"

"I'm okay, *Mom*." Dani teased. "I just need to talk, if you're not too tired."

"Where did you go? The beach?"

Dani nodded. "Did they grill you about David and me?"

"I wouldn't say that, but of course they're curious. They asked if you were out with him this evening."

"What did you tell them?"

"As little as I could. I told them you had gone for a long walk, that you needed some time to yourself." Liz took in Dani's worried look and went on to explain. "I sort of had to tell them that much; they wanted to know why you didn't invite him to dinner here."

"But you didn't tell them about Lupita blackmailing him, did you?"

"No. I didn't mention her."

"Good," Dani said.

"So what excuse did you give David when he called this afternoon, if you don't mind my asking?"

"Not at all; I need to talk this through with you, please."

"I'm listening," Liz said. "So what did you tell him?"

"That this was a family-only affair."

"He thinks you were here, then?"

"Yes. He kind of invited himself. He wants to meet everybody. But I just couldn't deal with that. Not on top of this whole Lupita thing."

A few seconds passed in silence. "Blackmail," Liz said, shaking her head. "I guess you have to believe him about that. You can hardly ask her."

"I considered that. But then I decided she'd just lie, and maybe retaliate against him."

Liz nodded. "Uh-huh. Just as well that you don't confront her."

Dani looked at Liz, appraising her friend's expression for several seconds, and then looked away.

"Dani?"

"Yes?" Dani looked Liz in the eye. "What?"

"Did you?"

"Did I what?"

"Confront her."

"Not exactly."

"Do you want to tell me what that means?"

"He's a wimp, Liz."

"We were talking about Lupita."

"Yes. That's what I meant."

"How did you 'not exactly' confront her?"

"I just helped her to see that she should leave him alone from now on."

"And did she agree?"

"I was persuasive."

"Do you need to tell me what happened?"

Dani shook her head. "No. I'm okay with it. If you don't know, nobody can put you on the spot."

"Are there going to be repercussions?"

"No."

"What keeps her from retaliating?"

"Given her situation, she can't."

"Is she ... did you?"

"Are you trying to ask if I killed her?"

Liz locked eyes with Dani, but didn't say anything.

After a moment, Dani said, "She's a strong woman. She's not happy about her new situation, but she'll get over it with time. Probably."

"Was that what you wanted to talk about?" Liz asked.

"No. I'm still trying to sort out my feelings about David."

"Do you believe what he told you about Lupita, then?"

"More or less. It's moot now anyway. But I'm troubled that he couldn't handle it on his own."

"Does he know?"

"Know what?"

"That you persuaded her to back off."

"Not yet. I'm thinking I should tell him in the morning."

"You're going to see him in the morning?"

Dani nodded. "For brunch."

"Do you want to keep seeing him?"

"He's so kind and gentle. Not to mention being a real hunk to look at."

"That sounds like 'yes' to me," Liz said.

"But he's a wimp," Dani said.

"Is there an alternative explanation for his behavior?"

Dani frowned. "What are you saying, Liz?"

"Besides his being a wimp, can you think of a reason he would have put up with Lupita?"

Dani's mouth opened and closed a few times. "Uh, I haven't thought about it. Do you think — "

"I don't have any opinion. Just asking," Liz said. "If he weren't a wimp, would you keep seeing him?"

"Maybe."

"Why?"

"Because he's fun?"

"Is he?" Liz asked.

"I think so."

"And that's all you were looking for, isn't it? When we went to the club the other night? Someone who would be fun to go out with a few times?"

"Yes."

"Are you looking for something more than that right now?"

"I don't know. I hadn't thought of it like that. Should I be?"

"I can't answer that, Dani."

"I see. What do you think I should do?"

"Take small steps. You're meeting him for breakfast?"

"Right."

"If that goes well, invite him back here for lunch. Let's see how he fits in with everybody."

"You think that's okay?"

"Sure. And if it's not, you'll be closer to some answers, maybe."

"Thanks, Liz." Dani stood up and hugged her friend.

## 11

I t was just after sunrise when Phillip, a steaming mug of coffee in his hand, stepped out onto the veranda. There was no sign of life aboard either *Diamantista II* or *Vengeance* when he put his coffee down on the table and reached for a chair.

"Good morning, *señor*." Martínez had approached from the shadows, making just enough noise to alert Phillip to his presence. "I hoped you would come out early this morning. Are *Señor* Berger and his wife still asleep?"

"I think so; they haven't come out of their suite, anyway."

"Good; I see the yachts are still dark, so we have a few minutes, yes?"

"I expect so, but we should walk around like we did the other day, just in case. Can I get you coffee? It'll only take a ... "

Martínez shook his head, smiling. "Thank you, but I have already had breakfast."

As he turned and began to walk toward the flower beds in the front of the mansion, Phillip fell into step beside him. "I wondered if you'd lost your inside source, José."

Martínez looked at him and smiled, shrugging. "You mean because I waited to get in touch?"

Phillip nodded.

Martínez said, "I thought it best to give General Olsen some time to learn what he could. Now, at least, we know they are taking this seriously. I was offended on your behalf that they chose such an inexperienced person as your contact at first. I'm glad they saw their error."

"What's next, José?"

"Next? We should discuss my clients' requirements."

"We haven't made a commitment to you yet; you still haven't told us — "

"Excuse me, Colonel Davis. You and I both know what the appointment of General Olsen means. I appreciate that you must maintain a posture of negotiation, but I know your side is in the game, as the saying goes, yes?"

Phillip shrugged. "If you say so."

"Yes," Martínez said. "For now, let's work on the assumption that your people are committed. I need to equip a light infantry battalion. Only weapons, though. Uniforms and transportation are not a problem."

"So, 550 people, then?"

Martínez nodded. "Let us say 600, *señor*, to be safe."

"Eastern-Bloc weapons okay?" Phillip asked.

"Hmm." Martínez stroked his chin and looked down at the flowers. "I suppose that's necessary. Many of our people are veterans, though, so that will mean a bit of extra training. Maybe more ammunition than if you provide U.S.-made weapons."

"I don't understand," Phillip said.

"Veterans of your Gulf wars, *señor*. We are no longer dealing with a bunch of old men from home. We have a new generation, and they are battle-hardened."

"I see."

"Are U.S. weapons available? The price isn't critical," Martínez said.

"Everything is available. That isn't the problem. I can ask, but I know the preference will be foreign-manufactured."

"Ask, please."

"And you still want delivery in the Everglades?"

"Yes. Is this a problem?"

"Maybe. We aren't talking about a couple of pickup trucks with a few cases of rifles, here."

"Ah, of course," Martínez said. "I should tell you that delivering in small quantities would be good. We will do this a couple of platoons at a time, let's say. This makes a difference, yes?"

"Yes. That's much more manageable from a logistics' perspective. What kind of interval between shipments?"

"Let us say two weeks, for now," Martínez said.

"Can you take delivery somewhere like the Shark River Entrance? Whitewater Bay?"

"Yes. That would be excellent."

"Do you have anything else for now, José?"

"The cost? And method of payment? I will need to make arrangements, of course."

"Of course. I'll have to get back to you, now that we know the scope of your requirements."

"I'll be in touch, *señor*." With that, Martínez let himself out the pedestrian gate and got into a nondescript pickup truck driven by another man.

ORTIZ SAT on the bench at the Bayfront Park Amphitheatre facing the fountain. He picked up one of the two cups of coffee that sat next to him and took a sip, watching the old crone pushing a grocery cart along the sidewalk. As she approached, he could see that the cart was filled with bulging plastic bags that contained various discarded bits of clothing. He was downwind, and the homeless woman was still several yards from him when he wrinkled his nose at the sour odor wafting his way.

She gave him a gap-toothed grin and pushed the cart up to the end of the bench farthest from him. Still grinning at him, she sat down on the bench. When she reached for the extra cup of coffee, he said, "Sorry, but I'm expecting someone."

She nodded and took a sip of the coffee. "Yes, David. You called, and I came. You like the disguise?"

His face reflected his surprise. He gave her a closer look and saw that her "missing" teeth had been blackened temporarily. "You smell like a garbage truck. Thanks for not hiding in my car this time."

"I was here working on another case, so I was in the neighborhood. I knew you'd be meeting Dani Berger at the yacht club in a little while for breakfast. That's not too far from here. What's up?"

"I had a visitor last night after we talked."

"I know. You're wired, remember?"

"Then you already know about Lupita Vidal."

"Yes. South Beach can be dangerous at night, I guess. I'm on a tight schedule, here. What's on your mind?"

"Lupita."

"What about her?"

"Did you, um ... have someone ... "

She shook her head, making a clicking sound with her tongue. "Why would you think that?"

"Never mind the bullshit. Did you arrange that beating?"

"Of course not. You know we don't operate that way."

"Yeah, and I believe in Santa Claus and the Easter Bunny, too."

"So your mind's made up. Why'd you even bother to ask, then?"

"I wanted to know why. I'm reporting directly to Cruz, now. Is that what you wanted? Because if it is, you really screwed the pooch on this one."

"I told you, we had nothing to do with it, David. It's good that you're closer to Cruz, though. And why would you think we'd screwed the pooch, by taking out Lupita, which I assure you we did not."

"Because, she was key to the Haitian connection. That's why."

"She's just an enforcer, David. They'll get somebody else, no sweat."

"She was more than that. She was the go-between for Cruz and Santos."

"Yeah. After Cruz took over running you last night, we thought maybe he'd put you in that role."

"I wouldn't bet on it."

"And why's that?"

"He was sleeping with her."

"So? Do you have some kind of moral hang-up? Or is he just not your type?"

"That's not relevant, so I'll overlook how disgusting your remarks are."

"Not relevant why, David?"

"Cruz is straight. I worked damn hard to make Lupita think I had the hots for her."

"So? You didn't score with her; you told us that. You said she just liked to tease you. So what?"

"So one of the ways she teased me was by telling me all about what she did with Cruz."

"That's sick, David."

"Yeah, mostly. But while she was making me sick, she also let slip some details of what he had her working on between him and Santos. Now I'm cut out of that."

"You'll find a way. I'm sorry this is making your life more complicated, but I told you we didn't have anything to do with what happened to her."

"Then who did?"

She shrugged. "Maybe one of the Haitians got the drop on her? Or maybe somebody wants in on Cruz's exploitation racket."

"Nobody knows he's behind that. As far as everybody knows, it's all Santos's doing."

"Yeah, but everybody knew she worked for Santos, David. It could have been somebody wanting in on his game."

"Shit! You're right. I missed that. Too focused on Cruz. My fault."

"Okay, that's why we work in teams. Now we've got some catch-up work to do with her out of play. Any ideas?"

"You got somebody that could take Lupita's place?"

"What? You think I'm a madam? Wait! Don't even think about being a smartass. You got a real suggestion?"

"Connect me with somebody who could be the muscle for Santos and Cruz."

"And you'll be the go-between?"

"Yes. Find somebody I can bring in to solve their problem."

"That's not a half-bad idea, David. Male or female?"

"Either, actually. I think that relationship between her and Cruz was just a casual thing, not a critical element. It just kind of happened because of the two personalities. The main thing would be somebody that would be trustworthy in Cruz's eyes."

"What have you got in mind?"

"Somebody brutal, with a dirty secret that I could use to hold over their head. That would probably work. I could hint at the secret to make Cruz think I was in control. Their story would have to check out, though. You follow?"

"Yeah. Let me work on that. I'll get back to you."

"Make it fast. I don't know how long the window of opportunity will be open. They may have somebody in mind already."

"Okay. Anything else?"

"You passed along the tip about them buying arms?"

"Of course. Why?"

"What am I supposed to do about that?"

"Nothing. Your orders are to play along with them. We're

focused on the Haitians. The exiles are always planning invasions, but nothing ever comes of it."

"You sure about that, Mary?"

"Yes, David. I gotta run. I need to shower and change before my next meeting."

"WHAT'S WITH YOU, DANI?" Liz asked, frowning. "I've never known you to listen to the morning news."

Dani shrugged, pushing a button on the radio at the chart table to pause its scan of the AM broadcast band. "I'm sentimental, I guess. When I was a child staying here with Mario and Gina, we'd start every day with coffee and the eight o'clock news. Reading the news on line's not the same, and being here in Miami — " She paused, holding up a finger.

"The victim of last night's vicious attack in the garage of an upscale South Beach condo has been identified as Ms. Lupita Vidal, a resident of the building. The motive for the savage beating is unknown at this time. A Miami Beach Police Department spokesperson has declined to comment, as the investigation is ongoing. Ms. Vidal is currently recuperating at Mount Sinai Medical Center, where her condition is listed as 'fair.' Police are asking anyone with potential information to come forward, even anonymously. Speaking of that, this station received an anonymous tip that the assailant was a woman who spoke Cuban Spanish; she was seen leaving the garage shortly before police arrived on the scene. Police were summoned by a security guard who saw part of the attack via security cameras. And now, a word from ... "

Dani switched off the radio, shaking her head. "Unbelievable."

"The coincidence?" Liz asked, scowling. "Were you the anonymous tipster?"

"Why would you think that, Liz? You think I'd be that careless? That woman's on security tapes. I'd have disabled the cameras."

"Only if it suited you. I'll bet she was wearing a mask."

"You're probably right. I'll bet she wanted the word to get out that Vidal got her ass kicked by another woman."

"Think the police will find any trace evidence?" Liz asked.

"Not if the attacker knew what she was doing. Sounds like she might have been a pro, to take down a cage fighter like Lupita. Pros don't leave a trail. I'll bet David will be relieved to have that bitch out of his hair."

"Did he know?"

"Know what?" Dani asked.

"That you were going to beat her up," Liz said.

"What are you saying, Liz? You don't think I did that, do you?"

"Of course not," Liz sneered. "She's still alive."

Dani shook her head. "I'm disappointed that you think I'd kill with such little reason. We talked about that last night. Lupita didn't deserve to die. She just needed a little behavior modification therapy."

"I guess she got that," Liz said. "You're still meeting David at the club, right?"

"Ten o'clock, yes. Are you still offering lunch?"

"Sure. How about two o'clock?"

"Perfect," Dani said.

"Is it all right if I invite the others? They all want to meet him."

"That's fine. I suspect Papa and Anne have plans, but invite whoever's available. I'll warn David that he's going to be on display."

"You think he'll be uncomfortable? I could — "

"He'll be okay with it, Liz. I was teasing. He wants to meet everybody."

"Okay. Let's get you put together."

"How long do I have to keep this up?" Dani asked.

"Keep what up?"

"All this girl foolishness?"

"Until you don't want to play anymore, or until we sail back to the islands."

"I'm already wondering if it's worth the trouble. What do you think?"

"It's not my decision. You're the one trying to catch him."

"Guess I'd better go get started. Even if this is catch and release, I still want the satisfaction of landing one."

## 12

"Shitty coffee," Tony Santos said.

"Yeah, but nobody knows us around here," Manny Cruz said. They sat on adjacent bar stools looking out the window of a chain coffee shop near the Interstate in North Miami. "You get any more out of Lupita?"

"Nah," Santos said. "They got her doped up pretty good. But I don't think she knows any more than she done told me."

"And the cops?"

"Yeah, well, she didn't have much choice but to talk to 'em. They were all over her from the beginning."

"No, Tony. I was wondering if you'd gotten anything from them."

"Oh. Yeah, but not much. They got the surveillance tapes from security in her building, but that's about it."

"Have you seen the video?"

"Nah. One of the cops on my payroll told me about it. Like Lupita said. Skinny woman about her height with a blackjack. Cop said she didn't waste no moves. Beat the shit out of Lupita in no time flat."

"Did they get her face in the video?"

Santos shook his head and took a sip of coffee, making a face at the taste. "She had on one of them ski masks. Dark clothes. Cops and the building security guy figure she slipped in behind somebody's car and hid."

"So they think Lupita was the target? This wasn't some kind of random mugging gone bad?"

Santos laughed.

"What's funny?"

"'Random mugging gone bad.' Jesus, Manny. Think about that. Some dumbass woman decides she's gonna mug somebody and picks Lupita? Gimme a break. Lupita woulda kicked a mugger's ass without breakin' a sweat. You know that. This wasn't no random nothin'. Somebody put a fuckin' hit on Lupita."

"Then why not kill her?" Cruz asked.

Santos shrugged, rolling his heavy shoulders. He looked at Cruz and raised his eyebrows. "Yeah. Why not? While we're askin' questions, might as well throw in 'Who?' don't ya think? Somebody musta been tryin' to tell us somethin'."

"She worked for you, Tony. What do you know about her?"

"You're askin' me? You're the one was sleepin' with her. I figure you probably knew her better'n me."

"There wasn't anything to that except kinky sex. How'd you find her to begin with?"

"She was workin' our buildings in little Haiti. I spotted her a few times and got curious so I tailed her for a while. To see what she was doin'."

"And what did you discover?"

"She was collectin' for a two-bit loan shark. I watched her kick the shit out of two guys that laughed at her when she told 'em their time was up."

"What happened?"

"She stopped 'em on the street and they laughed at her. One of 'em put the moves on her, like she was a hooker, you know?"

"Then what?"

"She played along. Went back to their place with 'em and closed the door. Two minutes later, she came out, countin' her money, and then the ambulance came. They hauled the guys away wrapped up in bloody sheets. Coupla women, too. One of the men's sisters, she said."

"She said?"

"Yeah. I hired her on the spot. Right then, while we watched 'em loadin' the ambulance."

"What about the loan shark?"

"She said she'd square it with him. Offered to set me up with his clients, if I wanted."

"What did you do?"

"Shit, Manny. It was easy money. I couldn't see no problems. I shoulda maybe cleared it with you. You want in on it? There's room for more money."

"No, thanks. Not my kind of business. I'll stick to investing in property."

Santos nodded and took a sip of coffee.

After a moment, Cruz asked, "Do you think that loan shark might have been behind the attack?"

Santos looked at him for a second and shook his head. "He wasn't happy when Lupita cut him out. Made some kinda stink about it with her. They found him in the Miami River a few days later. Suicide. He jumped off a bridge, the cops figured."

"Those bridges aren't that high," Cruz said, frowning.

"Musta hit somethin' in the water; broke his neck, they said."

Cruz took a sip of coffee. "You got anybody that can fill in for her?"

"I'm lookin', Manny. If you got any suggestions, let me know, okay?"

"Yeah. You going to do your own heavy lifting for now?"

"Not much choice. Most of them Haitians are chickenshits, anyway. It don't take much muscle. Lupita had to kick ass more often 'cause the ones that didn't know her didn't take her seriously. Besides, she liked doin' it, you know? Me? I'm an ugly son of a bitch. I can mostly just look at 'em hard. That's all. But I do need somebody besides me. Let me know if you hear of somebody."

~

"GOOD MORNING, DAVID," Dani said, as she approached his table.

He put his coffee mug down and stood to greet her, smiling. "You look especially pretty this morning," he said, giving her a light kiss on the cheek.

"Thanks," she said, beaming, as she sat down and let him adjust her chair.

"I missed you last night; I've been spoiled by your company lately. Did you have a nice evening?" he asked.

"Yes, thanks. I needed a little time to sort out my feelings."

"I understand. I was halfway afraid you'd call and tell me you didn't want to see me this morning."

"Oh, David! I'm sorry. I never meant to cause you that kind of anxiety. I was just feeling swept off my feet; I needed some time to think. That's all."

"Well, anyway, I'm relieved. Should I get the waitress over here? Did you want breakfast?"

"Actually, I'd like for you to come out to Star Island for lunch, so maybe I'll just stick to coffee."

"That's great! So I'll get to meet your family?"

"Well, whoever's there. We didn't have time to make any big plans. My partner in the boat's going to feed whoever's around. That's Liz Chirac; she's the ship's cook and my best friend. My father and stepmother may not be there; I don't know what their plans are. This was kind of spur of the moment."

"I'm excited, Dani. Coach me a little; I want to make a good impression. Who am I likely to meet? Do your folks live there?"

Dani chuckled. "Slow down, David. My father's best friend

lives in Miami. They're business partners as well; they have been since before I was born. He's about to celebrate his 75th birthday, and Papa rented this place to throw a surprise party for him. A bunch of close friends are coming, okay?"

"I'm with you so far. Where do your folks live, just out of curiosity?"

"Papa and my stepmother live in Paris. They spent some time in the Bahamas on *Vengeance* with me and Liz before we got here a few days ago."

"Nice. Who else is staying there?"

"Phillip Davis. He may be around for lunch; I don't know. He's retired, now, but he was a career Army officer for 20 years, and then he was in business with my father and Mario."

"Mario?"

"Mario Espinosa. It's his birthday party. He's also my godfather, by the way."

"And will he be there?"

"No. It's not his birthday, yet. It's a surprise party, so he doesn't know we're all gathering. Now, about Phillip. He's quite a bit younger than my father; he was like a big brother to me when I was growing up. He's married, but his wife's not here yet. She's a French Customs officer; they live in Martinique."

"Wow. My head's swimming, Dani. Where'd you grow up, anyway? I know you lived in the States, mostly, after you were an adult, but that's as far as we've gotten."

"My mother lives in New York. I lived with her during the school year, more or less. But the rest of the time, with my father."

"In Paris?"

"Mostly down island. Papa's in the import/export business, and back then, he was spending most of his time in the Caribbean. He's from Martinique, originally, like your mother. So I was kind of a vagabond, growing up. I spent a lot of time with relatives and friends of his in the islands."

"And where was this Phillip guy?"

"Different places in the Caribbean and Latin America."

"I see. I guess I'll get it all straight, once I meet some of these people."

"You will. Don't worry. They're easy people to be with. Oh! And I almost forgot to mention Paul Russo and his wife, Connie Barrera. They have a boat that's a sister ship to *Vengeance,* and they run charters like Liz and I do. They're good friends of ours. We taught Connie to sail, and she bought her own boat. We're sharing the dock with them."

"So she owns the boat with her husband?"

"Well, now they're partners in the boat, but that's another long story. Liz and I introduced them. Paul's a friend of Mario's. They can tell you about themselves."

"Cool. I can't wait. Thanks for all the background. You'll probably have to help me out along the way, though."

"I will," Dani said, pouring herself a mug of coffee from the thermal carafe that was on the table.

They smiled at one another, drinking coffee in silence for a few minutes. Dani reached across the table and took his hand.

"Did you see the local news this morning?" she asked, breaking the silence.

He shook his head. "No. Why?"

"So you didn't hear about Lupita?"

He frowned, breaking eye contact for a moment. He looked back at her and shook his head. "Lupita Vidal?"

"Yes."

He swallowed and licked his lips. "She was on the news?"

"She was attacked last night. From what they said, she was badly beaten. She's in the hospital."

"Who did it? Did they say why?"

"No. Something about a woman who spoke Cuban Spanish, but I guess they don't know much."

"That's hard to believe; I mean she's a professional fighter. I ... " He looked away.

"What, David?" She squeezed his hand, and tipped her head forward, looking up at him, encouraging him. "You what?"

"I've heard about her, like, breaking people's arms and stuff. I told you she was the enforcer for this slum lord guy in Little Haiti, right?"

"Yes, and a blackmailer. Maybe she took some pictures she shouldn't have." She released her grip on his hand and patted him on the arm, a soothing touch. "I guess you don't need to worry about her anymore."

He gulped, and then reached for his coffee. Taking a sip, he shook his head. "I guess not."

"I'd better get back to the boat and get her ready for company," she said. "Liz will be busy with lunch preparations, I'm sure."

"Can I bring anything?" Ortiz asked.

"Just your appetite; Liz is a gourmet chef, seriously. The gate's at the end of the main road. If it's not open, just give me a call on my cellphone."

CRUZ WAS THREADING his way through the traffic on I-95 South when his cellphone rang. He stole a glance at the caller i.d., saw that it was Ortiz, and accepted the call.

"Yeah?" he barked.

"Manny?'

"Yeah, Ortiz. What's up?"

"I just had coffee with Berger at the yacht club. She's invited me to lunch at the compound in a couple hours. I'll probably meet some of the people there, but she wasn't sure who'd be around."

"Did she mention any names?"

"Yeah. She thinks her father and his wife won't be there for lunch, but she mentioned a Phillip Davis. She said he used to be in business with her old man. Also, Liz Chirac, her partner in the charter yacht, and another couple — Paul Russo and Connie Barrera."

"Davis we knew about, but who's the couple?" Cruz asked.

"They run another charter yacht in the islands. She said it was a sister ship to hers. Barrera's a friend of hers. She and Chirac taught Barrera to sail, and introduced her to her husband, this Russo guy."

"Any mention of why these people are there? Barrera and Russo, I mean. I never heard of them."

"Yeah. This whole thing's a surprise birthday party for Mario Espinosa, and — "

"I know that, Ortiz." Cruz clenched his jaw and shook his head, frustrated. "Barrera's friends with the two girls, but why would she and her husband be invited to Espinosa's party?"

"She said Russo's a long-time friend of Espinosa's."

"Wild card," Cruz grunted. "See what you can find out about him."

"Yeah, okay. No problem. Anything else?"

"Yeah. Behave yourself with those people. You need to get invited back, remember."

"I got it, Manny."

"Good. You got anything else?"

"Not really, but she did mention hearing about Lupita on the news this morning."

Cruz felt the hair on the back of his neck stand up. "Say what?"

"I said, 'She — '"

"I got that, Ortiz, but why the fuck did she even mention that?"

"Uh ... um ... "

"Ortiz? Does she know you and Lupita knew one another?"

"Sorta ... "

"What the fuck does 'sorta' mean, Ortiz?"

"Remember when I picked Berger up in the club a couple nights ago?"

"Yeah. What's that got to do with Lupita?"

"I was supposed to be setting Berger up for Lupita to snatch her that evening, and — "

"You were what? Where the fuck did you get that idea from?"

"Lupita. She told me to invite Berger out to dinner, and on the way, Lupita was going to kidnap her."

"Lupita said that?" Cruz asked.

"That's right," Ortiz said. "And then she called and interrupted me and Berger just as I was asking her out to dinner. She told me to ditch Berger for the evening and meet her on the beach."

"And did you?"

"Yeah, sure. You told me Lupita was running things, so yeah. That's what I did."

"You met Lupita on the beach, and then what?"

"I gave her some shit for interrupting me and Berger like that. Lupita was screaming at me over the phone, and Berger heard her. Lupita thought it was okay, because she was speaking Spanish. She didn't know Berger's fluent."

"So what did Lupita want with you?"

"She told me the plans changed. There wasn't going to be a snatch, and I was supposed to make Berger fall in love with me and get inside the compound."

"She told you that on the beach, right? Not where Berger could hear?"

"That's right."

"So Berger heard Lupita's name from the phone call?"

"Yeah. I knew she did. I bitched about it to Lupita, and Lupita said to tell her she was, um ... a ... a distant cousin, or something, and she was calling about some kind of family emergency. Like, she needed to borrow some money from me, or something."

"Why the hell did she make up a story like that, Ortiz?"

"I don't know. I mean, we knew I was going to have to tell Berger something to explain why I ran out on her that night, right?"

"Yeah, okay. So Berger thinks Lupita's your cousin, or something?"

"Distant cousin. That's why she mentioned hearing about her on the news, I guess."

"She say any more about Lupita? Ask any questions?"

"Just asked if I knew about the attack."

"And what did you tell her?"

"Played dumb. She caught me off guard with that; I didn't know it made the news."

"Me either. She buy it?"

"My act, you mean?"

"Yeah. What did you say?"

"That I hadn't heard, and Lupita was kind of like the black sheep, that I had as little to do with her as possible. I said I wasn't surprised, that Lupita ran with a pretty rough crowd."

"Okay. Well, stick to that story, if it comes up again."

"Yeah, I will. I don't think she'll mention it again. She's kind of distracted, you know?"

"Distracted?"

"Yeah. She said she was feeling swept off her feet." Ortiz chuckled. "That's what you're paying me for, remember? To sweep her off her feet."

"Right. Well, keep it up. With Lupita gone, we really need you in there."

"No problem. I'll call you after lunch, okay? It might be pretty late this afternoon."

"Yeah. Fine," Cruz said. "Oh, Ortiz?"

"Yeah?"

"You think of anything else about that Martínez character? I'm still trying to figure out who jumped Lupita."

"No. But I didn't forget. I'll let you know if anything comes to me."

# 13

"Any progress on getting your man into the compound?" Maldonado asked.

Cruz worked his right index finger in between his collar and his neck. Under Maldonado's scrutiny, his shirt seemed too tight. "He's going to lunch there today, Willy."

"It's about damn time," Maldonado said. "I don't know what his problem is. Martínez comes and goes like he owns the place."

"Yeah, well, Ortiz has a different agenda, Willy. We both know that."

"Yeah, yeah. I want to know who's there besides Davis and the Bergers. You understand that? Does Ortiz?"

"Yes, we do. We already know that — "

"Save it," Maldonado said. "Put it in your report after Ortiz gets inside."

"As you wish, Willy. But — "

"I *wish* to know who's there and what their connection to J.-P. Berger is. And make sure Lupita gets some pictures of them all. She can take a kayak and paddle right up to their seawall."

"Actually, there's a problem with that," Cruz said.

"What problem? Just cut her loose from whatever she's

doing. This might get hot without much warning. We need to be able to show Ortiz in frequent contact with Berger and his people."

"Lupita's out of action, Willy. Somebody jumped her last night and — "

"Jumped her? Lupita? You're shittin' me."

"No. Beat her to the point where she can't get around. She's gonna need a lot of physical therapy, word is. She's in the hospital."

"Shit! Who?"

"We don't know. Some Cuban woman, Lupita said."

"What did you have her doing?"

"Working for Santos, mostly. She was keeping the Haitians in line, until she started running this thing with Ortiz."

"She piss somebody off?"

"Not that we know of."

"She conscious?"

"Yeah."

"What did she say happened?"

Cruz related what Lupita had told Santos, leaving out the fact that Lupita's assailant had mentioned Ortiz.

"Cops?" Maldonado asked. "They involved?"

"Yeah. The building security people saw the attack on closed circuit video and called them."

"Shit, Cruz. How much does she know?"

"The rough outline."

"Give it to me, what she knows."

"Alpha-66 and some of the other groups are planning an invasion. We're looking to buy weapons from J.-P. Berger. I had to tell her that much to make sure she knew why we wanted Berger's daughter in our control."

"She know about Martínez?"

Cruz swallowed hard, his mind racing through his options.

"I didn't tell her, Willy, but she's sharp, and she's been

watching the place on Star Island. She's probably seen him around there."

"How long's she going to be in the hospital?"

"Several more days, at least."

"Is she doped up?"

"Yeah, they're keeping her drugged for the pain. Santos said she's half out of her head; doesn't know what's happening."

"So you're running this Ortiz kid yourself?"

"Yeah. It's the only choice I have."

"He know about Martínez?"

"I don't see how he could. He's nowhere near as sharp as Lupita."

"But you do think she knows about him? Tell me why you think that, Manny."

"She spotted him the first time he went to Star Island; asked about him by name. Him and Davis both. I think she overheard them, maybe with that parabolic microphone thing."

"What did you tell her?"

"Nothing, Willy. I just blew it off, you know."

"Good. Keep me posted on Ortiz's progress."

"You want me to do anything about Lupita?"

"Nah. Just get her back on her feet. We need her."

"Should I be looking for somebody to take her place?"

"No. Too risky to bring in somebody new at this stage. Why? You got somebody in mind?"

"No, but Santos needs to hire another collector."

"That's your business, Manny. Do what you need to do; the real estate business is part of your cover, but keep it separate, you understand? We made an exception for Lupita, and now I wish we hadn't."

"Okay, Willy. No problem."

"Good. Get back to work."

"GOOD MORNING, RICK," Phillip said. "Did I catch you at a bad time?"

"Not at all," Olsen responded. "The connection's way better on these things than the old encrypted phones."

"Yes. You sound like you're in the room with me."

"Good. What's on your mind this morning? Any news from Martínez?"

"Yes." Phillip recounted his earlier conversation.

"How does that strike you?" Olsen asked.

"A little on the loose side, frankly, but I've never dealt with him before."

"Yeah, I agree with that. I don't like flying blind on this. You still don't have a way to contact him?"

"Correct. I did a little fishing on whether he lost his inside track when my original contact was killed. I didn't get anything conclusive, though."

"I hear a 'but' in your tone."

"Yeah. He may be behind the killing. Or some of his backers may be. He certainly wasn't surprised by it. Any more news on that?"

"Not really. They still don't have a murder weapon."

"They probably won't find one, then. Unless he left the weapon behind for some reason, a pro would have gotten rid of it where it won't be found."

"Yeah. That's what they figure. You think Martínez is capable of that kind of thing?"

"Yes. No doubt on that score."

"Ordering it? Or doing it?"

"Either one. Why?"

"I don't know. The Director asked, but he didn't share his thoughts."

"Do we have any resources to call on, Rick?"

"What do you have in mind?"

"I'd like to know more about Martínez; where he is when he's not digging in the flower beds, for a start."

"You want somebody to tail him?"

"It crossed my mind. What do you think?"

"He's a seasoned agent. It wouldn't be easy, and it might spook him."

"That's one possibility," Phillip said.

"You've got another one in mind. What?"

"If I were in his position, I'd expect it. The absence of an effort to follow me would make me think I wasn't being taken seriously."

"That's a point. Give me a little time on that one. I'll get back to you."

"Okay."

"On a similar subject, we got the details on the license plate from the car that he sent for you."

"It took long enough. I was about to get one of my MPD friends to run it."

"A word of caution on that, Phillip. I know your friend Russo's there with you, and he's trustworthy. But beware of the MPD."

"That's why I held back."

"Okay, good. Anyway, the plate was stolen. It belongs to a local lawyer; no reason to think he's connected to this, but his car's the same model as the one you were in. Color and everything matches."

"That's worrisome."

"Yes, I agree. Martínez, or whoever's behind him, put some effort into the details. Not only that, but we found the car in long term parking at the Miami airport, and guess what?"

"What?"

"The plates had been returned. Whoever did it just borrowed them."

"Security cameras in the parking lot?" Phillip asked.

"Yes, but they didn't catch anything. The angle wasn't right."

"This is pretty thorough, for a bunch of geriatric exiles."

"Well, yes. There's a new generation playing the game, and not all of them are saints."

"What are you hinting at, Rick? A criminal element?"

"Yes. That level of sophistication is beyond what I'd expect from the old exile operations."

"I see your point. That's another good reason to find out a little more about Martínez."

"Right. I'll see what I can do. I need to run his requirements list up the flagpole and see what the response is, too. I'll let you know."

"It'll be interesting to see the timing between your answer and Martínez's next contact."

"Yes, won't it? Take care, Phillip, and call if you think of anything else."

"THIS IS BEAUTIFUL, Dani. I had no idea." Ortiz ran a fingertip over the high-gloss varnish that coated the chart table. "This is like glass; I can see my reflection."

"Thanks. It takes a lot of work to keep the bright work up like that, but it's more or less expected by our clients."

"I've never seen inside a yacht like this. It's like ... I don't know ... like being inside a piece of antique furniture, or something."

"Have you sailed, David?"

"No, not really. Just little boats, like at resorts. You know, the kind of boats they have on the beach?"

"Yes. Well, the principles are the same, but the experience is a bit different."

"I'd love to try it sometime."

"We can arrange that. We'll have to pick a day when Liz and I won't be missed, though."

"I'm surprised that two people can sail a boat like this; it seems so big."

"She can be a handful, especially if the wind pipes up. But it's what we do."

"When did you learn to sail, Dani?"

She chuckled. "I don't remember; I grew up around boats. Some of my earliest memories are of sailing with my father."

"And does he still sail?"

"Sure. He owns a few big crewed yachts based in the Mediterranean. When they're idle, he uses them. When I was in my early teens, I worked as deck crew on them."

"So have you owned a lot of boats?"

"Owned? No. This is the first one I've actually bought. I don't count some of the little ones I had growing up down in the islands. They were more like the kind you sailed off the beach."

"And the one tied up next to us? You said it's a sister ship. Was it built in the same factory?"

She grinned. "No. Boats like these are custom built. They're built in boatyards, or shipyards, not factories."

"But it looks identical."

"They're both built to the same design. A naval architect named Herreshoff drew the lines. The original was named *Bounty*. There have been quite a few built over the years, but no two are alike. When people commission the construction of boats like these, they modify things to suit themselves. Not usually anything major, but there's still a lot of variation."

"Interesting. This is like a different world to me. I mean, you could go anywhere you wanted on a boat like this, right? Anywhere in the world?"

"Well, not quite anywhere. There has to be enough water for her draft."

"Draft?"

"She draws close to six feet. That's the depth of water it takes for her to float."

"And when you go somewhere, you have your home with you. That's really cool. I think I could get interested in living like this. Can we look at the one next door, too? I'd like to see the differences."

"We'll ask Paul and Connie after lunch. Let's go up and see how Liz is doing. She and Paul decided to cook indoors instead of aboard."

"She and Paul? I thought Paul went with Connie."

"He does. But he and Liz are both first-rate chefs. When we're all together, the two of them try to outdo one another with their newest recipes."

"Sounds like I'm in for a treat."

"No doubt. I did — "

She was interrupted by a man's voice, calling from the dock. "Dani? You aboard?"

"That's Phillip," she said, mounting the companionway ladder. "Coming!"

As she emerged into the cockpit, Phillip said, "Liz sent me to tell you lunch will be ready in about five minutes. They're setting up in the outdoor dining room. Besides, I wanted to meet your friend."

She stepped aside, giving Ortiz room to climb into the cockpit. "David Ortiz," she said, "meet Phillip Davis."

Ortiz scrambled onto the dock and took Phillip's hand. "Pleased to meet you, Mr. Davis. Dani's told me a lot about you."

"It's nice to meet you, too," Phillip said, his grip firm, his eyes locked on Ortiz's. He nodded and released his grip. "Call me Phillip."

"You're from Martinique?" Ortiz said, as the three of them began walking up the dock.

"Well, I live there, now. My wife's from there, but I grew up in Georgia. Dani told me your mother's family's from Martinique."

"That's right, but I don't know much about it. I've never been there. Her parents lived in Cuba before Castro. When things got bad, they went to Martinique. It was my grandmother's family that lived there, actually. My father was from Cuba."

"You told me your parents came from Cuba on a raft, David," Dani said, frowning. "When your mother was pregnant."

"Uh, right," Ortiz said. "That's right. I was born in Miami. Dani said you were retired from the Army, Phillip."

"Yes," Phillip said.

"Where were you stationed?"

"Different places. Later in my career, I was a military attaché in Barbados, but I actually worked all over the Caribbean basin."

"David," Dani said, "I don't understand why your parents came from Cuba to Florida on a raft if they'd left Cuba after Castro to live in Martinique."

"Well, it's pretty convoluted," Ortiz said. "I'll tell you about it later, okay? No need to bore everybody with that tale. Were you ever in combat, Phillip?"

"I was too young for Viet Nam, and I was tied up down island during the actions in the Middle East."

"You must have been a pretty senior officer by then," Ortiz said, ignoring the looks Dani was sending his way.

"I guess," Phillip said, watching Dani, trying to catch her eye.

"I would have thought a senior career officer would have been sent where the action was," Ortiz said.

"Trying to understand the how and why of military assign-ments is a short route to insanity," Phillip said as they stepped onto the veranda. "Nice chatting with you, David, but I'll excuse myself while Dani introduces you around. I need to make a quick call; I'll catch up with everybody shortly."

# 14

Martínez sat in the tiny back room of a restaurant off Calle Ocho in Little Havana. He sipped at a thimble-sized cup of strong, sweet Cuban coffee while he waited for Maldonado. Before he'd finished the coffee, there was a tap on the door and Maldonado entered.

Pulling out the other chair, Maldonado sat. "Did you check out the room?"

"Yeah," Martínez said, pointing at the cellphone-sized electronic device on the table. "The room's clean; we can talk. What's wrong?"

"Why do you think something's wrong?"

"You call me and demand a meeting in the middle of the morning when I'm waiting to hear about what Davis told Olsen? There had better be something wrong, Willy."

"Calm down, José."

"Don't tell me to calm down. What the hell do you want?"

"Did you catch the news about Lupita?"

"News? What news?"

"She made the local news this morning. Somebody beat her up pretty badly."

Martínez studied Maldonado for several seconds. "Well, what's going on? Tell me the rest."

"We don't know who did it or why. She said it was a woman with a blackjack who spoke Cuban Spanish."

"Did the woman say anything?"

"Nothing of importance. She just cursed Lupita and worked her over. She had to be a pro."

"Yeah, to take Lupita down, I would say she was a pro. Have you talked to Cruz about this?"

"Yeah," Maldonado said. "He's got no idea."

"You believe that?"

"I've got no reason not to, José."

"Even with the Haitian business?"

"You mean the undocumented Haitians Cruz and Santos are bringing in?"

"Yeah," Martínez said. "I've never liked that."

"It's one more problem for the Americans to deal with," Maldonado said. "Besides, it's given us a good place to hide the troops for the invasion."

Martínez shook his head. "Yeah, that's true. I just don't like all the other stuff he's into."

"He's self-sufficient, José. He and Santos can provide Haitians for whatever you want: sex, domestic help, construction labor, hotel maids, highjacking trucks, smuggling drugs, you name it. It's not all bad; it's made this operation possible. If we had tried to hide the mercenaries in the Everglades, somebody could have spotted them. We couldn't have used one of the exile camps. We talked about that; we didn't want the exiles involved. They can't be trusted. Cruz's rentals are a much safer place to put them."

"How can you say that? The risk if he gets busted for any of the things he's into ... it could expose those guys ... " Martínez shook his head.

"How is he going to get caught?"

"The troops aren't Haitian, for one thing," Martínez said. "They don't fit the neighborhood."

"They're from the D.R.," Maldonado said. "Who's going to know the difference?"

"The Haitians. That's who."

"Santos keeps them in line."

"And that's another thing. Santos isn't one of us, either."

"You mean because he's from the D.R., too?"

"Yes. This whole setup depends on Cruz and Santos, and they've got all kinds of vulnerabilities. If they go down ... "

"Hey, that's not our problem, José. Cruz is one of those successful, Cuban-American entrepreneurs — the kind the exiles brag about. We've got what the Americans call plausible deniability. There's no DGI connection — not one anybody can prove, anyway. Not before we could silence him, if he went down."

"You make a good point," Martínez said. "Maybe we should rethink how this 'American-sponsored' terrorist invasion is going to be exposed. We could take him down with it. He'd make a much better scapegoat than Ortiz."

"Yeah, that's true. Ortiz is a small fish at best; Cruz would make a much bigger splash. You think about that, José. My hands are full right now with the setup. At least Ortiz is making some progress getting into Berger's entourage."

"He is?" Martínez asked.

"Yes. He's having lunch there this afternoon. The girl is falling for him, it seems."

"Good. Too bad Lupita's not able to get audio and video," Martínez said.

"All is not lost, there," Maldonado said. "If he takes the girl back to his place, it's wired. Lupita took care of that."

"Okay. At least she got that much done. I do wonder who took her out, though. And why."

"Yeah, me too. But that reminds me, José. She knows about you."

"What?" Martínez raised his voice. "How? What does she know?"

"I don't know, but she mentioned your name to Ortiz. He brought it up when Cruz was questioning him about Lupita."

"That is not good," Martínez said. "How could she have learned about me?"

"Was she around when you were meeting with Cruz?"

"Never. I never met with him. Not in person. Only on burner phones."

"Maybe she overheard."

"That would have been careless on his part," Martínez said. "What did Ortiz say?"

"Cruz asked him if Lupita had mentioned any new men in her life, or something like that. He said the only name he'd heard was Martínez."

"Shit. What did Cruz say?"

"He played dumb. He told Ortiz he couldn't think of anybody with that name and asked if she'd said anymore about him, but Ortiz said no."

"Where is Lupita, anyway?"

"Mount Sinai."

"Is she conscious?" Martínez asked.

"Yeah, but Cruz says she's drugged out of her mind. Pain medication."

"The cops involved?"

"Yeah," Maldonado said. "Cruz said they were there right from the start. Building security called them right after it happened."

"Did she tell them anything?"

"Cruz said Santos had one of the cops on his payroll checking. So far, all they know is what I told you about the Cuban woman. You worried she'll talk?"

"It would be better if she didn't," Martínez said. "Who knows what she might say if she's all doped up?"

"You want me to send somebody to talk with her?"

Martínez thought for a moment and then shook his head. "I'll take care of it."

"WELL, WHAT DO YOU THINK?" Liz asked, after Dani left to walk Ortiz back to his car. She and the others lingered over the remains of lunch.

"He's handsome, all right," Connie said. "And he seems nice. I mean, not like he thinks he's God's gift to women, or anything. Just a regular guy."

"Did I catch that he's in the real estate business?" Paul asked.

"That's right," Liz said. "I didn't hear that come up, though." She gave Paul a curious look.

"You mentioned it the other day, I think," Connie said. "Maybe I passed that along to you, Paul."

"Yes, I think you did. Any idea what he does, exactly?" Paul asked.

"I picked up from the bartender at the yacht club that he's a sales agent for some brokerage firm." Liz said. "He entertains people at the club using a business membership, but the broker's name escapes me."

Paul shook his head. "It wouldn't mean anything to me anyway, unless he was a crook of some kind. I don't know much about Miami real estate."

"There was one thing that seemed a little odd," Phillip said.

Everyone turned to look at him.

"Well?" Connie prompted. "Tell us."

"When I went down to *Vengeance* to tell them lunch was almost ready, Dani introduced him to me. We were making small talk, and he mentioned that she'd told him I was from Martinique. I expanded on that a little, and then asked about his family ties there. Dani had told us about that, remember?"

"Right," Liz said.

"When he answered," Phillip said, "Dani tried to clarify something about his folks coming from Cuba, and he sort of cut her off."

"He cut her off? That explains why she seemed irritated when we first sat down," Liz said. "I noticed she was tense about something. What happened?"

"He said his mother was from Martinique, or actually, that her folks were. She and his father were living in Cuba before Castro and they went back to Martinique after the Revolution."

"But wait," Liz interjected. Phillip nodded at her, and she continued. "Dani said his parents came to the States on a raft while his mother was pregnant with him. That had to be long after the Revolution. Something's wrong with the timing there."

"That's what she was trying to get at," Phillip said. "She mentioned that, specifically, and he put her off. He was wanting to talk about my military career instead, and she tried a couple of times to get him to address the other."

"Really?" Liz asked. "Now why would he cut Dani off to talk about your military service?"

"I don't know," Phillip said. "I'm sure he's getting an earful about it by now, though." He grinned and shook his head. "She was not happy, and we all know how that plays out. But he does seem like a nice young man."

"Excuse me," Liz said, as she took her cellphone out of her pocket. "It's Dani," she said, as she accepted the call. She stepped away and spoke quietly for a few seconds, shrugged, and returned the phone to the pocket of her shorts.

Sitting back down at the table, she said, "Nothing exciting. She wanted to let me know they're going over to South Beach for a little while, and that she'd call me if she wasn't going to be back in time for dinner."

"I guess they must have smoothed things over," Connie said.

"I couldn't tell," Liz said, "but I did notice she was acting a bit annoyed during lunch. She's been like a giddy teenager about him ever since she met him, but I think the old Dani's back with us."

"That's good; I like the old Dani better," Connie said, with a grin.

"I've got an appointment to keep," Phillip said. "There's a car coming for me in a few minutes. I'd better get moving. Great lunch, you two. See you all later." He turned as he went into the house, giving them an abbreviated wave.

"An appointment," Liz said. "I wonder what he's up to?"

PHILLIP WAS STANDING under the portico in front of the villa when the car pulled in. He recognized the Mercedes sedan from the earlier rendezvous with Martínez. As he committed the license plate number to memory, he registered that it was different from the previous one he'd given to Olsen. When the car stopped, he walked around the front and rested his left forearm on the driver's side windshield. Leaning toward the driver's window as it lowered, he used the phone in his left hand to snap a photo of the vehicle identification number.

"Can you give me a second?" he asked the man behind the wheel. "I'll be right back." He darted back inside before the man could answer. He returned in less than thirty seconds, and the second man opened the back door on the driver's side and held it while he got in.

"Good afternoon, *Señor* Davis," Martínez said.

Phillip said, "Sorry to keep you waiting, but I realized as you pulled up that I hadn't told the others I was leaving."

"No problem, *señor*," Martínez said, as the man who had held the door for Phillip got in behind Martínez. "I thought we would ride and talk, this time, instead of taking you to the safe house. It is best to avoid patterns, yes?"

"Yes, I agree, José."

"And how is General Olsen today, *señor?*"

"He's well. He sends his regards, but he hasn't received an answer yet."

"I understand, *señor.* These things take time, I know. I have some progress on my side; I hope that perhaps it may smooth the way."

"Okay," Phillip said. "What's changed?"

"I discussed your concerns about the source of the weapons with my principals, *señor.* It seems I was mistaken about their preference for U.S.-manufactured weapons. They pointed out to me that ammunition for Eastern-Bloc weapons will be more readily available where we are going, so it simplifies the logistics."

"I wondered about that," Phillip said.

"You should have mentioned it, *señor.* I'm disappointed in myself that I didn't think of it. I was simply thinking that our fighters were accustomed to U.S.-issued equipment."

"It's not a big problem, José. If they've seen combat in the Middle East, they probably know the Eastern-Bloc arms as well as our own. But in any case, we can provide training for a cadre, if your principals wish. Aside from the expense and the political issues, we have a much bigger inventory of Eastern-Bloc weapons, so we can deliver more quickly."

"That is good to know, *señor.* I understand that General Olsen is waiting for an answer from your government, so this is perhaps too early, but I wanted to let you know that we would be prepared to receive a sample order as soon as two days from now."

"At the Shark River Entrance?"

"We think it would be less likely to be noticed if you can deliver inside Whitewater Bay."

"We can do that. It will be easier to handle the transfer in protected water."

"Yes," Martínez said. "And for a platoon-sized shipment, we would pay cash, so we could expedite the sample shipment."

"I'm not sure that will be acceptable, José. Moving cash is

more risky than moving the weapons, with all the government focus on money laundering. It would be safer for both sides to arrange an electronic transfer from one offshore account to another."

"I see. Well, I'm sure we can work that out."

"I'll ask, if you wish, but I'm afraid I know what the answer will be," Phillip said.

"No, *señor*. We'll pay as you wish. I only thought it might be more profitable the other way."

"I'm sure my people appreciate your flexibility," Phillip said. "What else can we cover now?"

"I think this is all for now, *Señor* Davis. As always, it has been a pleasure. My friends will take you back to the villa now, yes?"

"Good afternoon, José."

"Good afternoon, my friend," Martínez said, as he got out of the car.

## 15

"You're all still here," Phillip remarked, pulling out the chair he had occupied at lunch.

"We were just lingering over the wine," Liz said. "You weren't gone very long."

"No; I had my meeting in a car this time. Did you get the text I sent you, Paul?"

"Sure. You'd just gotten up from the table when I got it."

"Have you run it by Luke?" Phillip asked. Luke Pantene was Paul's old partner and had taken his place as the head of the Miami PD's homicide department when Paul retired a few years ago.

"Yes. We got lucky; he was in the office, so he tracked down the vehicle i.d. number right away. Needless to say, it didn't match the plates."

"Stolen?" Phillip asked.

"Right the first time. The VIN says the car's registered to Manuel Cruz Realty Enterprises, LLC. The plate didn't match, so Luke didn't give me anything on it."

"What's going on," Connie asked. "I saw you messing with

your phone, but I thought you were playing solitaire, like Liz and I were boring you or something."

"Never," Paul said, smiling at her. "Now you know."

"No, now I'm even more curious. What are you and Phillip up to?"

"I'll defer to Phillip on that one," Paul said. "It's not mine to talk about."

Phillip took a deep breath and looked at the others, pausing with each until he made solid eye contact. "I'll tell you what I know so far; I'm likely to need your help before this is over. Liz, you can tell Dani, but remind her not to say anything to Ortiz. He's not one of us."

"What about J.-P. and Anne?" Liz asked.

"J.-P.'s in the loop; I don't know whether he's filled Anne in or not, but that's up to him."

"Okay," Liz said. "What's the big secret?"

"I've been approached by a guy I used to run into from time to time, back when I was still working. He's a mercenary, as best we know. He claims to represent a consortium of Cuban exile groups who're planning yet another attempt to overthrow the Castro government. They're looking for weapons."

"Weapons where?" Paul asked. "Here?"

"Yes. Delivered to one of their training camps in the Everglades."

"Isn't that illegal?" Connie asked.

Phillip shrugged. "It depends. We're — "

"Who's we?" Paul asked.

"J.-P. and I," Phillip said. "Neither of us is willing to do this without the U.S. government's blessing. We wouldn't ever have, but this time it's even stickier than usual."

"Because of the change in our diplomatic relations with Cuba?" Connie asked.

"That, and because of the domestic delivery. Let me give you a quick overview of what's happened so far."

Everyone listened as Phillip summarized events since his first contact with Martínez. "Any questions?" he asked.

"I take it that your government contact, this Rick Olsen, doesn't have the go ahead yet," Paul said.

"That's right. It's obviously sensitive, and nobody knows whether this Martínez is to be trusted," Phillip said.

"How will they determine that?" Connie asked.

"I don't know," Phillip said. "They asked for my opinion, but I couldn't help them. I've run across Martínez a number of times, but I never dealt with him on anything. Olsen's trying to arrange a tail, but I haven't heard anything on it yet."

"You said you'd need our help," Liz said. "Doing what?"

"For one thing, keeping an eye out for Martínez. He's come into the compound at least a couple of times, posing as a gardener. He's the only gardener I've seen here, so you can pick him out. We don't know where he's hanging out when he's not here. I was carrying a tracker today, thinking we'd find that house he took me to last time, but we just rode around the block."

"You couldn't have planted it in the car?" Liz asked.

Phillip smiled. "I didn't want to take a chance that they'd find it later. They could have played us, then. They're pretty sophisticated. Don't forget, they've got somebody inside whatever agency it is that's running Olsen."

"You don't even know what agency you're working for?" Connie asked.

"No. I never did. That's the way it works."

"That's nuts," Paul said. "How do you know you can trust them?"

"I don't. I've worked with Olsen before; I trust him personally. That's why they brought him in, I'm sure. He was retired, like I was."

"But whose payroll were you on before you retired? CIA?" Paul asked.

"The Army's," Phillip said, fixing Paul with a steady look.

"You trust him personally," Liz said. "What does that mean, exactly?"

"I know he won't get me in trouble if he can help it," Phillip said.

"If he can help it?" Connie said. "That's comforting. Why would he not be able to help it?"

"Orders," Phillip said. "Everybody's ultimately expendable."

"How can you live like that?" Connie asked.

Phillip shrugged. "I've done all right so far. It's only a little different from being in combat. When you join the military, you give the government a blank check; they can fill in any amount they want, up to and including your life."

"But that's different," Connie said.

"Maybe, but we're wandering off the subject now. Your questions are good, but in my line of work, you have to constantly re-evaluate your situation. You're always in business for yourself. Remember, we're not committed to anything right now."

"What happens next?" Paul asked.

"When we're done, I'll tell Olsen that they're ready for a sample shipment as soon as we get the go ahead. That's when I'll need help, probably."

"For the sample shipment?" Paul said.

"Yes. I need to get in touch with Sharktooth. We'll need a big power boat. We'll pick up the shipment in the Bahamas, on the west side of Andros Island. The delivery is in Whitehall Bay, up the Shark River from the Gulf. Somebody'll need to ride with him, but I'll want help securing the delivery area as well. I'll keep you posted."

"Where are J.-P. and Anne, anyway?" Liz asked. "I haven't seen much of them."

"Anne hasn't spent much time in the States. J.-P.'s showing her the sights."

"And how about Mario's birthday?"

"I don't know when this will all come together; it could be before or after," Phillip said.

"Before or after what?" Dani interrupted, a scowl on her face as she approached the table.

"You're back!" Liz said.

"I sense I missed out on something. What's going on?"

"I think we're done," Phillip said. "I need to go call Olsen and see about the next step. Liz, why don't you fill Dani in, and we'll get back together in a few hours over dinner?"

Liz nodded, and Dani said, "Good. I need to talk to you anyway, Liz."

"MARTÍNEZ WANTS to move ahead with a sample order?" Olsen asked.

"Right," Phillip said.

"And how did you leave it with him?"

"I reminded him that we had not yet made a commitment," Phillip said, "but he's pushing for a close. His view is that your appointment itself is a commitment of sorts."

"He has a point, I guess," Olsen said. "Can you tell if he still has inside information?"

"He hints that he does, but I can't tell."

"Where do you stand as far as being ready to deliver?" Olsen asked.

"In terms of the sample order?" Phillip asked. "A couple of days."

"Hmm," Olsen said. "How's J.P. feeling about this?"

"What do you mean?"

"Is he inclined to go for it? Or is he in wait-and-see mode?"

"Are you asking whether he would do it without government concurrence?"

"Yes, that's my question."

"I don't understand why you're asking that," Phillip said.

"I'm trying to read between the lines, myself," Olsen said. "I can't tell quite what's going on here. I'm getting some strong signals that our Uncle wants this to happen, but he doesn't want to be the one who says, 'Do it.'"

"Cold feet?"

"Not exactly. I think they want it both ways."

"What's going on, Rick?"

"This is purely guesswork on my part, you understand."

"Okay, go ahead and guess."

"I think someone in the chain of command wants to make a sting operation out of this, Phillip."

"And who gets stung? Are you thinking they want to burn the exiles?"

"Yes. Then they could say to the world that we're tough on terror."

"I don't like the way that feels."

"I don't blame you. See what J.-P. thinks and get back to me. Maybe I'll get some clarification in the meantime."

"I don't need to talk with him. There's no way we'll do this without the government's okay."

"What if you talked Martínez into a delivery outside the U.S.?"

"That doesn't change anything. There are other people Martínez can turn to if his principals want that. J.-P. and I have too much history with the U.S. to play games like that. You of all people should know that, Rick. I'm surprised you'd even ask."

"I wouldn't have, personally. You follow?"

"Yes. Tell them no."

"I already did."

"Then why are we having this conversation?"

"'No' wasn't an acceptable answer."

"What are you saying, Rick?"

"They're thinking of busting the delivery. There was a suggestion that if you didn't go along, there was a high probability that you and J.-P. would get caught up in the bust."

"If we don't go along, there won't be a delivery, so there won't be a bust."

"Don't be naïve, Phillip."

"You're suggesting that if we don't go along, they'll frame us and bust the exiles anyway? What, with their own people providing the weapons?"

"I didn't say that, did I?"

"No. It's just my suspicious nature, Rick. What's the percentage for them in that?"

"I'm not sure. It could just be some zealous bureaucrat at work, but who knows?"

"Given that, what guarantee do we have that they won't say one thing and do another?"

"You're asking me why you should trust them if they're willing to blackmail you into this?"

"Yes, exactly."

"A fair question. You want me to ask them?"

"Not yet. I need to think this through and talk it over with J.-P."

"Fair enough, Phillip. I'll pass along the latest from Martínez. Anything else?"

"Yes. What about the tail on Martínez?"

"No answer on that. They're dragging their feet. I'll let you know when and if."

"Thanks, Rick. I'll be in touch."

"WHAT'S GOING ON, Liz? What did I miss?"

Dani was sitting in *Vengeance's* saloon, and Liz was busy in the galley, opening a bottle of chilled white table wine. She poured two glasses and took them to the saloon. Putting one on the table in front of Dani, Liz sat down across from her.

"A mercenary Phillip knows from years ago has approached him about buying weapons for a group of Cuban exiles planning to overthrow the Cuban government."

Dani forced a laugh and took a sip of wine. "Big deal. There's been a new plot like that once a week ever since I can remember."

"Maybe so, but Phillip seems to be taking this seriously. Anyway, he may want some help if the plot turns out to be real. On to the important topic, now. How did David like lunch?"

Dani took a gulp from her glass. Swirling the remaining wine, she peered into the glass as if she were reading tea leaves. After several seconds, she swallowed the wine in her mouth and looked up at Liz, her countenance fierce. "That little asshole." She shook her head and drained the glass.

"Uh-oh," Liz said. "Sorry I asked."

"No," Dani said. "I need to talk about this."

Liz nodded and took a sip of her wine, waiting. Dani stood and went back to the galley. She retrieved the open bottle and brought it back to the table, pouring herself another glass before she sat down.

"Do you remember my telling you about his parents coming here from Cuba on a raft?"

"Yes," Liz said. "When his mother was pregnant with him, right?"

Dani took a smaller swallow of wine. After a moment, she said, "Yes. That was one version of the story, anyway."

"Is there another version?"

"Several. When I introduced him to Phillip, the story was a little different."

Liz nodded.

"Actually, a lot different. As in, his parents went to Martinique when things got rough after Castro."

Liz shook her head. "What about the raft?"

"That's what I wanted to know."

"And did you ask him?"

"Yes. I tried to when he was spinning the tale to Phillip, but the little shit cut me off. He wouldn't answer me; he just kept talking to Phillip."

"What did he tell Phillip?"

"That his parents went to Martinique to live with his grandmother's family after Castro came to power."

"But you challenged him right then, I'm sure."

"I damned sure did, the jerk."

"And what did he say?"

"That it was convoluted, and there was no need to bore Phillip. Asshole."

"You pursued this with him after lunch, I take it?"

"I did." Dani drained her glass again, and filled it.

"That's three," Liz said.

"What?" Dani barked.

"Three glasses. In less than five minutes. Slow down, or you'll regret it before morning."

"You're not my mother. Get off my case. I'll get smashed if I want to."

"Well, at least in the morning, you'll have a reason."

"A reason? For what?"

"To feel sorry for yourself. This is great wine, but it'll give you a bitch of a hangover."

"I can handle it."

"I know; I've seen how you handle it, but suit yourself. Did David explain himself?"

"He tried, but he just got in deeper and deeper. There was no raft. He just made that up. Thought it sounded romantic. All the little barflies he picks up fall for it, I guess."

"Did you two break up?"

"I don't know. I cursed him for lying to me. Then I threw my drink in his face and walked out on him. Does that count?"

"It could, I guess. How'd he react?"

"Surprised at first, and then scared."

"Scared?" Liz asked. "Did you — "

"No. I didn't lay a hand on him. But I sure as hell wanted to, and I guess he could tell. He said I was acting like Lupita, the shithead. That's why he was scared. She didn't have my self-control."

"That is scary," Liz said. "A woman with your temper, but without your monumental self-control. Wow!"

"Don't you make fun of me," Dani said, her eyes tearing up. "I need you on my side." She choked back a sob.

"I'm on your side. I shouldn't have said that. You did well not to smack him."

Liz held her arms out and Dani put her wine down, spilling half of it. She leaned into Liz, putting her head on Liz's shoulder. Liz stroked her back for a minute, comforting her as she would a child.

Dani sat up and sniffled, wiping her nose on the back of her hand. "Thanks, Liz. Guess I won't land this one after all, huh?"

"I don't think he was worth it," Liz said, measuring Dani's reaction. "Not even for catch and release."

Dani grinned sheepishly and shook her head.

"You okay?" Liz asked.

"Yeah. Thanks. Tell me about this deal of Phillip's. I wouldn't mind a chance to kick some ass."

"I don't know about that. I was worried about how to tell you this. You okay on the David situation?"

"Yes, I think so. Why?"

"I found out something about him this afternoon. At least I think I did."

"About David? What? How?" Dani frowned. "Tell me."

"The mercenary Phillip's been talking to picked him up in a car this afternoon for a meeting. Phillip sent Paul a text with the vehicle i.d. and the license plate number. He's trying to figure out whether this man's trustworthy."

"Okay. What's that got to do with David Ortiz?"

"The car belongs to a company called Manuel Cruz Realty Enterprises, LLC. Does that name mean anything to you?"

"No." Dani shook her head. "Why?"

"Because the bartender at the yacht club told me the other day that David Ortiz works there, for Manny Cruz. David entertains customers at the club on their corporate membership."

Dani thought about that for a few minutes. "He never mentioned where he worked. I knew he sold real estate, but the agents are pretty independent, you know? It never occurred to me to ask where he worked. Did you ask the bartender about him?"

"No. We were talking while I was waiting for my lunch, talking about men. You know, like ... Well, anyway, she saw me looking out the window at him and mentioned that he'd hit on her a time or two, but he wasn't her type."

Dani's face flushed. "Damn him. I can't believe that makes me jealous."

"Go easy on yourself, Dani. Emotions aren't rational; it's normal for you to feel a little sore and abused about now."

Dani nodded, thinking. Liz waited.

"That's probably not a coincidence, you know?" Dani said, breaking the silence.

"I had the same thought," Liz said.

"Did you mention it to Phillip?" Dani asked.

"No. I wanted to talk with you about it first."

"Good," Dani said. "I've got a plan."

"What's that?"

"I'm going to call David and apologize. I'll tell him, um ... "

"You want advice on that?"

"Sure, coach."

"Just apologize. Don't give him any excuses. But where are you going with this?"

"Oh, he made it clear he was really sorry; he wants to make it up to me, didn't want to lose me, all that stuff. You know."

"Okay. So you apologize. Then what?"

"We're going to take him sailing tomorrow. Just you and me and him, out in the Gulf Stream, out of sight of land. I'm going to find out what the asshole's up to."

"Should we tell Phillip?"

"We'll kind of have to; he'll see us getting on the boat, Liz."

"No. I meant about the coincidence."

"Oh. No, not yet. Let's keep that between us for now, until we know more. I don't want Phillip's nose in that just yet."

"Are you sure?"

"Yes. This is my kind of game. Trust me."

"Okay, coach," Liz said, grinning.

## 16

---

"**D**o I understand this correctly, Phillip?" J.-P. Berger asked. "Olsen thinks there is some bureaucratic infighting going on?"

"He only mentioned it as a possibility. I've never been able to tell what he thinks, precisely. He did present that as his personal opinion, though."

"Does that mean it is not an official communication from your government?"

"It might."

"What do you think, Phillip?"

"I think there are some factions in the U.S. government who don't agree on how to handle this situation. The right-wing hard-liners are in favor of backing the exiles, but the moderates see us resuming diplomatic relations. Our dealings with the Cubans have thawed significantly in the last few years. The moderates see this as a betrayal of sorts. And then there's the argument that we'd be as guilty of terrorism as any of the extremists in the Middle East for allowing the exiles to mount an operation from our shores against a sovereign nation."

"What do you think would happen if we walked away from

this? It's small change, in a business sense," J.-P. said. "Is Olsen's warning about repercussions plausible?"

"Maybe. It wouldn't be the first time our government has tried to do that kind of thing. Or, I should say, some person in our government. I don't think it would be prudent to ignore the possibility that we'd be blamed whether we participate or not."

"How can we protect ourselves? Do you see a way?"

"We're already in the middle. In effect, we're in a crossfire. We have Martínez and the exiles on one side, and the U.S. government on the other. Or maybe factions of the U.S. government on a couple of different sides. We need to break out and get behind our adversaries. Ambush them, in effect."

"How would we do that?"

"We start by trusting no one. Not the exiles, not the U.S., and not Olsen. Consider what would happen if the DGI found out about this from a credible source in the U.S. government."

"A leak to the DGI?"

"Yes."

"But where does the leak come from?"

"I don't know yet. Some agency that's outside this operation, and has something to gain from both sides by stopping it or exposing it."

"But we'd be betraying the exiles," J.-P. said. "That has some implications that I don't like."

"I understand your worry, but so far, we have only Martínez's say-so that the exiles are even involved. Some local Cuban-American realtor named Manuel Cruz is helping Martínez with the logistics of our meetings."

"Did Olsen tell you this?"

"No." Phillip told J.-P. about Paul's information on the car. "I've held this back from Olsen. I asked him earlier for some help in tracking down Martínez, and he hasn't delivered."

"You think he's holding back information on Martínez?" J.-P. asked.

"Or somebody is. When I asked, Olsen said, 'They're dragging their feet.' But I don't know who 'they' are. I'd already guessed something strange was going on there. In the old days, Olsen would have committed to surveillance on Martínez without checking."

"He had more leverage then," J.-P. said.

"Yes. That's my point. For whatever reason, he's nothing but a messenger boy here, and I don't even know who he's working for."

"But I thought he was working for the Director."

"He's working for some director, no doubt. And it's somebody he knows, or he wouldn't be there. But I'm not getting the sense that he trusts whoever it is. Bear in mind that there are lots of 'directors' floating around in our security services. More now than there used to be when I was active, and there were plenty then."

"So, we are on our own," J.-P. said, with a grin.

Phillip grinned back. "Yes. Just the way we like it."

"What's our goal here, then?"

"To come through this intact. 'First, do no harm.' Since we don't know who's on which side, it's hard to plan farther ahead than that. If we can figure out who's good and who's not, we can adjust fire along the way, so to speak."

"I have an idea," J.-P. said.

"What are you thinking?"

"We're overlooking Mario."

"I thought you didn't want him involved."

J.-P. shrugged. "Well, like other people, he's tried to retire from this business. Besides, I didn't want to risk spoiling the birthday surprise by bringing him into this."

"What's changed?" Phillip asked.

"Our risk assessment. What looked straightforward has become complex. And nobody knows the exile community better than he does. I can ask him about this without letting him know we're all in Miami. The surprise will not be spoiled."

"If you can do that, it might be a big help."

"I can do it, but it will have to wait until morning. If I were in Paris, I would be asleep now, so I can't call him tonight. Early in the morning, though, I will call and ask him about this Manuel Cruz, and José Martínez. Anyone else?"

"Not that I can think of."

"Good. Call me if you do think of someone. I will see you at breakfast."

"WHAT DID you learn at your lunch, Ortiz? Who was there?" Manny Cruz was sitting with his feet on his desk, his tie loosened, and a drink in his hand.

"I'm making good progress with the girl. We had a little spat this afternoon after lunch, but everything's cool now. She just called and asked me to spend the day sailing with her and Chirac tomorrow."

"That's good. But come on. I don't have all night. Who was at the lunch?"

"Dani and her partner in the boat; that's Liz Chirac. Phillip Davis. I got to talk with him for a couple of minutes, but nothing new, there. And a couple from another boat. Connie Barrera and Paul Russo, their names were. Husband and wife. They run the same kind of charter business down in the islands as Berger and Chirac."

"What are they doing there? You get their connection to the others?" Cruz asked.

"Yeah. Barrera's a friend of Berger and Chirac. She chartered their boat one time and got interested in sailing. She'd just wrapped up some kind of deal and was looking for what to do next. They taught her the business, and she bought her own boat."

"She was married then? Or not?"

"Not. She was single. She was looking for a cook, and they fixed her up with Russo."

"He's a cook?"

"Yeah, but — "

"How'd they know him?"

"He's a friend of Berger's family. He met them through Mario Espinosa. You know Espinosa's Dani Berger's godfather, right?"

"Yeah. So Barrera and Russo, they didn't know one another before?"

"No. I told you, Berger and Chirac introduced them because Barrera was looking to hire a chef for the boat."

"Russo must be from Miami, if he was Espinosa's friend. How about Barrera?" Cruz asked.

"Grew up in California. Last lived in the States up in Savannah," Ortiz said.

"She Cuban?" Cruz asked.

"No. I asked her if she was Mexican, you know, because of California. She about bit my head off. Told me she was American, that her family was in California when it was just the Spanish and the Indians."

"Okay, so she's sensitive about it. Must be some history there. What was she doing in Savannah?"

"She was a partner in some kind of health care business, is all she said. She got bought out and went to the Bahamas to chill for a while. Then she chartered *Vengeance* to learn to sail."

"And Russo?"

"What about him, Manny?"

"You said he was a chef. He worked in Miami?"

"Oh, yeah. But not as a chef. He's retired from the MPD. Cooking and sailing were his hobbies."

"MPD, huh," Cruz said, sipping his cocktail. "You sure you don't want a drink?"

"No, thanks, Manny. I'm good."

"Anybody else around there? What about Berger's parents?"

"They're staying there, but they weren't around for the lunch. He's from Paris, and his wife's never spent much time in the States, so he's spending most of his time driving her around, sightseeing."

"Okay. So that's it?"

"As far as meeting people. But I learned that Phillip Davis's wife is coming in the morning of Espinosa's birthday, along with a couple from Dominica."

"From Dominica," Cruz said. "And who are they?"

"Friends, apparently. I guess they're friends of Espinosa's."

"You got names?"

"That was kinda strange, Manny. Their names are Sharktooth and Maureen."

Cruz put his drink down and lowered his feet to the floor.

"Sharktooth?" He leaned toward Ortiz.

"Yeah. Weird, huh?"

"You get a last name?"

"I asked, but Dani said he never uses one."

"What the hell? Why Sharktooth?"

"He's got a water taxi in Dominica, takes the tourists on dive trips and shit. He's got these big, dried shark's jaws mounted on the bow of his boat. That's the boat's name. Sharktooth. She said that's all he answers to."

"Keep your ears open; see if you can get any more on him."

"Sure. You want me to ask about Russo's time with the cops?"

"No, that's okay. Don't ask too many questions, I'll get Santos to use his connections on that."

"Hey, that reminds me," Ortiz said. "Any news on Lupita?"

"No change. Whoever it was that did it fucked her up pretty good."

"Santos have somebody to replace her?"

Cruz frowned. "Why do you care?"

"I just wondered. I know she collected rent from some of

those deadbeat Haitians for him. I figured he might need a replacement."

"Maybe. You interested?"

Ortiz laughed. "Not me. But there's a guy who does odd jobs for a fellow I know who might be."

"Odd jobs? Like what?"

"Collections. The fellow I know? He's in the numbers racket. He makes book sometimes, too."

"How do you know him?"

"I showed him some houses back when I was with the other broker."

"So how do you know this guy that works for him?"

"The guy — my former client, that is — he lives in the neighborhood. I see him every now and then. He's got a younger brother he wants in the business, and he's trying to find a place for this odd-job guy."

"You know the guy? The one looking for work?"

"To see him, yeah. You know, just like, to say hello. That kind of thing."

"You know anything about him?"

"He's kind of scary looking. Haitian, speaks broken English with a strong Creole accent. Short, built like a gorilla, lots of tattoos. Maybe done some hard time, I'm guessing."

"Can't hurt for Santos to talk to him. You got a name?"

"François. That's all I know."

"I'll tell Santos tonight. Get this François to give him a call."

"Okay."

"You got anything else?"

"No. I'll give you a call if I get anything while I'm out on the boat tomorrow."

"Yeah. Good night, Ortiz. Good work."

"Thanks. 'Night, Manny."

～

LUPITA VIDAL WAS in a drowsy state, neither sound asleep nor fully awake. The wall-mounted television in her hospital room was set to a music-video channel, the barely audible sound coming from the hockey-puck-sized speaker on her pillow.

She was in a moderate amount of pain; the nurse had just brought her evening medication, helping her to take the two pills and holding the glass of crushed ice and water so that the straw reached her lips. Lupita had tried to speak to the woman, to ask her to turn the damned television off, but her voice had come out garbled. Even Lupita couldn't understand the words she'd tried to form.

She wondered why she couldn't give voice to her thoughts. It must be the painkillers, she supposed. When she had awakened a little while ago, she had resolved to spit out the pills the next time. She didn't like being drugged. By the time the nurse arrived with her evening dose, she had thought better of it.

As the drugs wore off, the pain swept over her in ever stronger waves, every muscle and joint screaming for her attention. She'd swallowed the pills with relief when the nurse finally came; it wouldn't be long, she knew, before she slipped away again.

"Lupita?" she heard, from the edge of consciousness. Was it the television? She forced her eyes open, realizing as she did that someone was in her room. A janitor, she thought, catching a glimpse of a roll-around mop bucket as he pushed it closer to her bed. *Why did he call my name?* she wondered. She decided it was the medication. She must be hallucinating.

"Lupita Vidal?" She heard him for sure, that time. There was no doubt. She gurgled some meaningless phrase and gave a little nod, the movement sending fresh ripples of pain down her neck and into her shoulders. The pain brought a momentary lifting of the fog. She cut her eyes toward him, careful not to move her head.

She recognized him. She tried without success to say his name, making a mumbling sound.

"Yes," he said, leaning down close to her face. She smelled his breath, tinged with garlic and tobacco. "Yes, you know who I am, don't you? Blink once for yes, twice for no."

She blinked once.

"Good," he said. "Have you told anybody about me?"

Confused by the drugs and his unexpected presence, she searched her memory for the answer, but she couldn't grasp what it was.

"Once for yes, twice for no," he reminded her.

She blinked once, confused.

"Did you tell the cops?" he asked.

The cops had been asking her questions. That seemed like a long time ago. She had been in excruciating pain, and the police-woman had been chewing gum as she demanded to know what had happened. Had she told them about him? Maybe, she decided. She blinked once.

"That's too bad, bitch. At least now you'll die knowing why I killed you." He grinned at her and took something from the pocket of his overalls. She watched, still not quite understanding what was happening.

He snapped off a plastic cap that protected the needle of the disposable syringe and picked up the clear plastic IV tube that ran from the bag of liquid hanging next to the bed down to a needle in her arm. He emptied the syringe into the IV line. He put the disposable syringe in his pocket and picked up the mop.

"You won't feel a thing," he said. "Rest in peace."

She closed her eyes as she heard him push the mop bucket out of her room.

## 17

"Mario said to give you his regards." J.-P. said, stirring sugar into his coffee. He and Phillip were in the kitchen, sitting at a counter that gave them a view of *Vengeance* and *Diamantista II*. The bright work on the boats glistened as the early morning sunlight was refracted by the dew on the varnish.

"You didn't tell him I'm here, did you?"

"No. We did not discuss anybody's location. He did not ask, and of course, I did not wish to spoil our surprise. I told him only about the situation with the exiles."

"Did he know this Manuel Cruz?" Phillip asked.

"Yes. Manny Cruz, he says the man calls himself. He is one of the younger men involved in the anti-Castro movement. Cruz is active in Alpha-66. Mario knows him only by reputation. He took some time to explain to me the intricacies of politics in the exile community. He stressed that your government and the news media tend to oversimplify things."

Phillip laughed. "Yes. I'm sure he's right. Nobody would have a broader perspective than Mario. So tell me, what did he say?"

"He reminded me that ethnicity and politics are not the same thing, and the difference might be critical. Even organizations like Alpha-66 and the others are not monolithic. There have been people from Cuba living in Florida for centuries; not all of them came to escape the communists. The ones who fled Castro and formed these organizations didn't all have the same views, either. Their motivations were individual. Some wanted to return to the way things had been under Batista; they had amassed great wealth, some of them. Their motives in wanting to overthrow Castro had as much to do with greed as with patriotism. Then there were some who wanted to make their country a true democracy.

"Mario pointed out that early in the post-revolutionary era, the wish to overthrow Castro created some alliances which have not survived. Added to that, the older generation is beginning to give way to younger ones. There are three generations which have come of age in the U.S., plus there are the people who have come here much more recently. They all share cultural bonds, but there is a great deal more ethnic and economic diversity in their ranks than there was in the '60s and '70s."

"Did he have any hard advice, J.-P.?"

"I am making a summary of what he told me; it is not too much longer. And yes, he did have advice, but he said that first I must make you and your government contact listen."

"I'm listening."

"This man Cruz is a strange one, Mario says. His grandfather was a wealthy attorney with many commercial interests in the days before Castro. Much of his wealth was in the form of real property; he lost that when Castro came to power. Still, he came here as a rich man, as did many of his contemporaries. His son, Manny's father, was born here and grew up as an American; he prospered, and the family is more wealthy now than they ever were in Cuba. This is not an unusual story, according to Mario, except for Manny Cruz. Why would he want to overthrow the Castro government? Cuba is where his grandfather came from; it means nothing to Manny, so why is he so active in Alpha-66?"

"I see his point. Did he have any ideas?"

"He doesn't trust Manny Cruz, because there is no obvious motivation for his behavior. Mario says this is true of many of the younger members of the militant groups. He says the organizations have become social clubs for some, and a cover for criminal undertakings for others. They have been infiltrated for years by agents of the U.S. government and the Cuban government. Mario jokes that most of the members are undercover agents for somebody.

"There are several well-known cases. He mentioned a man named Avila who was once the Chief of Operations for Alpha-66. In 1992, he turned himself in to the FBI and confessed that he was a senior operative for Cuba's DGI. They had planted him in Alpha-66 with the mission of conducting what amounted to terrorist raids on Cuba to help Castro justify his anti-American policies."

"Is that true?" Phillip asked.

"Mario thinks it probably was, but there's no way to know. He also mentioned the Cuban Five, also called the Miami Five. They were DGI agents who infiltrated several of the militant exile groups and collected evidence of terrorist activities directed against Cuba from the U.S. The Cuban government tried to get the U.S. to act on the evidence, but what happened was the FBI arrested the DGI agents and they ended up in federal prison for being in the U.S. as illegal agents of a foreign government."

"Okay, J.-P. I understand why Mario thinks we should be careful. Did he know anything about Martínez?"

"No, he didn't. But he did mention another name. There's a man named Guillermo Maldonado who shows up at social gatherings in Miami from time to time. His friends call him Willy. He's supposed to be a rich playboy from Argentina, but Mario says some of the old timers think he's a Cuban agent. Some of them knew his grandfather when he was in law school with Fidel before the Revolution. This man looks just like his grandfather, so they're sure it's him, and there are some strange gaps in his background, according to Mario's friends. His advice was that if Maldonado's involved, Raul Castro is behind this."

"Okay. I've heard enough," Phillip said. "How about you? Do you want to do this deal?"

J.-P. grinned and shook his head. "No. Now, how are we going to get out of it? Your friend Olsen says we must go ahead or your government will frame us."

"I need to digest this," Phillip said. "I want to try to make sense out of what Olsen is up to, given what you learned from Mario. It's clear that Olsen doesn't think we can walk away from it, but I don't think he's telling me the real reason the government's pushing us to go forward."

"You think it is a setup of some kind," J.-P. said.

"Without a doubt," Phillip said. "We need to figure out who they're trying to nail, and why."

ORTIZ WAS GETTING DRESSED when he heard the hammering on his door. Shoving the tail of a polo shirt into the waistband of his cargo shorts, he rushed to the entryway and put an eye to the peephole. Manny Cruz stood there, looking around like he was worried that someone would see him. Ortiz turned the deadbolt and opened the door, stepping back to let Cruz enter.

"What's up, Manny? I gotta hustle; I'm due at Star Island in a few minutes."

"Yeah, okay. This won't take long. Glad I caught you, though. I didn't want to do this over the phone. There's a couple of things you need to know before you get mixed up with those people again."

Ortiz nodded. "Okay."

"First thing, Lupita's dead."

"You're shitting me. Dead? How?"

"They think a heart attack, but they don't know for sure, yet. They're going to do an autopsy. The hospital called Santos early this morning. A nurse went in to check on her and found her at around midnight."

"I don't believe that. Lupita? No way she had a heart attack. She was what? Late twenties?"

"Twenty-seven, yeah," Cruz said.

"And she was a damn long-distance runner, besides doing all that mixed martial arts stuff."

"I hear you, Ortiz. Santos and I figure somebody finished her off. Maybe whoever beat her up; maybe somebody else."

"That doesn't make sense, Manny. If it was whoever did the beating, why not just kill her then?"

Cruz shrugged. "It was in that parking garage. Maybe they heard somebody coming. Who knows?"

Ortiz was shaking his head. "Un-fucking-believable."

"Believe it. Santos is beginning to think it must have been something to do with the Haitians."

"You mean, she kicked the shit out of the wrong person, or something?"

"More likely she had some kind of side deal going on that we didn't know about. Now that she's out of the loop, Santos discovered that she let a couple of them slide on their rent for several months."

"But he would have noticed the shortfall," Ortiz said.

"Yeah, except there wasn't a shortfall."

"I don't understand."

"She was making up the difference, Ortiz. We're not talking high finance, here. She could have done that, no sweat."

"Yeah, but why would she?"

"She was obviously getting something in return. Drugs, maybe. The people she let slide, they're dealing."

"I never saw her using," Ortiz said.

"Neither did I, but she could have been. Or she could have

been getting shit for somebody else. There's no way to know now, unless the people in those units talk."

"Is Santos going to ask them?" Ortiz asked.

"Yeah. He and the new guy."

"New guy?"

"Your pal, François. Santos talked to him last night. They hit it off. Santos said to tell you he was a good find."

"Glad it worked out."

"Yeah. You got anymore where he came from? We can always use muscle."

"Not right off the top of my head, but I'll keep my eyes open. What else? You said there were a couple of things."

"Yeah. See if you can pick up anything else on that Russo guy."

"The retired cop?"

"He's not just a retired cop. He ran MPD's homicide department."

"Okay, so he was a bigshot."

"Not just that. He was also MPD's liaison to the JTTF."

"JTTF?"

"Joint Terrorism Task Force. Every damn law enforcement organization you ever heard of, and some nobody even knows about, probably. Guys in jobs like that, they stay connected. You know what I'm saying?"

"Yeah. Like Davis?"

"Yeah, that's right. It's probably not an accident that they're both in this thing. We knew about Davis, but Russo's a surprise. Check him out, but watch yourself. You can't trust people like them."

"All right. I need to haul ass, Manny."

"Have a good time on that boat with those two gals, Ortiz. Sounds like some kind of wet dream." Cruz laughed, pleased with the low-brow pun. He opened the door and left, closing it behind him.

Ortiz shook his head and looked at his watch. He was going to have to miss his morning contact if he wanted to be on time for the sailing trip. Then he remembered that they would have heard his conversation with Cruz, so they would understand. Not only that, but they'd know everything he could tell them anyway.

"THIS IS AWESOME!" Ortiz said, watching Dani as she bent to tweak the main sheet. Her muscles rippled under her smooth, bronzed skin, and the skimpy string bikini she wore was all but indecent, especially when she worked the sails.

"Beautiful, huh?" Liz asked from behind the helm.

He turned to look at her, embarrassed that she'd caught him staring at her friend. She gave him a knowing smile as she leaned over to engage the autopilot, the tiny top of her own bikini affording him a distracting view. She stood and shifted her stance, feet well apart, bracing herself against the boat's motion.

He swallowed hard when she looked him in the eye. She smiled again and leaned back, raising her elbows and pushing them out to the sides, stretching her arms as she moved her hands to the top of her head. She held his gaze, and gave him an impish grin as she shook her strawberry blond hair free. Putting the hair clamp in her teeth, she ran her fingers through her mane, letting the wind carry it out behind her as she shook her head.

She grasped a handful of hair close behind her head and pulled it tight, smoothing it around the sides of her head. Then she twisted the mass into one long skein and worked it into a fresh bun on the back of her head, never losing eye contact with him. She took the hair clamp from her teeth and put it back in her hair, grinning at him.

"So, you like it?" she asked.

"Um, uh ... " he stammered.

"She means the sailing, David," Dani said, slipping her arms around his chest from behind, pulling him back against her as she planted a series of light kisses across the tops of his shoulder blades.

"Like I said, it's awesome," he said.

"Good," Dani said. "Now that we're out of sight of land, let's leave *Vengeance* to Liz. Or vice-versa."

"Okay, but where are we going?"

"I put the cushions on the foredeck; you and I can have a little privacy up there while we get some sun."

She took his hand and scampered out of the cockpit, leading him along the leeward side deck. When they reached the bow, she dropped his hand and flopped face down on the cushions.

"Join me," she said, reaching into a small locker on the side of the coachroof and pulling out a tube of sunscreen.

As he settled to a sitting position beside her, she handed him the sunscreen and said, "Do my back?"

"I'd love to," he said, squeezing lotion into his hand.

As he began to spread it along her spine, he stopped to massage the knots of hard muscle around her shoulder blades. He chuckled as she moaned with pleasure.

"More," she said.

"Yes ma'am," he said, rolling to a kneeling position. He shifted his weight to put one knee outside each of her thighs, straddling her as he began to put his weight into the rubdown.

"You've got some serious muscles, lady," he said. "You work out often?"

"My whole life's a workout," she said.

"I guess so," David said, pausing to add more lotion as he moved down to the base of her spine.

"Mm," Dani said, arching her back, catlike. "You're good at this."

He chuckled, but didn't say anything. He began spreading lotion around the edges of her bikini bottoms, working a finger under the cloth every few strokes.

"David?" she said.

"Uh-huh?"

"Tell me what you're up to."

"I was thinking that these were in the way," he said hooking an index finger under the string that spanned the side of her hip. "Liz can't see us; the sails block her view."

"That's not what I meant," she purred. "I'm talking about why you're here to begin with."

"I'm here because I've become very fond of you, and you invited me."

She rolled over between his knees so that she was facing him and put her hands on his chest. "Mm," she said, smiling.

"Since we're asking questions," he said, "what's with Liz and her come-hither act?"

She smiled up at him. "You find her attractive?"

"Uh ... "

"I thought so," she said, the smile turning to a scowl.

"Wait! I — "

"What, David?"

"Is this some kind of test? Or a trap?"

"A trap? What kind of trap do you think it might be?"

"To see how I reacted; maybe to see if I'd go astray?"

"And would you?" she asked.

"I told you, I've fallen hard for you, Dani. Liz is attractive, but it's you I want."

"Me? The *béké's* daughter?"

"What?" he frowned. "What's my mother — "

"I fell for that first lie, David. And the second one."

"The second one?" he asked.

"Ha!" she said. "Gotcha."

"Wait, Dani. I explained — "

"And speaking of lies, how does Manuel Cruz fit into this scheme of yours?" she interrupted.

He swallowed as he felt the color drain from his face. "Manny Cruz? What are you talking about? Scheme?"

"Manny?" she said, digging her fingertips into his pectoral muscles. "Is that what you call him?"

"I don't — OW!" he shrieked, as she clamped down on the tendons in his chest, her steel-hard fingers digging into his muscles, pinching nerves.

"You need to tell me what's going on, David."

"Don't!" he yelped, as her grip tightened again. "That hurts!"

"You're going to find out about hurts, if you don't explain yourself."

He grasped her wrists in his hands, gripping hard. "Dani, I'm one of those old-fashioned guys who doesn't believe using my size and strength against a woman, but if you don't let — "

She drove her knees into his buttocks, lifting him and throwing him over her head. Hooking her right hand into his left armpit, she guided his fall. Pulling down, she smashed his face into the leading edge of the coach roof as she slid from beneath him.

As he got his hands under his chest and began to lift himself to all fours, she was already on her feet. Dazed, he shook his head. Then she pivoted on her left foot and drove her right heel into his temple, knocking him senseless.

## 18

"You heard about Lupita?" Cruz asked. He was keeping up with the traffic in the northbound lanes of I-95, in North Miami.

"What about her?" Maldonado asked, turning in the passenger seat so that he faced Cruz. He had asked Cruz to pick him up so that they could meet in the moving car, making it less likely that anyone would see them together.

"She's dead," Cruz said. "Santos called me. They think she had a heart attack, but they're doing an autopsy today."

Maldonado studied Cruz for a moment. Deciding that Cruz was getting too comfortable with their relationship, he said. "No."

"Yeah," Cruz said. "I figured you hadn't heard; it wasn't on the morning news."

"You misunderstood me," Maldonado said, his eyes like a snake's when Cruz glanced at him. "I already knew she was dead. I meant that it wasn't a heart attack."

"How do you ... " Cruz's question trailed off as he grasped the hidden message. "It's probably for the best, anyway," he said. "Something they won't detect in the autopsy?"

"I wouldn't know," Maldonado said, staring straight ahead.

"We got a replacement for her," Cruz said.

"I heard," Maldonado said, watching Cruz flinch. "Keep him out of my affairs. If you want to take that kind of risk, that's your business."

"You know something about him?" Cruz asked, worry lines creasing his brow. He flicked his eyes toward Maldonado for an instant.

"I don't need to know about him. He's not involved in our project. You understand?"

"Y-yes." Cruz drove in silence for a full minute.

Maldonado watched him from the corner of his eye, amused by the way Cruz kept rolling his tongue around in his cheek. The nervous tic told Maldonado that he'd made his point with Cruz. "Tell me, Cruz, what has Ortiz learned from his time with the Berger girl?"

Cruz rattled off a concise report on Phillip Davis, Connie Barrera, and Paul Russo. He augmented what Ortiz had told him with information from his other sources.

"Interesting," Maldonado said. "The Barrera woman has some connections to the drug trade, you say?"

"That's only rumor, Willy. Some people think she's a snitch of some kind; others say she's got her own operation, and she's turning her competitors over to the cops. Nobody knows for sure."

"Is she of Cuban descent?"

"No. Ortiz asked her. Then he asked if she's Mexican, and she bit his head off. Told him she was American. But the rumors have her connected with some new Mexican cartel. That's if you don't think she's some kind of undercover cop."

"And Russo's tight with the antiterrorist task force," Maldonado said. "That makes them kind of an odd couple, unless she's a cop, too."

"Or unless Russo's bent," Cruz said. "That's another theory I heard."

"That he's working with the drug smugglers?" Maldonado asked.

"Yeah, that's option one. Option two is that he's straight and his wife's using him without his knowledge."

"Hmm. Any sign of why they're hanging out at Star Island?"

"Russo's an old pal of Espinosa's, and Barrera's tight with Dani Berger and Liz Chirac."

"I don't like it. There's too much coincidence. Can Ortiz find out more about what they're all doing together?"

"He's working on it; he's got the Berger girl eating out of his hand. They've gone out for the day on the yacht with the other girl."

"Chirac," Maldonado mused. "What do we know about her?"

"Not much. She's Belgian, worked for the EU in Brussels. She met Berger while she was on a sabbatical in the islands a few years ago, and they bought the yacht and went in business together. She's the chef and first mate; Berger's the captain. They've built up a nice business."

"Either one of them got a man in her life?" Maldonado asked.

"No. Not long-term, anyway. Neither one's been married, either. Berger was engaged once, though, years ago."

"Anything interesting about that? Her fiancé?"

"No. She was working in her mother's family's business, and so was the guy. She broke off the engagement and ran away to sea. She and her mother are estranged."

"Ran away to sea? That's odd. Why would an attractive young woman do that?"

"It's not so odd for her. Her father owns several big crewed sailing yachts that work the charter trade in the Med. She crewed on them in the summers from the time she was a kid. The sea's in her blood, from what we got."

"What's the mother's family business?"

"Investment banking. It checks out clean."

"Okay. Tell Ortiz to stay with it. Take the next exit; there's a coffee shop on the right as you get off. Drop me there. You have anything else?"

"Yeah. They're expecting another guy and his wife to show up before Espinosa's party. They're from Dominica. The guy's been in business with Berger and Davis for a long time. That probably means Espinosa, too, given that he's coming to the party."

"Who is he?"

"We don't know yet. All we have so far is Sharktooth and Maureen."

"What the hell? Sounds like a nightclub act of some kind. You don't have his real name?"

"Ortiz asked, but the Berger girl said the only name he uses is Sharktooth. We're working on it."

"I'll see if I can learn anything about him," Maldonado said, as Cruz pulled into the parking lot of the coffee shop.

THE WOMAN SAT in her cubicle in the office building on Northwest 20th Street in Miami. She was dressed as a bag lady again. When David Ortiz had failed to make their morning rendezvous, she had opted to come in to the office and check the audio and video feeds from his apartment. She sipped coffee as she listened to his conversation with Manny Cruz.

Cruz talked freely; it was clear that he had no idea that someone had piggybacked on his surveillance. She made a note to have someone get a copy of the autopsy report on Lupita Vidal; both men sounded and looked surprised at her death, but the circumstances were suspicious.

She pondered who might benefit from having Vidal silenced. She agreed with Ortiz that it made no sense for the person who beat Vidal to have waited this long to kill her. That meant Vidal had at least two distinct enemies, each capable of violence. She wondered what Vidal had been doing.

It was possible but improbable that some of Vidal's victims could be behind the beating, except that the nature of the attack itself argued for a professional thug having done it. The Haitian refugees she mistreated might have sought revenge, but not in that manner. Her death, if not from natural causes, implied her involvement in some criminal enterprise besides Cruz's trafficking operation.

Ortiz had mentioned that Cruz was involved in planning an invasion of Cuba. She had passed that up her chain of command in spite of her own skepticism. There were always rumblings of that sort of thing from the exile community; nobody took them seriously these days. She couldn't fathom a reason why any of the exiles might have attacked Lupita Vidal.

She considered the idea that Vidal could have been involved with a rival trafficking operation, but that wasn't probable. There were no indications of such an activity. Cruz had a lock on exploiting Haitians, at least in the Miami area. There could be a rival operation elsewhere, she reminded herself. New York was always a possibility. She would check that out.

Meanwhile, she knew now why Ortiz had missed their regular contact; there was no reason for her to worry about him. He'd succeeded in planting François, which left them in a better position than they had been in.

With Ortiz covering Cruz and François working alongside Santos, they should be able to amass the evidence they needed to shut down Cruz and Santos. It was too bad that Ortiz was sidelined by Cruz assigning him to spy on the people at Star Island.

At least Ortiz was continuing to build credibility with Cruz. She reminded herself that Ortiz's relationship with Cruz had allowed him to engineer the replacement of Vidal with François. Sometimes a roundabout route was the fastest way home.

She did hope that Ortiz would manage to keep her informed, but she understood that he might be hampered by his effort to seduce Danielle Berger. She shook her head; that was an aspect of this work that she detested.

The idea that one of her agents was being paid to take advantage of an innocent young woman angered her beyond reason. But that's what it took to do this job, sometimes. She'd be less angry if she didn't know how much Ortiz enjoyed his role. She just had to suck it up and charge ahead. Innocent people got hurt in operations like this all the time. She could hope Ortiz might end up learning a bitter lesson one of these days, but she also hoped it wasn't on her watch. She didn't need the grief.

DRESSED in their normal attire of shorts and polo shirts again, Dani and Liz sat in the cockpit discussing their prisoner. Ortiz, still unconscious, was hog-tied, his wrists pulled up to his ankles behind his back. They had left him on the foredeck until they figured out what to do with him.

"You looked like you were enjoying that a little too much, Dani," Liz said, disengaging the autopilot and tweaking their course to take advantage of a wind shift.

"The massage was okay," Dani said. "But I could feel his eyes crawling over my backside. That was disgusting."

"It can be, sometimes," Liz said.

"You mean sometimes it's not?"

"If it's the right guy, it can be exhilarating."

Dani shuddered. "He's not the right guy, then, the creep."

Liz laughed. "Anyway, that's not what I meant."

"I'm not following you," Dani said.

"I meant the whole thing: orchestrating the set-up, the tease, the take-down, all of it. Especially when you smashed his face into the coachroof."

Dani grinned. "My timing was nearly perfect, wasn't it? I

threw him and brought him down just as *Vengeance* was rising to meet him. It was almost like she wanted to get her licks in, too."

"That's what I meant. The broken nose was enough. That kick to the side of his head was over the top."

"I've told you before about stopping before you're sure your opponent's out for the count, Liz. Besides, he had it coming, the bastard, playing with me the way he has been."

"Maybe."

"What do you mean, maybe? He was using me, Liz. His link to Cruz says it all. The asshole was taking advantage of my vulnerability."

"Your vulnerability?" Liz laughed. "All that aside, I think he had some genuine fondness for you, Dani. I agree that he was using you, but one thing doesn't preclude the other. He followed you into your trap like a puppy. I think he really was falling for you. But don't worry; you took care of that."

"If he was falling for me, he sure helped himself to an eyeful of your little show, Salomé."

"I was right in his line of sight, Dani, just like you planned. You couldn't see his face. I promise you; he was embarrassed. He couldn't look me in the eye. I'd give him a passing grade on that test. I'm not sure why you put me up to that anyway, if you'd already decided to kick his ass."

"I was just curious, Liz. You really think he likes me? Independent of whatever he's up to with Cruz?"

"I think he did, but I'm not sure it matters. He was still up to no good. Anyway, whatever he felt for you, you squelched it. Why are you even worried about that now?"

"I still want to learn how to do this girl stuff. I just need to find the right guy."

"I think I've created a monster," Liz said, shaking her head. "Your skills are adequate, at this stage. I'm not sure what more I can teach you."

"Aw, come on, Liz. I've still got a lot to learn. What you did with your hair — that was really something. I'd never have thought of that."

"You don't have enough hair to do that, Dani."

"You think I should let my hair grow out?"

"Let me think about that. We need to decide what we're going to do with your latest conquest. We're a good three hours from the dock, if we turn around now."

"Okay. Good point. Let's hold our course until after we question him. There's nobody around out here to wonder what we're doing. If we turn around, we'll be more likely to run into other boats before we're done."

———————

## 19

"Did you have a good run?" J.-P. asked, as Phillip joined him at the table on the veranda of the Star Island villa.

"Pretty good," Phillip said, his hair still damp from his shower. He pulled out a chair and sat down, pouring himself a glass of orange juice from the pitcher on the table. He took a sip. "Mm," he said. "Fresh-squeezed?"

J.-P. nodded. "Thanks to Anne."

"Where is she?"

"Resting. She says I've worn her out with all the sightseeing."

"Good," Phillip said. "Then I won't feel guilty about taking up your time this morning."

"What is it that you wish?" J.-P. asked.

"Running always stimulates my thoughts," Phillip said. "A couple of things occurred to me. I'm not comfortable with Rick Olsen, for one. I'm not sure who he's reporting to, and he's not at liberty to tell me."

"This is strange to me. I've mentioned that before. You are totally at his mercy."

"Yes. My comfort with him comes from the days when we were in the military. We were working under the direction of the agency, but the constraints were well defined. Our situation is different now. It's not that I don't trust Rick personally, but I worry that he may be naïve, in a certain sense. During my time with you after I retired from the service, I developed an understanding of how fuzzy the chain of command is in the civilian intelligence organizations."

"What are you saying, Phillip?"

"I trust Rick, but I don't trust the people around him, and I don't think he's cynical enough to guide us through this."

J.-P. nodded. "You are in the best position to make that evaluation. I don't know him or the organization as well as you do. I have always been held at a distance from people like these. You have some ideas about how we should proceed?"

"Yes. I'm going to be selective in what I share with Rick until we know more. I was ready to accept their decision on whether we should go ahead with Martínez, until Rick told me that they said we effectively had no choice."

"Do you have a plan to deal with them?" J.-P. asked.

"The beginnings of one, anyway. We don't know enough about this scheme the exiles have. Mario told you that Cruz is connected to Alpha-66, but Martínez claims to be working for a consortium of exile organizations. I'd like to at least know which others are behind him."

"You asked him, did you not?"

"I did, and he was evasive. He wouldn't name any of them."

"I could ask Mario; he knows all of the old guard in the exile community," J.-P. said.

Phillip smiled. "You read my mind."

"It is an obvious thing," J.-P. said.

"I should have thought of it sooner," Phillip said, shaking his head.

"Do not be hard on yourself," J.-P. said. "We did not have a reason to ask him earlier. I will call him now. Can you think of anything else I should ask him?"

"Not really, but it would be nice to know if there are any of the exile groups that we can rule out, as well as which ones are most likely to be behind Martínez."

"I will ask. What are you going to do now? I think you have some other ideas, no?"

"Yes. I'm going to call Olsen and ask for a meeting. I want to look him in the eye when I talk with him this time. And I want to make sure that we don't have an audience."

"An audience? I thought he gave you an encrypted phone of some kind."

"Yes, he did. He even hinted that it would explode if I called anyone besides him with it."

"You think it is not secure, then?"

"It was provided by the people he's working for — the same ones who are willing to blackmail us."

"Ah! I see. Where is it now, this device he gave you?"

"In the microwave oven in the kitchen."

"What?" J.-P. raised an eyebrow. "The microwave?"

"A microwave oven makes a good RF shield, a poor man's Faraday cage."

J.-P. grinned. "So you are thinking that this telephone may allow them to hear what you are saying, even when it is turned off?"

"Not when it's in the microwave," Phillip said.

"But what if someone turns on the oven? Might it activate the explosive charge?"

"It might, if there is an explosive charge. I taped a warning note to the microwave, asking people to talk to me before using it — that it was dangerous."

J.-P. laughed. "Have you heard from Martínez recently?"

"Not since late yesterday afternoon, but I'll bet he'll show up once I meet with Olsen."

"You are testing to see if Martínez still has an inside source."

"Yes. And if he does, then we'll know that we can use Olsen to plant misinformation with Martínez."

"To what end, Phillip?"

"I don't know yet. That depends on what we learn from Mario."

J.-P. laughed again, a deep, contagious belly laugh. Phillip joined in, and J.-P. stood up.

Slapping Phillip on the shoulder, he said, "I go now, to call Mario. I will be back soon. I think it is best if I am alone when I speak with him, yes? So that he does not hear some background noise that gives away my location?"

"Yes. We wouldn't want to spoil the surprise," Phillip said.

"THAT SHOULD DO IT," Dani said, crouching in front of Ortiz as she wired the pin in the shackle that secured the heavy chain wrapped several times around his torso.

"I should think so," Liz said. "Are you planning to go through with this? I mean drowning him?"

Dani looked over her shoulder at Liz and shrugged. "I could go either way; it depends on him, at this point. How do you feel about that? Does it bother you?"

"A little," Liz said, "but I'll get over it. I was more worried about what alternative we have. It's like that joke that Sharktooth tells."

"You mean the one about the man who has the Devil trapped in the oil drum?"

"Yes." Liz laughed. "We don't need any help holding him, but turning him loose might be a whole different story."

"As I said, it depends on him," Dani said.

"What could he say that would make you trust him that much? To let him go?"

"Probably nothing, but I have to give him a chance. Otherwise, it's cold-blooded murder. You don't think I'm that kind of woman, do you?"

Liz looked at her, keeping her face expressionless.

"Liz! Answer me, damn it!"

Dani's face flushed and she jumped to her feet, taking a menacing step toward her friend. Liz burst out laughing, doubling over and hugging herself. Dani paused, a grin replacing the anger on her face, and then she joined in the laughter.

"It wouldn't be cold-blooded, Dani. He provoked you. Let's get on with it. We need to be on our way back. We don't want to run into that four-knot outgoing tidal current in the Government Cut entrance channel."

"Right," Dani said. She turned to the bow pulpit and lifted the high-pressure wash-down hose. "Can you turn on the water?"

Liz reached for the ball valve near the gunwale and gave it a quarter turn. The hose stiffened in Dani's hand. She aimed the nozzle at Ortiz's face and squeezed, sending a solid stream of seawater up his nose.

"Kind of like water boarding," she said.

Ortiz lay on his left side, his wrists and ankles tied together behind him. As Dani played the water over his face, he gagged and began to cough. When his eyes snapped open, she released the lever on the pistol-grip nozzle.

After half a minute of coughing, Ortiz caught his breath and looked first at Dani, then at Liz, his eyes round with terror. "What are you — "

His question ended with a grunt as Dani kicked him in the solar plexus. The kick was delivered with measured force, just enough to let him know what she could have done. "We'll ask the questions, David. You speak when you're told to, okay?"

He nodded.

"Do you work for Manny Cruz?"

"Yes. I can exp-- "

She kicked him again, almost gently. "We'll get to that. Remember, just answer our questions for now, okay?"

He nodded.

"Cruz owns a real estate brokerage. Is that right?"

"Yes. I — "

Liz bent down, her index finger wagging back and forth in his face.

"Sorry," he said. She stood back up.

Dani nodded. "And are you a sales agent?"

"Yes."

"Is Cruz involved in anti-Castro activity?"

"Yes."

"Are you involved in that with him?"

"Uh ... " he cringed as Dani shifted her weight and drew her foot back. "Yes!"

She relaxed her stance. "Did he put you up to meeting me so that you could spy on my father and Phillip?"

"Yes."

"You son of a bitch," she murmured. "What did he tell you to look for?"

"At first, the plan was to kidnap you, to force your father to provide arms for an invasion of Cuba." He stopped, waiting for a cue.

"At first?" Dani said.

"Yes," he said.

"But the plan changed?" Dani asked.

"Yes. Martínez said we didn't need to do that, that it would be better to have me inside your group to report back. Or to do whatever they needed me to do, I guess."

"Martínez?" Liz asked.

"Not now, Liz. Hold that thought, though," Dani said. "So you knew who I was that night we met in the club?"

"Yes. Cruz told me and Lupita about you."

"Lupita," Dani said. "She worked for Cruz, too?"

"Yes. Actually ... " he paused, looking at Dani in alarm.

She nodded. "Actually what?"

"She worked for a guy named Santos."

"You told me she worked for someone with a lot of rental property," Dani said, squatting down and glaring at him, putting the hose nozzle against his upper lip and aiming it up his nose. "Was that Santos?"

"Yes," he said, flinching away from the nozzle. "Please? I'm cooperating, okay?"

Dani moved the nozzle back a few inches. "If she worked for Santos, why was she involved with Cruz?"

"Santos works for Cruz, but they keep that a secret. It was like I told you; Lupita beat people up for Santos. He and Cruz smuggle Haitians into the U.S. and then exploit them. The rental units are in Little Haiti."

"Why was she taking pictures of you and me?" Dani asked.

"Cruz put her up to it, I'm sure, but I don't know what he had in mind. Blackmail, maybe? In case your father didn't want to deal? I'm guessing. I know he put her up to bugging my apartment. Video cameras, too. They wanted me to take you there, and ... you know."

Dani tensed, drawing back to strike, but Liz put a hand on her shoulder, squeezing at first, then patting her when she felt Dani relax.

"Keep talking, David," Liz said. "What else can you tell us about Lupita? You met her on the beach, right? After you left Dani that first night?"

"Yes. The original plan was that I was supposed to take you out to dinner, Dani. When you and I left the club, Lupita and I were going to snatch you. She called me because Martínez changed the plan."

"How did you even know we were going to that night club?" Liz asked.

"Lupita was following you. She called me and let me know."

"That's the second time you've mentioned this Martínez," Dani said. "Who is he?"

"He seems to be the guy calling the shots on this whole invasion thing. I never met him; Lupita told me about him. She was in charge; she gave me my orders and reported back to Cruz."

"Not to Santos?"

"No. Santos isn't Cuban. He's from the Dominican Republic, so I don't think Martínez trusts him. Maybe he doesn't even know about him. See, Lupita was sleeping with Cruz. But then she got beat up really badly, and I started working directly for Cruz."

"Lupita met Martínez, but you didn't? Even after you started reporting to Cruz directly?" Dani asked.

"Right. But by then, Martínez had already pulled back. There was another guy telling Cruz what to do by the time Lupita was killed. 'Willy,' she called him. I don't know — "

"Wait," Liz interrupted. "Lupita's dead?" She looked at Dani, frowning.

Dani shook her head. "You said she was killed?"

"The hospital told Santos she had a heart attack, but we didn't believe it. She was super-fit, in her twenties, a professional fighter ... somebody took her out. At least that's what Cruz and I figured."

"Why would someone kill her?"

"We don't know; they have no idea who did it. She pissed off a lot of people, though. It could have been anybody."

Dani sat back on her heels, studying Ortiz. After about a minute, she said. "Well, David, it's been fun, but Liz and I need to get back to Miami before the tide turns. Do you know the story of Scheherazade?"

Ortiz frowned. "*The Arabian Nights*?"

"If you've run out of stories to hold our interest, it's time to say goodbye."

"I don't understand."

"Can you swim?"

"Not tied up like this. And this chain ... I'll sink."

"Mm," Dani said. "That's right. I guess this is goodbye, then."

"You could cut me loose and throw me over the side. That would give you a good head start, even if I made it back. How far out are we?"

"Probably too far," Dani said. "Besides, the Gulf Stream's full of sharks. It's better with the chain. It'll be quicker. You've been a good boy; I'll knock you out before we drop you, if you want."

"What are you ... you can't just dump me out here! I'm a federal agent."

"Bullshit!" Dani said. "Lupita was right; you're just a *pinguera*."

"When did you talk to ... wait ... I'm undercover. Seriously."

"You're going to be undercover, underwater. You're no federal agent, asshole."

"We've got a few minutes, yet, Dani," Liz said. "Let's see how good a story he can tell."

"I can prove it, if you'll make a phone call," Ortiz said.

"Not so fast," Dani said. "Tell us your whole story, Princess Scheherazade. Don't leave out anything. I'll give you five minutes. Then we'll see."

"WHY THE INSISTENCE on a face-to-face meeting, Phillip? What's going on?" Rick Olsen asked.

"I've gotten uncomfortable with this whole situation since our last meeting, Rick."

"Want to tell me why?"

"There are too many things that don't add up. I think someone in your chain of command is compromised. The — "

"My chain of command?" Rick Olsen's face was red. "Do you realize that's tantamount to saying the director is compromised?"

"Is it? I'm not clear on your chain of command, or even which 'director' we're talking about. Martínez seems to know more about what's going on in your shop than you and I do."

Olsen walked along the boardwalk without saying anything for several steps. Phillip let the silence hang until Olsen broke it.

"I interrupted you," Olsen said.

"That's all right. I'm not sure how much more I should say."

"You may as well talk it out, Phillip. You obviously didn't want to do this on the secure phone."

"That's another thing. I don't know how secure it is; the same people who threatened to blackmail me if I didn't go their way are the people who provided it."

"You have to trust somebody, Phillip."

Phillip stopped, and so did Olsen. Olsen faced him, looking him in the eye.

"There are some people I trust," Phillip said, holding Olsen's gaze.

"But I'm not one of them?" Olsen asked.

Phillip shrugged and began walking again. "Martínez is certainly not one of them, and neither is whoever you're working for."

"What are you playing at, Phillip? I don't understand what you want."

"You're asking me and J.-P. to go ahead with this on our own, without the government's blessing. Not only are we on our own, but you've told me we don't have a choice. We'll be left holding the bag if we don't go ahead, and there's no guarantee the government won't bust us along with Martínez if we do. Is that a fair description of the situation?"

"Yes, but ... you're saying you don't trust the government?"

"Is that what you thought I meant, Rick?"

"Possibly. I'm not sure."

"Good. Welcome to the game. You and the government can try guessing what's happening, for a change. I take it these people you call the government haven't seen fit to put a tail on Martínez?"

"They don't think it's warranted."

"Do they know the man who's giving him his orders?"

"You mean, among the exiles?"

"I survived 20 years in the field because I never made assumptions like that, Rick. I don't know who's pulling his strings. Do you?"

"I thought he was working for the exiles," Olsen said.

"So he says. There are all kinds of exiles."

"I don't think I can help you, Phillip. I can't figure out what you want."

"It's simple enough. We want to know who's trying to buy weapons from us and why."

"It's just a few rifles, Phillip."

Phillip stopped again, and looked at Olsen, who paused and faced him.

After a moment, Olsen said, "Well, okay, and some mortars and a machine gun or two. We aren't talking about starting World War III. They could probably scrape this stuff together at gun shows, given time."

Phillip stared at him for several seconds, shuffling his foot, his right hand fidgeting with the edge of his pants pocket. He nodded his head, smirked and said, "There's more. I think it's a deal-breaker for the exiles."

"What is it? What do they want? Air support or something?"

"A man-portable nuke."

Olsen's face went pale. "You didn't mention that before."

Phillip smiled. "No. No, I didn't."

"You and J.-P. can't deliver that." Olsen stared at him.

The expression on Phillip's face betrayed nothing. After a moment, he asked, "Is that supposed to be an order? The official government position? You're saying, 'Don't deliver it?' Or are you asking whether we can?"

"Are you wearing a wire, Phillip?" Olsen asked.

Phillip laughed. "What, Rick? You don't trust me?"

Olsen looked uneasy. "Let's say it was a question, then. Can you deliver it?"

Phillip laughed again. "Are *you* wearing a wire, Rick?"

Olsen's face flushed. "No, of course not. You want to pat me down?"

"It doesn't matter," Phillip said. "I'm not going to answer that question; you and the government don't want to be part of this, anyway." Phillip turned and resumed walking.

Olsen hurried to catch up with him. "What are you and J.-P. going to do?"

"What do you think? You aren't leaving us a choice, Rick."

"I meant about the nuke."

"What nuke? Who said anything about a nuke?"

"So that's the way it is, then?" Olsen asked.

"I know I've put you in a bind, Rick. Sorry about that." Phillip gave Olsen a smug look.

"I'll have to get back to you," Olsen said. "I need to run this up the flagpole."

"Be my guest," Phillip said, "but don't use that phone except to set up another meeting. Understand?"

"Remember who you're talking to, son," Olsen said.

"You're the one who said we were both retired, now, General. I'll give you a day; no more."

"That sounds like an ultimatum," Olsen said.

"It is."

"And if we don't get back to you in a day?"

Phillip shrugged. "I need to get back to the villa, Rick. I look forward to hearing from you soon."

## 20

"Did you two get the rental cars?" Phillip asked, looking at Connie and Paul. The three of them sat at an umbrella table on the veranda of the villa, drinking coffee with J.-P. Berger.

"Sure," Paul said. "No problem."

"We picked up some encrypted UHF walkie-talkies, too," Connie said. "I didn't like the idea of using the handheld VHF radios from the boat. There's too much chance of being overheard."

"Good," Phillip said.

"What are you planning?" J.-P. asked. "You must have been busy while I was talking with Mario."

"I asked Connie and Paul to get set up to tail Martínez," Phillip said.

"Have you heard from him again?" J.-P. asked.

"Not yet, but he should be in touch soon."

"So you have talked with Olsen, then?" J.-P. asked.

"Face to face," Phillip said, "as planned. I set a little trap." He told them about his mentioning a man-portable nuclear weapon.

"That should shake up whoever it is that Olsen works for," J.-P.

said. "A suitcase nuke ... " He grinned and shook his head. "Why did you pick that as bait?"

"Two reasons," Phillip said. "If Olsen's boss is legitimate, there'll be a big reaction from the government; it will force them off the fence. The other reason is that it's so far from what Martínez has mentioned that if he hears about it, he's bound to question me on it. Given how sensitive the government is about that kind of thing, if Martínez hears about it, it means his source is probably this mysterious 'director,' or someone very close."

"And if he does bring it up, what will you tell him?" J.-P. asked. "He knows he did not request it."

"But he assumes we're dealing exclusively with him," Phillip said. "I plan to make him a little nervous on that score."

"I know I'm new to this game," Connie said, "but I don't follow your logic."

"Martínez said he was working for a consortium of exile organizations, but he won't tell us which ones," Phillip said. "I'm going to hint to him that we have independent contact with one that he may or may not be representing."

J.-P. began to laugh. "What is that saying you Americans have about the fox and the chickens?"

"Setting the fox to guard the hen house?" Paul offered.

"Yes. I suppose it does not quite describe this," J.-P. said, "but certainly there is a fox on the prowl among the chickens, here."

"Speaking of the exile organizations," Phillip said, "how did it go with Mario?"

J.-P. said, "He is to have his weekly lunch with his friends at that place in Little Havana today, so our timing is right. I am to call him later this afternoon. But he thinks that there is no such plot. He believes that he would have heard of it by now. It is the old men — his contemporaries — who play at invasions, not the younger ones. The young ones are too busy making money, and the old ones are the tigers, but without so many teeth, now. This is his thinking."

"I suspect he's right," Phillip said.

"If there's no such plot among the exiles, then what's Martínez doing?" Paul asked.

"I don't know," Phillip said. "He's a mercenary; he's working for somebody who wants weapons. If it's not the exiles, there are plenty of other possibilities."

"Should I get in touch with some of the people I knew from the JTTF?" Paul asked. "They may know something."

"Not yet, please. Right now, we have a limited scope. The more people who know what we're doing, the more difficult it will be to pin down who the players are."

"No problem. I understand what you're saying, but the offer is there. I have enough recent contacts there to bypass the MPD. I know they're risky, when it comes to the Cubans," Paul said.

"I'm surprised at you, Paul," Connie said. "You don't trust Luke?"

"Of course I trust Luke. But if Luke starts asking those questions, word could get around the MPD through any number of channels. Then he'd be screwed, and so would we. I'll have to square it with him afterwards, but he'll understand."

Phillip's cellphone rang. Looking down at the caller i.d., he said, "It's an unknown local number — probably Martínez on a burner phone. Be ready to move fast; he'll probably want to pick me up and drive around."

As Phillip stood and walked a few paces away to answer the call, Paul looked at Connie. "Ready, skipper?"

She nodded. "Should we head for the cars?"

Before Paul could answer, Phillip rejoined them. "Game on! He's picking me up out front in five minutes. He's in a white pickup with landscaping equipment in the back. Where are your cars?"

"Parked on the shoulder of the causeway," Paul said. "We'd better hustle if he's coming in five minutes."

As Paul and Connie stood up, Phillip said, "Call my cellphone

when you're in position. I'll stall him for a minute or two if
need be."

Paul nodded and took off at a run to catch Connie, who was
jogging toward the gate already. When he caught her, they shifted
to a running pace.

"Good luck," J.-P. said, as Phillip stood and went inside the
villa.

ORTIZ DID his best to relax; his muscles were cramping, almost
bringing tears to his eyes. Being trussed like an animal bound for
market was more uncomfortable than he could have imagined.
At least he was on a soft surface now, and out of the sunlight.
Dani had removed the chain from around his midsection, and
she and Liz had used one of the ropes — the spinnaker halyard,
she had called it — to hoist him by his wrists and ankles.

He had yelled, surprised at the pain, thinking his shoulders
were going to be dislocated. Dani had threatened to knock him
unconscious, and he had stifled his complaints. They had swung
him around and lowered him through a hatch, dropping him on
the bed in the forward cabin. Once he was below deck, one of
them had reached down and unclipped the rope from the cords
that cut into his wrists and ankles, leaving him on his belly, still
immobilized. When he heard the hatch slam closed above him,
he had wriggled until he managed to roll onto his side, which was
marginally more comfortable.

As his initial relief that Dani had decided against drowning
him faded, he began to worry about what she had in mind. He'd
told her everything trying to persuade her that he was an undercover agent for Immigration and Customs Enforcement. She now
knew all about their investigation of Cruz. He'd even told her that
the higher ups discounted the significance of the invasion. She
had taken it all in, offering no reaction.

He had offered assurances that he wouldn't press charges against her and her friend in exchange for his release. That had provoked laughter from both women. At first, he couldn't make sense of their lack of concern. Then he remembered that Dani's father was an international arms dealer. The reprieve she'd granted him might only be temporary. She'd been unmoved by his threats and promises, looking at him with an expression of mild disgust.

She'd told him to shut up if he wanted to live through the trip back to shore. When he had continued to press his case, she had produced a roll of duct tape and torn off a strip to put over his mouth, but Liz had asked if he'd promise to be quiet. He'd nodded his agreement, and Dani had stuck the end of the tape to the edge of one of the counters in the stateroom, leaving it where he could see it.

"Just a reminder," she'd said, as they left him on the bed.

He'd heard Dani calling out commands, and the boat had lurched, shifting its angle. It had been inclined to the left when they had lowered him; now, it was leaning to the right. It had taken him a few minutes to puzzle out that they had turned around. The change in the sunlight coming through the port-holes confirmed it for him.

He'd initially been too stunned to think about anything beyond his immediate plight. Now that the shock was receding, he felt a wave of sadness sweep over him; he hadn't been lying when he told Dani he'd fallen for her. He'd led her on, taken advantage of her. He'd known there was no future for them, and he'd been prepared to use her for his own purposes. He'd manipulated her, but she'd gotten to him.

He suppressed that thought; there was no percentage in it. He knew he'd earned her contempt, and he regretted it. Still, he'd burned his bridges with her, and his cover would be blown with Cruz whatever happened with Dani. While he didn't know what she intended for him, he knew it wouldn't be good. There was steel in those blue eyes that he'd once found so charming. He needed to get away from her, and the sooner, the better.

If he could free himself from his bonds, he had a chance. If he were to jump overboard once they were in the Venetian Islands, he might be able to escape. There would be people around; Dani's options would be limited. Before he rolled onto his belly, he had seen that there were drawers along one side of the bed. Maybe he'd find a knife or scissors, or even a mirror that he could break. Anything sharp might allow him to free his hands, then he would be able to untie his ankles.

He worked his way back toward the drawers until he could feel one of the pulls. He hooked his numb fingers into the handle and tugged, but the drawer wouldn't come out. Then he remembered seeing Liz open one of the drawers in the galley the first time he'd been aboard. She'd shown him how to lift up on the handle before pulling it out. The drawer slides had a notch that kept the drawers from sliding out when the boat rolled. He lifted and pulled, feeling the drawer come free. He pulled it out onto the bed behind him, and then began trying to roll himself over so that he could see what was in it. He bumped the drawer and felt it tumble over the edge of the mattress. It crashed to the deck.

"What was that?" he heard one of the women ask.

Desperate, he rolled to the edge of the mattress and looked down. The drawer was upside down on the varnished teak. It took him a few seconds to make out what he was seeing. Then a chill ran down his spine.

Before he could do anything else, the cabin door swung open and Dani stepped in. She scanned her surroundings in the time it took her to get to the drawer and its spilled contents. She shook her head.

"Too bad you couldn't behave, *comepinga*. Lupita said you were a stupid *págaro*. And you've scratched my varnish, on top of your other offenses. That's going to cost you."

"You were the one who attacked her weren't you?" Ortiz asked. "You did it."

"Why do you think that, *pinguero*?" She said, as she bent to pick up the blackjack and the balaclava.

Before he could answer, she brought the blackjack down on the side of his head, and he slumped into unconsciousness. She put the drawer back in place and folded the balaclava, dropping it and the blackjack back into the drawer and pushing it closed. She retrieved the piece of duct tape that she'd torn off earlier and stuck it over his mouth. "Asshole," she muttered as she rolled him back into the center of the bed. "Scratch my cabin sole, will you?" She shook her head and left, leaving the door open.

"I'm puzzled, *señor*," Martínez said, flicking his eyes toward Phillip. He was behind the wheel of the white pickup truck, with Phillip in the passenger seat.

"Puzzled?" Phillip asked. "Why's that, José?"

"The agency thinks that we are seeking a suitcase nuke. This seems strange."

"You never mentioned a suitcase nuke," Phillip said.

"And that is why I am puzzled. You told General Olsen that we wanted one. Or so I am told, *señor*."

Phillip stared out the windshield, the muscles in his jaw working beneath his skin. His right hand rested on the dashboard, his thumb making a circular, rubbing motion against his fingers. He saw Martínez make note of his nervous gestures, and then he spoke. "I never told Olsen that it was you."

"What?" Martínez asked, turning his head to look at Phillip, then looking back at the road in time to avoid running into the car in front of them. He stood on the brakes as the traffic slowed at the west end of MacArthur Causeway. "Who else would it be, *señor*?"

Phillip looked at Martínez. Once the traffic stopped, Martínez looked at him, and Phillip smiled. "I can't tell you that, José. It would betray a trust. You wouldn't want me sharing your requirements with some other exile group, would you?"

Martínez looked at Phillip as he pondered this information. After several seconds, he nodded. "I see. Should we trust Olsen, *señor*?"

"We?" Phillip asked. "Do you mean to ask if you and your people should trust him? Or whether you and I should trust him?"

"Either one," Martínez said.

Phillip thought for a moment. "That's for you to decide, José."

"Do you trust him, *señor*?"

"I don't trust anyone, José. I can't help you with that."

"I cannot blame you, *señor*. It is clear there is a traitor in your organization. It could be Olsen, or the man who brought him in on this. There is no one else, I think."

"Why do you say one of them is a traitor?" Phillip asked.

"One of them is passing information to me," Martínez said.

"Does that make him a traitor?" Phillip asked, smiling. "We are on the same side, aren't we?"

"But of course, *señor*. I was overlooking that. Even so, this situation is strange, since there is someone else negotiating with you for weapons to invade Cuba."

"Did you get that from your source in my chain of command?"

"Yes, *señor*. Is it correct?"

Phillip grinned. "I can't tell you that, any more than you can tell me who is in your consortium."

"Of course not," Martínez said. "I think we are finished, no?"

"If you say so, José. Unless you wish to tell me who you're representing, I can't say whether one of your backers is branching out on his own."

"You are suggesting that you and I might exchange this information?"

"Perhaps. We should consider it. Otherwise one of us could be embarrassed."

"I will have to discuss this with my principals, *señor*, but I see your point. Shall I take you back to Star Island?"

"Yes, I believe so."

"What will you tell General Olsen about our meeting?"

"I think this should stay between us, for now," Phillip said.

Martínez nodded. "As you say, *señor*. Between us."

## 21

---

"Except for the garbage in the forward stateroom, it's a beautiful day," Dani said, as Liz trimmed the mainsheet. *Vengeance* surged through the swell on a close reach in 15 to 18 knots of northwesterly breeze.

"You didn't think he was garbage at first, Dani," Liz said. "I think I saw remorse in his eyes before you clobbered him. Where did you get the blackjack, anyway?"

"Oh, this little place off Collins Avenue. They had a lot of odds and ends, like tasers, and pepper spray. I picked it up on that walk I took the other night."

"So you were the one who worked Lupita over."

Dani shrugged. "I don't like strange women taking pictures of me. She had it coming."

"Did you know she was dead?"

"You mean, did I kill her?"

Liz fixed her with a steady gaze for several seconds. "Did you?"

"No."

"Could she have died from the injuries you inflicted?"

"Not likely. I'm sure she's had worse. I didn't even break any bones."

"What about a concussion?"

"I never touched her head. I wanted her conscious. All she suffered was heavy bruising."

"Heavy enough for them to keep her sedated and in the hospital?" Liz asked.

"She probably wasn't able to move much; I went for the big muscles first, and hammered them. Then I worked on the others."

"Where did you learn that? Dare I ask?"

"When they had me in that prison in St. Lucia. I found out all about it from first-hand experience."

"They beat you with blackjacks?"

Dani shrugged. "Batons. I thought about using one on her, but they're harder to conceal, and they're more likely to do serious damage. I have a feeling that Manny Cruz or his buddies did away with her because she knew too much."

They passed a few minutes in silence. Liz got up and tweaked the headsails. She sat down again, her back against the coachroof. "Dani?"

"Yes?"

"What are we going to do with him? Do you think he's really an undercover agent?"

"I don't know; he's not my idea of a hard-nosed fed, that's for sure. Paul should be able to find out, one way or another."

"Let's say he's not," Liz said. "What then?"

"Then he's probably a crook of some kind, and we can let the cops deal with him."

"And if they don't want him? Suppose they don't have anything to arrest him for."

"Then he's probably disposable."

"Not if they know we have him, Dani."

"We can turn him loose. He won't get very far. Miami's a dangerous city. Look what happened to Lupita."

Liz shook her head. "You're impossible. Imagine what's going to happen if he *is* a federal agent. We've kidnapped him and tied him up, not to mention half drowning him. And that crack on the head."

"You're right, Liz. I was restraining myself, because I was afraid I was angry about the way the bastard used me."

"What?"

"I should trust my judgment," Dani said. "I mean, sure, he broke my heart, but I shouldn't let that influence my decisions when it comes to how we should handle him."

Liz looked at her, frowning. "Now I'm completely lost. Your decision as to how we should handle him? What are you thinking?"

"Same as you, I believe. We should cut our losses. We're still in 1,500 feet of water. Take the helm and I'll get that chain. We should just get rid of him."

"But what about all the things he told us about Cruz and those other people?"

"He's already told us everything he knows. He's not much good to us now. Besides, I've realized there's a big hole in his story."

"What's that?" Liz asked.

"If he were a federal agent, he wouldn't have been willing to help Lupita kidnap me."

"I hadn't thought of that," Liz said.

"So I think we should go ahead and dump him," Dani said.

Liz looked off into the distance, her brow furrowed.

"You don't think so?" Dani asked after a long pause.

"He said Cruz wanted him to spy on Phillip and your father."

"That's what he said, yes."

"Do you believe him?"

"It's a reasonable scenario. Where are you going with this?"

"We need to let Phillip and J.-P. in on this," Liz said.

"I was going to tell them, sure. No matter what we do with him."

"I don't mean just passing along the information. They need a say in what happens to him. He might be useful."

Dani scrunched up her face for a few seconds, and then she grinned. "You mean we could feed them misinformation through him?"

"Maybe. I think we should give them the option."

"That makes sense to me. We can do that whether he's a fed or not. Getting rid of him is a separate decision. Good thinking, Liz. We'll just keep him aboard until we talk it over with them."

"Hello. The usual place? Just give me a time to meet. I'll need at least 30 minutes to get there."

The way Rick Olsen answered the encrypted phone brought a smile to Phillip's face. "Unless you've learned something new since we spoke, I think we can do this on the phone," he said.

"But you said it was compromised," Olsen objected.

"I have new information. I think the phone's safe, but even if it's not, we've got a bigger problem."

"You're the one with his ass on the line; I'm safe at home. What happened?" Olsen asked.

"I heard from Martínez."

"That was quick," Olsen said. "What did he want?"

"To know who was trying to buy a suitcase nuke," Phillip said.

"Wait a second. You said he wanted to buy one. What's going on here?"

"A test, Rick. Who did you tell about the nuke?"

"Only the director. Why?"

"I think you know the answer to that one."

"There was no nuke?" Olsen asked.

"Let's just say that if there were a nuke in play, Martínez didn't know it until your side told him," Phillip said.

"My side? I thought you and I were on the same side, Phillip."

"I hope we are. But, as you said, I'm the one with his ass on the line. You're safe at home."

"It had to be the director," Olsen said.

"Uh-huh," Phillip said. "You and he were the only ones who knew about it."

"You don't think I'd be talking to Martínez ..."

Phillip let the silence drag on.

"I see your point, Phillip, but I'm offended."

"I'm sorry, Rick. I understand."

"Where does this leave us?"

"It leaves me and J.-P. caught in the middle. I'm not sure about anybody else."

"You can't do this without us, Phillip."

"Don't take this personally, Rick, but if that's an order, your side is in no position to give it. If you think differently, then there's no need for us to continue with these contacts."

"But without us, you're blind," Olsen said.

Phillip laughed.

"It's not a laughing matter, son," Olsen said.

"From your perspective, I agree. From our perspective, we're already blind. We're thinking if you were blind too, it would level the playing field a bit."

"That would be a mistake. Is there a way I could change your decision?"

"So far, all you've offered us is the sleeves from your vest, Rick. This ain't our first rodeo, as they say where you hail from. Not even the first one we've ridden without Uncle Sam's help."

"Listen to me, Phillip. You can't believe you could do something like this inside the U.S. without our blessing and get away with it."

Phillip laughed again. "Listen to yourself, Rick. You made it plain from early on that we might not have your blessing. All we're doing is removing that little element of uncertainty. If we know we're on our own, we know what the rules are."

"The government makes the rules, son. Don't do this."

"Sorry, Rick. If you want to be in the game, we might give you a vote on the rules, but you have to pay your way if you want in."

"So if we agree to fund this — "

"You don't understand. You said yourself, this first install-ment's nothing. Any of us could buy the stuff out of pocket at a local gun show. If you want in, then you're in all the way — no more bullshit about who you're working for, or what we can or can't do."

"Phillip, I can't believe you're — "

"Rick, if you keep wheedling, I'm going to lose respect for you. Right now, I think somebody's taken advantage of you. If you get your people to deal with reality, give me a call. Otherwise, I think we're done."

"So are you going to do this, or not?"

"Call me, Rick. I hope you enjoy your retirement."

Phillip hung up the phone while Olsen was talking. He switched the power off and put it in his pocket.

"WHAT DID HE SAY, JOSÉ?" Maldonado asked. He and Martínez were in the safe house where Martínez had brought Phillip a few days earlier.

"He is very careful. He gives nothing away unintentionally."

"Did he deny telling Olsen that we wanted a nuclear weapon?"

"I challenged him by saying that he had told Olsen we wanted a suitcase nuke," Martínez said. "He appeared to be nervous when I confronted him on it. He avoided my eye, and he fidgeted with his hand. After a few seconds, he said, 'I never told Olsen it was you.' His reaction and words made me think he and Olsen are maybe dealing with someone else."

"And you think this was deliberate on his part?"

"As long as I have known Phillip Davis, he has never done

anything that was not deliberate. So, yes, I think he meant to make me think that."

"Do you believe it?" Maldonado asked.

Martínez shrugged. "It is possible. Davis himself has ties to some of the exiles, and Mario Espinosa is the Berger girl's godfather. He and J.-P. Berger have done business for decades."

"But Espinosa hasn't been active in any of the anti-Castro activities since the Bay of Pigs."

"That we know of," Martínez said.

"We would know," Maldonado protested. "Cruz runs Alpha-66."

"Do you trust him, Willy?"

"He's one of us. Of course I trust him."

"He wouldn't be the first DGI agent who turned on us."

"I don't think we need to worry about him. It was his idea to hide the troops among the Haitians when we were working on the plan. Did Lupita know about that, by the way?"

"It's hard to say. She and Cruz had a strange thing going; she may have."

"It's just as well that she's gone, then."

"Yes," Martínez said. "But there are the other organizations. It doesn't have to be Alpha-66 looking for a nuke."

"That's true," Maldonado said, "but all of them are run by toothless old men, now. Besides, we have good sources in Brothers to the Rescue and the other organizations. We've heard nothing about this. Why would they suddenly decide to get aggressive again after all these years, anyway?"

"For the same reason we're doing this," Martínez said. "The current situation is ripe with opportunity, or vulnerability, depending on your perspective. We have no monopoly on that insight. There's no heir apparent to Raul Castro, and he's announced that he's going to retire. There will be a power vacuum."

"But a nuclear weapon? It's a sledgehammer to kill a mosquito."

"Think of the threat of a nuclear weapon concealed in Havana, Willy. The leverage is far out of proportion to the actual threat. A handful of men could take over the government without firing a shot."

Maldonado stared into space for several seconds before he locked eyes with Martínez again. "How did you leave it with Davis?"

"He may be willing to trade information. We both needed time to think. I believe the door is open."

"He would tell us who the other party is? The one that wants the nuclear weapon?"

"I don't know, Willy. That's not the sort of thing that he can do if they want to stay in business. But he might be willing to back away from that deal without burning any bridges. Business is business with these people."

"Could this be a negotiating ploy? Is he trying to make a better deal?" Maldonado asked.

"I don't know if it's a ploy. It could be, but there are good reasons to think it is a real threat. I don't think we can gamble on that. Do you?"

"What could we offer him?" Maldonado asked.

"He indicated that disclosure of our principals would be a step toward establishing trust."

"And would he tell us who his other client is in exchange?"

"I doubt it," Martínez said. "But as I said, he could walk away from that other deal."

"Can we apply pressure through Olsen to sway him?"

"The word is, he doesn't trust Olsen's chain of command. So probably not. Between us," Martínez said, "I think we already put too much pressure on him through Olsen when he asked if the U.S. government would bless the deal."

"You know why we did that; we didn't have any options that

didn't risk the cover of our inside contact," Maldonado said.
"What if we disclose some of our 'principals' to him?"

"What are you suggesting? A bluff? There are no principals to disclose."

"We might be able to come up with some names that would be convincing," Maldonado said.

"I think that's too risky. You're forgetting how broadly connected these people are in the Miami area."

"You mean Espinosa?"

"Espinosa, Davis himself, the Berger girl," Martínez said. "She's fluent in Cuban Spanish, remember? She spent a lot of her childhood here with Espinosa and his wife. They all have long-term ties here. And don't forget this retired cop, Paul Russo. He was part of the JTTF for years. He's probably got contacts we can't even imagine."

"Do you have any ideas for a solution?" Maldonado asked. "Or are you focused on why we can't do it?"

"Don't take that tone with me, Willy." Martínez's eyes looked like black marbles as he leaned into Maldonado's face. "You know what I am; what I can do to people who get in my way. Lupita was our first casualty on this operation. You could be the second."

Maldonado swallowed hard and looked away, fighting for composure. He turned back to face Martínez and said, "Sorry, José. There's a lot at stake, and I'm frustrated."

"Giving vent to emotions gets people killed," Martínez said. "There may be a way to do this, but we need to find out how Ortiz is getting along with the girl. Go and talk with Cruz. And find out how the troops are doing. Are they behaving themselves in Little Haiti? I'm worried about them getting bored; we don't need any problems that might attract the attention of the cops."

A buzzing sound came from Martínez's pants pocket. He looked surprised as he stood and took out a cheap cellphone. He gave Maldonado a forbidding look and went outside to take the call.

"What did he have to say?" J.-P. asked, as Phillip put away the phone after his call with Olsen.

"The trap is sprung," Phillip said. "And he wants to know who's trying to buy a suitcase nuke."

"Who did he tell?" J.P. asked.

"He said he only told the director."

J.-P. frowned. "What do you think, Phillip? What should we do?"

Phillip shrugged. "I don't know, but I don't think we can trust whoever Olsen's working for."

"I agree with that. Do you think they will follow through with their threat to expose us if we back out?"

"Is that what you want to do?" Phillip asked. "Back out?"

"It must be our decision, Phillip, not mine alone. But I am not comfortable with this. I heard from Mario while you were out. Nobody knows anything about this invasion — none of the exile groups. Mario's friends have checked."

"That does put things in a different light," Phillip said, scratching the back of his neck and looking at the floor. He took a seat across the coffee table from J.-P.

"Yes," J.-P. said. "I have been trying to understand what this could mean."

"I have to believe that Olsen's people know this, whoever they are," Phillip said. "They must have sources inside the exile groups; almost everybody does."

"Who could Martínez be working for, if not the exiles?" J.-P. asked.

"Almost anyone, I suppose. There's no telling where those weapons might end up. He could even be plotting an attack in the States."

"But would Olsen be involved in something like that?"

"I don't think so," Phillip said. "Not knowingly. But I'm not sure what's going on with him, so I'm not inclined to share anything else with him. Martínez is looking to arm a light infantry platoon with this first shipment. Whatever his objective is, there must be people to carry the weapons. If they aren't coming from the exile community, where are they?"

"And who are they?" J.-P. asked. "You think Martínez really could be working for a terrorist group planning a strike in the U.S.?"

"I can't rule it out. He's been a soldier of fortune for a long time. I don't know what drives him, other than money and excitement."

"Do you think he's going to respond to your offer to trade information?"

"Maybe. He knows we won't tell him who wants a nuke, but that doesn't mean we can't do some kind of trade. The problem is, he has to suspect that we know the exiles aren't his clients, and he's not about to tell us the truth about who's behind him."

"Mario suggested that this could be a reprise of the Avila scheme that he mentioned earlier," J.-P. said.

"To give the Castro regime some anti-U.S. propaganda?" Phillip asked. "I thought of that, but Martínez would still need troops. Where's he going to find 30 trained people in Florida?"

Before J.-P. responded, Paul Russo joined them. "We lost Martínez," he announced, sitting down next to Phillip on the couch. "We followed him to a gated community in Coral Gables. Connie and I tag-teamed him, so he wouldn't spot us. She called me to tell me; she had the last leg. She's a few minutes behind me."

"How many houses in the gated community?" Phillip asked.

"A dozen or two."

"Enough to give him some cover, then. If he's even staying there."

"He is," Paul said. "We waited to see if he came out."

"He could be pretending to be a gardener, or something," Phillip said. "Hanging out in there."

"Caretaker," Paul said.

"How did you find that out?"

"Connie gave the guy in the gate house some line about wanting to hire the gardener in the white truck that just drove in. I don't know what she said, exactly, but she got his phone number."

"She got Martínez's phone number?" Phillip asked, his eyebrows rising.

Paul gave him a rueful smile. "And the guard's, too. You know Connie."

"The guard had a number for Martínez?" J.-P. asked.

"Martínez is supposedly working for some outfit that house-sits and does handyman work while the homeowners are away. She got his business card from the guard."

"It's probably bogus." Phillip said. "Can you do a reverse lookup on the number, in case it's not?"

"Tried it already. It's a prepaid cellphone — no address."

"No address, huh?" Connie said, sitting down next to Paul. "You mean I undid my top button for nothing?"

"Not for nothing. At least we know he's staying there," Paul said. "Too bad you couldn't find out which house."

"I was worried that the guard would get suspicious if I asked that. I couldn't think of a plausible reason to ask more questions, once I had a way to get in touch with Martínez."

Paul nodded. "Right. Good thinking. I ran the plate on the truck. It's registered to a one-man landscaping company, but the owner says he rented out the truck and equipment to a guy for a couple of weeks so he could take his kids to Disney World."

"Look," Phillip said, standing and moving to peer out the window. "Dani and Liz are coming in to the dock."

"Let's go give them a hand," Connie said.

"WHO WERE you talking to just now?" Maldonado asked, when Martínez came back into the safe house.

"Our inside source," Martínez said. "That call was on my burner; that's how I knew it was an emergency."

"What's going on, then?"

"Olsen's gotten suspicious. I think they may be about to burn him."

"Really? They'd waste a guy like him? With all his connections?"

"That's why they'll kill him. He's dangerous because of those connections. He could wreck this whole thing with one phone call."

Maldonado shook his head. "I couldn't understand why we brought in somebody like him in the first place."

"Because he used to be Davis's boss. The trust was already established, and Davis would not have worked with that kid who was his initial contact."

"How will it go down?"

"You mean Olsen?" Martínez asked.

"Yes. Killing somebody like him is risky," Maldonado said.

"He'll commit suicide."

"They won't buy that," Maldonado protested. "Why would a man like him kill himself?"

"Remorse," Martínez said.

"Remorse? For what?"

"Killing that kid who made the first contact with Davis. The gun that was used will be found in Olsen's possession. It may even be the way he kills himself. That would be fitting, wouldn't it?"

"How do you know this?"

"You ask too many questions, Willy. You don't want me to answer that, do you?"

Maldonado swallowed with some difficulty and shook his head. Martínez smiled at him.

"We were still discussing what to do about Davis when that call came in," Maldonado said. "Now we've lost our source of information about what he and J.-P. Berger are thinking."

"When one door closes, another one opens," Martínez said. "The last you heard from Cruz, Ortiz was about to score with the girl, wasn't he?"

"Yes! You're right. I should check with Cruz. Ortiz was going to spend the day sailing with her, though, so Cruz may not have heard from him yet."

"That's all right. We have plenty to occupy us for the moment. I need to make sure the Olsen problem is handled. I'll be out for most of the evening."

"Then I should have the information from Ortiz when you return. I have plans for dinner with Cruz," Maldonado said.

"Be careful when you leave here. I think I may have been followed when I dropped off Davis. I saw a stunning woman behind me a couple of times in traffic, but if she was tailing me, I lost her. It could have been nothing."

∾

"How was the sailing?" Connie asked, as she caught the coiled line that Liz tossed her. *Vengeance* was coasting in, her starboard side a few feet off the dock. The breeze was pushing the boat away, and Dani looked tense as she worked the helm.

"That's the forward spring line," Liz said, reaching to pick up another hank of line. "Cleat it to stop us, please. It was a nice day out there, but we've got some things to cover with everybody."

Connie walked along the dock until she found a cleat about half a boat length from shore. She wrapped a couple of turns of the spring line around the cleat and took up most of the slack. She looked up at Dani, who was behind the helm, her eyes on Connie. She caught Dani's eye and nodded, indicating that she had the line secured.

Dani shifted the transmission into forward and eased the throttle open until the line took a strain. Satisfied that Connie had judged the length properly, Dani applied more power, and cranked the helm slightly to port. The diagonal thrust from the propeller working against the spring line pushed the boat sideways, bringing her up against the dock.

The forward spring line was bar-tight as *Vengeance* squeezed the fenders that protected her topsides from the edge of the dock. Dani handed Connie a coil of line, one end of which was secured to the bronze cleat on *Vengeance's* starboard quarter. As Connie bent to cleat the stern line, Liz stepped off onto the dock, bow line in her hand. She tied it off, and she and Connie both gave Dani thumbs-up. Dani throttled back and took the transmission out of gear. She leaned over and shut down the diesel.

"Where's David?" Connie asked.

"He's tied up below," Dani said, scowling.

Connie raised her eyebrows. "Paul's making rum punch; it's time for sundowners on the veranda. Will he be joining us?"

Dani shook her head. "He's tied up — literally. Son of a bitch. He may still be unconscious. We'll leave him here for now. We need to talk. Are Phillip and Papa around?"

"Yes. Paul put them to work helping with the *hors d'oeuvres*. What happened?"

"The short version's that Ortiz is a spy for Manny Cruz and this Martínez character that Phillip's been working with." Dani stepped off onto the dock.

"I'm sorry, Dani," Connie said.

Liz stepped between them and put a hand on Connie's arm, shaking her head.

"It's okay," Dani said. "I'm over him, the asshole. We just need to figure out what to do with him." She hopped over the lifelines like a cat, landing on the dock. "Let's go get some rum punch and we'll tell you about it."

"Okay," Connie said, as the three of them walked up the dock. "This could take a while. We've got some news from this end, too. I hope Paul made lots of *hors d'oeuvres*."

They found the three men standing at an umbrella table on the veranda, waiting for them. There was a tray of drinks and snacks on the table. As they approached, the men each pulled out a chair and held it for the three women to sit.

"Where's David," J.-P. asked. "I was expecting to meet him, finally."

"That can still happen, Papa," Dani said, with a wry smile, "but first, we need to tell you what we've learned about him. Liz, would you start?"

Liz nodded, but before she said anything, J.-P. spoke.

"Is he still on *Vengeance*?"

"Yes," Liz said. "He's indisposed now. We'll explain."

J.-P. nodded. "Please."

"When you came back from your meeting yesterday, Phillip, Paul told you that the car Martínez sent was owned by Manny Cruz."

"Right," Phillip said. "By his realty firm, actually."

"I recognized the name, but I didn't want to say anything about it until I had a chance to talk to Dani." She gestured for silence as Phillip and J.-P. both leaned forward, ready to interrupt. "You'll understand. Just let us tell you. When Dani was having lunch with David Ortiz at the yacht club that first day, I was inside chatting with the bartender. It was just the two of us, and we were talking about men. Nothing special, just idle chatter.

"She saw me staring out the window, watching David and Dani. Then she mentioned that she knew David, that he entertained customers at the club often. She said he used a company membership; he worked for a real estate company owned by Manny Cruz.

"Once I heard you connect Manny Cruz to Martínez, you see why I had to talk to Dani before I said anything."

Everybody nodded. "Yes, so you must have told her last night," J.-P. said.

"She did," Dani said. "I was already suspicious of him. I'd caught him in a couple of lies that had seemed senseless. Once Liz told me about Cruz and Martínez, the lies seemed ominous instead of dumb. He'd been wanting to go sailing, so I called him last night and invited him on the trip today. Once we got out of sight of land, we questioned him. Based on his answers, I wanted to dispose of him out in the Gulf Stream — had him all packed up, wrapped in chain. Then Liz pointed out that we should let you have a say in deciding what to do with him."

"What did he tell you?" J.-P. asked.

"He works for Cruz, all right, and not just in the real estate business. Cruz assigned him and a woman named Lupita Vidal to kidnap me. They were going to use me for leverage in Martínez's negotiations with you. Ortiz picked me up in a club at South Beach that first night, planning to snatch me when we went out to dinner.

"Before that happened, Martínez changed their plans. He wanted Ortiz to seduce me and become part of the group here. His job was to spy on us and report back to Cruz."

"Who would then tell Martínez what Ortiz had learned,"

Phillip added.

"Almost, but not quite. There's another player; the only name Ortiz has is 'Willy.' Willy fits between Martínez and Cruz," Dani said.

Phillip and J.-P. exchanged glances, and J.-P. shook his head. "Go ahead, please," he said. "What about this woman, Lupita Vidal?"

"She's dead; out of the picture," Dani said.

"Is her death related to this?" Phillip asked.

"Possibly, but only in a peripheral way. She was, um, mugged a couple of nights ago, and in the hospital, all doped up. Ortiz thinks they killed her because she knew too much and they were afraid she might give something away. The police were questioning her about the mugging. She was a prize fighter; hired muscle for Cruz and another crony of his named Santos. Cruz and Santos are smuggling Haitians into the States and exploiting them. Santos runs that part of Cruz's empire."

"Okay," J.-P. said. "This is consistent with what we have learned. Is there more that we can get from Ortiz?"

"Maybe," Liz said. "Dani?"

"He claims he's an undercover agent for Immigration and Customs Enforcement. ICE is investigating the trafficking operation, and Ortiz claims he was supposed to infiltrate Cruz's side of the racket. He was convincing enough so that Cruz trusted him with spying on us. Liz suggested that if that's true and we can find a way to trust him, we could make a double agent out of him. That's the basic story."

"Should I make a call?" Paul asked. "If he's with ICE, I can probably verify his identity pretty quickly."

"Yes," Phillip and J.-P. said, in chorus.

"Excuse me," Paul said, and left the table.

"While we wait for Paul, Phillip can tell you the balance of what we know," J.-P. said. "Then we will all be together in our understanding, I think."

## 23

---

"This new guy, François?" Santos put his coffee cup down and added cream.

"Yeah? What about him?" Cruz asked. "How's he working out?"

"Good," Santos said. "He's doin' real good. Learned his way around quick, too. And he ain't as much of a pain in the ass as Lupita was."

"That's good to hear. Everything quiet in the rentals?"

"Yeah, pretty much." Santos chuckled. "François, though, he did kick the shit out of a couple of them assholes from the D.R."

Cruz looked alarmed at that. "What happened?"

Santos shrugged. "No big deal. He was makin' the rounds in the building where we put 'em, pickin' up the rent for the week. They gave him some shit, told him they didn't have to pay no rent, that they were my guests." He grinned and shook his head.

"You didn't explain that to him before you sent him in there?"

"I did, but I guess he forgot. Cost them guys a busted nose and a few teeth, is all. I 'splained it to him when he told me 'bout it. Won't have no more trouble, I don't think."

"Those men are tough," Cruz said. "He's lucky he didn't get hurt."

"You ain't seen tough like François, Manny. One look at him an' the Devil gonna cross the street to keep outta his way."

"As long as he knows to leave them alone. We should have them out of there in a few more days, anyway."

"That's good. He knows to leave them alone, but he don't like it much. He says they're takin' up room he could be makin' money on. He gets a cut on the rent he collects, see. Besides, he don't like 'em 'cause they ain't Haitian. Says they're makin' trouble with some of the women."

"He noticed they weren't Haitian?"

"Yeah. He knew they were from the D.R. right off."

"How?"

"Takes one to know one, I guess; he's from Port-au-Prince, remember?"

"No, I didn't know that. I thought he was American-born, for some reason. He said they were making trouble with the women? What kind of trouble?"

"Messin' with some of the ones that're married, what he said. He figures the husbands are gonna get into it with 'em."

"Shit! We gave those bastards women to keep them out of trouble. What the hell are they doing?"

"I don't know, Manny. You know how some guys are. Goddamn animals, those guys. It ain't the first I heard of it, either. You want me to tell François to teach 'em a lesson?"

"Not yet. We need those guys in one piece. Besides, there's thirty of them. He may be tough, but nobody's that tough."

"That's what I told him, but he just grinned at me. His fuckin' teeth are filed to points in the front, Manny, like some fuckin' vampire."

"Tell him to keep away from them; I'll take care of it."

"How are you goin' to — "

"I said I'd take care of it, Santos. I need to get back to my office. You got anything else?"

"WHAT ARE YOU DOING HERE?" Dani asked, as Sharktooth approached the table where they were all snacking on the *hors d'oeuvres*.

"Paul let me in. He was on the phone. He said everybody was out back."

"That's not what I meant," Dani said, as everyone shifted position, making room for the chair that Sharktooth dragged over from the other table.

"We thought you and Maureen were coming with Sandrine in a couple of days," Connie said.

"Plans changed," Sharktooth said, grinning. "They still be comin' in a couple of days. I been talkin' wit' Phillip 'bout a little business we doin'."

"We were just filling everyone in, Sharktooth," Phillip said. "A lot has happened since we spoke last. Did everything work out all right?"

"Yeah, mon. No problem. I pick up *La Paloma* like we plan, an' meet the ship on the wes' side of Andros in the little bay."

"Did they get you loaded with no problem? "J.-P. asked.

"Yeah, mon. Mos' of the work on *La Paloma* done befo' I pick her up. They jus' load the shipment an' seal up the compartments wit' fiberglass."

"Where did you leave *La Paloma*?" Phillip asked.

"Lef' her in a marina in Marathon. Easy run up to Shark River from there. You got a delivery date yet?"

"No, not yet. Things are fluid right now," Phillip said. "Will *La Paloma* be okay where she is for a while?"

"Mm-hmm," Sharktooth said. "She be jus' fine. I change the registration, too, jus' in case something go wrong."

"Who's she registered to now?" J.-P. asked.

Sharktooth grinned. "Manuel Cruz."

Phillip and J.P. laughed.

"If it all comes apart, we can give the feds an anonymous tip and dump the whole mess in Cruz's lap," Phillip said.

Sharktooth nodded, but didn't say anything.

Dani broke the silence. "You've already brought the weapons in, I take it?"

"Given that we don't know who to trust, J.-P. and I decided to do it before anybody expected it. Harder for them to arrange any surprises, that way."

Dani nodded. "What kind of boat is *La Paloma*?"

"A 40-foot sport fisherman that one of Clarence's people found in the Turks and Caicos. A little beat-up, but still fast and seaworthy."

"Sounds perfect," Dani said. "Like she won't attract any attention."

Phillip shrugged. "If she does, that's why she's in Cruz's name. How about the marina, Sharktooth?"

"I used Cruz's name and paid cash for a month's dockage." Sharktooth said, grinning. "I wiped her down for prints."

"I see you found everybody," Paul said, joining the group.

"What did you find out about Ortiz?" Dani asked.

"Nothing yet. I talked to Luke; he has to make a few calls. He knows the woman who runs the undercover ops for ICE in South Florida. They're both on the JTTF. She's out in the field, though, so it'll take him an hour or two to get in touch with her. He did confirm that there's an ICE investigation going on in Little Haiti. He knows about it because of MPD's investigation into the murder of that Lupita Vidal woman you mentioned, Dani. He'd like to talk to Ortiz about her at some point. That much of Ortiz's story checks out."

"So they do think someone killed her?"

"Yes. The death was suspicious, so they did a preliminary investigation. The security videos picked up a janitor who went into her hospital room for a few minutes about the time her heart stopped. He disappeared after he left her room, and there wasn't supposed to be a janitor working there at the time, anyway. The ME's still waiting on tox screens, but they think the janitor injected something into her IV."

"I THINK NOW we have told you everything, Sharktooth," J.-P. said. They still sat around the table on the veranda. Sharktooth had devoured the *hors d'oeuvres*, and Paul and Liz had made another tray just for him.

"Uh-oh," Phillip said, standing up and reaching into his pocket. "That's a text on the phone Olsen gave me." He pulled the phone out and entered an access code on the screen, turning away to avoid the glare of the setting sun as he studied the message.

"What does he want?" J.-P. asked. "I thought you were no longer going to work with him."

"I did, too," Phillip said. "It's an odd message; nothing to do with the exiles. It's a personal warning. He says he thinks the man he's been reporting to is an agent of the Cuban DGI, but he doesn't say why. He says I should watch my six, and I shouldn't trust Martínez or any of the exiles. He overheard this director talking with someone about how they didn't need him anymore, because they had a mole in our operation."

"They didn't need Martínez anymore?" Connie asked. "I'm confused."

"Sorry," Phillip said. "My fault; I wasn't clear enough. Not Martínez — they don't need Olsen any more. He thinks they're going to kill him."

"The CIA?" Dani asked.

"I don't think so," Phillip said. "I'm not sure exactly who he's working for. Everything's changed since Olsen and I worked with the Agency. But it sounds like the DGI has at least one plant in there — maybe Olsen's boss. They've left him locked in an interrogation room for the last couple of hours. He says he heard Martínez talking outside the door, telling somebody that he'd just do it there, that it would be easier to move a body than a prisoner."

"I'm surprised they let him keep the phone," Dani said. "Amateurs."

"He told me earlier that they didn't know about the phones; he got them from somewhere else, because he didn't trust them. He mentioned that when I told him about the leak; I was suspicious of the phones."

"You said he told you the phone was booby trapped," J.-P. said.

"Yes. They were paired, somehow. If you tried to call any number besides the other paired phone, it would blow up. He said they were lethal. Same thing if you entered the wrong access code more than three times in a row."

"Is there anything we can do?" J.-P. asked. "I know you had some history with him."

Phillip shook his head. "I have no idea where he is." His thumbs flew over the screen of the phone as he spoke.

"You're sending him an answer?" Paul asked.

"Yes. He asked me to acknowledge receipt. If I don't hear back from him immediately, I should assume he's dead and proceed accordingly."

"What does that mean?" Dani asked. "Proceed accordingly?"

"I don't know what he meant," Phillip said, "but I think we're doing okay. Ortiz has to be their mole, and we already found him. If he's really undercover with ICE, we may be able to use him the way Liz suggested. We'll have to wait for Luke Pantene to get back to us, unless somebody's got a better idea."

## 24

"Okay, Luke," Paul Russo said to his old partner at the Miami PD. He had taken the call on his cellphone while he and Liz were preparing a light supper. After several platters of *hors d'oeuvres*, no one was too hungry. Paul listened for a couple of minutes and then said, "Sure, we're all here, and I don't think anybody's got any plans. Should we delay dinner until the two of you get here?"

He listened to Pantene for a few seconds and said, "Okay, then. We'll go ahead. I'll tell the others you're coming. See you when you get here."

"What's going on?" Liz asked, as Paul slipped the phone back into his pocket.

"He connected with that woman at Immigration and Customs Enforcement. She acknowledged that she had an agent undercover as David Ortiz, but she won't confirm his identity without seeing him. Luke's going to bring her by here this evening."

"Are we feeding them?" Liz asked. "I have some more shrimp in the freezer on *Vengeance*."

"No, he said it would be a while — maybe a couple of hours. She's out in the field somewhere right now."

"Should we get Ortiz off the boat and clean him up a little?" Liz asked.

"Probably. I'd forgotten about him, honestly," Paul said. "I mean, I knew he was there, but ... out of sight out of mind. I've got supper under control if you want to go fill the others in."

"Thanks. I'll do that," Liz said.

A few minutes later, she and Dani, accompanied by Sharktooth, opened the door to *Vengeance's* forward cabin. Ortiz was in the same position he had been in the last time Liz had looked in on him, but he had regained consciousness. He twisted himself around on the v-berth to look at them, making muffled sounds as he tried to speak.

Dani moved close to him. "Okay, David. We've got partial confirmation of what you told us about ICE. You aren't in the clear yet; we still need someone to confirm that you're who you say you are. Are you following me?"

He nodded. "Mm-hmm."

"I'm going to untie you, but don't do anything stupid. Sharktooth here isn't as gentle as Liz and I are."

He nodded again, and Dani took a folding commando knife from Sharktooth's hand and flicked the 5-inch blade open with her thumb. Reaching across Ortiz, she cut the cord binding his wrists to his ankles, and he straightened his limbs, groaning as he stretched his cramped muscles.

"Can you roll onto your stomach?" Dani asked.

When he complied, she clipped the cord that held his wrists together, and then she freed his ankles.

"It'll be less irritating if you take the duct tape off your mouth yourself," she said. "Or if your hands are still too numb, I'll do it. That's up to you. Can you sit up?"

He rolled to a sitting position, his legs hanging off the side of the berth. Stretching his arms, he flexed his fingers a few times. Picking at a corner of the duct-tape gag with the nail of his right index finger, he got a grip on it and peeled the tape away.

"You ladies sure know how to show a fella a good time," he said. "Any chance of a drink of water?"

"Sure," Liz said, heading for the galley. "Coming right up."

Dani watched as he probed the area over his right ear with his fingers. "Any signs of concussion?" she asked. "Nausea, double vision, anything?"

"Nope. I've got a hard head, I guess. It's tender where you hit me, but there's not even any swelling. I'm amazed."

"Dani, she an artist wit' a blackjack," Sharktooth said, grinning, as he cleaned his fingernails with the big knife that Dani had returned to him.

Ortiz looked warily at Sharktooth as he accepted a glass of water from Liz. He took a couple of swallows and then drained the glass. "Thanks, Liz."

"You're welcome." She took the glass from him. "More?"

"Not just yet. What happens now?"

"We're going up to the house," Dani said. "Paul and Liz are serving shrimp curry for dinner while we wait for a couple of people to come identify you."

"Okay. I'm starved. Who's coming?"

"Paul Russo's former partner, Luke Pantene. He runs homicide for MPD. He wants to ask you about Lupita's murder," Dani said.

"Ask me about Lupita's murder? I'd think you'd be the one he was interested in."

"Watch your mouth," Dani said. "I told you that you weren't in the clear yet." He locked eyes with her for a second. Then he nodded and looked away.

"I don't know this Pantene. Who else is coming?" he asked.

"The woman you're reporting to," Liz said. "I don't have a name, but Luke knows her. She was worried about you because you'd missed your last two check-ins."

"Mary Weatherby," he said. "Known as the ICE Queen."

"Charming," Dani said. "Does she know you call her that?"

"Everybody calls her that. She thinks it's funny," Ortiz said. "About that shrimp curry ... "

"Think you can walk okay?" Dani asked. "Sharktooth can give you a hand, if you want."

"I think I'm okay, thanks, but stay close, Sharktooth, just in case."

"WHAT HAS CRUZ LEARNED FROM ORTIZ?" Martínez asked. He and Maldonado sat in the living room of the safe house, sipping drinks. Martínez had brought back a bottle of Saint James Reserve that he'd found in a ramshackle liquor store in downtown Miami. They savored it over cracked ice, with just a splash of water.

"Damn, this is good," Maldonado said, swallowing the sip that he'd been rolling around in his mouth. "Where's it made, anyway?"

"Martinique," Martínez said. "What about Ortiz?"

"Cruz hasn't heard from him yet; he thinks that's a good sign. Figures they're probably out in the ocean, out of cellphone range. He thinks Ortiz probably scored, as long as they've been gone."

"Has Cruz tried calling him?" Martínez asked.

"Yes. It goes straight to voicemail; like the phone's either turned off or out of range. Cruz is going to keep trying; I told him to call me as soon as he makes contact, no matter what time it is." He took another sip of his drink. "I can't believe the French can make rum this good."

"They've been making it there a long time," Martínez said. "It's a favorite of mine from when I used to hide out in Fort-de-France. It's not easy to find in the States, and it's damned expensive. I only drink it on special occasions, to celebrate."

"We're celebrating, then?" Maldonado asked. "You accomplished your mission?"

"Of course, Willy. It was like that saying, shooting fish in a barrel."

"So he shot himself. Same gun?"

"Yes."

"Did he leave a suicide note?"

"No. That's too obvious. It's better to be subtle."

"Then the gun is the only connection?" Maldonado asked.

"Not that subtle." Martínez took a sip of the rum and smirked. "They might miss it. Remember who we're dealing with."

"So there was another clue?"

"A clipping from the newspaper about the kid, with the mention of his surviving children underlined. All wrinkled up in the pocket of his suitcoat that was hanging on the back of the chair. He'd been drinking, too. Poor old bastard." Martínez shook his head. "But now we only have Ortiz to tell us what's going on. We dare not use the director if we want to frame Olsen as the leak."

"We should be okay," Maldonado said. "Worst case, we can go back to the original plan and snatch the girl."

"I don't know; without Ortiz and Lupita, that might be a challenge. I don't trust those men we brought over for the attack to kidnap her."

"That reminds me," Maldonado said. "Cruz said Santos is happy with the new guy."

"What new guy are you talking about?" Martínez asked.

"Did I forget to tell you?" Maldonado asked. "Ortiz found a Haitian thug to take Lupita's place."

"You didn't mention that. Is he sleeping with Cruz, like Lupita?" Martínez grinned.

Maldonado laughed. "I didn't ask. Cruz says he's a real tough guy. He got crossways with a couple of our mercenaries from the D.R. over a misunderstanding about rent and kicked their asses."

"What?" Martínez growled, a scowl on his face.

"It's cool, José. No permanent damage, and Santos told him to stay away from them. They've been causing some problems with women, though."

"I thought Cruz was providing women," Martínez said. "That was part of their deal."

"Yes, he is. I guess a couple of the guys decided they liked the looks of some married women in the building. The husbands were getting upset. Cruz asked if you could tell them to chill out before Santos's new muscle decides to do it. He doesn't like people from the D.R."

"But what about Santos? He's from there."

"Santos is paying him. I guess that changes things for him."

"Does Cruz know anything about this new guy?"

"I don't think so. He had Ortiz send him straight to see Santos. François, his name is. Cruz didn't want any contact with him. But he did say Santos told him François has done some hard time in the U.S. prison system. He's got a lot of jailhouse tattoos. Oh, and his front teeth are filed to points. 'Like a vampire,' Santos told Cruz."

Martínez relaxed a bit and took another sip of his drink. "Well, at least he doesn't sound like an undercover cop of some kind. Tattoos, maybe a cop would do, but filing his teeth? That's far out."

"ARE YOU ALL RIGHT, DAVID?" Mary Weatherby asked, as soon as Luke and Paul escorted her into the living room of the villa where the others were gathered.

"I'm okay," Ortiz said. "A little stiff, but I'll live."

"Glad to hear it. I've been worried. The second time you missed your check-in, it alarmed me." She looked around at the others.

"I've told Ms. Weatherby as much as I know about the situation," Luke said, "but we haven't met everybody, so I'll ask you to introduce yourselves. Mary?"

She nodded to Luke. "Thanks. I'm Mary Weatherby, the Assistant Special Agent in Charge of Immigration and Customs Enforcement's Miami Field Office. We cover Florida, Puerto Rico, and the U.S. Virgin Islands. I'm responsible for undercover operations; David works for me. Call me Mary."

When everyone was introduced, Luke Pantene took the floor again. "Paul's told me a little about what's going on here, and I've passed that along to Mary. The two of us cross paths fairly often. Right now, MPD's investigating the murder of a woman named Lupita Vidal. That overlaps with an undercover investigation that Mary's running. ICE is looking into a human trafficking operation that appears to be run by Manny Cruz. Vidal worked as an enforcer in his organization. I know Cruz also popped up in your dealings with this Martínez character who claims to want to buy weapons to overthrow the Castro regime."

"We picked up some pieces of that invasion plot through David's work with Cruz," Mary said. "Frankly, I blew it off because some of the exiles are always plotting to attack Cuba, one way or another. We know Cruz is nominally involved in Alpha-66. Now I hear from Luke that this one may be real. He says you've had some contact with the CIA about providing arms."

"Let's clear that up," Phillip said, "or maybe add to the confusion." He explained how he knew Martínez and summarized what had happened so far. "As for the CIA, I dealt with them when I was a military attaché some years ago, and when Martínez approached me, I called the last contact number I'd been given. I ended up meeting with an unnamed agent shortly after the call.

"The results of the meeting were leaked to Martínez as soon as it was over. Then I got a call from a former commanding officer of mine. He was also a mentor of sorts. He told me he had been brought in from retirement to act as my contact. I told him about the leak, and he explained that he was reporting directly to 'The

Director.' They had discovered the leak and dealt with it by short-
ening the chain of command.

"Over the course of several contacts with him, I realized that
the leak was still there. I told him, and he passed that to the director. The last I heard from my contact, he was in some kind of
trouble. I need to stress that I'm not sure what agency I was
dealing with. My old mentor wouldn't confirm or deny that he
was working for the CIA. That made J.-P. and me nervous about
the deal."

"Can you tell us who your contact is?" Luke asked, "Your
mentor, that is?"

"His name's Rick Olsen," Phillip said. "He's a retired Brigadier
General."

Pantene's eyes opened wide. "I'm sorry to tell you, but Rick
Olsen's dead, Phillip. An apparent suicide, in the last hour or so.
When did you last speak with him?"

"We spoke by telephone a few hours ago. I wouldn't bet that it
was suicide."

"My guys are investigating," Luke said. "It's early days, yet. Did
he have a cellphone that you know of? We couldn't find one in
his effects, which is odd, these days."

"Yes, but tell your guys to be careful." Phillip told them about
the modified iPhone that Olsen had given him. "He had the mate
to it. From what he said, making a call to any number other than
the mate would cause the phone to explode. So would entering
the wrong unlock code more than three times in a row."

"Interesting," Luke said. "We didn't find any kind of cellphone.
Can I have the one he gave you?"

"I don't see why not," Phillip said, taking the phone from his
pocket and handing it to Luke. "Where was he found?"

"Bayfront Park. He ate a gun, right there on a park bench.
Some jogger found him and called it in. Did he normally carry a
pistol?"

"I don't know," Phillip said.

"So where do you stand with this arms deal?" Mary Weatherby asked.

"On hold," Phillip said. "It's not going to happen without the government's blessing; that's the way we operate."

"And you haven't received it?" she asked.

"No. Olsen waffled when I pressed him." Phillip explained their 'damned if they did, damned if they didn't' dilemma. "We'll err on the side of not breaking any laws," he finished.

"How quickly could you deliver," Weatherby asked, "if we turned this into a sting?"

"More quickly than you could get approval, probably, assuming we agreed to participate. We aren't in the business of delivering military weapons to people inside the U.S., or anywhere else, without appropriate approval."

"I understand that; Luke's vouched for you."

"Are you still in contact with Martínez?" Luke asked.

"I don't have a way to reach him," Phillip said, "but he has an uncanny way of knowing when to get in touch with me. I expect I'll hear from him soon. What should I tell him?"

"Sandbag him, for the moment," Weatherby said. "We need to get our ducks in a row. Interdicting illicit weapons shipments is within my scope of responsibility. How big a shipment are we talking about?"

"He wants to equip a light infantry battalion," Phillip said.

"So we're talking about a few hundred people," Weatherby said. "We'll need a task force to handle that."

"Well, he's talking about a first shipment to equip a platoon," Phillip said. "Deliveries would be spread out over several weeks, so we wouldn't be dealing with a battalion-sized force."

"Okay," Weatherby said. "Good to know. That's more manageable, but I'll still want reinforcements. Do you know where to find Martínez?"

"We tried to follow him after his last contact with Phillip,"

Paul said, "but he lost us at a gated community in Coral Gables. We couldn't very well follow him in there."

"Where in Coral Gables?" Ortiz asked.

Connie gave him the address. "Why do you ask?"

"Cruz has a house listed for sale in there. I staged it for showing a few days ago, and then he pulled it, said he didn't want it shown yet. He didn't say why, but I can guess. My bet is Martínez is holed up there."

"There is another person who may be involved," J.-P. said. "Dani said you mentioned someone named Willy."

"Yes. Martínez dropped out of sight a few days ago, and somebody called Willy started talking to Cruz about this invasion thing. But that's all I know. Just Willy — no last name, nothing."

"I think this must be Guillermo Maldonado," J.-P. said, "He is — "

The cellphone that Phillip had given to Luke Pantene rang, interrupting J.-P.

Phillip said, "Why don't I answer it and see who has the mated phone?"

Luke gave him the phone, and Phillip stepped into another room.

"Speaking of calls, I'm overdue to check-in with Cruz," Ortiz said. "That is, if we want to keep my cover intact with him. I'll be vague — tell him everything's going according to plan."

"Do it," Weatherby said.

"Where's my phone, Dani?"

"In a drawer under the chart table. Come with me; I'll get it for you."

---

## 25

"I heard from Cruz," Maldonado said. "He just got a call from Ortiz."

"And?" Martínez asked.

"Everything is going well. He spent the day on the yacht with the two women, and he's just finished dinner with the whole group."

"Okay. What are his prospects with the Berger girl? Solid? Are they getting along?"

"He's spending the night with her on the yacht," Maldonado said. "That sounds positive to me."

"Yeah," Martínez said. "Good for him. Did Cruz give him the message?"

"What message?"

"About him being our main source of information now that Olsen is gone."

"Yeah, he did. Ortiz is cool with that. He passed along some information already," Maldonado said.

"Tell me."

"Two things. There's a new arrival, a man from Dominica that

they call Sharktooth. Ortiz says he's a giant. He couldn't get any
other name for him, though."

Martínez chuckled. "Yeah, he's a big man, all right. Nobody
ever found out what his real name is."

"You know about this man?" Maldonado asked.

"Yes. He's part of that group from way back, one of Berger's
partners for as long as I've been around. Get the word to Ortiz to
watch his step. It's easy to underestimate Sharktooth. He's big and
black, and he speaks mostly patois. Sometimes, he passes as a
Voodoo *houngan*. He can give the impression that he's not bright.
About the time you decide he's not all there, he'll blindside you."

"Blindside how?"

"That depends. He's a genius, for one thing. PhD from Whar-
ton. And he can move faster than any man I've ever seen,"
Martínez said. "He's dangerous in every way you can think of. Oh,
and besides the Queen's English, he's fluent in French and
Spanish."

"Wow. From the way Ortiz described him to Cruz, I had a
different picture. Dreadlocks to his waist, bald on top. I wouldn't
have been surprised to hear he had a bone in his nose."

"I wouldn't be surprised, but it would be there only to mislead
somebody," Martínez said. "Like I said, a dangerous man. You said
Ortiz had two things. What else did he learn?"

"Yeah. Besides this Sharktooth showing up, Ortiz overheard
Phillip Davis talking with somebody on the phone about Olsen.
A few minutes later, he heard Davis tell J.-P. Berger that Olsen
killed himself."

Martínez smiled and nodded. "Anything else?"

"Not yet, but he'll call later. They're sitting around talking.
He's trying to pick up as much as he can while he, ah ... entertains
the girl."

"Perfect," Martínez said. "That's exactly as we planned it. I
should call Davis soon, then."

"WHAT DID HE SAY?" Weatherby asked, as Ortiz came back into the room after his call to Cruz.

"He gave me a big pep talk; they've lost their other source of inside information. That means they're counting on me for insight into what's happening here."

"That tracks with what I was told," Phillip said, pulling out his chair and sitting down. He handed the modified iPhone back to Luke Pantene.

"Who called you?" Pantene asked.

"Wait a second; let's finish one thing before we start something else," Phillip said. "What else did Cruz have to say?"

"Not much, except that I should stay alert. 'Shit's gonna start happening fast, now,' he said. I'm supposed to suck up to Dani and be ready for further instructions soon. That's about it." He squirmed in his chair as he tried to ignore the cold stare that Dani focused on him.

"Okay, thanks," Phillip said. "Sorry, Luke; I didn't mean to be rude. Just worried about losing details."

"No problem," Luke said, nodding.

"Back to your question," Phillip said, "whoever it was didn't identify himself, but the implication was strong that he was Olsen's boss — whatever 'director' he was reporting to." He paused for a moment. "Luke? Mary? Any thoughts on what agency we're dealing with?"

"Typical," Mary Weatherby said. "Directors in our intelligence services are as common as bank vice-presidents, or English sparrows. He could be anybody. Do you know where he is, physically?"

"No," Phillip shook his head.

Luke nodded. "Ever since all the shakeups and consolidations after 9/11, there's no making sense out of the intelligence organizations. What did he say? Anything besides the news of Olsen's death?"

"I think I got a kiss-off," Phillip said. "He told me they wouldn't replace Olsen, and that I should work directly with Martínez from now on."

"Does that mean the U.S. government concurs in this invasion?" J.-P. asked.

"I pressed him on that point," Phillip said. "I got a non-response. He said, 'Work with Martínez. Nothing has changed.' Then he hung up. When I called back, I got a recording that said the number wasn't in service."

"That quickly?" J.-P. asked.

"It was a recording, J.-P. Don't draw any conclusions from it, except that they're not going to answer any more calls," Phillip said. "It could have come from the voicemail associated with that number. Or anywhere."

J.-P. nodded. "He gave you conflicting instructions."

"He certainly did," Phillip said.

The group fell silent as everyone thought about what they had learned. After a couple of minutes, Phillip said, "There are a few more bits of information everyone should have." When everyone was looking at him, he resumed speaking. "J.-P. asked Mario Espinosa to find out which exile groups might be involved in this. The answer is puzzling; none of them knows anything about it. The next piece of information is that this man you mentioned, David, this 'Willy,' could be a suspected DGI agent named Guillermo Maldonado. His nickname is Willy. One possibility is that the Cuban government is behind this — not the exiles."

"Why?" Weatherby asked.

"Back in the '90s, a DGI agent named Avila surfaced here. He claimed he'd been funding Alpha-66 and other exile organizations in anti-Castro attacks. He said his mission had been to help Fidel justify some of his anti-American posturing."

"Whoa!" Mary Weatherby said. "We need to think about that. But why now?"

"That's a fair question," Phillip said.

"Suppose they staged an invasion and then accused the U.S. of harboring terrorists?" Phillip suggested.

"But there's been a thaw in relations over the last few years."

"Yes, but maybe Raul Castro doesn't want rapprochement anymore," Dani said. "Look what happened to the rest of the communist countries, once we exported capitalism. But where are their troops? A platoon's roughly 30 people, right?"

"Right," Phillip said.

"If there were 30 exiles mixed up in this, Mario's friends would have picked up on it," J.-P. said.

"Unless they were mercenaries, not exiles at all. That's where Martínez's roots are," Phillip said.

"Hold that thought," Weatherby said. "I need to make a phone call; I may know where the troops are quartered."

As she left the room, Phillip's personal cellphone rang. He stepped outside to answer; he wasn't surprised to hear Martínez's voice.

"We must talk, *señor*. Walk up to the causeway and watch for my truck in the next few minutes."

PHILLIP WAS STANDING in the shadows on the shoulder of the MacArthur Causeway, outside the guard rail. He was at the corner of the Star Island turnoff, watching for the white pickup truck. He spotted the westbound truck when the driver signaled for a right turn. The truck pulled out of the traffic lanes, stopping at the corner opposite Phillip. He stepped out of the shadows and approached the passenger door.

"Good evening, *señor*," Martínez said, as Phillip buckled his seatbelt. The truck accelerated back onto the causeway, headed toward Miami. I was sorry to hear about the general."

Phillip didn't respond to that. "What's on your mind, José?"

"Can you deliver in 24 hours? At midnight?" Martínez asked.

"We could, but you haven't paid us yet."

"You wish to use the same account from years ago?" Martínez asked. "In the Bahamas?"

"That will work," Phillip said.

"Good. We have the number. When I drop you off, I will make the call. You will have the money first thing in the morning. We will pick up the shipment at midnight tomorrow night in White-water Bay. We will be in four 50-foot ocean racers. You come in from the Shark River Entrance, yes?"

"Yes." Phillip said. "I think we can make that happen, as long as there are no unexpected problems."

"We will take steps to guard against unexpected problems, *señor*."

"It's short notice, José. Can I reach you somehow if something goes wrong?"

"I will know, *señor*. Do not let anything go wrong from your side. I believe you have been told that there could be ... repercussions ... Is that the word?"

"What do you mean?"

"We know that Olsen warned you that this was not optional, if you and *Señor* Berger wish to avoid difficulty with your government."

"Is there anything else, José? I need to get back and get to work to make this happen."

"Nothing, *señor*. I will see you at midnight."

Martínez pulled off onto the shoulder. He had turned around at the west end of the causeway and was now across the road from where he had met Phillip a few minutes earlier. "Good night, *señor*."

"Good night," Phillip said, as he got out and closed the door.

The truck sped away toward the beach while Phillip waited for a break in traffic so that he could cross the causeway to reach the Star Island entrance.

## 26

"No, Santos. Don't use François; I want you to handle this yourself. It's critical, and François hasn't been with us long enough. Besides, we don't want the girl harmed, and who knows what he might do to her. We fully intend to turn her over to them when we pick up the weapons."

"Okay, okay. I got it, Manny. Pick her up, but treat her good. What about Ortiz? How come he can't do this?"

"Because they don't know he's one of us. We need to preserve his cover. He has more to do with them at Star Island."

"You don't want me to take him too, then?"

"No, leave him. We want him to go back to the compound and keep an eye on them. Don't worry about him; I'll explain it to him after you've got the girl, but you need to make it look like a real snatch. Wear a mask, so he won't know it's you. Ortiz will be surprised; he won't know what's happening. He'll probably put up some resistance, so be ready."

"So he don't know I'm coming, then?"

"No. He thinks he's taking her upstairs to his place and keeping her there."

"He might call the cops or somethin'," Santos said.

"No. The first thing he'll do is call me to tell me he lost the girl. I'm going to act surprised and tell him he needs to play it straight. I'll tell him to call her father, like he has no clue what's going on. And at that point, he won't know shit, except what I tell him."

"I don't get how this is gonna work, Manny."

"Just do what I told you. Maldonado and I will handle the rest."

"Okay," Santos said. "So I'm gonna jump him in the parking garage at his place and snatch her. Then what?"

"Take her out to where the boats are hidden. You can stash her on one of them. Lock her up in the cabin if you want, but make sure there's nothing there she can use to break out, okay?"

"Yeah, yeah. Then what?"

"Stay there and keep an eye on her. Just make sure you don't attract any attention. That shouldn't be a problem, as far back up in there as the boats are."

"How long I gotta keep her there?"

"The delivery's at midnight. Sometime in the evening, Martínez will show up with the troops. He'll let you know what to do once he's there, but the basic plan is we'll turn her over to Davis or whoever shows up with the weapons."

"All right. When is Ortiz gonna take her to his place?"

"I'm going to call him now; I'll get a time from him. Sit tight for a minute."

~

"DID YOU SEE DANI AND ORTIZ?" J.-P. asked, when Phillip walked into the living room.

"No. Where would I have seen them?"

"They left a few minutes ago; I thought you might have passed them on the entrance drive," J.-P. said.

"No, but Martínez dropped me up on the causeway and I

walked back in, so they might have been gone already. I could have missed them. Where were they going?"

"Ortiz got a call from Cruz, maybe 15 minutes ago. He wanted Ortiz to take Dani to his place."

"Ortiz's place?" Phillip asked. "Why?"

"Cruz thinks that Ortiz has seduced Dani," Liz said. "Remember, that was his mission, after they decided not to kidnap her."

"Okay, I got that. But why take her to his place tonight? Especially this time of night?"

"Ortiz thinks they probably want him to spirit Dani away; turn her into a hostage of sorts," Paul said.

"That may be," Phillip said. "Things are starting to happen, all right. Martínez wants delivery tomorrow night." Phillip glanced at his watch. "Oops! Make that tonight."

"We haven't discussed arrangements for payment," J.-P. said.

"The money will be in the account in the Bahamas by the opening of business this morning," Phillip said.

"What if we don't agree to go forward?" J.-P. asked.

"Martínez reminded me that Olsen told us we didn't really have an option."

"Yes, I remember that," J.-P. said. "But we always have an option."

"That's probably why they want to hold Dani hostage," Connie said.

J.-P. grinned. "Dani may have other ideas."

Connie chuckled.

Weatherby looked at J.-P., a frown on her face. "Aren't you upset? She's your daughter!"

He smiled. "Yes. My daughter, to the core."

"What do you mean by that?

"I am not worried. I am disappointed," J.-P. said.

"You think she's on their side, then?" Luke asked.

At that, J.-P. laughed. "No. She is my daughter. She only knows one side. They have no idea what they've done."

"I don't understand your reaction, then," Weatherby said. "Why are you disappointed?"

"Because we're going to miss the fun," J.-P. said.

"Fun?" Weatherby said. "She's in danger."

"You do not know my daughter, Mary. Nor do you, Luke. Not like the rest of us know her. I appreciate your concern, but Dani wears danger like most young women wear jewels. She *is* danger. She has not led a sheltered life. When this is over, you will understand."

"Well," Mary Weatherby said, "you should all know that Cruz and company bugged Ortiz's apartment a few days ago. Audio and video. We discovered that, and tapped into their feeds. My people will be watching what goes on there, if that's any comfort to you. We can have people there in a matter of minutes, if things look risky."

"That's good to know," Phillip said. "You mentioned before I left that you might have a line on where Martínez's troops are."

"Yes, I was coming to that. We took advantage of what happened to the Vidal woman a few days ago. Ortiz managed to introduce another undercover agent called François. He's working for Santos in Little Haiti, handling collections and other strong-arm tasks. He basically took Vidal's place."

"And?" Phillip asked.

"He reported that there are 30 men from the D.R. staying in three of the apartments. I called him while you were gone to get more details. They've only been there a few days. François tangled with a couple of them when he went to collect the rent. He messed them up a little, and afterward, Santos told him not to collect rent from them. He said they had a different arrangement. François complained about the loss of income — he gets a commission on the rent. Santos told him to mind his own business, and that it was only for a few days."

"That sounds like it could be our phantom platoon," Phillip said. "If it is, they'll probably be moving out sometime today. Any

chance of you or Luke putting somebody in there to
watch them?"

"Already in motion," Weatherby said.

"And we have the house in Coral Gables under surveillance,
too," Luke added.

"I take it you got the go-ahead to work this, then?" Paul asked.

"We did," Luke said.

Mary Weatherby nodded. "But it'll be several hours before we
have extra bodies at our disposal. I can push that, now that you
have a delivery date."

"Pushing might be a good idea," J.-P. said. "Especially if you
plan to intercept them."

"WELL," Ortiz said, as they approached the high-rise building
where his condo was located. "You're getting your wish."

"What?" Dani said. She had ignored his attempts at conversation on most of the drive, only acknowledging him when he
talked about the exiles and their plot.

"You wanted to see my place. It's on the sixth floor in the next
building on the right. There's a sliver of ocean view from the
balcony."

"What makes you think I wanted to see your place?"

"You said you did, once."

She scowled at him. "When?"

"The night we went to the Thai place for dinner. We were in a
club afterward, and some of my friends were talking about neighborhoods — "

"That was before I knew you were an asshole," she hissed.

"I'm truly sorry that I misled you; you do understand it was
for a good cause, right? In the service of our country, and — "

"Please," she growled. "Next you're going to tell me to lie back
and think of England, you miserable bastard."

"England? What are you talking about?"

"Never mind, David. You'd probably take it the wrong way."

"Dani, I know I was a shit. If I could start all over, I'd ... " he shook his head and flipped the turn signal, slowing as he came to the entrance to the building's garage.

"I wasn't lying when I said I'd fallen for you." He stopped to insert the keycard to open the door. While it rolled up, he looked at her. The light from the security lamp over the door gave her face a stark, sallow look, but he flinched when he saw her eyes. Such a rich, dark blue when she was happy, they were as cold as the arctic ice now, and as deadly as gun barrels. He shuddered and looked away as the door opened fully.

"Don't press your luck," she said, "and don't get any romantic ideas, either. What I did to Lupita, I could do to you. I'm halfway there already."

He didn't say anything as he pulled into the garage, creeping along until he came to an open parking space. He pulled in and shut the engine off, opening his door and stepping out of the car. Walking around the back of the car, he reached Dani's door as she opened it. She got out before he could help her. He saw a flicker of surprise in her eyes, and then there was an explosion of light and he felt himself slip to the floor as he lost consciousness.

Dani backed up against the inside of the open car door. A husky man with a stocking over his face was watching her, staying back out of her reach. She thought about pushing off the door to launch herself forward, but the unconscious Ortiz was in her way. Then she saw the pistol the man used to knock Ortiz out. The barrel was trained on her face, and the man held it with two hands as he shook his head.

"Don't," he said, in a normal tone.

She relaxed, and he nodded.

"Good," he said. "My orders are to see that you are not harmed. You will be our good-faith hostage. We will release you to your friends when they deliver the weapons tonight. You understand?"

"Who are you?" she asked.

"They call me Santos. Will you come with me without trouble? Or do I gotta handcuff you?"

"Where are we going?"

"Answer me, or I hurt you."

She studied the gun for a moment. "I'll come without a struggle."

"Good. Get in the car. You will drive. If you don't do like I say, I shoot you, but only so it causes pain. The first shot through your left calf, so you can keep driving. I know many places to shoot you without killing."

"That won't be necessary," she said. "I told you I'd come without a struggle."

He nodded and took a step back, giving her more room to get back into the car. "Climb over the console and fasten your seatbelt."

When she was buckled in, he sat down in the passenger seat and closed the door, keeping the pistol trained on her legs. "Back out of the parking place and follow the signs to the exit."

As she shifted into reverse and backed out, he took a knife from his shirt pocket, using his left hand. Keeping his eyes on her, he flicked it open with his left thumb and stuck the point under the roll of stocking below his chin. In one smooth stroke, he cut away the mask. Still watching her, he folded the knife closed and returned it to his shirt pocket.

## 27

O rtiz blinked several times; the light dazzled him, and at first, it had no definition. As he stared at it, it appeared to move. The motion slowed, and at last, the light was steady. He closed his eyes, thinking the light made his head hurt. The pain didn't go away. He opened his eyes, blinking again, wondering where he was. He'd been asleep; maybe he was hung over.

The surface beneath him was hard, unforgiving. He felt it with his right hand. "Concrete," he muttered. He turned his head to the right and saw the side of a sleek, red Porsche. That was familiar. To his left, several feet away, he saw a dark gray Mercedes roadster with the top down and the dark, tinted windows raised. Sitting up, he spotted foot-high numbers — "219" — stenciled on a white-painted concrete block wall.

As the throbbing in his head receded, he realized he was in his parking place in the ground-level garage beneath the condo building where he lived. He'd brought Dani Berger here. He recalled watching Dani getting out of his car, but after that, he couldn't remember anything. He looked around, confirming where he was. His car wasn't here; and neither was Dani.

He raised a hand to the side of his head and found his hair matted with blood. The area behind his right ear was tender to his touch. He'd brought Dani here at Cruz's instructions, expecting that he'd be told to take her somewhere else before morning. "Morning," he mumbled. "What time is it?" He looked at his watch. It was five minutes after one a.m. He'd only been out for a few minutes.

His memory was returning quickly. He had seen a look of surprise on Dani's face, and then his head had exploded in a burst of bright light. Somebody must have hit him from behind and taken Dani and his car. Putting his right hand on the concrete floor, he levered himself onto his knees. Leaning against the red Porsche, he rose to a standing position, testing his equilibrium. Feeling steady on his feet, he patted himself down. Nothing was missing from his pockets except his car keys, which were on a separate ring from the key to his condo.

"Not a mugger, then," he whispered to himself. He spent a few seconds thinking about what he should do. Cruz had sent him here, and his condo was bugged. Cruz would be wondering where he was, by now. So would Mary Weatherby and Dani's friends at Star Island. He pulled his cellphone out of his pocket and speed-dialed Cruz.

"Somebody sandbagged me and took the girl and my car," he said, when Cruz answered.

"Yeah?" Cruz said. "Who? Did you get a look at them?"

"No," Ortiz said. "What do I do now?"

"Stay cool, Ortiz. Have you called the cops?"

"No. Should I?"

"No, don't. That would waste too much time. I'll get somebody to work on it right away. We'll find her. Meanwhile, get your ass back to Star Island and let her father know what happened, okay?"

"Should I call them first?"

"Yeah, that's probably a reasonable thing to do. Call them and tell them; see if they have any idea who could be behind this. We picked up rumors that somebody else was trying to get her father to sell them a nuke."

"Somebody else?" Ortiz asked. "Like who?"

"Maybe some far-out, radical exile group. I don't know who they are, or if it's even real. Sounds like maybe it is, though."

"You don't know what happened? One of our people didn't take her for some reason?"

"You maybe got a concussion, Ortiz? Why the hell would one of our people take her? You *are* our people; *you* had her, man. You okay?"

"No. I mean, yeah, I'm okay. But I didn't know about the other exile group. Maybe I wasn't careful enough. I thought once I got her here, we'd move her somewhere else. You know?"

"Yeah, Ortiz. That was the plan, all right. I was going to have someone pick her up and then send you back to Star Island to tell her folks she'd been snatched by somebody. But now I don't know what the hell's going on."

"So what should I do, Manny?"

"Like we said. Call her people and tell them what happened. See if they got any ideas. Then go back to Star Island and hang out with them; help them figure out what to do, and stay in touch with me. The deal's going down tonight, so watch out for anything that might be suspicious, like we talked about, okay?"

"Yeah, okay. I got it," Ortiz said.

"Good. Glad you didn't get hurt bad," Cruz said. "I gotta go pass the word about this. Call me if anything changes." He disconnected the call.

Ortiz thought for a few seconds and then dialed Mary Weatherby's cellphone number from memory.

DANI GLANCED down at the dash display as Santos fiddled with the car's navigation system. She noticed that the pistol didn't waver, and he kept her in his peripheral vision. He'd done this kind of thing before. That was good in a way, she knew. It meant that he wouldn't shoot her by accident or in a moment of panic if something unexpected happened. On the other hand, it meant that he wasn't likely to slip up and give her an opening to escape.

"Flamingo," she said, when he had finished working on the touch screen.

"You know Flamingo?" he asked. "You been there?"

"Yes. I spent a lot of time in this area when I was growing up."

He was quiet for several seconds. "You know the way, then?"

"Yes, I think so. It's been a few years. The roads might be different now."

"Follow the GPS," he said. "It won't do you no good to try to make no wrong turns. That would make me mad."

"Okay," she said. "Flamingo's like the edge of the world, from what I remember. How long have you been going there?"

"Years," he said. "Why?"

"Has it changed much? Gotten built up in the last ten years?"

He laughed and shook his head. "No."

"So it's still around a two-hour drive?" she asked.

"Yeah. We ain't goin' all the way to Flamingo, though."

"I don't remember anywhere to stop along the way," she said.

"You know Coot Bay? Coot Bay Pond?" he asked.

"No. Why?"

"That's where we go. Coot Bay Pond."

"What's there?"

"We leave the car there and take a canoe."

"Into the Everglades, huh?" she asked.

"Yeah. Into the Everglades."

"Did you bring mosquito repellent?" she asked.

"Yeah, I got some. Don't worry. You gonna be fine, long as your friends deliver like they supposed to."

"Are we going to the delivery location?"

"You askin' a lot of questions."

"The conversation keeps me alert," she said. "You know, driving this late at night, no traffic. It's boring, kind of dangerous. It's easy to drift off. It helps to have somebody to talk to. Or I could maybe listen to the radio if you'd rather."

"That's okay. Maybe the radio later."

"We could talk about something else," she offered.

"Like what?"

"Boats. Sailing. The islands. I think I hear a trace of the islands in your voice."

He grinned at her. "You can tell where I am from, maybe?"

"Maybe. You aren't from one of the islands that used to be British."

"No," he said.

"Or French," she said.

"No. You right so far."

"Maybe I hear a trace of *Papiamento*, or it could be Spanish. I think Spanish."

He grinned, waiting.

"You don't sound Cuban. How about Puerto Rico?"

He shook his head.

"The Dominican Republic, then."

"Yeah," he said. "I'm from the D.R. You got a good ear."

"I've spent a lot of my life in the islands," she said.

"Which ones?"

"Up and down between St. Martin and Grenada. My father's from Martinique."

"You sound American," he said.

"My mother's from New York."

"So, you *are* American, then?"

"Except when I'm French."

"When are you French?"

"When we are working in the French islands."

"We?"

"My business partner and I."

"What business? Arms?"

"No. We own and operate a charter yacht."

"From which island?"

"Different ones. She's U.S. flagged, our boat. That makes it easier to attract American clients, but we pick up and drop off wherever the client wants."

"That sounds like a good life. How are you involved in this arms business, then?"

"By accident, I guess," she said. "My father and his friends are here to celebrate my godfather's birthday."

"Your godfather, he lives in Miami?"

"Yes, for a long time. He came from Cuba as a child, before Castro."

"Ah, so he is why you are being used as a hostage. Your godfather, he is part of this plot?"

"I don't know much about it," Dani said. "He and my father, they trade all kinds of goods all over the world. I'm just a simple sailor."

"I see," he said.

"So now you know about me. Tell me about you, Santos. How did you end up holding a gun on me and making me drive into the Everglades at 1:30 in the morning?"

"It is the long story, like they say. And not so interesting."

"We have the time, and we both need to stay alert. Tell me," she said.

He sat for a few seconds, looking out the windshield, watching her from the corner of his eye. "You know *Bahia de Samaná*, and the town of *Samaná*?"

"Only from hearing about them. We haven't sailed in there, but I hear it's beautiful."

He laughed. "Perhaps, for rich tourists, it is beautiful. And maybe it has changed. For a small boy whose parents died, it was not so beautiful. So as soon as I could, I left. I got jobs on the little freighters, and when I came to Miami the first time, I decided to stay here. It was not easy ... "

Dani kept him talking, noticing that the more he told her, the more he relaxed. Before they got to Flamingo, she would know his life's story.

"YES, of course I called Cruz, Mary," Ortiz said. He sat in the living room with the others, sipping coffee to stay awake.

"But you didn't go up to your place? You never left the garage?"

"I didn't want to go in there; I was worried that it would look out of character. I mean, we know they have it wired. I couldn't think of any reason I would go there under the circumstances, so I stuck to doing things that would be easily explained. Why?"

"I wondered if there was any sign of intrusion," Weatherby said.

"Wouldn't the listeners have picked up an intruder?"

"They should have, but remember, we didn't wire the place, so we don't know where the blind spots are."

"I didn't think of that. You want me to go back?"

"No. That would be even harder to explain. It's probably not important. I just wondered. You say Cruz played dumb when you told him?"

"Yes. I asked him point blank if one of our people — you know, *his* people — took her. He asked if my thoughts were scrambled from the blow to my head. 'Why would we do that? We already had her — you had her,' he said, or something like that. He said there were rumors that there was another exile organization trying to buy nukes from J.-P. and Phillip. He suggested they may have taken her."

"I imagine that he wanted you to come back here to spy on us," Connie said.

"Yes, I thought the same thing," Ortiz said. "I asked him about that; I told him I had figured they were going to send somebody to pick her up from my place so I could come back here, and he agreed that he had planned to do that. He basically asked why he would have me attacked when I was on his team."

"Are you persuaded by that argument?" Weatherby asked.

"Not at all," Ortiz said. "It's plausible, though, and he presented it, so I have to pass it along. My gut tells me he set this up thinking that it would make my story to you more convincing. He is a devious bastard."

"I think you're right," Luke said.

"Me, too," Weatherby added. "But as you suggest, we should keep the other possibility in mind."

"What about Dani?" Ortiz asked.

"We put out a statewide alert for your car," Luke said. "That's the best we can do for now, unless we have an idea as to where they're going to take her, or for that matter, who took her."

## 28

Maldonado put his cellphone down and grinned at Martínez. "You probably overheard enough to know that Santos has the Berger girl."

"Yes. What about Ortiz?"

"He has no idea what happened. As best Cruz can tell, he was only out for a few minutes. Santos was careful not to hit him too hard. He called Cruz when he came to; Cruz planted the idea of some rival exile group. Ortiz seemed to accept it. Cruz told him there were rumors of some group wanting to buy a nuke from Berger and Davis."

Martínez laughed.

"What's funny, José?"

"I was imagining that Ortiz would tell Davis that some exile group that's trying to buy a nuke has kidnapped the girl."

"He probably will; that's what we hoped, isn't it? To give Santos time to get clear with her?"

"Yes, of course," Martínez said. "I hope the irony is not lost on Davis."

"The irony?"

"Yes. Davis started the story of the nuke. Never mind, Willy. Santos took Ortiz's car?"

"Yes. I still think he should have switched cars. They'll put out an alert for it, you know."

"It was not necessary to change cars. I explained that to you. It would have left more of a trail for them to follow, if they found Ortiz's car right away. As it is, Santos will abandon the car in the Everglades. By the time it's found and reported, this will be history."

Maldonado nodded. "I hope that you are right, José."

"I'm right. Is Ortiz going back to Star Island tonight?"

"Yes. He's probably already told them. Cruz told him to call them right away, not to just show up there. He said Ortiz was acting a little confused, which he thought was a good thing. He wanted to make sure Ortiz behaved like a normal guy whose girlfriend was just kidnapped."

"Good. The phone call would be the right thing, and then going there."

"Will you call Davis? Or are you going to call her father?" Maldonado asked.

"Davis. Why?"

"Wouldn't it have more impact if you called her father?"

"I've never dealt with her father; I couldn't read his reaction as well as I can Davis's. Besides, I don't want to alarm him. This isn't a kidnapping for extortion. They've already agreed to all the terms. This is just a little assurance that they will fulfill their commitment. We've sent them the money almost 24 hours in advance of delivery, and we've never inspected the weapons. I will present it this way to Davis. I don't want them to sense that she is being threatened. This is business."

Maldonado nodded. "When will you make the call?"

Martínez looked at his watch. "Soon. I want to allow time for Ortiz to get there; my call should be an assurance, not a surprise."

"Sʜʜ!" Phillip said, looking at the screen of his cellphone. The incoming number was the one Martínez had used on his last call. "This is probably Martínez." He tapped the screen and said, "Hello," putting the phone in speaker mode so that the others could hear.

"Good morning, *señor*. I hope that I did not wake you."

"Hardly," Phillip said.

"I did not think so. I trust that by now, you have heard from Ms. Berger's friend."

"Yes."

"He is well, I hope? We did not wish him any harm."

"He's all right, yes," Phillip said. "So it was you, then."

"Not me, personally, *señor*. But yes. I wanted you to know that we have Ms. Berger. She is well, and being treated with respect. It is not our intention to cause her father to worry. We mean no harm to her or any of you."

"I'm not sure that's believable," Phillip said.

"I understand, *señor*. Personally, I did not feel this was necessary, but my, ah, principals, they are nervous. We have paid the money, but we have not yet taken delivery of the goods. Nor have we even verified that you have them ready to deliver."

"You know us better than that," Phillip said.

"Yes, I do. But as I said, my associates ... "

Phillip let the silence hang.

"*Señor*?"

"Yes?"

"You understand?"

"Don't expect me to condone your tactics. I thought you were trustworthy. Now I'm not so sure. You say your principals don't know us as well as you do. You should explain to them that actions like theirs may have unpleasant consequences for them."

"Threats are not necessary, *señor*. They are honorable – "

"That was no threat. They should watch their backs. You may have unleashed something I'm not at liberty to explain."

"I think all will be well soon, *señor*. Ms. Berger will be at the delivery location we agreed to. I know you will do as promised, and you have my word that she will be turned over to your people the moment we have our goods."

"I hope it goes as you say it will," Phillip said.

"It will, *señor*. Please convey my assurances to *Señor* Berger. I called specifically to reassure him, because there was a rumor that his daughter was in the hands of that faction which is trying to buy the nuclear weapon. That is not so. I personally guarantee her safety."

"You're a brave man to do that," Phillip said. "*Buena suerte*. You have anything else?"

"No, *señor*. Until midnight, then." There was a click as Martínez disconnected the call.

"Do you think it was wise to threaten them?" Mary Weatherby asked.

Before Phillip could answer, J.-P. spoke. "It is as Phillip said. They have no idea what they have done." He chuckled.

"To be clear," Weatherby said, "I intend to arrest these people. There will be no settling of scores tonight."

J.-P. nodded.

"I'm glad that we agree," Weatherby said.

"I don't think you quite understand, Mary," Liz said. "They'll be lucky if they make it to the rendezvous."

"What am I missing?" Weatherby asked.

"Dani," Sharktooth said. "She not signed up to your plan, see."

"But she's their prisoner," Weatherby said.

"Did you ever read O. Henry?" Connie asked. "You sound like a literate woman."

"Yes, I've read some of his work. Why?"

"How about *Ransom of the Red Chief*?" Connie asked.

Weatherby shook her head. "It's been since college. I don't remember that one."

"Too bad," Connie said. "I have a feeling we're going to see a re-enactment. If not, you should look it up later. It's one of his better stories."

"Okay, damn it, I want an explanation."

"The short version is they'll be sorry they ever met Dani," Paul said, "and at this point, it's out of our hands anyway. I'd vote for a little sleep. We're going to have a long day."

Phillip looked at his watch. "It's two o'clock. There's not much we can do until tomorrow. J.-P. can call the bank around nine to verify receipt of the funds, although I'm not sure that matters now. We'll have to leave here late in the afternoon to pick up *La Paloma* and make the drop in Whitewater Bay at midnight. Mary, have you and Luke got your resources lined up for the bust?"

"Yes," Luke said. "We'll need to work out all the details during the day, but they're committed. We'll have a couple of Coast Guard 45-foot RBMs and a 110-foot cutter standing by offshore, with a few other special-purpose craft, including an airboat in case somebody takes off through the 'Glades. The mission commander wants to let them pick up the weapons in White-water Bay and then intercept them in open water after they get into the Gulf. They'll have a chopper, too."

"Sounds good enough for now," Phillip said. "Let's everybody find a place to stretch out and crash. How about breakfast around 8:30?"

# 29

"There's a dirt road about 100 yards ahead on the right," Santos said. "Slow down and turn."

Dani flicked the turn signal on and took her foot off the accelerator. "You have a canoe or something here?"

"Yeah. Canoe and a coupla kayaks. We take the canoe. Follow this road as far as you can. It's not far."

"The undergrowth's going to scratch Ortiz's car," she said, hearing the scraping sounds.

"This is good. Just stop."

"There's nowhere to pull over," Dani said.

"No problem. Just stop. It don't go much farther."

She stopped and put the car in park, shutting off the engine. She turned and looked at Santos, waiting for him to speak.

"Good. I'm gonna get out; you stay put until I tell you." He brandished the pistol.

"Okay," she said, keeping both hands on the wheel.

Santos opened his door and got out, walking around the front of the car and facing her, the pistol trained on her through the windshield. He nodded and motioned with his left hand for her to come toward him. She got out, closing her door and locking the car with the electronic key fob.

When she was a few steps from him, he reached into his pants pocket with his left hand and withdrew a key ring. He tossed it to her and said, "Follow the road. The canoe is under a camouflage tarp on the right in a few yards." He kept the pistol trained on her and backed into the undergrowth, allowing room for her to pass him without getting too close.

She spotted the tarp, more from the change in the visual texture than from anything else. The moon was close to full, bathing the undergrowth in silvery shadows. Stopping, she looked over her shoulder.

He nodded. "That's it. Push the tarp back. The canoe's chained to a log. One of them keys will fit. Go on and unlock it."

She bent and fumbled with the keys until she found one that fit the lock. She took the padlock off the chain and snapped it shut. Holding the keys in her left hand and the lock in her right hand, she straightened up. "Got it," she said, moving to toss him the keys.

"No!" he barked, a wary look on his face. "Put 'em in your pocket. We need 'em for the boat."

She smiled at his caution and put the keys and the lock into the pockets of her shorts. He was a pro; he didn't want to be distracted by catching the keys. She'd been testing him; she'd wanted to pocket the lock. She wouldn't have taken him yet, anyway. She wanted to know where the boats were hidden, first. "Okay," she said.

"Flip it upright and drag it into the road," he said. "The water's straight ahead. Just grab that rope on the end and pull it along behind you."

Once she had the canoe in tow, she asked, "You want me to launch it?" She could see the glint of the moonlight on smooth water a few yards farther on.

"Yeah. Push the front end of it straight out from the mud.

Leave the back end on shore." He watched as she followed his instructions. "Good. You ever been in a canoe?"

"Yes," she said.

"They wobble," he said. "Don't do nothin' until I tell you. Be real careful when you get in. There's monster alligators in here."

She'd already noticed that one was watching from a few yards out in the water. The eyes and nostrils that broke the surface were the only giveaway. "I see one," she said, pointing.

"There's more. Big bastards, too. Get in the canoe and go up to the front. There's a brace thing across it. Step over that and kneel down facing out."

She stepped over the gunwale on the starboard side of the canoe, placing her left foot in the center. Dropping to a crouch, she grasped the gunwales with her hands, one on each side, and swung her right foot over.

She worked her way forward until she was past the forward-most thwart. Kneeling, she sat back against the thwart, keeping one hand on each gunwale. She felt the canoe shift as Santos heaved his bulk aboard. Glancing over her shoulder, she saw that he had put his left foot in the center, as she had done.

His left hand gripped the port gunwale; he held the pistol in his right hand, pointed in her general direction. Putting his weight on his left leg, he gave a strong thrust against the muddy shore with his right leg. The canoe lurched forward, spooking the big gator, which disappeared without leaving a ripple.

The canoe rocked and continued to drift forward as Santos settled into a kneeling position. "There's a paddle on the left side up there," he said. "It's held in with Velcro. Pull it loose."

When she had the paddle free, he said, "We're gonna go right straight up the middle. It's shallow, so use the paddle to push against the bottom. That's easier than tryin' to row this thing in a straight line."

"Paddle," Dani said, as she extended the paddle until she felt the soft bottom. She applied a bit of force, and the canoe moved forward.

"What?" Santos said.

"You paddle the canoe in a straight line. Row is something else; you do that with oars."

"Whatever," he said. "You know how to *paddle* this thing?"

"Yes."

"Good, 'cause in a few hundred yards, we're gonna be out in Coot Bay. It's a little deeper. Not so easy to reach the bottom with the paddle."

"That's okay," she said. "It'll be a lot faster if you put the pistol down and help paddle. You'd have plenty of warning if I tried to jump you, as unsteady as this thing is."

"All right, but I'll make us go all over the place," he said.

"I'll teach you how. You're right-handed?"

"Yeah."

"Then only paddle on the left side. Don't try to use much muscle. Put your paddle in the water when I put mine in. Stroke like you see me stroke. If you see us going off to the side, dip the paddle in and turn it so it's cutting the water like a knife blade as we coast. Then you can twist it to steer. Give it a try and see if you can keep us going where you want."

After a minute or two of erratic zig-zagging, Santos managed to hold a reasonably straight course. "That's pretty damn cool," he said.

"You're getting it, Santos. Now give me an idea of where we're going so I can help."

"We're about halfway to Coot Bay," he said. "There's a gap in the mud and grass straight ahead. We're gonna go through that and then straight across Coot Bay. There's a creek that leads out of Coot Bay into Whitewater Bay, then we follow the shoreline around to the right. It's maybe four or five miles to the boats."

"Okay, good. Let me know if you want me to help turn us one way or the other."

"I got it. This isn't so damn hard, if you know what you're doin'. Where'd you learn this?"

"Boats are how I make my living, remember?"

"Yeah. Good, 'cause I don't know shit about them."

"I thought you ran away to sea when you were a kid."

"Yeah, but I didn't learn nothin' about boats. I learned about mops and scrub brushes and liftin' heavy stuff."

"I NEED to go meet Cruz at the apartments and start getting the troops sorted out," Martínez said. "You're planning to be at the delivery, right?"

"Yes, but I'm only going that far. I want you and Cruz to carry on to Cuba from there without me."

"No front-line combat for you, huh, Willy? It's not the real thing, you know. They're going to be waiting for us. Cruz and those poor bastards won't have a chance. You wouldn't have to get your hands dirty."

"That's not it, José. You know I need to stay back here and manage the media coverage."

"Sure you do," Martínez taunted him. "Why are you even going to the drop? It's muddy and nasty. There will be snakes and alligators."

"Fuck you, Martínez. I'll be shooting video of the whole thing. We'll have plenty of moonlight. It would be a waste without the media coverage."

"Don't be upset, Willy. I'm just giving you a hard time. What are you going to do once we head out?"

"Santos will bring me back to Miami. I'll have to sort out the mess here, since Cruz won't be coming back."

"You have somebody to take his place?" Martínez asked.

"I think so. I'll run it through Ortiz and Santos until all the details are public. Once Cruz is executed, I'll call a meeting of my fellow investors and we'll pick a successor."

"Not Ortiz, then?"

"No," Maldonado said. "He's done a decent job so far, but he's not one of us. Not yet. There's a guy in New York that I have in mind, maybe."

"Anybody I know?"

"I don't think so. No reason you would. Why?"

"I like Miami," Martínez said. "I'm getting too old for this shit."

"You're only in your late forties, José. Phillip Davis is your age, isn't he?"

"Yeah, and he's retired."

"He's not, either," Maldonado said. "He's in the middle of this, just like you."

"Only because I put him in the middle. He hasn't been in the line of fire in years. Guys like me and Davis, we've used up our nine lives. They call it infantry for a reason. Ground war's a young man's game, Willy. I need to get out before somebody takes me out."

"You're serious, aren't you?"

"Yes, I am," Martínez said.

"How would we work it? I mean, people know you. Like Davis, for example. There are others like him that have run across you over the years."

"I'd have to be a different person. Maybe a little cosmetic surgery. Think about it, Willy."

"Yeah, I will. But first you have a job to do, José. How will you avoid getting shot when you hit the beach, anyway?"

"I'll keep my head down, don't worry. Besides, the men defending the beachhead all know me. I hand-picked them for this ambush. It's going to be a slaughter; Cruz will be the only survivor."

"And then what happens to him?" Maldonado asked.

"He'll confess, and blow the whistle on Davis and General Olsen."

"Why is he going to do that?"

"In exchange for clemency; he thinks he'll serve a few months in prison and then be released and deported back to the U.S.," Martínez said. "He's all set to be a hero with the exiles; the dumb bastard's talking about running for elected office."

"What a fool," Maldonado said. "Can't he see that could never happen?"

Martínez grinned and shrugged. "Who knows?"

"WE'RE GOING up into that little break in the mangroves," Santos said. They were following the northern shore of Whitewater Bay, a few yards off.

"That one?" Dani asked, pointing.

"Yeah, there's a little open area up in there, big enough for the four boats."

"Are they under cover?"

"You mean from the air?"

"Yes," Dani said.

"The trees close it off almost completely. Why?"

"Just curious. Are you going to want me to call my father or anything?"

"No. He's been told, by now. Besides, cellphones don't work out here, so don't waste your time once I lock you up."

"Okay. So you use satellite phones?"

"Yeah. What are you getting at?"

"It would go better for you if he knew I was all right; you don't know him. He's probably going nuts right now. It'll soon be dawn; he could have the Florida National Guard out with choppers, for all we know. My godfather's a big donor to the Governor's campaign fund. Maybe you should at least check with your boss."

"Stop here, before we get under the trees."

"Why?"

"They block the satellite. I got the pistol back in my hand, so don't do nothin' stupid, okay?"

"Okay." She looked straight ahead, listening to his whispered conversation. Smiling to herself, she considered her next steps.

"He said no calls to your father," Santos said. "Everything is fine; you got no worries. Come midnight, you be back with your friends. Now paddle us up in there."

"Whatever you say." With a few deft strokes, she took the canoe into the narrow channel.

About ten meters in, the mangroves opened up. Four sleek, 50-foot ocean racers were tied with their sterns to the mangroves on the opposite side of the little bay. The dark gray, matte finish made them almost invisible in the shadows of the trees.

"Take us to the outside of the one on the right," Santos said.

As the canoe scraped up against the side of the bigger boat, Santos stood up, facing the ocean racer. The canoe rolled in a violent reaction to his shifting weight. He grabbed the gunwale of the bigger boat to keep his footing.

Reaching out with her left hand, Dani laid her palm on the big boat, steadying them while she twisted to put the paddle in the canoe behind her. "Now what?" she asked.

"You see them steps in the side a little to your right?"

"The molded-in ones?" she asked.

"Yeah. Them," he said. "Go on and climb up there. Then stand there and don't move until I'm up. I will shoot you if you try to run. There's nowhere to go, anyway. Go on!"

Dani put both hands on the big boat's gunwale as her end of the canoe began to drift away from the side of the boat.

"Hold us!" Santos yelped.

"Okay," she said, putting her left foot up on the canoe's gunwale. She saw that he had lost his balance. He held on to the big boat with his left hand and had his right elbow resting on the big boat's gunwale, supporting most of his weight. His right forearm lay on the side deck of the ocean racer as he tried to lever himself up. The pistol, still gripped in his right hand, pointed away from her.

She lunged, thrusting hard with her left leg, pushing the canoe out from under Santos as she scrambled up onto the big boat's narrow side deck.

"Shit!" Santos yelled, as he was forced to hang on with his left hand and his right elbow. In his panic, he dropped the pistol on the side deck.

Dani, by now crouched on the deck in front of him, snatched the pistol and shoved it in her waistband. Santos, intent on not losing his grip, didn't notice.

"Help me up!" he barked, his feet scuffling in the bottom of the canoe, which was no longer below his center of gravity. Only his toes kept it from drifting away.

Reaching over his right shoulder, Dani hooked her fingers under his armpit, grasping and pulling as she grabbed a handrail behind her with her other hand. "I've got you. Calm down, now."

"Get me up before the fuckin' gators — "

"Try to pull the canoe back under yourself with your feet," she said. "No way I can lift you."

"Okay, but don't let me go," he said, doing as she suggested.

In a moment, he was able to plant his feet in the canoe and take his weight on his legs. Sighing with relief, he said, "Thanks. I owe you big — "

Before he could finish, Dani swung her right hand around. Her middle finger was stuck through the shackle of the big padlock she'd taken from her pocket. The body of the lock was cupped in her palm. She drove the big hunk of laminated steel into his left temple with all her weight behind it. His eyes rolled back and he gurgled as he began to convulse.

Muttering "Paybacks are a mother," Dani dropped down into the canoe as he collapsed into it. She held onto the big boat with one hand, watching until he grew still. Reaching behind her, she found the canoe's bow line. She made it fast to a cleat on the big boat's side deck.

Kneeling in the bottom of the canoe, she felt for a pulse in Santos's neck. Deciding he was dead, she rifled his pockets. She found the satellite phone and an extra, fully loaded magazine for the pistol. Pocketing both, she remembered the folding combat knife he'd kept in his shirt pocket. She retrieved it and considered what to do with his corpse. She might want the canoe later, and he was too heavy for her to lift.

She climbed back onto the ocean racer and looked for a length of rope. Finding several ready-made dock lines in a locker, she took one and got back into the canoe. She tied the dock line around the end of the midship thwart that was closer to the big boat and climbed back up. Pulling on the dock line, she managed to capsize the canoe, spilling Santos into the dark water.

She watched for a minute, seeing a pair of eyes that looked to be a foot apart break the surface a few meters away. She spotted the alligator's nostrils as it began to glide toward the inert Santos. She was awestruck at the speed with which the gaping jaws opened and closed. With a sound that was eerily like the flushing of a toilet, Santos and the alligator disappeared. The huge creature left barely a ripple on the surface as it swam away to conceal its prize.

## 30

P hillip woke up at dawn. He was tired, but his mind was racing. He splashed some cold water on his face, deciding to treat himself to coffee before shaving. As he walked into the kitchen, his cellphone rang. He looked at the screen but didn't recognize the number. With a shrug, he answered.

"Yes?"

"Phillip?"

"Dani?"

"Yes. I — "

"Where are you?"

"I'm at the delivery location. A guy named Santos knocked David out and made me drive him out here. From what he said, they wanted to use me as a hostage."

"What number is this you're calling from?"

"A sat phone that Santos had. Why?"

"I wondered if it was being monitored. He let you use it?"

"He's not in a position to stop me; I don't know if it's secure. I wanted to let everybody know I'm okay."

"Where is Santos?"

"He's gone to feed the alligators. He's fascinated by them, I think. He's not going to catch me, if that's what you're worried about."

"Hmm. I see. Think he'll be back soon?"

"I doubt it; he didn't give that impression when he left."

"What did he tell you?"

"Not much worth repeating. He said they'd turn me over to you when the transfer was made at midnight tonight, that they had no intention of harming me. I asked to call you or Papa, and he checked with somebody, but they told him you'd already been informed, and not to let me make any calls."

"How did you get his phone, then?"

"It fell out of his pocket before he left."

"Where did he leave you?"

"I'm on the boats; there are four big go-fast boats tucked back in the mangroves off the north side of Whitewater Bay. Fifty footers, I'd say. I'm in the forward cabin of one of them."

"Are you locked in, or can you get out?"

"Maybe. I don't know how long I have."

"Can you hold on a second? Somebody just came into the kitchen."

"Call me back," Dani said. "I want to look around this boat a little bit."

"You think it'll be okay for me to call back?"

"Yes, if you're quick. But if a man answers, hang up. 'Bye."

Phillip put the phone down. "Good morning, Mary."

"Hi. Who were you talking to?"

"Dani. She got her hands on a sat phone that Santos had."

"She okay?"

"Yes, she's fine. She's at the delivery site, on one of their four boats."

"Santos let her call?"

"I don't think so. I was worried that the phone might not be secure, so our conversation was guarded. My guess is that Santos is dead."

"How? He's a ruthless bastard, and damned careful."

"Dani's an easy person to underestimate," Phillip said. "She grew up doing this kind of thing. She said Santos had gone to feed the alligators and that she didn't expect him back soon."

"Gone to feed the alligators? What the hell?"

"She probably whacked him and sunk his body in the swamp," Phillip said.

"So why doesn't she make a run for it?"

"That's not her style. She wanted to check out the boat she's on, but she didn't sound rushed at all. That's another reason I suspect Santos is dead. She was calling from the forward cabin of one of the boats, and she was evasive when I asked if she was locked in. Knowing Dani, that means she's free and exploring."

"What did she mean by 'check out' the boat?" Mary Weatherby asked.

"I don't know. She said she didn't know how long she had; I took that as a question. I'm sure she wants to know when the others will be arriving, but I don't know what to tell her."

"I just heard from the surveillance team in Little Haiti, speaking of that. Martínez and Cruz showed up a couple of hours ago and rousted the troops. They had another man with them. They loaded everybody into three vans and drove off into the Everglades."

"Any idea where they were going?"

"Yeah. They were tailed. They're in an abandoned training camp that used to belong to Alpha-66, not far from Flamingo."

"That's close to the delivery site," Phillip said.

"Right. I'm guessing he's staging them there. The tail said it looked like they had food and some boxes of uniforms. Maybe web gear: packs, canteens, that kind of stuff. Probably didn't want to move them in broad daylight."

"Or have them hanging around where the boats are hidden, either. People fish down in there," Phillip said. "Not many, but still, if I were Martínez, I'd wait until dark to move the troops to the boats."

"Good morning, Mary, Phillip," Luke Pantene said. "I smell coffee."

Phillip opened a cabinet and handed Luke a mug. "Help yourself. Sleep well?"

"I slept some. Not long after we turned in, I got a call from the team watching the house in Coral Gables. Martínez and a couple of other men left the house and headed over to Little Haiti, to that building where the 30 men from the D.R. were. My guys handed off to Mary's people once they saw where they went."

"Probably Maldonado and Cruz," Phillip said.

"Not Maldonado," Luke said. "He came outside with them, but they got in three vans and drove away. He went back in the house. He's still there."

"We got a positive i.d. on Cruz at the pickup," Mary said. "And the other man's a driver who works for Cruz; we've seen him around, but we don't have a name for him."

"I'd better call Dani back," Phillip said.

"What?" Luke asked, surprise in his voice.

"Tell him, Mary," Phillip said, walking outside with his coffee and his phone.

"More eggs, anyone?" Liz asked, as she and Paul passed steaming platters around the breakfast table. When everyone declined, she said, "Now tell us what we missed while we were in the kitchen."

"I think everybody could do with updates," Phillip said. "I was on the phone with Dani while you and Paul were cooking, and I left Luke and Mary following up with their people."

"You talked with Dani?" Liz asked, surprised.

"Twice," Phillip said. "We've been hampered, because we

aren't sure the phone she's using is safe, so a lot of this is guess-work on my part, based on hints she dropped."

"Is she all right?" David Ortiz asked.

"Of course she is," J.-P. said. "The only question is how much damage she's done to the other side."

"That's a good summary," Phillip said. "As best I can tell, it was Santos that kidnapped her."

"That makes sense," Ortiz said. "She should be very careful with him; he's violent and unpredictable. I'm surprised he let her use her phone."

Phillip nodded. "Her cell phone won't get a signal; she's using a satellite phone that she got from Santos." He held up a hand to silence Ortiz. "Let me tell you what I think, then we can talk about it."

Ortiz nodded, and Phillip continued. "As best I can tell, she disabled or killed Santos and took his phone. I think she's been searching the four boats."

"What has she found?" J.-P. asked.

"The only comment she made was that the bilge was contaminated," Phillip said. "I can't think what she was trying to tell us. She described where they're hidden. She hasn't said much else. My guess is, she's not going to be there when Martínez and company show up. She did say something about hiding a canoe, so I expect she'll be watching from close by, hidden in the canoe. Once the action starts, she'll probably call and give us a blow-by-blow description. By then they will have discovered that she and Santos are missing, so it won't matter if they know she's got the phone. I'm guessing she and Santos took a canoe from where they left the car. I did a little map reconnaissance. The closest you can get with a car is about five miles from where I think the boats are."

"Where the boats, you t'ink?" Sharktooth asked, producing a battered topographical map of the area around Flamingo. He spread it on the table where they could all see it.

"Here." Phillip put a finger on a patch of mangrove swamp in the northeast part of Whitewater Bay. "It matches with what she's said, and there's three or four feet of water leading up in there from the open part of Whitewater Bay, where we'll make the rendezvous. You can see where State Road 9336 passes close to Coot Bay Pond." He moved his finger to illustrate. "That's where I'm guessing they started the canoe trip."

"Won't Martínez need that canoe to get to the boats?" Connie asked.

"She did say there were a couple of kayaks stashed where they got the canoe," Phillip said. "If I were Martínez, I'd bring my big boats into Coot Bay to pick up the troops. There's not enough water in that little Coot Bay Pond, according to the charts in my iPad, but it's only a few hundred yards from the road to Coot Bay proper, which has three to four feet, bank to bank. He'll probably march them through the swamp for that little distance. That's about what I know. Any questions? Comments?"

After a few seconds of silence, Mary Weatherby spoke. "Okay, Luke and I talked with the Coast Guard while Phillip was on the phone with Dani. They're all set; they'll move into a position a couple of miles off the Shark River entrance sometime between nine p.m. and eleven p.m. Someone from my shop will bring a couple of radios by here so we can communicate with them."

"What about ground forces?" Phillip asked.

"We have a team on standby to close off the area if necessary," Luke said. "We're holding them back for now. There's too much chance of them being noticed, given that Martínez already has his troops in the vicinity. They'll have choppers, and we'll only need about five minutes to have 50 people on the ground."

"Sounds good," Phillip said. "I figured Sharktooth, Paul, Connie, Liz, and I would be the delivery crew. J.-P. will stay here, reachable by phone. Where will you and Mary be?"

"Is there room on the boat? *La Paloma*?" Mary asked.

"Sure, if that's what you want," Phillip said.

"We couldn't think of a better way to have a front-row seat," Luke said.

"We've got around a three-hour drive to get to *La Paloma*, not allowing for traffic. Then we'll spend another three hours or so on the run up to Whitewater Bay. How long will we need to cut the weapons out of their hiding places, Sharktooth?"

"No more than half an hour, I t'ink. I lef' a big angle grinder on board to cut the fiberglass bins open. We probably do that offshore, yeah?"

"Yes. I think we should leave here late this afternoon to beat the traffic headed for the Keys. We can give *La Paloma* a good going over, make sure she's still fit for sea, and then go have dinner somewhere in Marathon, if that suits everybody. We should get out of there around eight, to be safe. There's no harm in getting to Whitewater Bay a little early. Questions? Comments?"

When there was no response, Phillip continued. "There is one thing that bothers me. We need to find a way for the Cubans to come through this without losing face. If we go through with the deal, it looks like the U.S. is harboring terrorists. On the other hand, if we just arrest everybody and tell the world that Cuba was trying to make the U.S. look bad, it'll scuttle all the recent improvements in our relationship. Either way, Cuba loses, and so do we.

"Yes," Liz said. "That's been worrying me, too."

"You've got my attention," Luke said. "Mary and I are already taking heat about that. Right, Mary?"

"Right. The suits are stressed out over that very thing. You might imagine that the State Department and the President are somewhat alarmed. Does anybody have any ideas? We're closest to what's happening, here. I'm sure the people up the line would at least listen to our thoughts."

Liz said, "I've been talking with Connie and Paul about this. They had the same worry. Connie's the smoothest con artist I've ever run across – no offense, Connie. She's got a great idea, but Paul and I couldn't get her to propose it. How about it, Connie?"

Connie nodded. "Okay, but it's just a standard scam. I'm not sure we can make it work here. That's why I didn't want to say anything."

"It's worth a shot, Connie," Paul said. "Tell them."

"Okay, here goes. In the game, it was referred to as the 'some other dude did it' dodge. Let's say you want to make the mark think you're innocent after you've ripped him off. You act sympathetic and lay the blame on somebody else. There's nothing magic about it; it's all in the presentation, kind of like sleight of hand."

"So how would that work here?" Luke asked.

Connie smiled, warming to her role as con artist extraordinaire. "We've got a couple of ready-made scapegoats in Maldonado and Martínez. The idea we could plant with the Cuban government is that those two have gone rogue."

"Gone rogue?" Weatherby asked, looking interested. "What do you mean? Can you elaborate on that?"

"Yes. Our story could be that those two saw this as an opportunity to stage a coup," she said. "We aren't sure who they wanted to put in power, but they wanted to depose Raul Castro. They were going to somehow turn this fake invasion into the real thing. The only challenge for us is to show how they could have done it, when the Cubans are expecting them. Of course, they don't know that we know they were expecting the invasion; we can't let on that we figured it out. The big problem will be convincing them Maldonado and Martínez had the wherewithal."

"That's great," Phillip said, grinning. "The suitcase nuke is a perfect solution to that problem."

"What?" Luke and Mary Weatherby asked, in chorus.

"What suitcase nuke?" Paul asked.

"The one they were planning to use on *Punto Cero*," Phillip said. "It's perfect; it all fits."

"I'm lost, now," Connie said. "What's *Punto Cero*? Point zero?"

"It's the 75-acre compound outside Havana where Fidel spent his last years; it would be a perfect target for someone staging a coup," J.-P. said. "Symbolic, yes?"

"I'm just expanding on your story a little bit, Connie," Phillip said. "We already fed them the idea that somebody was trying to buy a nuke to use against Cuba, but we didn't say who it was. If we lead them to believe it was Maldonado and Martínez and we include the nuke in the shipment, they'll draw their own conclusions."

"What's this about a suitcase nuke, though?" Luke asked.

"We stuck one in the shipment, on the chance that we could use it to frame them somehow," J.-P. said.

"Don't worry, Luke, Mary. It's not armed," Phillip said.

"I got the trigger in my duffle bag," Sharktooth said, a big grin on his face. "We not goin' to deliver any working weapons."

"What about the rifles and machine guns?" Weatherby asked.

"Firing pins in my bag," Sharktooth said.

"I hope you're leaving that bag here, then," Luke said.

"I t'ink so," Sharktooth said. "When we firs' start to do this, we don' know how everyt'ing be workin' out. Now, t'ings lookin' good, yeah?"

# 31

D ani was awakened by the splashes of paddles breaking the surface of the water in the distance. She had been napping off and on since she finished with the boats late this morning. After making sure the canoe was well hidden in the tall marsh grass, she'd stretched out in the bottom to rest. Slipping the satellite phone from her pocket, she punched one of the keys and checked the time. It was 10:30 p.m.

It was close enough to showtime that she could safely call Phillip on his own sat phone. She'd like to know what their final plan was. He should know about her handiwork, as well, now that they didn't have to worry about whether the phone she'd taken from Santos was secure. Even if their call were monitored, it was too late for Martínez and his people to react. Before she could place the call, she heard a man's voice. Deciding he was too close, she put the phone away and picked up the pistol. Maybe she would get a chance to call Phillip later.

"Not much farther now, Willy. Just through those trees."

"Santos better be there," the other man said. Willy must be Maldonado, Dani figured.

"He should have been waiting with the canoe, back there

where the kayaks were chained," the first man said. "Something's not right."

"Shit, he's probably screwing that damn girl, José," Maldonado said, chuckling, his voice getting louder. "I would be, if I had the chance. She's hot. I see the boats, now."

"Any sign of the canoe?" the first man asked. He would be Martínez, Dani thought.

Two one-man kayaks meant two men. Not having the canoe would mean an extra trip to pick up two more men to drive the big boats. She smiled at the thought of having unwittingly put a hitch in their plans.

"I don't see it," Maldonado said. "You think he took her somewhere?"

"I don't know, Willy. He knew not to mess with her."

"Hey, I never figured he'd rape her, José. It's probably consensual. She looked like a fine, hot piece of ass, from those pictures Lupita took. She probably got bored waiting. You know how women — "

"Shut up, Willy."

Dani heard a kayak bump into one of the big boats.

"Santos!" Martínez called, rapping on the side of the boat with his knuckles. There was no response.

"Now what?" Maldonado asked.

"I'll take a boat back and pick up the two drivers. If Cruz has made it through the swamp, I'll go ahead and pick up the first load of troops, while I'm at it."

Dani heard them board one of the boats.

"This is going to mess up the schedule," Maldonado said.

"We've got some extra time. Cruz will get the men through that stretch of swamp a lot faster than the time I allowed. It's only a couple of hundred meters."

"You want me to look for Santos and the girl while you're gone?"

"No. Forget that. Get your video camera set up. You'll have to work from one of the kayaks."

"The canoe would be better," Maldonado said.

"That's like looking for a needle in a haystack, Willy. I told you, forget Santos and the canoe. Focus on the mission."

"But we have to give them the girl, José."

"I'll tell Davis there was a change of plan and that she'll be waiting for them at Star Island."

"You think he'll buy that?"

"He's got no choice."

"But what if he doesn't, José?"

"Then we'll just waste them. Shut up and get to work."

One of the big V-8 engines roared to life. In seconds, it had been throttled back to an idle, the water-cooled exhaust burbling. If Martínez and Maldonado were still talking, Dani couldn't hear them over the engine. The second engine started, and ten seconds later, she heard two clunks as Martínez engaged the transmissions. She could feel the throbbing of the propellers through the water under the canoe's bottom. The vibration died out as the boat moved away.

Dani estimated the boat's displacement speed and did a rough calculation, deciding Martínez would be gone for about 40 minutes. It would be about 11:10 when he got back. Another 40 minutes for the other three boats to pick up their passengers and return would give them a comfortable margin before midnight.

She heard Maldonado moving around on one of the remaining boats. Rolling over so that she faced away from the boats, she got up into a crouch and put on the military-surplus camouflage poncho that she'd found on the second boat she had searched.

She pulled the hood up to hide her blonde hair and reached over the side of the boat. Leaning over the gunwale until she felt the bottom, she scooped up a handful of greasy mud and smeared it over her face and hands. The mud smelled of decay, but it would hide her pale skin.

She was already starting to perspire under the poncho, but it couldn't be helped. She had to cover her white clothing. Unlike in the predawn hours, the full moon was directly overhead; the boats weren't in shadow now.

She sat down in the bottom of the canoe facing the boats and leaned back against the midships thwart, adjusting her position so that her eyes were even with the canoe's gunwale. She watched Maldonado assembling his video camera; it was a big, professional-looking one, like TV news teams used.

Finished, Maldonado stood up and hoisted the camera to his shoulder, facing out toward the center of Whitewater Bay and swinging the camera back and forth. Dani picked up the pair of binoculars she'd taken from another of the boats and raised them to her eyes. Maldonado flipped out the monitor screen on the side of the camera and adjusted some controls.

She could see that the screen changed from black to a silvery gray. She couldn't make out the image, but it was clear that he had set the camera to work in the bright moonlight. Maldonado put the camera on the side deck and climbed over the side of the boat, disappearing from Dani's field of vision. She thought he must have gotten in the kayak.

In a moment, she heard another bump from the big boat, and his head and shoulders appeared, just above the big boat's gunwale. He lifted the video camera and then disappeared again. In a few seconds, Dani heard the rhythmic splashes as he paddled out several yards into the Bay.

Peering through the tall grass with the binoculars, she saw that he was sitting in the kayak with the camera on his shoulder, testing it, getting comfortable shooting from the kayak. After several seconds, he put the camera in his lap and picked up the double-ended paddle, turning the kayak around and returning to the big boat. Dani slipped back down to a more comfortable position, listening as he secured the kayak to the big boat and climbed back aboard.

With nothing to do but wait, she closed her eyes, confident that if she slept, the sound of Martínez's boat returning would awaken her. She realized that she'd been napping again when she caught herself listening to the sound of the engines, waiting for them to stop. When they went silent, she heard several men speaking in soft tones.

After a brief period, Martínez raised his voice above the others. "Silence!"

The murmurs stopped, and Martínez spoke again. "Cruz, you and your two men take those three boats back and pick up the others. When you come back, you'll see this boat waiting out in open water. Come alongside and shut down your engines. We'll drift out there until they show up."

Dani heard the other three boats start their engines and leave. As the sound faded, she heard Maldonado and Martínez talking.

"Are you ready, Willy?"

"Yes. No problem. *Buena suerte*, José."

"You got the extra set of keys to Ortiz's car?" Martínez asked. "It's a long walk back to Miami."

"Yeah, José. I'm good. Don't worry about me."

Dani crossed her fingers, hoping Martínez's boat would start; she didn't want him stranded so close by with ten or twelve men, even if they were unarmed. She released the breath she was holding when the twin engines rumbled to life and the boat moved away. Now she began to worry that she'd miscalculated the fuel consumption. Maybe the engines were more efficient than she thought. It was too late to change anything now. She settled back into the canoe to wait for midnight.

"THE COAST GUARD'S IN POSITION," Mary Weatherby said. "They've got us on their radar."

"Good," Phillip said. "Ask them if we've got any company out here."

Mary relayed his question. She wore a headset with a boom microphone. "Nobody within ten miles," she said. "They asked how long before we reach the entrance channel. Once we're in, they're going to come in closer."

Phillip touched a couple of buttons on the GPS display mounted above *La Paloma's* helm. "Five minutes to Flashing Green 'I' at the Little Shark River channel entrance," Phillip said.

She spoke into the microphone again and then said. "Once we're inside the entrance, they'll close up."

"Warn them that Martínez has shallow-draft boats. He may have someone with local knowledge who can lead them out one of the other channels into Ponce de Leon Bay," Phillip said.

Mary spoke into the boom microphone and listened for a few seconds. "She says, 'Roger that, captain.' They'll spread out enough to cover all the entrances, but they don't want to give the go-fast boats room to use their superior speed."

"Good for them," Phillip said. "Sharktooth, did I hear you call J.-P. a minute or two ago?"

"Yes. I asked him if he's heard from Dani. Or anybody else. Everyt'ing quiet, he say."

"Okay. I figured by now she might have decided to call one of us even with the risk that the phone could be tapped. The other side doesn't have any reaction time, now, even if they're listening. Maybe she's not where she can speak openly. Is Ortiz still there with him?"

"Yes."

"No call from Cruz? Or Martínez?" Phillip asked.

"No. Nothing."

"Damn. It's too quiet," Phillip said. "I was hoping Dani would give us a heads-up on what they're doing in there.

"Are you worried that they may have some trick planned?" Paul asked.

"They could. We should be ready for anything," Phillip said. "Hey, Sharktooth?"

"Yeah, mon?"

"Time to bring up our weapons."

Sharktooth grinned and went down into the main cabin.

"I'm good. I've got my Glock," Mary Weatherby said.

"Me, too," Luke added.

"Good, but you'll be better off with M4s, at least until we see what's up. Who's checked out on the M249?"

Connie and Liz both spoke up.

"Good," Phillip said, "but we only brought two that work. Let Sharktooth have one; he's big enough to shoot a machine gun like a rifle. The two of you take the other one. Whichever one isn't shooting can feed ammunition. I want everybody armed with a long gun, with a round in the chamber and the safety on. No pistols in a fire fight between boats, please. Save 'em for close work."

"Are you expecting a firefight?" Mary Weatherby asked.

"Yes, always. But I'll probably be disappointed," Phillip looked at her and grinned. "I hope I am, anyway." He throttled back as the banks of the Little Shark River closed in on both sides.

"We'll be into Whitewater Bay in about ten minutes," Phillip said. "Get yourselves sorted out. We'll be working our way through a bunch of little islands in a couple of minutes. Once we're out of them, the Bay will open up. It's around three miles across. I'll keep heading roughly east until we spot them. That should be easy, with all this moonlight."

"I'll advise the Coast Guard as soon as we spot them," Weatherby said.

"And is the ground team listening in?" Phillip asked.

"Yes. On the same frequency. They're acknowledging right along with the Coasties."

"Okay," Phillip said. "That's good. I wouldn't be surprised if Dani has something planned; she's had all day to get up to mischief. My bet is she did something to those boats. We're probably going to need boots on the ground before this is over."

"What could she have done?" Weatherby asked.

Phillip shrugged. "Hard to say. Sharktooth?"

"Yes?"

"Weapons check, please. We're almost there."

DANI HEARD the droning sound of twin diesels approaching at the same time Maldonado began to paddle out toward the four boats in the middle of the Bay. Once she thought he was far enough away not to hear her, she got to her knees and picked up a paddle, using it to push against the muddy bottom a few inches under the canoe. She eased the canoe forward until she had a line of sight out into the Bay.

Maldonado sat in the kayak, drifting, about 100 meters out from the bank. He had the video camera on his shoulder, apparently recording. The four boats were clearly visible out in the middle of the open area. They were side-by-side; Dani surmised that the occupants were holding them together. They all drifted as a unit.

The droning grew louder, coming from the west. Dani looked in the direction of the sound and spotted what had to be *La Paloma's* running lights. Someone on one of the four go-fast boats flashed a spotlight briefly in the direction of the approaching craft. The running lights blinked twice in response.

As Dani watched, one of Martínez's boats separated itself from the pack. When it was a few meters from the others, it started its engines. The rumble of the exhausts drowned out the sound of the newcomer's diesels. The pitch of the engines dropped as the driver shifted into forward. The boat began moving to intercept the approaching vessel, which was now easily distinguished as a sport fisherman.

Dani wasn't surprised when the engines on the go-fast boat sputtered and died. She was now sure that it was the one carrying Martínez. It had the most time on the engines since her tampering, so it would be the first to shut down. She picked up the binoculars, curious to see what would happen next.

The man at the controls tried in vain to restart the engines. After a couple of failed attempts, he stood up and moved aft to the lift-up deck over the engine compartment. When he raised it on its hinges, there was a loud popping sound, followed by a brief hiss, and then a fireball bloomed from the engine compartment, engulfing the whole boat as the explosion reverberated across the water.

Grinning, Dani watched as the men on the other boats scrambled into action. With no idea what had happened, they cursed and shouted for several seconds as debris from the burning wreck dropped all around them. As the men who had survived the explosion discovered that they could stand up in the shallow water, they began to converge on the three remaining boats.

She lowered the binoculars a bit to check on Maldonado, who was still recording. The dull crack of a medium caliber handgun being discharged drew her attention back to the three boats. They had separated from one another, and as the last of the survivors from the wreck clambered aboard, they started their engines.

*La Paloma* was by now coasting to a stop within two hundred meters of the remaining boats. Dani saw Sharktooth standing on the flying bridge, holding a machine gun like it was a toy rifle. She grinned and swept the glasses over the rest of the boat, seeing Liz sitting on the foredeck with another machine gun on a tripod, Connie next to her, ready to feed the ammunition.

The three go-fast boats began to move, their engines roaring as the throttles were opened. Dani imagined the rate of fuel consumption surging, and as if in response to her thoughts, the engines began to cough and sputter. One by one, the engines died. As the boats settled back into the water, Sharktooth and Liz opened fire, churning the water around each boat into foam.

The shooting stopped, and she heard Phillip's voice booming out from a loudhailer. "Stay in your boats. Remain seated and do not move. If you stand up, you die." He repeated his order in Spanish. After a brief pause, Liz and Sharktooth fired several short bursts each, sending tracers a few feet over the drifting boats, reinforcing Phillip's threat. Silence settled over the Bay. As the seconds dragged by, Dani heard helicopters in the distance, the chopping sound punctuating the roar of big outboards closer in.

She caught a glimpse of the first Coast Guard launch coming in from the west just as she remembered Maldonado. At first, she couldn't find him, and then she saw that he was paddling along the shoreline, staying in the shadows and making for the entrance to Coot Bay. She thought briefly of alerting Phillip via the satellite phone, but then she worried that Maldonado might ditch the camera. She wanted that video.

She picked up her paddle and went after him, the longer waterline of the canoe giving her a significant advantage in speed. When she had closed to within several boat-lengths, he sensed her behind him. She saw him glance over his shoulder, and then he put the paddle down and twisted around, a pistol in his hand.

His first shot went wide, and the momentum of the canoe carried it ever closer to the lighter kayak, which was dead in the water. The slender craft rocked as Maldonado tried to bring his pistol to bear. Dani raised her pistol in a two-handed grip and took careful aim, putting a round through his right shoulder. He screamed and his pistol flew from his hand, splashing into the water a few feet from him.

"The next one's going through your other shoulder," she said.

"No, please," he said. "I surrender."

She saw him lifting the video camera with his left hand. "Put the camera down, Maldonado, or I'll feed you to the alligators like I did Santos."

"Okay, okay," he said.

"You sit very still," she ordered. "I'm going to put the bow of the canoe where you can drop the camera into it. If you do that, maybe I'll let you live. You want to take a chance on life?"

"Yes, please."

"Good boy," she said. She took the paddle in her left hand, gripping it near the throat of the blade. Her fingers extended along the paddle's surface, she used it like an extension of her hand and maneuvered the canoe into place.

"Pick up the camera and lay it gently into the canoe," she said, as the bow of the canoe touched the left side of the kayak. She kept the pistol trained on him. When the camera was safe, she backed water with her paddle, opening up a distance of a few feet.

"I need medical attention, please," he said.

"Maybe, but that's not your biggest problem right now."

"What do you mean?"

"I mean you've pissed me off. I'm your biggest problem."

"How?" he whined. "I don't even know who you are."

"No?" she asked. "And here you told Martínez I was a fine, hot piece of ass."

"That was just locker-room talk. I didn't mean anything by it."

"Uh-huh. You need to learn to respect women."

"What? I — "

She fired a round into his kayak, near where she thought his feet were. "You still want to live?"

"Yes."

"Good. Here's the deal. You pull your right foot back so your knee is sticking up in the air in front of your face."

"What?"

She pumped another round into the kayak near his feet. "Do it!"

When he had positioned himself as she ordered, she said, "The next time you feel the urge to disparage a woman, remember that she might not like it."

"Okay. But — "

Her pistol barked and his knee exploded. She watched him, a cold look on her face, until his screams became whimpers. "Wait here," she said. "Someone will pick you up soon."

She paddled back into the tall grass and took out the satellite phone, entering Phillip's number.

"Phillip?" she said, when he answered,

"Dani? Where are you?"

"I'm all right. Maldonado's drifting in a kayak near the entrance to Coot Bay. He needs help. He caught a couple of stray rounds. I'm going to paddle back into Coot Bay Pond and pick up Ortiz's car."

"Okay. I'll get word to the people there to let you pass. What are you paddling?"

"A dark green canoe."

"Did you do something to the boats?"

"There's water in the fuel tanks."

"One of them blew up."

"I saw that. Tell everybody not to open the engine compartments. I tried to tell you earlier, the bilges reeked of fuel."

"How did — "

"I'm really tired, Phillip, and I feel cranky. I need a hot shower and some food. I'll tell you all about it back at Star Island, okay? Besides, I just got a low battery alarm on this phone. 'Bye."

"Goodbye."

# EPILOGUE

*Two days later at the villa on Star Island ...*

"WHAT TIME DID you get in last night, Phillip?" J.-P. asked.
Everyone had gathered for an early breakfast before Phillip and
Sharktooth went to the airport to meet their wives. This was the
first opportunity for them to talk as a group since the engagement
the night before last in Whitewater Bay, and since Mario
Espinosa's surprise party would be tonight, it was also their only
chance to work through the remaining puzzles.

"I didn't look at a clock; I didn't want to know," Phillip said,
looking around the table, his eyes bleary. "Late, I'm sure. I must
have been deposed by half of the lawyers in Miami yesterday. Did
they ever get in touch with you, Dani?"

"A couple of FBI agents came by late yesterday morning and
questioned me, but there really wasn't much I could tell them
that was new."

"What about the explosion that killed Martínez? Did they ask
you about that?"

She shook her head. "No. I was surprised they didn't. I even brought it up, and they said it wasn't their job. The woman in charge said somebody might be in touch later, after the forensic technicians were finished with the boats and the wreckage. All they wanted to know was what happened to Santos. Nobody can account for him."

"What did happen to him?" Phillip asked.

"He fell out of the canoe beside the boats and a big gator snatched him and swam away. You know how they hide their prey and let it ripen; he's probably somewhere out there, under a sunken log, I guess."

"How did you come to have his satellite phone," Connie asked.

"Like I told Phillip, I guess it came out of his pocket in the canoe."

"Maldonado told them that you shot him twice after he surrendered," Paul said. "That's what Luke told me. Luke said he'd been kneecapped."

"Really?" Dani asked. "He probably had it coming, but they didn't ask me about him. Where would I have gotten a pistol, anyway? I was a prisoner, remember?" She grinned.

"He was a mile and a half from the action when they picked him up," Phillip said. "They found him about where you said he was when you called me."

"The way Liz and Sharktooth were blazing away with the M249s, he probably caught a couple of stray rounds. Those 5.56 mm slugs carry for quite a distance."

"Four rounds, Luke told me" Paul said. "Two through the kayak, one through his shoulder, and one through his knee. They didn't recover the bullets."

"I'm not surprised. I was worried myself when you two cut loose with the machine guns. He probably saw me behind him and just assumed I shot him. What's going to happen to him and Cruz, anyway? You said Martínez bought it when his boat blew up."

"That's right," Paul said. "Here's what I've heard from Luke, so far. They're still working out everything they're going to charge them with. For the moment, they're looking at murder, conspiracy to commit murder, and a whole list of human trafficking offenses."

"Murder?" Liz asked.

"Olsen, and the other spook that you had your first meeting with, Phillip," Paul said. "And the State Department's involved, dealing with the Cuban government. The Cubans are making noise about extradition; it seems they bought the story about a coup, especially after their representative was shown the suitcase nuke."

"Can they actually be extradited?" J.-P. asked.

"Nobody's sure, but Luke said the threat of it got the two of them singing like canaries. Neither one of them wants to go back to Cuba," Paul said.

"But they must be looking at spending forever in prison," Connie said.

"Yes, but in a U.S. prison. They'd rather serve time here; they'd almost surely be executed if they were sent back."

"Executed? Would they not have been celebrated as heroes of the Revolution?" J.-P. asked.

"That's not an option for the Cuban government at this point. Since we busted them, the Cubans are forced to treat the two of them as traitors, or admit to plotting a bogus invasion for propaganda reasons," Paul said. "Or so the story goes, anyway."

"I got a question, Dani," Sharktooth said.

"What's that?"

"What made that boat blow up? I was bettin' Phillip it was cookin' gas, but he say ask you."

"Gasoline in the bilge. The tanks were full, so I had to drain out several gallons to make room for the water I added. I wanted to be sure they couldn't get too far, because I didn't know how you planned to stop them."

"The explosion was an accident then?" Liz asked.

"Not entirely," Dani said. "I found a flare pistol in their ditch bag, and I fastened it in the engine compartment. Then I ran a piece of fishing line from the trigger to the engine cover."

"So the only accident was that Martínez was unlucky enough to choose the wrong boat," Liz said.

"No," Dani said. "The accident was that nobody opened the engine compartments on the others."

Sharktooth said, "Cookin' gas work better, Dani. I tol' you that."

"I didn't have a wrench that fit the propane line. You always taught me to improvise, so I used gasoline."

Sharktooth's laugh rumbled like an approaching thunderstorm. "Good job," he said. "Gasoline ver' dangerous stuff."

"What about the Haitian trafficking victims?" Connie asked.

"ICE is handling that as routine business. Probably most of them will end up staying here, one way or another. But who knows what may happen with politics the way they are," Paul said.

"Speaking of ICE, what's new with you and David Ortiz, Dani?" J.-P. asked. "He seemed relieved to see you when you came in the other night."

Dani shrugged. "I was in no mood to talk to him then. He invited me to lunch at the club yesterday."

"And did you go?" J.-P. prompted. Then he looked around at the others and asked, "Or would you rather talk to your Papa in private."

Dani grinned ruefully and shook her head. "No, I ditched him, Papa. He's a mess. That boy's so confused."

"Will you see him again?" Liz asked.

"No."

"You seem subdued. Are you disappointed?"

"A little, I guess."

"Don't worry. You'll find somebody, soon."

Dani laughed. "That's not why I'm disappointed. I was geared up for a revolution, and all I got to do was blow up one lousy boat."


THE END

# MAILING LIST

Join my mailing list at http://eepurl.com/bKujyv for notice of new releases and special sales or giveaways. I'll email a link to you for a free download of my short story, **The Lost Tourist Franchise,** when you sign up. I promise not to use the list for anything else; I dislike spam as much as you do.

# A NOTE TO THE READER

Thank you for reading *Bluewater Revolution*. I hope you enjoyed it. If so, please leave a brief review on Amazon. Reviews are of great benefit to independent authors like me; they help me more than you can imagine. They are a primary means to help new readers find my work. A few words from you can help others find the pleasure that I hope you found in this book, as well as keeping my spirits up as I work on the next one. If you would like to be notified by email when I release a new book or have a sale or giveaway, please visit http://eepurl.com/bKujyv I promise not to use the list for anything else; I dislike spam as much as you do.

If you haven't read the other **Bluewater Thrillers**, please take a look at them. If you enjoyed this book, you'll enjoy them as well. The **Connie Barrera Thrillers** are a spin-off from the **Bluewater Thrillers**, and share some of the same characters. Dani and Liz taught Connie to sail, and they introduced her to Paul Russo, her first mate and husband.

In June of 2017, I released *Bluewater Enigma*, the thirteenth novel in that series. Now I've turned my attention back to Connie and

Paul for their eighth adventure. You'll find progress reports and more information on my web page at www.clrdougherty.com. Be sure to click on the link to my blog posts; it's in the column on the right side of the web page. Dani and Liz and Connie are keeping the blog alive while I work on the next book, so you can see what they're up to while I'm writing.

A list of my other books is on the last page; just click on a title or go to my website for more information. If you'd like to know when my next book is released, visit my Amazon Author's Page at ( www.amazon.com/author/clrdougherty ) and click the "Follow" link near the upper left-hand corner. I welcome email correspondence about books, boats and sailing. My address is clrd@clr-dougherty.com. If you'd like personal updates, drop me a line at that address and let me know. Thanks again for your support.

# ABOUT THE AUTHOR

Welcome aboard!

Charles Dougherty is a lifelong sailor; he's lived what he writes. He and his wife have spent over 30 years sailing together. For 15 years, they lived aboard their boat full-time, cruising the East Coast and the islands. They spent most of that time exploring the Eastern Caribbean. Dougherty is well acquainted with the islands and their people. The characters and locations in his novels reflect his experience.

A storyteller before all else, Dougherty lets his characters speak for themselves. Pick up one of his thrillers and listen to the sound of adventure as you smell the salt air. Enjoy the views of distant horizons and meet some people you won't forget.

Dougherty has written over 25 books. His **Bluewater Thrillers** are set in the yachting world of the Caribbean and chronicle the adventures of two young women running a luxury charter yacht in a rough-and-tumble environment. The **Connie Barrera Thrillers** are also set in the Caribbean and feature some of the same characters from a slightly more romantic perspective. Besides the **Bluewater Thrillers** and the **Connie Barrera Thrillers**, he wrote *The Redemption of Becky Jones*, a psycho-thriller, and *The Lost Tourist Franchise*, a short story about one of the characters from *Deception in Savannah*.

He has also written two non-fiction books. *Life's a Ditch* is the story of how he and his wife moved aboard their sailboat, *Play Actor*, and their adventures along the east coast of the U.S. *Dungda de Islan'* relates their experiences while cruising the Caribbean.

www.clrdougherty.com
clrd@clrdougherty.com

# OTHER BOOKS BY C.L.R. DOUGHERTY

*Bluewater Thrillers*

Bluewater Killer

Bluewater Vengeance

Bluewater Voodoo

Bluewater Ice

Bluewater Betrayal

Bluewater Stalker

Bluewater Bullion

Bluewater Rendezvous

Bluewater Ganja

Bluewater Jailbird

Bluewater Drone

Bluewater Revolution

Bluewater Enigma

Bluewater Thrillers Boxed Set: Books 1-3

*Connie Barrera Thrillers*

From Deception to Betrayal - An Introduction to Connie Barrera

Love for Sail - A Connie Barrera Thriller

Sailor's Delight - A Connie Barrera Thriller

A Blast to Sail - A Connie Barrera Thriller

Storm Sail - A Connie Barrera Thriller

Running Under Sail - A Connie Barrera Thriller

Sails Job - A Connie Barrera Thriller

Under Full Sail - A Connie Barrera Thriller

*Other Fiction*

Deception in Savannah

The Redemption of Becky Jones

The Lost Tourist Franchise

*Books for Sailors and Dreamers*

Life's a Ditch

Dungda de Islan'

For more information please visit my website

Or visit www.amazon.com/author/clrdougherty

# EXCERPT FROM BLUEWATER ENIGMA

Read on for a preview of *Bluewater Enigma*, the 13th novel in the series...

# BLUEWATER ENIGMA - CHAPTER 1

"I don't see her," Dani Berger said, fumbling as she rushed to enter the gate code into the keypad. "She's gone."

"Get a grip," Liz Chirac said, nudging her out of the way and entering the code. "She's here somewhere."

Liz swung the gate open and held it, stepping back out of Dani's way. Irritated by their flight's delayed arrival into Miami, they were impatient to be back aboard *Vengeance*. Liz watched her friend charge down the dock. The duffle bag slung over Dani's shoulder was bumping against her hip, bouncing as she hustled to the slip where they had left *Vengeance*.

By the time Liz closed the gate and caught up with her, Dani was standing on the floating finger dock on the east side of the vacant slip. She stared at the empty expanse of water, thunderclouds forming on her brow. Liz dropped her own duffle bag on the main dock next to Dani's and stepped out onto the float. She put a hand on Dani's shoulder, feeling the tension in her wiry frame.

"They must have moved her for some reason," Liz said.

Dani whipped her head around, glaring at her. "Or some asshole stole her," she snapped.

"Slow down, Dani. Who would steal a 60-foot sailboat with all these million-dollar, 100-mile-an-hour testosterone rockets next door?"

Dani shrugged Liz's hand from her shoulder, scrambling back onto the main dock. She climbed the nearest piling like a monkey going up a coconut palm. Balancing atop it as she scanned the marina, she said, "Not here, not in any of the slips." She jumped down, landing like a cat. "She's gone."

"But nobody steals a boat like *Vengeance*," Liz said. "What would they do with her? She's too slow to run with and too big to hide. They can't even sell her. She's too easily recognized."

"It happens, Liz. She's gone." Dani looked at her watch. "The marina office closed an hour ago. Let's go find a security guard." She picked up her bag and slung it over her shoulder, fidgeting while Liz retrieved her own duffle bag.

"Let's walk up to the office," Liz said. "If we don't run into the guard, maybe there's an after-hours emergency number on the door."

Dani nodded. "Yeah, okay."

"There's some explanation, Dani. You know how rare this kind of theft is. Boats like *Vengeance* don't appeal to joyriders. It would take a skilled crew, and how could they avoid being spotted with her?"

"They could have had as much as two weeks to get her out of sight," Dani said. "Drug runners used to steal boats like *Vengeance* all the time; she'd haul a lot of illicit cargo without attracting attention. Dope, guns, cash, whatever. Make a run or two and then ditch her before the authorities catch on. That's the way they used to do it."

"But that was eons ago," Liz said. "Smugglers are more sophisticated now."

"They do what works. When the law gets wise to one scheme, they try something else. Maybe they've gone full circle — back to the old ways. Miami was always a hub for that kind of thing," Dani said, as they walked up the dock.

They stopped, and Dani rattled the office door, rapping on the glass with her knuckles.

"There's nobody here," Liz said. She pointed at the card taped in the lower left corner of the window. "Let's call."

U.S. Representative Horatio Velasquez opened the car door for his wife, helping her into her seat as the photographers' flashes blinded him. He ignored the reporters' shouted questions, smiling and nodding as he walked around to the driver's door and got in.

"I'm not that fragile, you know," his wife, Miranda, said. "I'm only six months. Or was that for the press?"

"Everything's for the press, at this point," he said. "I've got a lot of ground to cover to catch up with O'Toole before the primary."

"Before the primary? You're a shoo-in for re-election. What's O'Toole got to do with it?"

"Think about it," Velasquez said.

"I don't understand," Miranda said. "O'Toole's in the Senate."

"This isn't about my seat in the House, Miranda."

"But I thought he was going to run for President. Are you going after his Senate seat or something?"

"Or something," Velasquez said. "I've always been aiming higher than the Senate; you know that."

"You're thinking about running against him for the nomination?" Miranda's eyebrows rose. "For President?"

Velasquez grinned at her. "I've got a shot; I'm a Cuban-American and this is Florida. I'm popular with all the key factions."

"But there's more to it than Florida, Horatio, right?"

"Of course, there is. Don't act so dim-witted. If I can beat him on his home turf, what do you think's going to happen with the nomination?"

She frowned. "He's marrying that Montalba woman, right? So he's got an in with the Hispanic community, just like you."

"Not just like me. Marrying into it's not the same as being born into it. You should have learned that by now. You'll never be anything but my Anglo wife. Besides, she's from Argentina."

"So?"

"So, that's not the same as having Cuban or Mexican heritage. Not in the U.S. And she's filthy rich, besides. So's O'Toole."

"I see your point about Argentina, but what's being rich got to do with anything? Isn't that a plus?"

"It could be, under the right circumstances, but we've already tried having a billionaire for President. I don't think we're ready for another one, yet. All that money can be made to work against him."

"Why haven't you talked to me about this?"

"I'm talking to you about it now."

"But Diego's about to turn one, and this one will be a babe in arms on the campaign trail."

"I know," Velasquez said. "It's perfect. I'll be the up and coming father of young children, positioned against an old, rich, white-haired Anglo bastard." He glanced at her, taking in the set of her jaw and the creases on her forehead. "Right?" he asked.

"It's all about you, isn't it?" she said, biting off the words as she blinked back tears.

"Think of it, Miranda. You'll be the first lady; our children will grow up in the White House. How can you say it's all about me? I'm doing this for you and our children. Not to mention for our great country and all the generations to come. Somebody has to straighten this all out. Don't you see that?"

"And you, Horry? You're the one to straighten out 'our great country.' Is that it?"

"Better me than a scumbag like O'Toole. Think of what it will mean for Diego and his little sister."

"I *am*. That's what *bothers* me. But I don't get a vote, do I? Except in the polling place, and you can bet I won't cast it for you."

❧

BEVERLY LENNOX STUDIED her dinner companion as he prepared to taste the wine the waiter poured for him. He was breathtaking. The dim lighting threw his dark eyes into shadow. She couldn't tell if they were dark brown or dark blue, but she'd like to find out. This was the first time she'd met him; their other contacts had been by phone.

She hadn't expected him to be so handsome. His voice on the phone had been smooth, and his manner, respectful, polite. She wasn't used to that. He wasn't at all the type who required her services. Most of the men Manny had sent her to had been repulsive.

Horatio Velasquez was the exception, and she'd been pleased when Manny had ordered her to become Velasquez's full-time mistress. It was an easy job. Velasquez was self-centered and arrogant, but he wasn't abusive. Besides, he kept up the pretense of being a family man, so his demands on her time were limited. She'd never had such a sweet situation before.

She'd been distressed when Manny had told her to expect a call from this man, Berto — no last name. She hid her reaction from Manny; she was skilled at that. It was part of her job. Still, she couldn't keep from asking if this meant she was no longer Velasquez's, exclusively.

Manny had laughed at her. "You do what Berto says," he'd ordered. "He is the boss. If he wants you, then you are his. You don't get to choose, you stupid *puta*. I need to teach you this again?"

Then he'd given her that special smile of his. Even now, the thought of that smile sent a chill down her spine.

When the waiter filled her glass, she realized that Berto must have tasted the wine and approved it. She'd been watching him, charmed by his style, as he'd sniffed at the little bit of wine the waiter had poured for him to taste.

When he'd closed his eyes and taken a sip, holding it in his mouth, her thoughts had wandered. Now, Berto was watching her, smiling as he held his glass out toward her.

She smiled back and lifted her glass, hoping she hadn't spaced out for too long. She was clean. She didn't do drugs, and she didn't want Berto to think she did.

"To your relationship with the Honorable Horatio Velasquez," he said. "May it be a long and pleasant one for you both." He smiled and looked her in the eye as he touched his glass to hers.

"Thank you," she said, raising the glass to her lips and tipping it slightly, but not taking any of the wine. She needed her wits about her.

"I wanted to meet you before I made my final decision," Berto said. "Manny is good at what he does, but some things are outside his experience. He's lacking in certain social graces." He paused.

When she didn't try to fil the silence, he smiled and nodded. "You're perfect. I envy Velasquez, in a way. Do you have any concerns about continuing with him?"

"No," she said. "He's easy enough to be with, and I think he's comfortable with me."

"I'm sure he is," Berto said, reaching inside his dinner jacket and withdrawing an envelope. He passed it to her and nodded his approval when she slipped it into her evening bag without looking at it.

"There are credit cards in your name. Don't concern yourself with limits on the cards; there aren't any. If you need cash, get an advance on one of them. Okay so far?"

She nodded.

He smiled and said, "There's also a passport for Velasquez, in a different name, of course. Follow the instructions in the memo that's in the envelope. You understand?"

"Yes," she said.

"Good. There's a number in there where you can reach me. If you have any questions or problems, call me directly. You will never hear from Manny again. He wishes you well, I'm sure. Are you all right with that?"

"With never hearing from Manny again?" she asked, in a neutral tone.

He smiled and nodded.

"Yes," she said.

"I thought you would be. And now, enough business. Let's enjoy our dinner."

# CHAPTER 2

"I thought you were going to jump through the phone and rip that marina manager's head off last night," Liz said, as the waitress poured fresh coffee for each of them. She and Dani were having breakfast in a pancake house around the corner from the hotel where they had spent the night.

"Just as well for him I got it out of my system while we were on the phone," Dani said. "I still can't believe the brass of those people."

"The marina management?"

"No," Dani said. "Whoever it was that marched in their office pretending to be a delivery crew." She shook her head and took a sip of coffee. "I guess I can't really blame the marina."

"He told you they had a letter with your signature on it?" Liz asked.

"That's what he said. He remembered it because of the timing. He said he wondered why we didn't just tell him about it when we brought the boat in, instead of sending the delivery crew in cold the day after we left."

"That timing is odd," Liz said. "Whoever it was must have known, don't you think?"

"You mean about us? Our travel plans?"

"Yes," Liz said.

"It almost sounds like they were watching us, doesn't it?" Dani asked.

"Yes, and showing up to take *Vengeance* while we were on the flight to New York, too."

"I'm missing something," Dani said. "What does our flight have to do with it?"

"If the manager had tried to call us to verify things, we couldn't have been reached."

"I didn't think of that. You have a criminal mind, Liz."

"You taught me well. He was going to call the police for us?"

"Yes. He offered. There's somebody they work with regularly, he said."

"Really?" Liz asked. "So this isn't such an unusual thing?"

"Yes, it is. He said they'd had a few go-fast boats stolen over the years, but never a big sailboat. But there's a fair amount of petty theft. People leave stuff out in the open on deck and then get upset when somebody takes it, from what he said. Anyway, they have a detective that they work with on a regular basis."

"What about our insurance?"

"He suggested we hold off until we talk to the police and get copies of everything from the files in the office."

"That makes sense. Do they have the letter that you supposedly signed?"

"He said he put it in our file himself."

"This seems a little too well put together," Liz said.

"Which part?"

"The fake delivery crew showing up the day after we put her in the slip, while we were en route," Liz said. "I keep going back to that. Somebody targeted us, specifically."

"Or *Vengeance*," Dani said.

"You mean like a theft to order?" Liz asked.

"It's not unheard of."

"I'm having trouble with that idea, Dani. How many *Bounty* replicas do you suppose there are?"

"I don't know. More than a few, I guess. The original was built in 1934. Connie and Paul didn't have a big problem finding *Diamantista II* when they decided they wanted one."

"But they're still not common," Liz said, "and each one was built to order, so no two are quite the same. It's not like a Beneteau 58 or something. If you put two of those side by side, nobody could tell one from the other."

"No, you're right about that. *Vengeance* is distinctive. You or I could pick her out of a crowd, even a crowd of her sister ships."

"That's my point," Liz said. "That's why I don't think it's a theft to order. Something else is going on here."

"Somebody could put her in a boatyard for a week and change enough stuff so we wouldn't recognize her, Liz. At least, not at a glance."

"But why do that?" Liz asked.

"Somebody wanted a Herreshoff *Bounty*," Dani said.

"Why not buy one, then? There are several of them listed; I checked on the web last night."

Dani sat back, frowning, as the waitress put their breakfast on the table. After the woman freshened their coffee and left, Dani asked, "What are you trying to say, Liz? That somebody wanted *Vengeance* because it was *our* boat?"

"That's the only thing that makes sense to me."

"Unless they stole her to make a drug run or two," Dani said, cutting a piece of fried egg and dredging it through the runny yolk.

"Then they would have just stolen her," Liz said. "Why go to the trouble of a forged letter from you authorizing a delivery crew to take her?"

Dani chewed the piece of egg, her brow wrinkled. She swallowed and said, "I guess that could have been a ploy to buy time, but I see your point. It does appear that they wanted *Vengeance*, but why?"

"I don't know," Liz said, "but I think there's more to this."

"Did you look closely at any of those listings online?" Dani asked.

"No," Liz said. "Why?"

"I was just thinking. We could settle with the insurance company and replace her, if any of them look attractive."

"I couldn't do that, Dani. She's not just another boat to me; she's home, my first love, all those trite, sentimental things. We're going to get her back. Just you watch."

"You're astonishing," Horatio Velasquez said, staring at Beverly Lennox's cleavage as she leaned over to put his breakfast on the table.

"I'm so glad you think so," she said, a shy smile on her glistening, dark red lips. "I have a surprise for you," she said, standing up straight, one knee flexed slightly, turning to the side to show off her figure.

Velasquez grinned, feasting his eyes, watching every ripple of movement as she untied the belt that held the diaphanous robe closed. She gave a theatrical shrug, letting the silk slide from her shoulders as she stepped in close, her pelvis inches from his face.

"What's this?" he said, reaching for the thick, creamy envelope, one corner of which was tucked behind the wispy triangle of her thong panties. He put the envelope beside his forgotten breakfast and hooked a finger in the thong, leaning toward her, his lips brushing her lower belly.

"Open it and find out," she purred, leaning over to kiss him on the cheek. "I'll wait."

He picked up the envelope, catching a whiff of the musky

scent that drove him to distraction. Folding back the unsealed flap, he took out a passport and an airline ticket.

"Surprise!" she said, watching as he opened the ticket.

"St. Lucia," he said. "But I already have a passport." He frowned as he opened it.

"Not like that one," she said.

"Jeffrey Harold Starnes," he read. "He looks a lot like me."

"There is a remarkable resemblance," she said, leaning against him to look over his shoulder, her left breast grazing his cheek. "But it's been altered enough so that it won't be matched to you by a scanner. He answers to Harry, by the way, so if I mess up and call him Horry, nobody will notice."

He turned, kissing the side of her breast, and looked up in disappointment as she backed away a little. "It looks like the real thing, but it's too risky."

"You worry too much," she said, pouting. "It's real, issued by the State Department, just like yours."

"How?" he asked. "Your mysterious *friend*?"

She smiled. "Let a girl have some secrets."

"Is he CIA or what?"

"If I told you, he'd have to kill us both. Just roll with it, okay? I knew you shouldn't use your own — talk about risky."

"Okay. Where are we staying? Somewhere private, I hope."

"We have a classic sailing yacht all to ourselves for the week," she said. "It'll be very private."

"But we don't know how to sail," he said.

"There's crew. A captain and a gourmet chef."

"Aw, damn," he said, frowning. "You'll have to wear clothes. Bummer."

"They're both attractive young women — one's French, and the other's Belgian. I'm sure they won't care what *I* wear — or don't wear. But you, on the other hand ... just don't get any ideas about messing with the help, hot stuff."

He grinned. "Like I said, you're astonishing. I thought you were kidding about arranging a getaway for us."

"Your schedule's still clear, right?" she asked.

"Absolutely, and I'm keeping it that way. No way I'm missing this."

"Good boy. Are you going to eat your breakfast before you go to the office?"

"It's cold," he said.

"I'm not." She slipped the thong from her hips and turned, striding toward the bedroom in nothing but her red spike heels.

GUILLERMO MONTALBA WAS SIPPING his second cup of coffee when the encrypted cellphone on his desk chimed.

"Yes?" he answered.

"Everything is set. The installation's done; it's all tested. Works great; you'll have Hollywood-quality video recordings. Did you give her the proximity key?"

"Yes, she has it. She knows to keep it with her credit cards. How close does it have to be to the sensor?"

"It's not that critical. If it's anywhere within a few yards, it'll wake the system."

"How do you avoid recording hours of garbage, then?" Montalba asked.

"The proximity device wakes the system. It doesn't start recording unless there's sound or motion in the immediate vicinity."

"Do I need to give her specific instructions about it? Like keep it in the room, or anything?"

"No, sir. It can even be left outdoors. It'll be fine, I assure you."

"What about retrieving the data?"

"There's ample storage for hundreds of hours. The preferred method is physical retrieval."

"I thought there was Wi-Fi." Montalba said.

"The system supports that for remote retrieval, but it's not well suited to this application. Unless we have a receiver in range for real-time streaming, the download speed's too slow. We'd have to shadow them within maybe 20 or 30 yards all the time to do that."

"How will you retrieve the data, then?"

"Swap out the disk drive. It only takes seconds."

"But that means you have to wait until nobody's around, doesn't it?"

"That's correct, but we can handle that. You said that retrieving it at the end of their stay would be satisfactory."

"Yes, that's right, but what if there's a failure?" Montalba asked. "How will you know?"

"The system is 100 percent redundant, and we can pass close enough periodically to stream a few seconds and make sure everything's working. We just can't sit next door and stream it all the time, okay?"

"Yes. What about the other stuff?"

"It's in place. Hidden, like where somebody would hide their stash. It's out of sight, but easy enough to find if you know what to look for."

"And you've got the fix in with the authorities? I don't want anybody going to jail."

"It's taken care of. They'll confiscate it and give them a lecture and a written warning, just as you ordered. Of course, they'll expect a bribe. Does the woman know where they need to be on that first day?"

"Yes," Montalba said. "She has written instructions. If there is a scheduling problem, she will let me know and I'll call you. About the bribe, though ... "

"Don't worry. They'll drop enough hints for even Velasquez to figure it out."

"Are they flexible on the amount?" Montalba asked.

"Yes. It's mostly for show. They're being well paid by our people."

"Excellent," Montalba said.

"Anything else?"

"About the equipment," Montalba said. "Can you leave it in place after this mission?"

"If you wish."

"And once it's awake, how long will it continue to function?"

"Indefinitely. It's powered from the ship's batteries, so as long as their electricity is on, it will record."

"What about the storage? What happens when it's full?"

"It loops back and overwrites the oldest recording, but remember, there's hundreds of hours' worth of storage, and it only records when there's sound or motion."

"If I have her leave the proximity key, can I eavesdrop on the crew after she's come back to the states?"

"Yes, sir. You'll have to let us know when to retrieve the storage, but that's it. Actually, it would be better not to rely on the proximity key, in that case. I'll just have them reprogram the system for continuous recording when they retrieve that data at the end of next week's exercise."

"Speaking of that, are your people set for her arrival?"

"Yes, sir. Still next week, is that correct?"

"That's correct."

"Please let us know if it changes. I'm going to give the team a little break until then, unless you object."

"No, that's fine," Montalba said. "Thank you. I'll be in touch."

# CHAPTER 3

"Well, that was frustrating," Dani said, stirring hot sauce into the bowl of black bean soup she'd ordered for lunch. She and Liz were sitting at a sidewalk table outside a hole-in-the-wall Cuban restaurant off Lincoln Road Mall in Miami Beach.

"I guess it went about the way I thought it would," Liz said. "The detective didn't offer much hope, did he?"

"No," Dani said, raising a spoonful of the soup to her lips, testing its temperature before she tasted it.

"But maybe they'll get fingerprints from that letter. Whoever it was did a good job of forging your signature."

"Yes, thanks to scanner apps for cellphones, no doubt. But I'm not holding my breath on the fingerprints."

"Why is that?" Liz asked.

"Anybody sharp enough to do that would have been sharp enough not to leave prints on the paper." Dani tasted her soup and added more of the pepper sauce.

"But the manager said the man took the letter out of an envelope and handed it to him. How could someone handle paper like that without leaving fingerprints?"

"Silicone's the way I'd have done it," Dani said.

"Silicone?" Liz asked, picking through her bowl of lobster salad. "How does that work? You mean like the grease?"

Dani shook her head. "The sealant. You spread a thin film over the pads of your fingers and let it cure. If you use the clear stuff, it's not noticeable. It fills the grooves, so the most you leave is a smudge, if there's even that."

"Where do you come up with that kind of thing? After all this time, you still surprise me."

Dani shrugged. "My misspent youth. How's the salad?"

"Good. Is your soup okay?"

"Okay, but not as good as what you make."

Liz smiled. "Thanks. It's the pork belly; that's my secret."

"Isn't fat just fat?" Dani asked.

"And silicone's just for flat-chested women, right?" Liz teased. "It's all in what you do with it."

"On a serious note, partner, what are we going to do now? We're missing the boat."

Liz looked at Dani's poker face until Dani lost it, choking on her mouthful of soup as she fought not to laugh.

"How long have you been waiting to spring that one on me?"

"It just came to me," Dani said, dabbing at her lips with her napkin. "Honest, it did."

"Uh-huh," Liz said, giggling and shaking her head. "Anyway, thanks. I needed that. I'm still in shock."

"I know. Come on back, Pollyanna. I miss you. It's just a boat," Dani said.

"I'm trying; I know you're right, and I feel silly for being so sentimental about her. But still ... "

"I feel the same way, Liz, but you just have to suck it up and move on. 'Illegitimi non carborundum,' as Phillip used to tell me when I was a sappy teenager trudging through the Central American jungle with him."

"What? That almost sounds like Latin."

"Almost," Dani said, spooning up more soup.

"But it's not, is it?"

"I don't know; fake Latin, I think. It means, 'Don't let the bastards grind you down.'"

Liz laughed. "I like that. That's a good thought to hold onto when we call the insurance people."

"It's going to be okay, Liz."

"You don't think they'll give us a hard time?"

"No. The agent's done business with Papa for longer than I can remember. They're not cheap when it comes to premiums, and they're not cheap when it comes to claims, either. You get what you pay for, and they know us. That counts for more than most people think."

"So what do you think they'll do? Are they going to mount some kind of search?"

"Yes. No doubt about that."

"How long?"

"You mean until they settle with us?"

Liz nodded, chewing a mouthful of salad.

"That's going to be up to us, most likely. They'll search for her, though. They'll want a recovery if they can manage it, but they'll pay us off quickly, if that's what we want. We've got a business to run; they understand that."

"I'd like to give it as much time as we can, Dani. Is that okay with you?"

"We'll take it a day at a time, how about? We don't have to set any deadlines just yet. It's not like we have a charter on the books right away."

"Good," Liz said. "Thanks. I'll work my way through this. *Non me dedam nisi pugnavero.*"

"What?" Dani asked. "You'll have to help me. Latin was a long time ago, for me."

"'I won't quit fighting,' roughly. I'm not letting the bastards grind me down. Not without a struggle, anyway."

"Atta girl!" Dani said. "Let's kick ass and take names."

READ MORE ABOUT *Bluewater Enigma* at www.clrdougherty.com

# ALSO BY C.L.R. DOUGHERTY

*Bluewater Thrillers*

Bluewater Killer

Bluewater Vengeance

Bluewater Voodoo

Bluewater Ice

Bluewater Betrayal

Bluewater Stalker

Bluewater Bullion

Bluewater Rendezvous

Bluewater Ganja

Bluewater Jailbird

Bluewater Drone

Bluewater Revolution

Bluewater Enigma

Bluewater Thrillers Boxed Set: Books 1-3

*Connie Barrera Thrillers*

From Deception to Betrayal - An Introduction to Connie Barrera

Love for Sail - A Connie Barrera Thriller

Sailor's Delight - A Connie Barrera Thriller

A Blast to Sail - A Connie Barrera Thriller

Storm Sail - A Connie Barrera Thriller

Running Under Sail - A Connie Barrera Thriller

Sails Job - A Connie Barrera Thriller

Under Full Sail - A Connie Barrera Thriller

*Other Fiction*

Deception in Savannah

The Redemption of Becky Jones

The Lost Tourist Franchise

*Books for Sailors and Dreamers*

Life's a Ditch

Dungda de Islan'

For more information please visit my website

Or visit www.amazon.com/author/clrdougherty

Made in the USA
Middletown, DE
12 February 2019